ROBIN AND RUBY

Books by K.M. Soehnlein

THE WORLD OF NORMAL BOYS

YOU CAN SAY YOU KNEW ME WHEN

ROBIN AND RUBY

Published by Kensington Publishing Corporation

ROBIN AND RUBY

K.M. SOEHNLEIN

KENSINGTON BOOKS
http://www.kensingtonbooks.com

KENSINGTON BOOKS are published by

Kensington Publishing Corp.
119 West 40th Street
New York, NY 10018

All Kensington titles, imprints, and distributed lines are available at special quantity discounts for bulk purchases for sales promotion, premiums, fund-raising, educational or institutional use.

Special book excerpts or customized printings can also be created to fit specific needs. For details, write or phone the office of the Kensington Special Sales Manager: Kensington Publishing Corp., 119 West 40th Street, New York, NY 10018. Attn. Special Sales Department. Phone: 1-800-221-2647.

Library of Congress Control Number: 2009943466
ISBN-13: 978-0-7582-3218-2
ISBN-10: 0-7582-3218-7

First Hardcover Printing: April 2010
10 9 8 7 6 5 4 3 2 1

Printed in the United States of America

For
Karen Woodhull,
Kim Soehnlein,
and Sonia Stamm

The truth will set you free—
but first it will make you miserable.

—Vito Russo

Part One

The City of Brotherly Love

Sometimes life throws you a job that you're not yet ready to do. The Friday dinner shift at Rosellen's had started deadly: just one table in Robin's section for the first hour, and then an unexpected surge of customers, and suddenly he was in the weeds, juggling an indecisive four-top and this party of eight professionals lobbing one highly specific demand after another: five different temperatures of steak; an omelet from the brunch menu but with egg whites only; two pepper grinders to be left on the table, even though he assured them that Rosellen's Upscale Southern Cuisine was perfectly spiced. One guy wanted his salad with dressing on the side; another wanted his salad with dressing "extra tossed," whatever that meant. The whole bunch of them seemed to be trying to prove that they were in charge, as if the monumental shoulder pads in their pin-striped power suits didn't already send that message. But the fussiness of their needs made them all seem like little kids.

Then they ordered wine. In thirty minutes' time, they ordered four fucking bottles! Uncorking wine is Robin's personal doom. You're supposed to keep up a conversation with the table while you finesse the captain's knife, and you're supposed to make it look effortless, like tying your shoes, but for Robin it's more like tying a tie: too short, too long, too short again, almost right but not quite. He sweated through the first Bordeaux, the bottle wedged in his armpit instead of in the crook of his elbow where it's supposed to be. The second one also took effort, but it came out more smoothly, and maybe he got too confident, because with the third bottle, he snapped the cork in two and had to return to the bar for a replacement. Rosellen would take that one out of his check.

Now here he is with a fourth red, so stressed out that he decides to just rest it on the floor, clamped between his feet. Bending over, he announces, "Ladies and gentlemen, whatever it takes," and yanks up with all his strength. *Splup!* The cork emerges, miraculously intact. Robin waves it in the air on the tip of the corkscrew, a little flourish, the end of a magic trick. A couple of the diners, already tipsy, put their hands together and applaud.

He sees all of this unfold in the enormous rectangular mirror on the wall behind the table, as if he is starring in a short, comic film about a clown in a crisp white shirt.

There in the mirror, he spots George across the dining room, mouth hanging open. George, who's not just a coworker but his roommate and his best friend, smiles at him, even as he shakes his head in disbelief. Robin simply shrugs and lets his gaze float upward, miming, *What else could I do?* Acting his part: the boy who just can't help himself. But he's also aware that the hostess and the bartender have witnessed the bottle-on-the-floor stunt, and so word of this will travel back to Rosellen, who won't be amused.

The shift ticks by in a kind of blur. The awareness of having messed up has a way of seeping out and saturating all his thoughts, leaving Robin feeling strangely indistinct, as if the separate edges of things are melting together. He starts to think he has a low-grade fever, and he touches his forehead, which is maybe a bit warm. Could he have picked up a cold, a summer flu? He touches his neck, poking at his glands, and that does it: triggers the mental spiral, the one he can't avoid, the one he still can't shut down, even after the test results assured him he was negative. This is not a cold, it's a symptom of the Big One, the first sign of the virus that's been lying in wait, ready to erupt and take him down, once and for all. . . .

"Do I feel a little warm to you?" he asks George.

George puts his hand on Robin's forehead.

"I'm having a freak-out, about, you know—"

"Shh. Not here," George says, looking around to see if anyone is in earshot. And then, more gently, he adds, "You're in a restaurant kitchen in the middle of June. Of course you're warm."

In spite of everything, Robin lets himself smile, though it's a smile with a tint of the gallows: *If you get sick, you'll never have to serve another table of yuppies another bottle of wine again.*

As he makes his way to the kitchen to check on his last order for the night, he feels a pinch against his thigh: the folded corner of the envelope he's been carrying all day in his pocket. He'd almost forgotten it was there. Now he rubs his fingertips along its smooth surface, as if it's a talisman that will remove all obstacles from his path.

It had arrived in the mail that morning, before he left for work: the letter he was sure would never be sent.

Congratulations. A slot in our London theatre program has become available for next spring's semester. Because you were first on the waiting list, we're happy to extend to you . . .

A semester abroad, studying theater. Only a handful of college juniors are invited. Someone has apparently backed out, and now Robin gets to take his place. A few months ago, when the original letter came, the one saying, "Sorry, but . . ." his mother had insisted he not give up hope, you never knew what might happen. She said she had a feeling about this one. One of Dorothy's famous "feelings." He didn't give it much weight. She was wrong as often as she was right.

But here it is on paper, his name, Robin MacKenzie, and the date, June 11, 1985, a few days ago, and the official signature of the Chair of the School of Drama. *Congratulations.* You won't be spending the spring of your senior year on campus, in Pittsburgh; you'll spend it in London. You might actually, one day, be an actor. You might even have talent.

Might, because amid the elation, he feels something else: the lingering pinprick of embarrassment from the original rejection.

George had retrieved the letter from their mailbox this morning. Robin was ironing their work shirts at the time. (George was useless with an iron, and not much better at most other household tasks, and Rosellen would probably send him home if he came to work in a wrinkled shirt.) After he read the letter, Robin went back to ironing.

"It's great news," George said. "Why don't you look like you're into it?"

"Because first on the waiting list still means second-best."

George put his hand on the back of Robin's head and rubbed, in that comforting way he had of asserting their friendship, and it did make Robin feel better, to know that George believed in him, wanted the best for him, wanted to see this as a prize, rather than some new setup for failure.

"You know I'll come to visit," George told him.

"I'll sneak you over in my suitcase. You might fit." A timeworn joke: at five-feet-seven, George is four inches shorter than him.

"Is Margaret Thatcher letting any more black boys into her country?" George asks. Race riots in England have been showing up in the news, and after what happened in West Philly last month, George has been paying attention.

Now, hours later, the letter is already rumpled. After sharing it with George, Robin called his mother and read it over the phone to her ("Didn't I tell you!" Dorothy proclaimed) and then listened as she repeated the news to his sister, Ruby. "You're so lucky," Ruby said, which gave him a moment's pause: was that it? Luck, and not talent?

By the time he was ready to call Peter, he'd read the letter so many times he nearly had it memorized.

Peter was the one person Robin was nervous about breaking the news to, because what would it mean to tell your lover that you'd be leaving the country for six months? He called but got no answer and couldn't leave a message because Peter didn't have an answering machine. Where had Peter been all morning? And then, when Robin finally got him on the phone, right before leaving for the restaurant, what did it mean that he said, "I'm glad that you're going"? Wasn't the idea of a separation even a little bit sad? "Oh, come on, Robin, I'm *happy* for you. This is what you wanted."

"You're going to visit me, right?"

Peter laughed as if the question was unreasonable. "I can't make promises for next spring."

"Why not?"

"Because I'm in school, too?"

"I'm just talking about a visit. Most people would want to visit their boyfriends in London."

And then they were having a fight: "That's not what I meant." "That's what you said." "No, you're twisting it around." "No, *you* never listen." It went on, and got loud, and then they fell silent, and finally Robin said, "I need you to come here. I can't stand being this far away from you for another weekend." *Here* meaning Philadelphia, where Robin has moved for the summer to live with George and wait tables at Rosellen's, while Peter stayed behind in Pittsburgh, at Carnegie Mellon, working on his dissertation.

Peter sighed and after a moment said, OK, he would come the next day, Saturday. It was the perfect, romantic end to the argument, and it reminded Robin why being in love with Peter had, from the start, given him a sense of security, a net beneath the high-wire act of being in a real relationship. He and Peter have so many interests in common, high and low: They could stand in front of a single painting in a museum for an hour and not run out of things to say; they could sit through *Desperately Seeking Susan* in back-to-back screenings and laugh at the same gags twice. Peter loved him. Why pick a fight? Why doubt it? Does the tightrope walker let himself fall in order to test the net?

"OK, Blanco, you're officially on probation," Rosellen tells him. "One more broken cork and . . ." She slices her hand across her neck.

It's 10:30 in the morning. Saturday brunch is just beginning, but Robin has been called into the small cluttered office out of which Rosellen runs Rosellen's. He stands across the desk from her while she shuffles through purchase orders and invoices. Her smooth bronze forehead and gold hoop earrings catch the overhead light. The smell of sizzling butter fills the air. He hates that smell; it stays in his uniform even after he washes it.

"If I wasn't so short-staffed, I'd let you go," she says. "You know I'm doing you a favor."

Of course I know, he wants to say, *'cause you never let me forget it.* But what he says is, "Sorry I keep messing up," as he tries to cope by picturing himself onstage, *finding his focus*, as his acting teachers say. The focus here is on keeping a paycheck coming in. Paying his half of the rent. Proving to everyone—to Peter, to his mother—that coming to Philly this summer wasn't just a foolish, impulsive move. He stops the nervous tapping of his foot and turns on his smile to lighten the mood. "Rosellen, if I could afford it, I'd buy ten cases of wine, and I'd practice at home until I got it right."

"You know I pride myself on my wine list," she says. "Some folks think African Americans don't know about good French wine."

"Luckily none of the African American waiters mess up like I do," he says. "Blame it on Whitey."

"I not blaming *Whitey*," she says coolly. "I'm blaming you."

Rosellen's is a new restaurant. New, as in opened less than a year ago, on South Street, west of Broad, but new in concept, too. Early reviews in the Philly papers have dubbed Rosellen's cuisine "Yuppie Soul

Food," words that she has banned everyone on the premises from ever speaking. She's coined her own term, "New U.S.," which stands for Upscale Southern, and which Robin is supposed to recite as he greets his tables.

So far, the local press has been kind. There aren't many like Rosellen: a female African American chef. That's another term, "African American," that she makes them all use, instead of "black," which is how George has always referred to himself. Rosellen is strict about language. Chinese are "Asians." Street people are to be called "the homeless," never bums or bag ladies. She herself is a lesbian, and though she doesn't make too much of that with the press or the customers, she sometimes talks with Robin and George about "the struggle of the lesbian and gay community." Rosellen is George's cousin, which is why Robin works here, the only reason, because not only is Robin a pale, blue-eyed white boy, he also has no experience beyond busing tables at an Italian restaurant in a New Jersey mall, near where he and George grew up. Rosellen has a soft spot for George; they're the two gay members of the Lincoln family. So she agreed to meet Robin, and after pronouncing him "easy on the eyes," she threw a few shifts his way. During his first week, he knocked a glass of wine across a table onto a customer and had to comp the entire dinner.

As Robin leaves her office, George is standing with Malik, the other waiter on duty. "This sister is fly," Malik is saying. "Tonight it's *all* going on."

"*Word*," George answers. "But keep it safe. Pack a rubber."

"She's got the contraception. She already told me, one of them diaphragms."

"Brother, you gotta think about disease."

"Maybe *you* do," Malik says, taking a step away.

Robin feels his face heating up. But George remains calm. "I'll tell you straight up, everybody has to protect himself."

"She's no freak," Malik says, as he heads off to a customer.

Robin scans the dining room. Malik and George have two tables each, but no one has been seated in his own section.

George turns to Robin. "Did you get a yellin' from Rosellen? She cut you with your captain's knife?"

"She made me fall on it. It's a bloody mess back there." He lowers his voice. "Maybe I should just go back to Pittsburgh and live with Peter. Save myself rent for the summer."

"Oh, you've been paying rent?" George asks, arching an eyebrow.

"I will be. You know I will—"

"Kidding," George says, but Robin can't help but feel bad; George pulled a hundred dollars out of his scholarship money to cover him this month. George shrugs. "I told you, it was cheaper than paying the dry cleaners to iron my shirts."

George carries a basket of cornbread to a four-top of pale Germans, two men and two women in their late twenties who stare with open, eager faces as he recites the ingredients in the omelet of the day. Robin sees how George doesn't try to flirt and charm. I'll act like him today, Robin thinks. Won't try to please everyone. Slow and steady. Calm and unemotional. No broken corks. No sweat on my brow. You're on probation, so play it safe. Of course, George, with his Malcolm X glasses and his two-inch fro pinched into baby dreads at the tips, fits in here in a way Robin never will. If Robin said "word" or "brother" to someone like Malik, if he said that the special of the day was "dope," as George just did, he'd sound like an actor miscast for his role.

Maybe living in London will suit him better. Maybe it'll even be less expensive than here; he hasn't checked the exchange rate yet. He hasn't thought about the everyday details because it hasn't quite seemed real, this offer. He's read about the program, the courses, the apprenticeship at the cavernous, concrete National Theatre. He's studied the photos of this place in the brochure, all cool and silvery. He's placed himself on that dark, modern stage, rehearsing in a pool of light where nobody can touch him, where there's nothing to worry about but entering a life someone else has dreamed up. But he hasn't actually called the program back and said, yes, I accept.

Peter's Honda CR-X, a little metallic-blue hatchback, rolls into view on South Street. From the alley behind the restaurant, Robin watches the car slow down, blinker flashing. Peter's face is in profile through the open driver's side window, his wide jaw and thick neck both covered in dark stubble. His hair looks puffy, slept-on, windblown. He rushed to get here; just the idea of it gives Robin a hard-on, the idea of Peter waking up and without even a shower, getting in the car to be here before the day was old.

Robin stamps out the cigarette he's been smoking and pulls a little tube of Binaca from his pocket. *Whoosh* goes the minty mist into his mouth. He runs his tongue over his teeth, trying to cover up the "ashtray breath" that Peter always complains about.

Robin waves. Peter sounds the horn, which makes a funny little Japanese-model toot, not the resonant honking of a big, American car. Just before Peter kills the engine, Robin hears a snippet of "Point of No Return," that Exposé song on the dance-mix tape he made for Peter.

He steps to the window and leans in for a kiss. Peter's eyes dart around, as if someone might see them, before he accepts a quick peck. When Peter gets out of the car, he puts some distance between them, as if Robin is planning to pounce on him right there in the open air. Depending on his mood, Robin can find Peter's discomfort adorable or annoying. Right now it just seems like a fact, one of their things: Robin pushes for public affection while Peter cautiously withholds.

"Are you doing okay?" Peter asks. "Did you get through your shift?"

"Rosellen put me on probation."

"What does that mean?"

Robin shrugs. It's not really clear, is it? "Maybe it would have been easier if she fired me."

"You don't need her, now that you're going to be a famous actor."

"Because actors never have to wait tables?" He's thinking now not just about rent money he owes to George, but the expensive tickets he plans to buy for next month's Live Aid concert at JFK Stadium. He had hoped to have them already, a surprise gift for Peter.

Peter's eyes look a bit glazed from the drive. Robin wants to drag him back to the apartment as quickly as possible and throw him into bed. Peter will want a shower first. "I can't get dirty 'til I get clean," he likes to say, though Robin's on a campaign to convince him that the smell of sweat during sex is a good thing.

Behind them, the restaurant's kitchen door swings open. It's one of the dishwashers, Cesar, the tall one with the Sacred Heart tattoo on his forearm, the one who tells menacing and vaguely queer stories of reform school in Puerto Rico, where he grew up. He tosses an overstuffed heavyweight trash bag into the Dumpster, then catches sight of Robin. "Hey, Blanco, got a smoke?"

Robin nods.

Cesar struts over, pulls a Parliament from Robin's pack, and takes the Bic from Robin's hand. After he lights his own, he holds the flame, and Robin, mesmerized by the way Cesar's dark eyes lock on to his, pulls out a cigarette for himself, too, and lets Cesar light it. They often smoke together on breaks. But as soon as he inhales, Robin wishes he hadn't. He senses Peter shuffling around uncomfortably.

"This is Peter," Robin says. "This is Cesar."

"Hi. Nice to meet you," Peter says, thrusting out a hand. "I'm a friend of Robin's."

Cesar squints through the smoke. "Another college boy," he says, taking Peter's hand and giving him what Robin can see is a crushing grip.

"I was his T.A.," Peter says, shaking it out.

"What's that, tits and ass?" Cesar laughs, but Peter just looks confused. "*This* one's got the ass," Cesar adds, reaching out to swat Robin on the butt.

"Cesar!" Robin protests. He hears the edge of flirtation in his own voice, the subterranean longing he knows he feels toward a lot of the rough-looking guys in the kitchen, especially this one. It's not the first time Cesar's smacked or pinched or grabbed Robin's butt, usually with some comment about how much Robin's *got going on* back there. "Pretty fresh for a white boy," Cesar likes to say.

"Jesus," Peter grumbles, after Cesar has gone back into the kitchen. "I think he broke my finger."

Robin reaches out to take Peter's hand, to rub the offended spot, but Peter pulls away. "What did he call you?"

"I'm the only white guy," Robin says. "So I'm 'Blanco.'"

"He was white, too. Hispanics are white."

"Puerto Ricans don't consider themselves white."

"Sure, OK," Peter says, sounding eager to change the subject. "Hungry? I'm buying."

"Anything but soul food." Robin takes another puff of the cigarette. There's no smoking in Peter's car, a restriction that he is not yet used to, even after eight months of dating. When you're raised in a home where your mother smokes, and where she lets you smoke with her, it's odd to be forbidden your habit. But Peter's grandmother has emphysema, and he talks often, with pity and condemnation, about this hacking, skeletal woman. Robin knows that smoking is not such a good thing, not for someone who's only twenty and has been smoking since he was thirteen. A third of your life, he thinks. At twenty-six it'll be half your life. You're definitely quitting soon.

"Put out that cancer stick and get in the car. We need to talk."

Peter starts the engine, and the music kicks in again, Latin girls harmonizing, *"Takin' meeeee, to the point of no return, ah-ah-ah."* He flips on the headlights, though it won't be dark for hours; it's a habit he grew up with in rural Canada, driving twisty back roads. "Better if they see you coming," he always says. "You never know who's out there." He drives with both hands on the wheel, perfectly placed at 10 and 2.

As they turn onto South Street, Robin glances one last time through the restaurant's plate-glass windows and catches sight of George, gliding through the dining room, looking surprisingly adult from this distance, filling out his white shirt like a grown man. He's not the skinny, dorky teenager Robin befriended in New Jersey all those years ago. They've already said a hurried good-bye, with plans to hang out tonight, as they do every night, though it seems unlikely that they'll spend much time together, with Peter here now. George doesn't like Peter. They've only met a couple times. After the first visit, George was evasive. The second time, Robin pushed for an opinion, and George admitted, "He doesn't seem right for you. Kinda uptight." Robin tried to defend Peter: yes, he could be a little stiff, but that was a sign of maturity, stability, trustworthiness. George was unconvinced. "You're just seeing what you want to see."

Peter had had his own strong reaction to George: "He sees me as his competition." Robin told him he was being ridiculous.

George is working the post-lunch bridge-shift, the first wave of dinner guests responding to Rosellen's "Black Plate Special," a couple hours of a fixed-price menu. The customers now are mostly people from the neighborhood: African American seniors and young mothers with kids in booster seats. Half the tables are empty. After sunset, the next wave of yuppies will start their advance, already fueled by cocktails imbibed elsewhere. Many of these people are only a couple years older than Robin, but they've already staked out their upwardly mobile careers. The women travel in track shoes and switch to high-heeled pumps on the sidewalk. The men put styling mousse in their expensive haircuts, which look shiny as helmets, making them look like slick warriors for Big Business.

Robin is amazed by how robust and healthy these people seem, almost robotically fit, because the other phenomenon he was all too aware of these days was the exact opposite: all those men, gay men, getting sick and frail. He hadn't been so aware of them in Pittsburgh, but Philadelphia was a different story: the hairdressers and antique dealers who used to spend their weekends at bathhouses were now staying home and growing full beards to hide the purple lesions on their faces. OK, it's not just bathhouse queens, he admits, it's lots of guys, which is even scarier. Robin thinks uneasily of Donovan, living one floor up from his mother in Manhattan. He isn't some creature of the night, doesn't seem like a West Village leatherman; he's just a boring guy with a 9-to-5 city job, and now, not even thirty years old, he's sick with it. Robin used to enjoy their passing flirtations in the elevator, but last time he visited his mom, he saw what was happening to Donovan, and he actually began taking the stairs so that he wouldn't have to face him. He checks his own skin now all the time, fretting over every blotch and zit, constantly feeling his neck and his armpits for swollen glands.

Peter wears a white T-shirt tight enough to show that he keeps himself in shape, but not so tight to read as *flaming*, the word he uses to talk about gay guys he thinks are "too obvious." His pale blue tennis shorts hug perfectly the meat of his thighs. His arms are smooth except at the wrist; his legs are wildly hairy from his ankles to his cock, a swirling, black pattern. Peter Savas, my hunky Greek graduate student, Robin thinks, glad again that fate threw them together last semester, when Peter was leading Robin's section of Renaissance Art, an elective Robin had enrolled in at the last minute; glad, too, that Peter broke the rules and had sex with him, keeping it quiet until the semester ended. He's never had a real boyfriend until Peter; never left half his clothes and a toothbrush at a guy's apartment; never gotten to know a lover down to his daily habits: Peter puts honey in his coffee, hangs his shirts in the closet according to color, speaks Greek on the phone with his ailing grandmother during regular Sunday calls.

But "need to talk," is still in the air, buzzing like a gnat. "Talk about what?"

"Oh, you know," Peter says lightly. "Us."

"You're mad that I made you come here."

"You didn't *make* me," Peter says, which sends Robin into an anxious consideration of a frayed patch on the cuff of his shirt. He tugs at the cottony tendrils while silently adding up the reasons Peter most definitely *is* mad at him:

I left Pittsburgh instead of staying with him this summer.

I took this job to make money, now I complain I don't make enough.

I call all the time, whining about how I miss him.

I smoke cigarettes and let bisexual dishwashers feel my ass.

At least you're not cheating on him! You're spending all your time at the restaurant, or hanging out with George at the apartment, having a totally uneventful summer. You haven't been breaking out your fake I.D. to go dancing with the queens at Equus and Key West, or hanging around the Steteler Hall men's room at Penn, where everyone knows you can get a blow job; you haven't been putting yourself in the way of temptation; you haven't been risking infection. . . . Robin remembers their last argument, when Peter visited three weeks ago. The fight had been about Robin not having a driver's license, about the burden Peter said that put on him. It did no good to remind Peter that driver's ed wasn't even *offered* at the arts high school Robin attended. What was the word Peter threw at him? *Unexamined.* As in, "A lot of your behavior goes *unexamined.*" It seemed like such a ridiculous charge, because Robin feels like he examines every thought, emotion, and action until he drives himself crazy.

"I was serious when I said you should come to London with me," Robin says.

Peter smiles indulgently. "Yeah, well, my dissertation . . ."

"You can study the Renaissance in London."

"The *Italian* Renaissance?"

"Italy, England," Robin says, with an exaggerated flap of his hand.

"Philadelphia, Pittsburgh," Peter says coolly.

"Look, I'm really sorry," Robin says. "I'm calmer now. Yesterday I felt really anxious about everything. At least now we get to spend the weekend together."

"It's not London," Peter says. "It's not your phone call." Then, with a contemplative tilt of his head, he adds, "It is and it isn't."

Robin falls silent, scolding himself. *Why are you so bad at this?* When emotions get messy, he never quite understands what he's supposed to *do*. In bed it's different. He can take charge. He can push Peter to try new things. Peter's only been out and sexual for a couple of years. Sex for Robin is something else he's been doing since he was thirteen, since those first boys he messed around with in Greenlawn, and it only got more intense once he moved to Manhattan.

Robin runs his hand along Peter's thigh, lets his fingers creep under his shorts. "You believe that I've been missing you, right? I know I said it a million times on the phone, but I'm not sure you really *believe* it." His fingers move higher, and Robin can see the effect he's having on Peter. He thinks about going down on him right here, as they move through traffic on Broad Street, an exciting image bound up in all the sex-in-car scenes he's read in books—the teenager in *Peyton Place*, distracted by the suddenly exposed breast of the bad girl in his passenger seat, driving headlong into an oncoming tractor trailer . . . or the philanderer in *The World According to Garp*, getting a blow job that turns into a dismemberment when another car rear-ends theirs and the woman sucking bites down hard. Sex in cars ends badly. But doing the things he shouldn't has always made his dick throb.

Peter says, "You're going to get us killed," and pushes his hand away.

Robin's face warms up in shame. He hates that Peter seems so distant, but it's important to listen. That's what George always says, that Robin doesn't really *hear* what people are trying to tell him.

They drive through the narrow, brick-lined streets of Center City. The softly burning light on the old buildings is both soothing and unsettling. Like so many things, it seems too beautiful to trust. A couple years ago, visiting George at Penn, where he's majoring in premed, Robin decided he wanted to live in Philly one day. In part, it was the appearance of the charming, history-bound architecture at golden, late-day moments like this. And in part it was simply that this wasn't New York. He needed space from New York, the city that has owned him for so long, which is why he went to college in Pittsburgh, why he moved in with George this summer, why he set his sights on London. He needed space from his mother in her Manhattan apartment; she is too much the shaper of his life and has been for years. And he needed space from his past, all that sexual adventure that now seems to have marked him, along with every other guy having sex with guys, as endangered.

Peter has chosen an old-fashioned Greek restaurant in the midst of the gay neighborhood. "How do you know about this place?" Robin asks, and Peter mentions his ex-girlfriend Diana, who goes to college at Temple. Robin met her a few weeks ago: a high-strung, curvy girl who seemed to have the same dubious response to him that George had to Peter. What was that about, this doubt among friends?

Inside, the hostess, a woman with big, pretty eyes and big, shapely breasts who looks like a more Mediterranean version of Diana, leads them to a corner table. She might be as much as ten years older than him, or she might be a very mature teenager. Girls are like that; they look like women much earlier than boys look like men. Case in point:

his own sister. For years he called Ruby "peanut," and then he turned around, and she was nineteen, in college, this imposing young woman with a tough attitude who wore only black.

All these faces are suddenly crowding his mind: Ruby, Diana, this waitress who looks like Diana. It's as though he's erecting a protective female wall between himself and Peter's air of masculine control.

Robin looks up from the menu and sees that Peter is staring at him with an admiration so unexpected and intense it looks almost mournful. "You're so handsome," Peter says. "When you space out, and your face relaxes, you're like an angel."

"OK, something's wrong," Robin says.

Peter sighs. "I'll order for us first."

Robin digs his cigarettes from his pocket.

"Don't," Peter says, even though there's an ashtray on the table, white and royal blue and etched with an image of the Parthenon.

Robin fingers his cigarette, wondering how long he can hold it without lighting it. The clock on the wall says 6:32.

"I'm glad you called me," Peter says.

"You are?"

"Sure. I had the whole ride to think."

"About us."

"It's really about me." Robin can hear the wind-up in Peter's voice, and then he's on a roll, reciting something like an autobiography of his twenty-eight years on the planet: raised with a drive for material success inherited from his father, an importer of Greek foods who wanted Peter to carry on the family business. Scarred by the overwhelming repression of his Orthodox family. Wasting too many years with a girlfriend he barely touched. It took so long to discover himself! Only in grad school, when he began to study great gay artists like Michelangelo and Leonardo, was he able to break free and to live in a more *examined* way.

Robin waits for Peter to get to the moment when he entered his life, toward their time together. These eight months have been so substantial to Robin, but now, placed in this chronology, they shrink to some kind of footnote, one brief stop along a larger, more essential path that Peter is traveling. And, really, they haven't even shared eight full months. There was the furtive beginning, student and teacher sneaking extracurricular sex. There was a lengthy separation during Christmas break. Then at last came four months when they lived as boyfriends, spending nearly every night in Peter's off-campus apartment. But that was cut off by Robin's move to Philly at the end of May, and since then, there have been just a couple of visits. *Why didn't you just stay in Pittsburgh with him, you fool?*

"Meeting you has been so special to me," Peter is saying. "You're this interesting, handsome, younger guy, but you've had so many experiences, living in New York, and growing up in a such a troubled family. You're sort of exotic to me, you feel very modern. It's been amazing to have gotten close to you—"

"Do you ever think," Robin interrupts, "how weird it is that we met at a school in Pittsburgh? Neither of us is from there, which makes it seem like we were *meant* to find each other." He's riffing now, scrambling, because he can feel where Peter's monologue is leading.

And sure enough, Peter says, "It's just not the right time in my life to be in this relationship," and then, "What we've had has been important to me, but I can't really commit to it," and then, "I hope we can move on to some other kind of friendship without the pressure to try and make a sexual relationship work."

Peter is saying the words and Robin is hearing them, they're accumulating weight and solidity. "Given everything I just outlined, the only conclusion that I can reach is that we should break up."

He feels it like a physical impact.

This is actually happening.

You're being dumped.

"I hope you understand," Peter says, and Robin shakes his head no.

The waitress appears and sets down a platter of various mushy substances, shaded beige to gray, and a basket of pita cut into long strips and fried into crispness. Quick upon her heels is a doughy busboy, who refills Peter's water glass with a messy splash. The sound of the ice being jostled by the water becomes for Robin the very sound of his relationship being dismantled, and before he knows it he has lighted the cigarette in his hand.

He looks at the time. 6:39. Over the course of seven minutes, his relationship has ended.

The inhaling and exhaling of smoke seems to organize his ability to speak. "I'll give you credit," he says calmly. "You drove all this way. You could have said this over the phone."

Peter smiles shyly and drops his gaze downward, happy to take the compliment. Robin tells himself, Beg for a second chance. Let the tears flow. Show him how you feel. No, fuck that. You should say the meanest thing you can think of and then throw your ice water in his fucking face.

Peter says, "I'd love to know how this sounds to you."

"Shitty."

"Tell you what. I won't say anything else. I'll let you lead from here."

Robin nods and smokes his cigarette. He doesn't know where to look.

Peter says, "Meantime, how about we eat? This is hummus, this is baba ganoush, and this is tzatziki." He points as he identifies each one, then grabs a pita slice, dips, and eats. Robin puts out the cigarette and then does what Peter does. Dips and eats. Chews and swallows. He compliments the food, as if this will somehow counteract everything that Peter has just said to him.

"The tzatziki's good," Robin mumbles. "I've never had it before."

"Yogurt and mint," Peter says, mouth full.

As the meal proceeds, Robin notes Peter's every facial expression and gesture. He seems satisfied, or at least relieved. Where is the doubt, the remorse? Robin's own thoughts return to a fantasy he's sometimes indulged since meeting Peter, the one about moving in with him to a little cottage by a creek on a bucolic patch of land in the western Pennsylvania countryside, while Peter finishes his dissertation and Robin decorates the house, cooks meals, auditions for summer stock plays. He has no idea where this vision originated or how he, a city boy who loves taxis and tall buildings and restaurants, could possibly remain satisfied out in the boonies. The fantasy curdles, and he sees himself staring at a closed door, behind which Peter types out pages of whatever it is he has to say about Renaissance art. He sees himself going quickly insane, snapping and turning against Peter, who has ruined his life by promising him love that he can't deliver, sees himself creeping up on Peter's bed, a kitchen knife in hand, the blade poised above Peter's heart . . .

His mother once admitted that she fantasized killing his father after he asked for a divorce. Dorothy had seemed absolutely bonkers to Robin at the time, beyond the realm of understanding or sympathy. But now he sees that he's just like her, and that hurt finds hurt and magnifies it.

What will she say when he tells her about this, about Peter? *Peter's really quite provincial. You need someone more sophisticated. I had a feeling this wouldn't work out.* George will say it more simply: *I never trusted him.*

When the bill lands on the table, Robin doesn't budge, even though his pockets are full of tip money. They have always split their costs, but not this time. This one's on Peter. And then, as the waitress takes the money away, Robin is seized with panic. Has he just given the breakup his blessing, letting Peter pay his way out of their relationship? It's all suddenly so real: not a scene he's starring in but his actual life.

Outside the restaurant, they linger under the bright summer sky. The heat of the day has passed, but the humidity clings, and under his work clothes, his skin is grimy, coated in burnt butter. He resists the urge to light up again. "Will you stay over tonight?" he asks, as Peter jiggles the car keys.

"I've got somewhere lined up," Peter says, nodding vigorously. "But I'll drive you home."

"Lined up? With Diana?"

"Mm-hmm."

There's something suspect about Peter's behavior. He keeps nodding as he lets himself into the car.

Robin looks into the empty hatchback. "Where's your bag? Where are your clothes?"

"They're already at Diana's."

"You went there first? Before you picked me up?"

Peter nods. "I figured you'd need some space—"

"You had this all planned out." He gets in, slams the door. "You said it's all about you and your path in life and your fucking destiny, but it's about me, about what's wrong with me. Why don't you just say it?"

Peter starts the ignition and without looking whooshes into traffic. A blare of a car horn startles them both into a shaky calm.

"OK, yes," Peter says, his gaze on the road, "there are some things about you—not that you're a bad person, but there is the difference in our ages—eight years is a lot—and the fact that you have all of your twenties still ahead of you, whereas I want to figure out other things, start settling in to my adult life."

"I've already *had* my twenties. I had them in my teens."

"There's also that," Peter says. "Your history."

Robin feels his heartbeat quicken. "You mean my sexual history."

"Yes," Peter says, softly but emphatically. "Especially after the last time."

The last time: The sex they had, during Peter's previous visit, three weeks ago. That hot, hot moment when Peter slipped inside Robin unsheathed, and Robin let him thrust, thrust, thrust. Thirty seconds like that, maybe sixty, maybe a whole minute and thirty seconds. A tiny span of time that felt eternal. They both knew what was happening. Robin even said an encouraging *yes,* but finally Peter froze, cold realization on his face. "What are you doing?" he asked, and pulled out.

"I haven't been with anyone since I've been with you," Robin says. "And I haven't wanted to, either."

"With this virus, when I sleep with someone, I'm sleeping with *everyone* he's *ever* had sex with."

"Well, that's only a *few* dozen people," Robin says and then neither of them says anything more.

His head is flooding with chatter, noise he wants to float away from. He pushes the play button on the cassette deck. Exposé mixes into Lisa Lisa singing "I Wonder If I Take You Home," a perky song that he understands now is really an anthem of doubt. Robin snaps it off after just a few measures.

As Peter heads along Walnut Street toward West Philly, Robin imagines leaping from the car and running back to the restaurant, which is really a wish to run backward in time, to just a short while ago, when Peter was still his boyfriend. But in fact he feels paralyzed, rigid with the horror of being discarded by this man he was sure was the right one, the safe one, the one who would prevent him from chasing after his every dangerous impulse.

The ride passes in silence. They cross over the Schuylkill River, past the big neoclassical train station and into the Penn campus, mostly quiet now that the summer is here. Peter reflexively locks the doors as they move into the surrounding neighborhood, where once-stately, now-dilapidated single-family homes are the outward sign of the poverty and crime that runs deep here. Peter pulls up to the curb in front of the row house where Robin and George share an upper-floor apartment. On the neighboring stoop, two teenage boys turn their attention to the car; these two, sometimes along with a couple more just like them, dressed in backward baseball caps and shiny tracksuits, are always here, staring at Robin as he comes and goes, never saying anything directly to him but often talking loudly among themselves in a way that unsettles him, because they're letting him know whose turf this is. For the first week he would offer a hello, but he never got a verbal reply, and one time he heard one say what sounded like, "Crackers tryin'a take over the 'hood." After that he just moved past quietly.

The fact is that Robin picked exactly the wrong time to move into West Philly, just a week after police helicopters dropped a bomb on a separatist black commune twenty blocks away. There was still smoke rising from the ruins on Osage Avenue when George helped Robin lug his bags up to the apartment, and the first call Robin got from his mother was an urgent plea that he get out of there quickly. In the weeks since, he's quietly wondered if he should have listened to her. But it became a point of pride to not flee the heat, to be one of the few white faces in the crowd at Clark Park last weekend when the neighborhood demonstrated against police brutality. Plus, how could he leave George? He needed to show George that he was *down* with him.

George claimed that the Stoopers, as they'd dubbed the boys outside, always said hello to him, but when Robin and George went in or out of the building together, he never heard any of them speak to George.

Usually Robin puts on his butchest demeanor when he sees them, adopting a toughness that doesn't come naturally. But right now, he simply doesn't have the energy. "You suck," he says to Peter, slamming the door behind him. "And not in a good way."

"Don't leave angry."

Robin throws his hands in the air. "I *am* angry," he shouts, "and you don't want to stay over, so I guess I'm going to leave. Angry."

Peter hangs his head and mutters, "OK, then. Let's talk tomorrow."

Robin stares through the window at the dashboard. His gaze lands on the tape deck. Peter never listened to dance music before he met Robin. He pushes the eject button and the plastic cassette pops forth. He sees his own handwriting on the label. It reads, "Dance With Me."

"I want it all back," he tells Peter. "Everything I ever gave you." The words are borrowed from somewhere, a book, a movie. He long ago learned the importance of an exit line.

He hears Peter pull away from the curb, and then there's a swell of laughter among the Stoopers. He hears one of them use the word "punk," which George recently explained to him has nothing to do with punk rock and everything to do with getting it up the ass.

He takes the two flights up to his apartment quickly, past the first floor, where their landlord's daughter is raising a bunch of kids, where the cry of an infant is almost a constant. The old wooden stairs creak beneath him, and as he gets closer to his third-floor flat, he realizes there's music coming from behind the door.

He enters, and there's George: naked and dancing.

Robin gets an eyeful of the muscular triangle of George's back and the high, hard curve of his ass, shaking with the music. Prince's seductive falsetto rings out over an amplified beat, *I really get a dirty mind,* while George shakes his index finger at some invisible lover, his masculine body softened by his sassy pose.

Robin feels the first smile of the day breaking across his face. "Is this a free show, or are you looking for tips?"

George spins around, startled to be discovered. He lets out an embarrassed whoop, shields his crotch, and dashes by, near enough for Robin to reach out and slap his ass. Robin can feel the damp heat rising off George's skin.

Through the bathroom door, George shouts, "I came out of the shower, and I heard this song, and I was, like—"

"Empty apartment, dance naked."

"You know I love me some Prince."

"I'll come in more quietly next time." Robin affects this kind of flirtation with George sometimes, a little steam valve meant to release whatever tension might naturally build between gay friends sharing an apartment but not a bed. This tension wasn't something he'd expected going into the summer, since he and George did not, it seemed, have any unresolved questions about who they were to each other. But George isn't the diminutive science geek he was in high school. He's been building up his body, dropping to the floor of the apartment once a day for push-ups and sit-ups in a tank top that reveals the sweet dusting of hair at the center of his developing chest. Robin has imagined running his fingers over those newly tight muscles, and he imagines more than that in this moment. But then George reemerges from the bathroom in his ugly plaid robe. Its indigo and turquoise stripes seem designed to make its wearer look as unattractive as possible.

"I thought you'd still be at work," Robin says.

"I asked to leave early. I thought you were out with Peter."

"He ordered us Greek food and then broke up with me."

"What?"

The phone rings, and Robin grabs it, wishing for Peter, but instead it's someone named Matthias. "*Mah-TEE-uss,*" in some northern European accent, calling for "*Gay-org.*" George takes the phone without explanation and stretches the cord as far as it goes, which in this case means back into the bathroom.

Robin steps to the window, propped open because they have no air conditioning, just a ceiling fan that stirs up the heat. *Maybe Peter's out there, maybe he came back and is waiting for you to notice him, ready to apologize and ask you for another chance.* But, no, just the neighborhood boys doing their thing. Above the trees on 41st Street, the sky is a haze of pastel twilight, a glimpse of a fading day.

At the far end of the living room is a waist-high countertop that opens to the kitchen. George walks from the bathroom to the fridge, pulling bottles of Old Latrobe from a six-pack he probably bought at the corner bar on his way home from work. He hands one across the counter to Robin, who drinks deeply, feeling the earthy, cold liquid move into the hollow center of his torso.

"So, what happened?" George asks him.

"You first. I want details."

"About?"

Imitating the voice on the phone, Robin says, "*Matthias.*"

"Did you see him in the restaurant today?" George asks.

"One of the Germans?"

"He's actually Danish. The tall guy, with the punky hair?"

"*That* guy? How'd you know he was gay?"

"He practically followed me into the kitchen. You should have seen Cesar's reaction to that." George looks down at the floor; he might be hiding a smile. "I gave him my number."

"Wow. That's superfast. Maybe some kind of record for you."

"What was strange was how he was so sure *I* was gay," George says. "That never happens. Especially with white boys."

"Georgie, when you stare—"

"I know, I need to wear dark glasses."

"Because *your eyes go up and down a man*—"

"*—like searchlights.* Thank you, Joan Crawford."

"That was Rosalind Russell."

George slugs from his beer until foam spills from his lips. Then he wipes his mouth and lets out a resonant belch.

"That's right," Robin says. "Wash down the gay movie reference with a brewski."

"He's leaving town tomorrow."

"Ah, *that's* why you left work early. You're gonna see him tonight."

"Maybe." George steps around to Robin's side of the counter and hops up onto one of their two barstools, his bare legs dangling below the robe. "Hey, I looked up something in the university catalog today. It's not too late for me to apply for semester abroad programs. How slammin' would that be, if I was in London at the same time?"

"That would be *major*." In an instant, the entire picture of London seems to click into place: the two of them sharing a flat, Robin going off to rehearsal, George doing an internship at some kind of national health clinic, meeting up at night to go dancing at that world-famous club, Heaven . . . "But wait—don't change the subject, Georgie. You need to *get* some."

"OK, we both know it's been a long time." He arches his back and howls, "Matthias, have your way with me." The robe slouches open. Robin finds himself staring again, staring at *George*. So weird.

George says, "I'll call this guy back. I will. But first tell me what stupid Peter said to you."

Robin frowns. He relocates to the couch, facing the window, looking out at the dimming sky. Where to start? How about this: "He thinks I'm going to give him the virus."

"Don't even joke."

"I'm not."

"You took the test, Robin."

"They say it can hide for a while in your bloodstream. Undetected."

"I know," George says. "But you can't make yourself crazy about every penis that's been in your mouth."

Robin doesn't say what he's thinking, what George is probably thinking, too. It's not so much penises-in-mouth that worries him, it's cocks-up-ass. In New York City. For years now. Only lately did anyone recommend using a condom, only lately did they even have a name for this: AIDS.

George follows him across the room. "What did he actually say to you?"

"Something about the last time, when I let him fuck me with no rubber."

"You *what*?"

"Not for very long. He didn't shoot." Robin feels his face warm up; he knows how this must sound to George, can see him getting agitated.

"But that's riskier for you than him. Why is he putting it all on you?"

"I'm the one with the history."

"Fuck Peter," George says, cresting. "Fuck that hairy white boy. He's putting you at risk and laying blame on you. He's the one breaking up with you. It's not your fault."

"You never liked him."

"Now you know why. He's a mind-fucker."

"You might be right." Now he might cry. Yeah, just cry yourself a river. George can handle it.

As Robin wipes moisture from his eyes, the phone rings again. Peter! But no, it's George's mother.

Mrs. Lincoln calls every few days to provide family updates, especially about George's older sister's upcoming marriage and the latest triumph his younger brother has scored on his way to the state track and field championships. While his mother talks, George cradles the phone at his neck, with little more to say than, "Uh-huh," "Yeah," "Really?" and so on. The joke around the apartment is to let the dishes pile up until the next call from Mrs. Lincoln, when George can get them done while she fills his ear with chatter. It's a joke that hides a reservoir of uneasiness: His parents don't ask him about anything but his schoolwork. He's the brain in the family, as he's been told since childhood, so as long as his grades stay high, they don't need to know anything else. The Lincolns are all overachievers. Mr. Lincoln is a county administrator involved in local politics; Mrs. Lincoln has gone from schoolteacher to secretary of the teacher's union. Robin knows, though it's rarely discussed, that George's courses in premed are guided more by his parents' deep desire for a doctor in the family than by any dream George ever held.

When at last he hangs up the phone, George wraps his fingers around his neck and gasps, "Help! I can't breathe. My mama sucked the air outta the room. Right through the phone!"

Robin resists saying what he wants to say: Come out to them. You're not going to have a real relationship until they know who you really are. The last time he tried to encourage this, George said, "You don't know black folks, do you?" It was the first time, in all their years of friendship, that George ever said anything like that to him. Living here in this neighborhood, at this time, Robin thinks, no, maybe I don't.

Now, George walks to the kitchen and stares into the fridge. "I'm gonna make a snack. Want some frogs' legs?"

Robin grins and says, "Hold the formaldehyde."

* * *

This joke goes back to high school, freshman year, when they were lab partners in biology. George had a knack for science, a natural aptitude and a lack of squeamishness when faced with the series of animal dissections—long worms, huge, crunchy grasshoppers, bulbous frogs—that made up the bulk of their lab work. Robin felt lucky to have George by his side at those scratched-up wooden lab tables, helping him cope with the sickly smell of preservatives that rose up from the puny, pickled organs. George could name the systems of the body, could explain what a recessive gene was, could tell a kingdom from a phylum. Robin did his best to keep up, though mostly he just cheated off George. But you don't stay friends with someone for years simply because he lets you see his test answers.

In the middle of Robin's freshman year, his younger brother, Jackson, was injured in a playground accident, and, after a couple months spent comatose, died in the hospital. For Robin, everything fell apart, and when he finally picked himself up and looked around at what seemed to be a changed world, the only one of his school friends he was drawn to was George Lincoln. It wasn't that their friendship was especially deep; in fact, the opposite was true. He found that he and George had a lot to talk about, none of it in any way related to Jackson's death. It started with the simple discovery that they each had subscriptions to *Time* magazine, and they would spend study hall in the library talking about the hostage crisis in Iran or the Soviet invasion of Afghanistan, talks that for Robin were a great distraction from the sadness and tension that had taken over his family, from the earnest-eyed teachers treating him like someone delicate and broken.

At Greenlawn High School, it wasn't common for a black kid and a white kid to become close friends, after-school friends, unless you played sports together, which neither of them did. To make friends across the color line, you had to work against all these unspoken rules, like who sat where and with whom on the school bus or in the cafeteria. They never talked about it. It seemed to Robin it would be rude to do so; his parents had raised him not to "see color." Talking about race, they insisted, was a kind of racism, and so, for years, he never raised the subject. This summer, things have shifted. Like George's remark about him not knowing much about black folks. Like everyone at work calling him Blanco. Like all the little ways George has made it clear that the two of them are different, and have all along been living essentially different lives. It's only now, being a white guy in a largely black world, that Robin has begun to understand that silence around race is its own kind of racism. Working at Rosellen's, living in this apartment, in this neighborhood, it's like he's decided to sit on the black side of the cafeteria, and everybody, maybe even George, maybe even Robin himself, keeps wondering what he's doing here.

The summer after Jackson died, Robin's parents announced their divorce. When Robin told George he'd be leaving New Jersey with his mother and his sister and moving into an apartment on West 71st Street, George said, "That's on the same subway line as my grandma's." She lived in Harlem, and George visited her every few weeks. In a city full of bad neighborhoods, Harlem was supposed to be one of the worst, though Robin couldn't imagine it was much worse than 72nd and Broadway, around the corner from his new apartment, an intersection frequented by so many junkies it was known as "Needle Park." There was even a movie about it, though he was too young to see it.

The first time George took Robin on the A-train to his grandmother's, it was the bright middle of the day, and Harlem seemed to Robin like a lot of places in New York in 1979: run-down but active; dirty, druggy, and menacing in the shadowy corners but also lively wherever people gathered in the light. The old brownstones on Grandma Lincoln's block were stately in the slanting winter sun, and inside, amid the upholstered wooden furniture, the dust motes floated in beams that looked plucked from a Rembrandt. Grandma Lincoln was only fifty-five, but she seemed ancient and timeless. She was the first person Robin met after moving to the city who struck him as a genuine New Yorker. Dorothy's college friends, dropping by to gossip and drink wine, didn't count. They'd all come from somewhere else. More than that, Grandma Lincoln's was the first black household in the city into which he'd been invited. She made them coffee, like they were grownups, and served them cake that she'd baked from scratch. Grandma Lincoln called her freezer "the icebox" and still had a black-and-white television in her living room, with aluminum foil wrapped around the V-shaped antenna. After cake and coffee, she put on the TV, let a soap opera run in the background, and kept up an intermittent conversation with the boys. When the image got staticky, she'd say, "Adjust the rabbit ears for me, George-honey." When it was time to go, she told Robin, "You're a good-looking boy, but too skinny. Come back here and I'll feed you a proper meal, with or without Little Georgie."

Robin started calling George by these sweetheart nicknames: George-honey, Little Georgie. George claimed to hate this, but Robin couldn't resist.

During another of George's visits, Robin decided to test him. As they walked through Central Park, George in a wool coat and canvas sneakers, Robin in the belted trench coat, silk scarf, and pointy-toed boots he'd taken to wearing after reading Oscar Wilde and deciding he wanted to be a dandy, Robin said, "I have a crush on someone," and then revealed that *someone* was Alton Humphrey, a boy in his new high school. He hoped this wouldn't end his friendship with George, but thought that it might; he figured it was a risk worth taking, if they were going to stay friends.

George nodded as he listened and then said it was probably a phase that Robin would outgrow. He said what he'd heard Dr. Ruth Westheimer say on her sex-advice radio show; in puberty, boys had "experimental" ideas, but they usually outgrew this "phase" as their hormones came into balance. *Homosexual tendencies* were nothing to worry about. Nothing permanent. He told Robin that his "androgynous wardrobe" was part of that, too, as if Robin himself hadn't put it all together.

Robin didn't tell George about the sexual experiences he'd already had, orgasms shared with boys from Greenlawn (the names would have shocked George: Scott Schatz, the quiet burnout who cut school all the time; Todd Spicer, the beautiful stoner who drove Robin to school in the morning) and, more recently, now and then, with a man he met in New York. This man, a piano teacher his mother had hired but could not afford to pay after a few lessons, invited Robin to his apartment on Lexington Avenue, where Robin would drink wine, disrobe, and then masturbate onto him. On the way out he'd slip a few bucks into Robin's pocket. Giving George the full picture would have been pushing things too far, too fast. So Robin simply shrugged his shoulders, saying that the concept of a phase was "interesting," and thus he let George talk his way into maintaining their friendship, which for some reason he seemed to want to do, despite Robin's deviant confession.

Then there was the night when George came into the city to meet Robin, who had gotten the dates mixed up and was out at the theater with Dorothy. Ruby was out, too, so no one answered the buzzer at their apartment, and George wound up stranded at the diner on West End Avenue, killing time and contemplating whether or not he'd have to head up to his grandmother's to sleep, probably waking her up because it was so late. After that, Dorothy decided George should have a key, so that he could come and go as he pleased, so that he wouldn't have to take a late-night subway ride to Harlem if Robin messed up their plans. Robin remembers George taking the key and trying it in the lock, remembers the feeling that George was now part of their family. Robin was sixteen, George a half year older.

Another weekend, not long after that: George came into the city with a plan to stay overnight. "Let's *shoot* for who sleeps on the floor," George said. Scissors, paper, rock: Robin lost two out of three. In the middle of the night, having woken himself up with a stiff shoulder and a nearly numb arm, he pulled himself groggily into the single bed and pressed up against George. Then he couldn't fall back asleep. He hadn't spent a full night in bed with a boy since Scott, back in freshman year, and he longed to wrap himself around George the way he had with Scott. Robin had thought of Scott as his first love, but he had no photos of him, and after four years, and so many new experiences, the memories had begun to fade. What he felt for George wasn't what he'd felt for Scott, but there in bed, George's warmth was magnetic, the smoothness of his legs against Robin's a temptation, the chuff of his breath like a feather tickling Robin's neck. Robin got hard. He let his hard-on push through the fly of his underwear and poke into George's hip. He felt the pulse of his blood like a bass line beating inside the mattress. Something had to be done. He let a hand slide onto George's rib cage. George's breathing shifted, but he didn't wake. I'll just leave it at this, Robin thought, that's all for now, as his thoughts raced with every possible thing he might do with George. The things he'd done with others, that he wanted to do with his crush, Alton. And in the midst of this cataloging his mind wandered and drifted and led him into sleep, and when he woke in the morning, George had relocated to the sleeping bag on the floor.

Over breakfast there had been a bit of nervous joking about it. "You were going to get the bed no matter what," George said.

"I couldn't sleep on that hard floor," Robin replied.

"Yeah, well *I* couldn't sleep squished up with you under that little blanket, snoring like someone's *grandpa*."

"I don't snore. You snore!"

That was all. There was no more sneaking into bed with George after that. George wasn't going to be his boyfriend. Nor would George be scared away. He's your friend, Robin told himself, just let it be. Don't ruin it just because you want a boyfriend.

George came back from his freshman year at the University of Pennsylvania announcing that he had "big news." As soon as he and Robin were alone, he spilled it: "I'm bisexual." George had had sex with a guy he'd met in a political science class. He'd gone to bed with him, and a little while later, he'd gone to bed with this boy's ex-boyfriend, too. Both of them were white, one of them a fellow biology major like George, the other a theater major, like Robin. Robin almost didn't believe him. "Why didn't you say anything before," he wanted to know. "What took you so long?"

George had been as calm about this as he was about nearly everything else. "I didn't feel anything until I met Michael," he said. "And then I liked it, and I figured I should try it again, so Michael set me up with Neal, and I liked that, too, maybe even a little more." Neal was the one George now had the crush on. George said Neal was "very sensual," a phrase that made Robin laugh; it seemed so incongruous coming from George.

At the time George was also dating a girl named Jeanette, who wasn't white, and who had no idea about these boys. George had visited her over winter break, met her family, had sex with her. Robin found himself getting angry about the whole thing. He called George a hypocrite. George protested, "You of all people should understand." There were tears in his eyes. Robin knew he should have been supportive of his friend, but he couldn't block the feeling of having been wronged.

"You're devious," he told George. "The truth is in your actions."

George fought back: Robin was "irresponsible" about his own sex life, and probably "dishonest," too. "You use your blue-eyed privilege to get what you want," he accused.

They shouted "fuck you" back and forth a couple times. Then they retreated to their separate colleges on opposite sides of Pennsylvania, unable to quickly repair what they'd so suddenly damaged, and the silence lingered for weeks.

It was impossible, during that brief period of hurt, for Robin not to attach to George the images of other boys, boys he'd had sex with who turned around and went back to their girlfriends before the cum dried. Alton had turned out to be one of them: whispering about love while he put his cock roughly inside Robin's ass. Alton was now engaged to a girl he met on vacation in the Hamptons. Engaged at twenty-one. There had never been a closet for Robin, not really, not since that first kiss with Scott in high school. Sure, he had been evasive at times, even sneaky when necessary, withholding information from acquaintances and strangers for the sake of safety or comfort, but he never lied to himself about the nature of his desire.

The faces of all these boys hovered in his mind when he thought about George dating a woman and sleeping with a guy. How could George be one of the liars, the users? But eventually he had to admit that George hadn't lied to *him*.

"I'm going to come visit you this weekend," Robin announced over the phone, six weeks after their estrangement began.

George responded: "It's about time."

In Philly, Robin discovered that George had given up his girlfriend. "I've come to the conclusion that my inclination is more homosexual than heterosexual" was how he put it. He also announced that he was going to stay celibate for a while because of all this disease spreading around. Not only the big one that was in the news all the time, the so-called "gay cancer," but all the other venereal diseases, too. He got a case of crabs from one, or both, of the boys he'd had sex with, and rather than admit this to Jeanette, he made a bunch of excuses about why he couldn't see her. "Eventually," he said, "she dumped my ass."

"Good," Robin said, and after that, everything was okay again.

George encouraged Robin to slow down his own sex life. "This thing has killed thousands of men who have sex with men," George said. "More than four thousand in 1984 alone." George was spending a lot of time learning all he could about viruses, in particular this newly discovered immunodeficiency virus that was the likely cause of AIDS. He gave Robin a pamphlet, made by a gay organization who did a presentation on campus, called "How to Have Sex in an Epidemic," which advised things like reducing the number of partners, not exchanging bodily fluids, using condoms for anal sex, for oral, too, if you want to be totally sure, and since then, Robin had followed the guidelines. But memories of certain nights, certain guys, came to him like flashes from half-remembered dreams, distressing reminders of what couldn't be undone.

* * *

George leaves to meet the Danish guy, and Robin paces between the living room, kitchenette, and the narrow hallway at the back that leads to their bedrooms, the doors facing each other, mirror images. He's freshly showered, buzzed on Old Latrobe, smoking cigarettes instead of eating a pint of Häagen-Dazs, which is what he really wants but won't allow himself, even for the sake of self-indulgent comfort. He swings between moods: missing Peter, hating Peter, wanting to beg him for another chance, wanting to scratch his face. But without Peter here, without even a phone number where he can be reached, it's all an abstraction, a mental carousel. He puts the dance tape, the one he took from Peter's car, into the boom box. The music instantly conjures up the night, several weeks ago, when he sat here compiling and ordering the songs, timing out each one so they'd fit on two sides of the cassette and none would be cut off. All of it for Peter, to be close to Peter. *Why didn't you see this coming?* It's one thing when a relationship is fizzling and you both know it and can simply move on. But this is a true shock, and he can't work his way around to any thought but this: *It's your own fault*.

He stops the music and tries the TV instead, the portable set with the patchy reception and the rabbit-ear antenna wrapped in foil, just like Grandma Lincoln's. He turns the dial between channels and finds only that unfunny comedy with Nell Carter and some post-Vietnam drama with Jan-Michael Vincent as a vet on a secret mission in a supersonic helicopter. He needs a better distraction. Aside from George, he only knows a couple of people in Philadelphia, one a transplant from New York, the other a friend of a friend from Pittsburgh, but when he calls them neither answers. Of course not, it's Saturday night.

He could call Ruby now, he thinks. She'll listen to his tale of woe. But he remembers that she's gone away for the weekend with her boyfriend, Calvin, down the shore. He thinks about calling his mother, but there's the risk that she might say something infuriating in the name of good advice. Besides, they have a standing phone date on Sunday afternoons, on her dime, so he decides to just wait until tomorrow. Tomorrow is an important one: June 16, Jackson's birthday. They'll reminisce, and get a little weepy, and Robin will pull out the photo of himself with Jackson and Ruby that he had laminated and now keeps in his money clip, and he'll give it a closer look, to mark the occasion. The picture was snapped on the first day of school the year Jackson died. The three of them stand in the driveway in Greenlawn:

Robin and Ruby offering their best smiles, Jackson with an exaggerated toothy grin and scrunched-up eyes, the "monkey face" he always gave to the camera. He did it to annoy Dorothy, whose insistence on the first-day-of-school photo had been, like so many of her proprieties, something that Jackson saw as "dumb." Now, years later, as pictures on photographic paper have largely replaced pictures in his mind, Robin sees Jackson's obnoxious expression as a kind of eternal statement. Jackson would always be remembered as someone who didn't stand still, didn't flash pretty smiles to the camera, didn't want to be sentimentalized. He was, at his core, a bratty boy. Robin won't say this kind of thing to his parents, when he talks to them in separate calls tomorrow, though he and Ruby have often talked about it. Part of the sadness of losing their little brother is that he never got to be anyone else, never got to grow out of his brattiness and become someone they might have liked more.

In his bedroom he finds his well-worn paperback copy of *Franny and Zooey*, its white cover, with a single green stripe and black calligraphic letters, smudged with fingerprints. The inscription, in his mother's handwriting, says, *"We must all find a way."* Beneath her signature she wrote the date, Christmas, 1978, which was right after Jackson died. Robin read *Franny and Zooey* in a trance that winter, too young to understand the story's philosophical bent. What he took from Salinger's novel was simple desire: he fell for the young hero, Zooey Glass, the smart, caustic, and handsome actor who smoked cigarettes in the bathtub while arguing with his mother about what was wrong with his younger sister, and it was that image that led him to announce, the next year, that he'd *found his calling.* It's embarrassing to remember all this now, the impulse of a fifteen-year-old to choose a path borrowed from a novel, because acting, like life, has proved to be much more difficult that he ever imagined. He still doesn't trust himself onstage; "acting" at this point seems like an accumulation of lessons and missteps and fleeting moments that might be breakthroughs or might just be small technical improvements.

He suddenly understands why London has been weighing on him so heavily: It's a test. It might be his one real chance to find out if he's got what it takes. To discover if he's talented, as opposed to just easy on the eyes or lucky.

Then he remembers Calvin's screenplay.

He opens another beer and carries it to his bedroom. On the wobbly card table that substitutes as a desk, he finds the dog-eared page where he last left off.

> INT. NIGHTCLUB, NEW YORK CITY—AFTER MIDNIGHT
> Synthesized music, bright flashes of light, but we only see one table on screen. In a booth, seated, CARTER looks back and forth between BENNETT and AGNETHA, who sip their cocktails and smoke. (Characters must shout to be heard.)
>
> BENNETT
> I'm bored. Where's my nose candy?
>
> CARTER
> Don't pressure me, you pretentious fucks.
>
> AGNETHA
> You're a tyrant. You bore me.
>
> CARTER
> Boredom is a neurological impossibility. Scientists have shown that what you experience as boredom is actually the motivational part of your brain shutting down. Boredom is *fear*.
>
> BENNETT
> (sarcastic)
> I find that scary.
>
> AGNETHA
> The hell with this, you cocksuckers.
>
> CARTER
> We could go back to my place, snort blow, and play truth or dare.

The script arrived in the mail earlier this week, a sloppy pile of typewritten sheets thickened in spots with Liquid Paper and a cover page announcing "*Entering and Breaking*, by Calvin Kraft." The role Calvin had in mind for Robin was Carter ("overeducated and handsome"), a twenty-year-old rich kid who seemed a lot like Calvin: too smart for his own good, letting insults fly whenever he opened his mouth, then retreating into sulkiness.

The first time Robin met Calvin was when he showed up at the apartment on 71st Street to take Ruby out. That night, Robin had plans to meet a friend, but he lingered out of curiosity and to satisfy his mother, who wanted his opinion on the new boy in Ruby's life. Calvin turned out to be one of those tall guys who carry themselves with a stoop. His blond hair hung greasily across his eyes; you wanted to push it out of the way. His mother insisted Calvin call her Dorothy, saying, "Even my children call me Dorothy. I haven't been Mrs. MacKenzie for years." There was some awkward small talk, the four of them suffering through introductions. Then Robin mentioned that he was on his way to the movies to see *Amadeus*. "They say Milos Forman's filmmaking is outstanding," Calvin said, pronouncing the name "*ME-lowsh*," and then, in what Robin would come to recognize as Calvin's characteristic ability to recalibrate featherlight small talk into cutting insult, he continued, "There's no way I'll see it. The subject matter is retrograde, no matter how contemporary they try to make it. Film's supposed to look to the future. Opera's a dead art for dead souls."

Dorothy gasped in shock.

"Uh-oh," Ruby said, a giggle in her throat as she took in their mother's reaction.

Dorothy was a devoted subscriber to the Met, and there wasn't a milestone in Robin's life that wasn't marked by the background crescendo of an aria on the turntable. There might have been one playing at that very moment, perhaps something from Mozart meant to send Robin off to the movie.

A year later, Dorothy had yet to warm to Calvin, though Robin had forgiven him the blunt first impression, especially since Ruby seemed contented enough. She seemed to take some rebellious pleasure in the way her boyfriend didn't kowtow to their mother. It had been so long since his sister had dated anyone. (Had she ever, seriously?) Calvin and Ruby spent a lot of time together, though they didn't display a whole lot of physical intimacy. And besides, Robin found Calvin amusing, despite his pretensions.

So Robin had invited Calvin to visit Carnegie Mellon with Ruby and Dorothy to see him perform. He'd been cast as Brick in *Cat on a Hot*

Tin Roof. Before the show, knowing his family was in the audience, he'd been nearly sick with nerves. The director had complained that Robin was sometimes too self-conscious onstage, and so that night he decided to try something new, to underplay rather than go for broke. Onstage, he could feel the other actors struggling to adjust to his reined-in presence, but he also felt for the first time that the role was a natural extension of him rather than a mask he put on and took off. His drama professors were always talking about the "performance breakthroughs" that happened when "you got out of your own way." Robin wondered if maybe he'd finally had one.

Calvin was teeming with praise, his opinions carrying loudly through the backstage dressing rooms. "You found the fault line between sorrow and rage," he proclaimed. This was an embarrassing compliment to receive in front of the rest of the cast, some of whom clearly thought Robin's changes had been disruptive. Even his mother had been more subdued.

Later, in the men's room of the restaurant where they were having a celebratory dinner, Calvin cornered Robin at the urinal. He was working on a screenplay that he wanted Robin to see. He said it was inspired by *Liquid Sky*, a film that had opened a couple of years before and that was still playing at one Manhattan movie theater at midnight. Robin had seen this "new wave" film and found it unbearable. It reminded him of a certain kind of underground nightlife that always seemed out of reach on his trips downtown: arty fashion plates speaking in flat voices that seemed to signify detachment or irony or some other kind of superiority. But Robin agreed to look at whatever Calvin wrote.

For months now, Calvin had been leaving Robin biweekly answering machine messages saying, "It's coming soon, I'm wildly inspired, I'm rewriting it with you in mind, it's going to blow you away." But when the screenplay arrived (the *original* copy, which made Robin take notice), Robin found that "Carter," though clearly the hero, the last man standing, was anxious and full of himself and not particularly likable. If he'd been a muse to his sister's boyfriend, what did this character say about him? And was the script any good? He couldn't tell. It was certainly repetitious; there were three long phone conversations between Carter and his best friend, Bennett, during which Bennett snorts coke and rambles on about sex and disease, while Carter quietly masturbates (the notation in the script reading, "We don't see but we are left with no doubt that Carter is pleasuring himself"). Carter is described, in one scene, as "hungry for something new." In Calvin's cover letter to Robin, he wrote, "Nudity is optional, but I want to test the limits. Feeling dangerous?" It was a dare, and also weirdly coy. Robin wondered if he should warn Ruby that her boyfriend had some of the telltale signs of a closet case.

He looks up from the script and his gaze lands on the movie poster he's Fun-Taked to the wall: Brad Davis looking outrageously humpable as a French sailor in *Querelle.* A fantasy unwinds of Calvin's film as a wild success: beautifully shot, smartly edited, a cool soundtrack laid on top. It gets picked up by a New York distribution company, gets a long theatrical run at the Bleecker Street Cinema, gets reviewed by J. Hoberman in the *Village Voice.* Robin gets written up in *Variety* as "Someone to Watch."

Unlike some of his classmates, he wasn't out hustling for an agent, didn't go on a thousand auditions, hadn't acted upon the conventional wisdom that said, "If you don't get cast in a feature film by the time you're twenty-one, you'll never have a career." Maybe he was lazy, just didn't have the hustle in him. Or maybe he was wise, taking his time until he was sure of his own talent. When you've been told your whole life that you're good looking, it's easy to doubt that anyone values anything else about you. Good looks get attention, but not all attention is a good thing.

Peter first noticed him for his looks. Robin would catch him staring from the podium at the front of the lecture hall. Robin knew that stare. Men who wanted sex used it, dirty thoughts raging behind their eyes. He's fallen for it so many times, letting guys do things to him just because being *wanted* still felt, even after many years, like an opportunity that might not come again.

Without warning, everyone he's ever had sex with is in the apartment with him now, crowding him, heavy breaths on the back of his neck, damp as drafty air. There's one in particular: his name was Darren, a dancer with haunches like a thoroughbred and a dazzling white smile. He worked on a cruise ship, performing in some kind of Broadway revue, and he had docked in New York for half a week. Darren had spotted Robin at a bar in the West Village, Uncle Charlie's, and had rescued him from a drunk in an ugly knit sweater whom he couldn't shake. By the time Darren shipped out again, Robin had lost track of what day it was. He'd followed him back to the small hotel room where he'd been put up for the week, and since then had hardly seen the light of day. After the second day, they'd scrapped the condoms. Darren had assured him he didn't have "it," and Robin, not yet nineteen, didn't know not to trust a stranger with a voice like music and the body of a satyr.

He wonders, not for the first time, did Peter ever see beyond the surface, did he care about me beyond his lust? Was Peter simply hot for him, while Robin was convinced they were falling in love?

The phone clangs, snapping him from the dream. The ringer is loud; there's only one phone in the apartment and they need to be able to hear it from every room.

"Hello?"

"Hi, Robin." It's Peter.

"I was just thinking about you!" He tamps down his excitement, and adds, "On and off, all night."

"I'm just saying hi. I was a little concerned."

A little concerned is a start, something to work with. "Can I see you?" Robin asks.

"Um, I could swing by in the morning."

"Not tonight?" Robin already knows this isn't what Peter wants. He pushes anyway, "I just think, if we could talk—"

"Yeah, um, but my plans . . . I'm on my way to meet . . ." He cuts himself off.

"You caught me by surprise, and I didn't get to ask everything I wanted to."

"I'm meeting Diana and a bunch of her friends at this place. It'll be crowded."

"A bar?"

"A club."

"Which one?"

"I forget the name. Something with an R."

"Is it a gay club?"

"I think it's mixed. New wave music. Diana wanted to go." Silence. "So, yeah, just saying hi."

No invitation is forthcoming. "Okay, then. Tomorrow. Come by around noon."

After he hangs up, Robin is all agitation. Why bother calling if . . . ? And then he gets an idea. On Peter's last trip, he and Robin went to the gay bookstore, Giovanni's Room, and spent an hour browsing. Peter bought him a gift, a copy of *The Memoirs of Hadrian*, about a gay Roman emperor, a book that Peter said helped him realize how ancient and storied the history of homosexuality was. The guy behind the counter was friendly, sort of flirty, and gave them all sorts of tips about things to do in the city. Sure enough, when he calls the bookstore now, the boy who answers is happy to field Robin's question about a mixed club that plays new-wave music and starts with an R. "Revival," he says without hesitation. "It's on 3rd Street, in a building that used to be a bank. You can tell by the big columns out front."

The location is on the far side of Center City, too far to walk, and too expensive a cab ride. He could take SEPTA, but at night it's a scary few blocks between apartment and train stop, and he usually runs most of the distance, clutching his keys between his fingers like brass knuckles.

He opens the last beer in the fridge. Has he already drunk four?

There's a noise in the hallway. Robin turns to see the door opening. In walks George.

Robin peers past him. "Are you alone?"

"Yeah."

"That was quick."

"Yeah." George drops onto the couch and slumps. He eyes the beer in Robin's hand. "Open one of those for me?"

"Last one." He passes him the bottle. George chugs halfway to the bottom.

"Didn't go well with the Prince of Denmark?"

George shakes his head, shutting his eyes for a moment, as if clearing his vision. "Turns out all he wanted was a quickie."

"Wham, bam, thank you ma'am?"

"More like, wham, bam, thank you, Sambo."

Robin chuckles, but the look on George's face is grim. His body is tightly coiled.

"I get to his hotel room, he gets on his knees before we even get past the small talk. He starts going down on me, saying stuff like, '*Oh, your byoo-tee-full black pee-niss, your smood black skeen.*' And then he's like coming, and it's over."

"He didn't get you off?"

"I couldn't even stay hard. *I vould like to see your black pee-niss orgasm.*"

"Did you tell him we say 'African American' now?"

George doesn't smile. "So I've been racially fetishized and blue-balled all at once. He probably gave me gonorrhea on top of it." George stands and walks to the bathroom, taking the beer with him. He leaves the door open.

Robin follows, as George starts the water for the shower. He's already pulled off his shirt and is kicking off his shoes. The troubled expression on George's face is somehow unfamiliar, and it takes a moment for Robin to realize what it is: A mixture of anger and sadness that comes from being insulted. His feelings are hurt. This is not the usual even-keeled, easily amused George.

"He's a fool," Robin says.

"He's a fucking colonialist motherfucker."

Robin feels like he's on thin ice, but he wants to try again. "I mean, he's a fool not to take his time with you. You're looking foxy."

"Please," George mutters. "Don't you start, too."

George steps into the shower, closing himself in behind the opaque curtain. Robin gets his second glimpse today of George's naked back and ass. It seems especially perilous this time, in the midst of this discussion, and he glances away, his eyes trying to rest on something neutral: a stain on the linoleum, a burn mark from one of his cigarettes.

"The thing is," George is saying through the hiss of the water, "I knew this guy was blunt, but that seemed normal enough. I didn't expect to fall in love. I thought I'd get a little something more than *'your skeen is so smood und shiny, Gay-org.'* "

"You can't expect anything from men," Robin says. "Men suck." He waits for a response, and when he doesn't get one, he steps out of the bathroom. He hates seeing George like this, and he hates that his own reaction is all mixed up with some buzz of desire. This buzz can't be about George. It's the four beers he drank. It's Calvin's dirty screenplay. It's the still lingering effect of Peter's blue tennis shorts tenting up in the car, Peter tempting him before cutting him loose.

Later, George joins him on the couch for the network news, which is saturated with coverage of a hijacked TWA flight that's been diverted to Beirut. A passenger has been killed, his body dumped on the tarmac. Then the story shifts to local news, the ongoing investigation into the Philadelphia police department over the bombing of MOVE. There's a quote from Ramona Africa, the only woman who survived the conflagration, saying the police fired on her as she ran out of the flames: "No one was supposed to survive."

George says, "I'm gonna grow out my dreads and call myself George Africa, and then I'm gonna live among my people and fight the Man."

"What about me?" Robin says. "You're all I got, George Africa."

"Except you're going to London, so fuck you, Blanco."

There's something distinctly not-jokey in George's voice, but Robin doesn't know what to do with it. His mind begins to zoom forward to a day when George no longer wants to be his friend, no longer wants anything to do with him.

Impulsively, he stands up and blocks the TV.

"No more news. It's Saturday night. We should get out of the house. Do you feel like driving?"

"I got a parking spot right out front."

"Well, I have an idea. This club. It's called Revival."

"What kind of music?"

"New wave mostly."

George curls his nose. "I can't dance to that. And what if your ID doesn't get you in?"

"If it doesn't work out, we don't have to stay."

He doesn't tell George until they're well on their way why he wants to go there. "Aw, man," George says, and slaps his hand on the steering wheel.

"Sorry," Robin says. "I need to do this. I'll make it up to you."

George falls silent, but he doesn't turn the car around.

He drives a two-tone Cadillac Seville, gray with a black roof, a late seventies model with a short, slanted trunk. His parents passed it on to him when he moved to Philadelphia, and it's already been broken into twice this summer. The hood ornament and the hubcaps have all been stolen, and the passenger side window no longer rolls down. George pulls up to a fire hydrant across the street from the club, hazards flashing. Robin checks out the crowd lined up behind a velvet rope stretched between two classical columns. Everyone's in some kind of black and white getup, with jagged, asymmetrical haircuts, and heavy black boots. Ruby and Calvin would blend right in. "Are we really in Philadelphia?" Robin asks.

"Those folks are so pale, we could be in Boston."

"That's just face powder," Robin says.

"I wasn't talking about their makeup."

"There are black people in line," Robin says.

"And they'll be waiting out there all night. All four of 'em."

"Or they'll be let in first to make the club more interesting."

"I hope they brought more than one form of ID."

Maybe this was a bad idea. Robin can usually talk his way into a gay bar, but a trendy place like this? His fake ID might not pass inspection; he hates that at twenty, it's legal for him to drink in New York, but not in Pennsylvania. The fact that George didn't bother to dress up won't help get them past the doorman. He's wearing aqua blue medical scrubs and a T-shirt that reads EMBARGO SOUTH AFRICA, NOT NICARAGUA, like an undergrad going to breakfast in the dining hall.

"Tell you what," Robin says. "I'll do a lap through the parking lot. If I see Peter's car, we'll stay. If not, let's just go to the package store, and we'll drown our sorrows at home."

"Even if you find him, you're just going to piss him off."

"No, he'll talk to me. Peter's a talker."

"A bullshitter is what he is."

"Wait here for me, OK?"

Robin gets out of the car and makes his way past the parking lot attendant, who eyes him silently. Robin was right to wear black shoes, black trousers, and a white T-shirt with the sleeves ripped off, the most "new wave" stuff he owns. The sign says parking is four dollars; Peter wouldn't have paid that much. Robin walks to the far side of the lot, to an alley where cars are parked tightly together. He takes a few steps along the sidewalk, and then he spots Peter's Honda at the curb.

Indecision takes hold: Maybe instead of going into the club, he could leave a note. A note on the windshield, so he knows you're serious about wanting to see him tomorrow, so he doesn't wake up and think he can blow you off.

A movement inside the Honda catches his eye. There's someone in the driver's seat. And maybe someone on the passenger's side as well.

Robin slides stealthily alongside the parked cars, craning his neck for a clear view through the hatch. In the streetlight filtering into the car, he can definitely make out Peter. The other person sits facing Peter, in profile. A younger guy: glowing skin, light-colored hair, sharp cheekbone. The upturned collar of a polo shirt frames the back of his neck. Peter seems to be talking to him. Why does he look so serious?

Who is this guy reaching out his arm, resting his hand on Peter's shoulder, halting Peter's speech in mid-sentence, this guy Peter is suddenly leaning toward, closer, closer?

This guy who is kissing Peter on the mouth.

Robin sprints to Peter's window. He looks down at the back of Peter's head as he kisses this other guy. And before he knows what he's doing, Robin is banging on the roof of the car and shouting Peter's name. The night fills with the sudden thunder of fists on metal.

Peter breaks out of the kiss. His face is a mask of alarm shifting into recognition. "What are you doing here?" he asks and opens the door.

"What are *you* doing here?" Robin repeats, and when Peter stutters the beginning of some kind of explanation, Robin finds himself shoving Peter nearly back into his seat.

I'm going to hurt him, Robin thinks, as he raises his hand.

But then there's some other force upon him, other arms, belonging to this other person, the passenger, who has run around the car and is behind him now, pulling.

Robin wriggles sideways, frees himself, and gets a look at this guy: skinny, tiny waist, bony arms. Blond hair the color of Robin's and blue eyes much like his, too. A puffy lower lip and a soft chin. A smooth, hairless face.

Now all three of them are standing in a tense, triangular face-off. "Calm down, Robin," Peter says. "Just calm down."

"Ohhhh," the kid says. "You're *Robin*."

"And who the fuck are you?"

Peter answers for him. "Douglas is, was, one of my students."

"Hi, Douglas," Robin says, his voice calm for a split second before he's shouting, "What the fuck are you doing making out with my boyfriend?"

"Ex-boyfriend," Douglas says.

Robin swings his arm and lunges, ready to smack this boy on the mouth, the mouth that Peter just kissed, but Douglas blocks the blow, grabs Robin's fingers, and twists. There's a struggle for a moment, the two of them intertwined, and then Robin turns the momentum around, getting Douglas's arm in his grip, yanking it behind him. "Ow!" Douglas shouts.

Peter yells, "Stop it, Robin, stop it!"

With a rush of force he didn't know he had, Robin pushes Douglas into the street. He watches as Douglas stumbles and falls to the pavement.

There's a sudden glow of headlights, a car approaching from the end of the alley, the sound of tires on asphalt.

Peter rushes to Douglas and pulls him out of the way. The approaching car stops, blinding them with light, not the elevating light of the stage but the overpowering light of interrogation. Robin backs away, but Peter is suddenly on him, spinning him around, shoving him toward the Honda, pinning him facedown against the door. Robin smells the dry dust on the window and the mechanical odors of the engine. The will to struggle seeps away, replaced by the sensation, the vision, of lying in bed on his stomach with Peter on top of him; Peter has just finished fucking him, the heat still lingering, their bodies compacted and trembling.

Then there's another voice shouting, "Let him go." It's George, silhouetted in the headlights. It was George's Cadillac that came down the alley. "Get off him, Peter."

"George. Hey . . ." Peter loosens his hold, but Robin remains against the car, depleted.

George has something in his hands, brandished like a club—it *is* a club, it's The Club, the weighty, metal steering-wheel lock that everyone uses these days.

"Oh, my God," Douglas says.

George looks over at Douglas, then back at Robin. "Are you all right?"

Robin nods.

"He's not all right, he's crazy," Peter says. "You owe us an apology."

"Us?" Robin asks.

"I'm calling the police," says Douglas, standing behind Peter and sucking up snot, wild-eyed, defiant. He's shaking his injured hand. Robin wants to charge at him all over again, land a powerful blow on that pure, pale skin. He feels the strength he is capable of, the harm he could cause. This knowledge of his capacity for violence is old and powerful; it runs through him in a line straighter than a sword. But he stops himself, because he sees the look on Peter's face: mortified, disappointed, maybe even disgusted.

"Why were you kissing him?" Robin asks.

"Why are you even here?" Peter snarls.

"He's obviously stalking you," Douglas says.

Douglas, you're scrawny and annoying, you have empty eyes and a weak chin. Peter will use you for as long as he wants, he'll fuck you without a condom and blame you for it, then he'll leave you for someone younger who looks just like you. He doesn't say any of this. The words stay trapped in his throat.

"George, do me a favor, talk some sense into him," Peter says.

"No one's doing you any favors," George says. Firmly, he takes Robin by the arm and says, "I don't want to be here if the cops show up."

Robin nods. He understands.

Driving away, Robin feels like they're escaping the scene of a crime, like he's in some movie where you yell to the taxi driver, "Just go!" without any sense of where to. They pass through a neighborhood Robin doesn't know: unpopulated, vaguely industrial, marked by chain-link fences, heavy machinery, rubbish at the side of the road. He stares out the window into a desolate, inert night marked by the eerie glow of a rising full moon.

"Did I just make an ass of myself?" Robin asks.

"Now you know what kind of person Peter really is."

"But what if he *wasn't* cheating on me, what if he just ran into this kid at the club and the kiss was some spontaneous—"

"They were in his car," George says. "They were *at it.*"

"So you don't think I overreacted?"

"You were in shock. That can make it difficult to control your impulses."

"Maybe." But it doesn't feel like shock as much as its opposite: not something unexpected, but something long dreaded, coming to pass. Earlier, at the Greek restaurant, Peter made it sound like he wanted to be with someone his own age. Robin knows why Peter lied, and this knowledge is the tip of something sharp poking his skin, jabbing and jabbing, drawing pinpricks of blood that Robin licks away but can not stanch. The rage that surfaced was bigger than simple anger at Peter and his boy toy. It was the fury Robin holds in check all the time, and has for years and years. He lets some out every now and then, throws something across the room, slams a door hard enough to jiggle the hinges. But not in public, not with his fists.

George says, "The only other time I saw you lose it like that was a long time ago. After your brother died, after the funeral."

Robin looks at him. "Jackson's funeral? You were there?"

"Yeah, I was there!"

"I don't remember that day too well."

"I was hanging out with Ruby and some kids from school. We all saw it: You got in a fight with your cousin. You looked like you were gonna asphyxiate him."

Memories of Jackson's funeral exist in fragments: a Catholic mass, a limousine ride to the cemetery, their house full of people, all those neighborhood women carrying covered dishes, his mother in an expensive black dress. And then, yes, fighting with obnoxious Cousin Larry on the roof outside Robin's bedroom window. How did they wind up on the roof? How did Robin's fingers wind up squeezing Larry's neck? Or was it the other way around? Had it been Larry who was choking him? Robin holds some sensation in his body: his own breathing is too short, too shallow, his head is burning up. . . . For days after the funeral, Robin lay in bed with a fever that spiked so high it nearly put him in the hospital. The illness had the effect of erasing what happened, so that images of that day now rise up and veer off without warning, like bits of a dream, impossible to grasp. He can't at all picture George there, though of course he would have been. A lot of kids from school came. It was a big deal in Greenlawn: a local kid in an accident, in a coma, dead at age ten. "Coma Boy," that's what they used to whisper about Jackson in the halls of Greenlawn High. Robin was Coma Boy's Brother.

Remembering this, his heart races. His throat goes dry. The idea of Jackson's birthday looming tomorrow dredges up pain from deep inside, not the pain of grief or loss but the pain of blame, of responsibility. He was there when it happened, the accident that started everything. They were fighting on the playground slide, Robin and Ruby and Larry and Jackson, a confusing scuffle that ended with Jackson tumbling to the pavement and landing on his head.

He says, "It's like I was some other person." George reaches over and ruffles the back of Robin's hair, rubs his neck, grips the tendons.

Robin breathes into the force, banishing the image of Jackson's fall, as he always eventually does. "I'm sorry you had to see that. With Peter."

George allows himself a smile. "I'm glad I did."

Robin sees admiration on George's face, and there's more to it than just George's loathing of Peter. It's like yesterday at the restaurant, George smiling while Robin opened that wine bottle on the floor. It's a little bit dangerous, being appreciated for being wild, for the ways you break the rules. With a start, Robin realizes how far they've come from their early days of talking current events in study hall and riding the subway to Grandma Lincoln's. Nor is George's reaction here some methodical, unemotional response, like after Robin first came out to him.

He's changed; they've changed each other. Peter is back there somewhere, turning into the past, and George is right here at his side, as he's been all along.

Robin realizes he needs to say something more. "Hey, I'm sorry for before, when you came back from your date? You were feeling bad, and I tried to make a joke. And then I tricked you into bringing me to that club."

George nods, and Robin can see him taking this in. Then he seems to get an idea, and a faint smile appears at the corners of his mouth. "How about this: I take *you* for a ride, without telling you where we're going."

Robin laughs. "Should I be worried?"

"Just a little," George says, and now he really seems amused. He says, "It'll be a good distraction. For both of us."

George drives them to the Schuylkill River, to an unlit stretch of city park wedged between the riverbank and a row of gloomy warehouses. Tonight, the full moon, so bright it looks blue, casts a glow on the water that shatters the liquid surface into a black-and-white checkerboard. On the far shore, tiny pairs of headlights whoosh along an elevated section of the Schuylkill Expressway.

They walk toward the river down a slope covered in trampled grass, but Robin stops before they get too far. "Where are we?"

"Well," George says. "Have you ever heard of Judy Garland Park?"

Robin laughs nervously. "Judy Garland wouldn't last a minute here."

"Yeah, but you know the expression, *a friend of Dorothy*?"

Now Robin gets it, and as his eyes adjust he can see that, yes, there are men standing at intervals along the riverside fence going north toward the Walnut Street overpass, and figures moving around the perimeter, toward some railroad tracks that snake from one of the warehouses into a dark thicket of trees. A freight train sits like a monster waiting in the dark, silently watching them.

He's been to the cruising grounds in Central Park, a series of overgrown trails called the Ramble. Once he even backed himself up against a tree trunk while an older guy, who looked like a father of three from Spanish Harlem, with flecks of gray in his mustache, sucked his dick; but Robin got nervous quickly and zipped up before it went very far. But that was in the daylight.

"Come on," George says, and leads him down to the fence. Robin wonders how he should stand: facing the river with his back toward the park? That feels sort of vulnerable, like someone could sneak up on them from behind. But looking outward puts them on display, inviting action. Is that what George wants? Is he hoping to hook up tonight? Robin faces sideways, leaning on his hip.

"So you come here for sex?" Robin asks him.

George clears his throat. "Mostly, I watch."

"I didn't know you were a Peeping Tom."

"I'm not creepy about it. I just like to be *around* it. I guess you could classify me as a bit of a voyeur. Everyone's either a voyeur or an exhibitionist." He adds, "*You* are an exhibitionist."

"I'm a *thespian*," Robin says, deliberately using a word he finds ridiculous. "It goes with the territory."

George pulls his wallet from his pocket. From the billfold he fishes out a flattened joint. "Gimme your lighter."

Robin's never seen George with pot before. "You're full of surprises tonight."

"Blame it on the full moon."

"Oh really?"

"Yes, really. Anecdotal evidence suggests that the moon can influence our circulation, like it does with tides. Our bodies are mostly water."

"I'm glad there's a scientific explanation."

"There almost always is."

George leans forward, matching paper tip to flame; a moment later, he erupts into coughing, smoke swirling furiously around him. "I'm still new at this," he says.

Robin takes one deep hit, and right away feels himself melting. He leans back into the fence for support, as a wave takes hold like a warm embrace. It's so seductive: *Hey there, remember me? Remember this feeling?* Yeah, I remember, Robin thinks. He smoked so much of this stuff in high school, in New Jersey, when all you had to do was walk into the courtyard between classes and someone would get you high. George never did; he wasn't part of that scene. Robin never buys it anymore; he doesn't *hold,* as they used to say. He can't get anything done when he's stoned, though he can get into plenty of trouble.

"Since when do you buy pot?"

"Cesar *gave* it to me. He told me to share it with you." A faint smile curls George's lips; behind his glasses, his eyes are already glazed and goofy. He makes a stab at Cesar's accent. *"Tell Blanco, he smoke a little of this, he be less uptight."*

"Uptight! Is that what they say about me?" Robin thinks of himself as friendly and talkative with the customers, eager to hang out at the bar with the waitstaff after closing, cool with being singled out as "Blanco." But then of course he gets frazzled a lot, and walks on eggshells when Rosellen is near, and when he's in the weeds he knows he can get bitchy with the busboys and dishwashers. He says, "I am not long for that job."

George says, "He keeps talking about my ass."

"He does that with me, too!"

"Me and you and Blanco, we should all party together."

"Do you think," Robin asks, "that he's totally trying to engineer a three-way?"

He can't quite make out George's reaction, but Robin feels himself thrust into a pornographic dream: the two of them, himself and George, bent over, Cesar naked and erect behind them, taking turns and barking out dirty names in *Español*.

That's the other thing he remembers about smoking pot. It's the on switch to horniness.

"OK, George, admit it. You don't come here just to watch."

"Well, think of it like this. You go to a museum to look at paintings. You just want to be around the art. It doesn't mean you wish you were a painter."

Robin considers this. "The first time Dorothy took me to MoMA, and I saw *Starry Night*, I wanted to go home and throw paint all over a canvas."

"Maybe I'm just waiting for the right inspiration. One time, this guy talked to me for a while. He was kind of a clone, a big Italian guy with moustache. He wanted me to follow him that way." He points toward the railroad tracks. "Didn't seem wise."

Robin peers into the darkness. "I'll say."

"I walked with him to his pickup truck, but at the last minute I changed my mind. I've realized that I'm just not into doing it with strangers." George takes another puff, smaller this time. He stares with almost comic intensity into Robin's eyes and announces, "I better stop or I'm going to be too high to care."

Robin doesn't ask, *Care about what?* because the silence that follows is full of suggestion, and even with the moonlight on George's glasses, Robin can see into his eyes, can see what might happen next, if they'll let it.

From out of nowhere, there's a swirl of red and blue light and the shrill of a siren. Back at the curb where they just parked, a car is slowing down. A police car. It comes to a full stop. The doors open. "Fuck," Robin says, the warmth of the high shifting instantly to panic. He grabs George by the arm and says, "We're outta here." But the way out is where the cops are. He looks upriver, toward the overpass, where men are scattering like birds.

George says, "Come on," and pulls him toward the train tracks.

Together they move into the shadows, stumbling alongside the freight cars. The ground is difficult to walk on; there's garbage everywhere, and loose, sharp stones between the ties. He slips on a beer bottle and tumbles into George, who pulls him by the arm through some bushes into a tiny overgrown clearing at the river's edge, a leafy, protected area you might call a "fort" if you were a kid playing in the woods.

George whispers, "I've never seen pigs here before. The guy with the truck, he told me they don't bother with this place."

"Maybe they want their dicks sucked."

"You've got a dirty mind, Robin."

"You're the one who hangs out here."

Through the bushes, beams of light flicker in the dark. He hears rustling; footsteps moving closer. Cops on foot, wielding flashlights, which means nightsticks and guns, too. Robin's blood pounds in his ears, and he shivers from the damp river air, from the effect of the high, from nerves. Their pot smoke is probably still lingering in the air, back by the fence. He starts preparing a story: *Officer, we were going for a midnight stroll and got lost. We're tourists trying to find our way back to our hotel. We were looking for a little lost dog, a hound dog that follows its nose everywhere.* His mind leaps to police dogs, big growling canines trained to sniff out dope smokers and cocksuckers. Is this really happening? Hiding from the cops in the bushes in the middle of the night, stoned? George is supposed to be the sensible half of their friendship, the responsible one. What was he thinking?

One of the flashlight beams swings in their direction, and Robin shrinks deeper into the darkness.

Then a burst of static slices the air. He gasps, then covers his mouth.

Another loud burst. It's a walkie-talkie. There's a muffled communication, voices trading information, hard to make sense of. Robin picks up the word "suspects." *Suspects?* Are they suspects? Did that little bitch Douglas actually call the cops on them? What if they have George's license plate number? If the two of them are arrested, who will they call? Rosellen? His mother?

"Should we surrender?" Robin whispers.

George shushes him, softly but insistently. Then he takes Robin's hand and squeezes and doesn't let go. Robin suddenly realizes how much scarier this must be for George. Philly cops are not going to look kindly at a black kid, growing dreads, with the stink of pot on his clothes.

Out on the tracks there's more static, more talk of suspects, and then a sudden rush of footsteps and crunching gravel. Miraculously, the sounds are traveling away. The flashlight beams disappear. Hand in hand, they continue to wait this out. A silent minute passes, maybe two, maybe five, who knows how long, but at last they hear a siren and a screech of tires. Robin breathes deep, in and out. George stays, "Stay here," then lets go of his hand, steps out of the brush, and takes a look. The air seems to get colder when George's body pulls away. It's a moment of pure loneliness.

At last George returns and says, "All clear."

After all the activity, the park is deadly quiet. They pass only two men, white guys wearing worn, tight jeans and black leather jackets. The men slow down to stare at them, and one of them lifts his chin and nods suggestively. Robin looks away, unsettled by how gaunt this guy seems. He used to fantasize about older men, who were experienced, who were strong, whose bodies had hair and muscle tone, so different than the pale awkward boys in high school. But older men now seem entirely dangerous. Not dangerous like cops. Dangerous like death. George picks up the pace, and Robin follows.

In the car, they rub their arms to warm up. In astonished, relieved voices they go back over everything that just happened; already, with their fear behind them, it has become a thrilling misadventure.

"Another night in the City of Brotherly Love," George says.

"Never a dull moment."

"So, Robin—"

"What?"

"Do you regret that you moved here?"

"No," Robin says quickly, too quickly, really, because it masks the truth: he doesn't yet know.

"Seems like you're not that into it."

"I'm getting used to it."

"Philly can be pretty rough."

Robin nods. Carefully, he adds, "Seems like it's changed you."

"To what?"

"I'm not really sure. One minute you're George Africa. Then you're George the Voyeur."

"I'm just me. You gotta stop thinking of me as Little Georgie. I haven't been that guy for years."

"I know that." And then it occurs to him that he has a similar question for George. "Do you regret inviting me to live with you?"

"It had to be done."

"What does that mean?"

George does something surprising then: he sheds his glasses, folds them, tucks them on the dashboard. He shifts in his seat, drawing closer to Robin.

Blame it on the pot, on the full moon, on the adrenaline rush of their escape from the cops. It's in the air. You might be misreading this, Robin tells himself. But there's only one way to find out. He slides closer, too.

George's mouth is floating toward his. The remaining gap between them closes. There's a pinprick of static electricity when their lips make contact.

George's mouth is warm and wet, his lips a little rough. He keeps his eyes closed. Robin's eyes stay open, he wants to see this, it's so new and unexpected, unexpected even though he was ready for it. They kiss shyly, a string of individual kisses. Maybe if he doesn't think about the fact that this is *George,* his best friend, practically his brother, George whom he's never kissed before, if he lets this be about the kiss and not the kissee, there will be nothing to worry about. His dick is pinched inside his briefs. He tugs at the fabric to free things up. His other hand is braced against the dashboard, as if to keep him from lifting off like a traveler in a hot-air balloon.

Then George tilts his head just the slightest degree, a tiny but unmistakable surrender that sends a shudder through Robin. At last he closes his eyes, he bears down, he accelerates. Little pecks become one complete kiss, mouths open, tongues moving, and time disappears into their bodies. Their hands are moving, nervous but unstoppable, finally dropping into each other's laps, groping for hard-ons.

Which is when Robin feels himself hit a limit. "Wait, wait," he insists. "Needle off the record." He takes George by the shoulders and gently lifts him upright.

George blinks. His lids are heavy, drowsy, like it's morning and he's waking from a dream. Robin can see that he's still inside the kiss. "Greetings," he says, with a grin.

"I just want to be sure you want to," Robin says.

"Duh."

"Because this is out of the blue, right?"

"Not exactly."

"But, we've never . . ."

George stares at him. "I'm pretty sure that I've been dropping hints."

"Like dancing naked in the apartment?"

"That was just a coincidence. Other things."

A week ago, back home after a murderous dinner shift, George gave him a backrub that felt so good, and ranged so far and wide that Robin had to cover up his hard-on. George noticed and made a joke that "A happy ending costs extra." Robin was so flustered all he said was, "You better get yourself a boyfriend, Georgie. Don't let those hands go to waste."

But this is different. Not a reaction to something; an intention.

There's the sound of an engine starting up. Across the street, a pickup truck pulls out of a spot and rolls alongside them. George stares at it. "Hey, look! It's the guy who hit on me that time."

"Are you sure?"

"Yeah, see that, above the turn signal?" Robin looks there, at a diamond of bent metal, shining in the light. George says, "I remember that dent."

Aglow in the passing headlights, glasses off, shirt unbuttoned, mouth raw from contact, his friend is absolutely not, Robin sees, Little Georgie from high school. He tries to recast him: not as his best friend but as a sexy stranger, a hot opportunity arising out of nowhere. When he thinks of it this way, there's no hesitation. No emotion to get in the way. Yeah, he realizes, I'd have sex with this guy.

George leans in for another kiss, which gets Robin stiffer. He hasn't actually softened up since this started. If the kiss is any indication of what actual sex would be like, that just might be reason enough to push this further. He scans ahead to tomorrow. He doesn't work on Sundays. He can't remember if George works brunch or dinner. That could mean the two of them home all day, figuring out how to deal with what happened the night before. And what if Peter calls? Will there be some last-ditch attempt to make things right again? Does what's happening here have anything to do with Peter, or is this completely separate?

Neither of them speaks as they begin the drive back to their apartment. But the silence seems to hum, like the resonance of amplified music after a speaker has cut out. Maybe it's too much for George; he flips on the car radio, tuned to the community radio station he listens to lately. Right now there's a Bob Marley song playing. Robin has never really understood reggae, but right now, with his head still thrumming from the joint they smoked an hour ago, it seems to fit the mood.

George finds a parking space on their block, and Robin lets out "Yes!" as they pull to the curb. Parking the car sometimes means walking the worst blocks in the neighborhood, unlit, mostly empty stretches where muggings are a fact of life. The zone where the university bleeds into the neighborhood is the worst of it, because college students are known to carry wallets full of cash, and wear watches and gold chains, and to carelessly shut out the world with headphones attached to a Walkman. Robin's years living in cities have stripped him of all of these, even his wallet (ever since he was pickpocketed on the New York subway, he has used a money clip, kept in his front pocket), but that doesn't make him any less a target. George warned Robin about this before he agreed to move here, and every time he feels his stomach clench, he remembers that he said, "If you can handle it, Georgie, I can handle it."

They shuffle down the sidewalk with a meter of empty air between them, hands stuffed in pockets like school chums. The walk carries for Robin memories of late-night treks to other apartments, those penultimate steps when he finds himself barely able to contain his excitement, or, on less successful nights, when he is overcome by last-minute doubt and scrambles for a way to back out. But this walk is unlike any of those, because it feels so absolutely ordinary: Robin and George are simply going home.

They enter the apartment as they usually do. George unlocks the door, kicks off his sneakers, and nudges them to the wall. Robin steps past him to the bathroom and leaves the door open while he pees. *Exhibitionist*. He avoids the mirror as he washes his hands. He doesn't want to tempt the truth his eyes might reveal (apprehension? eagerness?); he just wants to move without deliberation into whatever comes next.

He hears the refrigerator door open and close, another familiarity. George is forever searching their generally empty fridge for a snack or a sip of something. Robin always comes upon him staring into the shelves as if patiently awaiting an arrival.

Robin goes into the living room and looks to the answering machine. A little rectangle of red light strobes.

"Wait," George says from behind him. "You don't need to talk to him now."

Robin pauses, index finger poised above the play button. "You think it's Peter."

"Who else?"

George hands him the newly lit end of the roach, and Robin steps away from the answering machine. Strange to realize he's not going to listen to whatever Peter's left on the tape. That he's going to wait, so he can be with George.

He is still holding smoke in his mouth when George leans into him. The onrush of the high and the wetness of the kiss meld into a surge that sets Robin's hands in motion. He raises George's T-shirt and caresses his back, brushing lightly up his spine. George shivers. "You need to warm up these mitts," he says, reaching around to cover Robin's hands with his own. He guides them down his back, past the elastic waistband of his scrubs and over the slope of his ass, which is hairless and hard. George mutters, "Hot damn," with a deeply satisfied growl that Robin registers as the most unguarded expression either of them has allowed thus far.

George shoves Robin onto the lumpy cushions of their beat-up couch. Robin locks arms and legs around him. Their differently angled cocks slip across each other under layers of fabric, hard against hard.

A pillow wedged under Robin's head shoots over the armrest, knocking the answering machine from the end table. The device dangles on a wire for a moment, then dislodges and clatters atop the carpet. The ejected microcassette is a tease: Is Peter's apology recorded there? Robin's eyes meet George's and then they both laugh: at Peter's expense, at Robin's, at all of this.

No longer is he imagining George a stranger. His own awareness of the moment won't allow it. And yet: this is George, but not the George he knows. George's mouth is all over him, clothes are coming off, little giggles are emitted as they shuffle and adjust and gasp at each new sensation, but there's something serious running beneath it all, some intensity of purpose. Robin reaches between George's thighs and wraps his fist around a shaft swollen thick. He strokes to the root and back up to the damp tip. Then he dives forward and sucks George into his mouth. "Oh, yeah," George says, which inspires Robin to give it his all.

Above him, he hears George say, "Don't worry, I won't come. And if I get too pre-cummy, just stop."

It takes Robin a moment to understand what George is trying to communicate: *how to have sex in an epidemic.* This is how it's supposed to go now, how it should have gone with so many other guys. A plan: voiced, agreed upon. An understanding of what they won't be doing.

Though part of him wants to taste it.

"You better hit pause on this tape," George warns, seizing up until Robin relaxes his grip. George's mouth hangs slack while he holds back his breath and a premature burst. He stands up, naked and erect, wearing only tube socks, white with red stripes. "This couch is working against us," George says. "It's not wide enough, and it's not long enough."

"Your place or mine?" Robin asks. Robin has the wider bed, a double to George's twin.

But George guides them to his room, saying, "Let's break mine in."

Their rooms are identical in size and laid out in mirror configuration. But where Robin's is tidy, George's is a mess. The furniture came with the rental: a banged-up table, now cluttered with opened envelopes, unopened textbooks, crinkled bills and scattered coins from shift-tips; a wooden chair draped in George's hideous robe; a tall shelving unit crammed with summer clothing and crowned with an emerald-green bottle of Polo. A pile of unwashed laundry spills out of the closet and fills the air with body smells: pits, feet, dirty underwear. Near the bed is a white tube of K-Y Jelly and a balled-up hand towel.

George has pushpinned above his bed a handful of postcards purchased in a gift shop on South Street: Albert Einstein lit celestially from behind, Harry Belafonte with his shirt blown open, Prince looking slick and sleazy, doe-eyed Sal Mineo dreamily hanging on Elvis's every word. The last image is a dark-skinned black man in a dress shirt and tie loosened at the neck, a cigarette poised impatiently, eyes wide as dollar coins, a man not lovely but formidable. "Remind me who he is," Robin says.

George points to a book splayed facedown on the pitted carpet, scarlet and navy letters on a cream-white dust jacket: *Another Country, a novel, James Baldwin.* "Oh, right," Robin says. "Dorothy has this book."

"Please don't mention your mother while we're . . ."

"Sorry."

As George fusses with a fitted sheet that has come undone from the bed, Robin flips the book over and scans the opened page: someone named Vivaldo is about to bottom for someone named Eric. Robin reads aloud, "*He whispered into Eric's ear a muffled, urgent plea.* There seems to be gay sex going on here."

George says "Here, too," taking Robin's prick in his hand.

Robin grabs George the same way, as if they are enacting the handshake of a secret society. George's dick is the same length hard as it is soft; sex hasn't made it longer, just stiffer, fuller, unlike Robin's, which nearly doubles when he's aroused. "I'm a grower. You're a show-er," Robin says, looking downward, comparing himself to George with a self-conscious pang.

"Don't you start talking about my 'beautiful black penis.'"

"It *is* beautiful."

"I like yours, too."

He looks him in the eyes and says, "Now what?"

"OK," George starts, "I know this might sound weird and unexpected"—he bobbles his head nervously—"but can I ask you to do something?"

Robin says, "Sure," but worry grips him, mindful of the equilibrium they've maintained thus far, fearful of the irreversible act, the one that will ruin everything.

"Can I watch you?" George asks.

"Watch?"

"Just you. Masturbating."

"You mean, instead of . . . ?"

"Just for a little while." George forces an uneasy laugh. "I warned you. I'm a voyeur."

"I thought that was just . . ."

"What?"

"Something you said so you could explain why you haven't gotten laid."

"No, that's what I wonder about. How another guy jacks off."

. . . The memory again of the piano teacher, Mr. Morris. He wore a musky cologne that would linger on Robin's clothes after their lessons. His large hands seemed too weighty to move so quickly on the keys. Robin wondered how they would feel on his skin. *I can't touch you,* Mr. Morris said, *but you can show me how you touch yourself.* And later, when Robin hesitated, when he questioned whether he should once again take his clothes off and stand apart and touch himself for money, whether there wasn't something wrong about it, Mr. Morris told him, *Beauty is a blessing to be shared, like a talent for music* . . .

"Will I be watching you, too?" Robin asks.

George shrugs.

"OK, then," Robin says, as if something has been decided.

They climb onto the bed, one at the head and one at the foot. Legs stretched, nearly touching. Robin frowns, trying to figure this out. "You start," George says. "Just do what you do." Robin nods seriously, and grips himself, one hand wrapped tight, the other roaming, stirring up extra sensation. He slips into a kind of privacy, his eyelids fluttering, drooping, squeezing shut. . . . Morris had a lover who had been some kind of artist, had made collages of illustrations cut from Time/Life how-to guides, history books, gay porno magazines, all that shredded, varnished paper. But the lover was gone, something had happened to him, the art was all that was left behind. . . .

He comes back to the moment, looks at George, who says, "Close your eyes again."

Robin does as he's told, but something has shifted. He senses that to be watched and wondered at could be a peril perhaps more risky than their back-and-forth groping thus far. It strikes him as out of balance. He can hear the sound of George stroking himself and wonders why he can't watch, too. And this has the effect of increasing the hunger he feels, feels for George, just an arm's length away. George says, "Tell me what you're thinking about."

"I'm trying to picture you right now."

"I'm touching myself."

"I like the way your voice sounds," Robin says. "Really deep and confident."

There was giggling earlier but not now. Now his heart is beating so fast. He and Peter have never done anything quite this purposeful. All their sex was the same: horizontal, sweaty, lots of rub-a-dub. It always just *happened.* But this, George is making this happen.

George continues to speak, to instruct. "Do that, touch there, don't stop." He gets more commanding the longer Robin keeps at it.

Hips thrust, toes curl, teeth grip a lower lip.

"I'm close," Robin says.

"Not yet. Take your hands off your penis. Put your hands on your hips. Catch your breath. Try to hold back."

He wonders if all along he's wanted George to admire him like this, if some part of him craved this kind of attention. Has he been angling for this all along, since they've lived together? *Exhibitionist.* But if that's so, then why does this feel like such a surprise?

"All right. You can look."

For a split second he worries that he'll open his eyes to some strange sight, like George contorted into a crazy position or wearing some kinky outfit, but no. He's naked, his body tense with stimulation. George has a different jacking method, two hands pumping at once, maybe because he's bigger and needs more friction. Robin shuffles closer, nearly touching George, who leans back against the wall.

He doesn't have much left in him.

He has said so many things to George over so many years, but never before this: "I'm coming." This one is new.

And then he's everywhere, exploding, and then George is too, loudly, swearing, "Damn, damn, damn . . ." Robin feels a wild, exhilarating confusion that contains the need to burst into laughter, or perhaps break into the tears that have been held in check all day.

They lie on the bed, bumped up against each other. Robin reaches out and finds George's hand and squeezes, and George does the same, holding tight, like earlier, in the bushes, hiding from discovery.

George mumbles, "We'll sleep well now."

The bed is too small to allow anything but tangling together, more so because there are damp spots to avoid, but Robin finds he has no desire to cross the hall to his own spacious mattress. To leave George's room would mark the end of something he's not yet ready to give up.

Whatever just happened, he can't walk away from. He wants a cigarette, but George doesn't let him smoke in here. So he backs himself into George, letting George spoon him from behind, their arms braiding together. He listens to the roar of blood rushing in his ears, aware that the pot hasn't yet let go its sensory hold. George's sweat-slicked body rises and falls behind him. Soon George is snoring, hushed and contented.

Eventually, Robin sleeps. He can't tell for how long, or how deep; no dreams mark the shift. Then suddenly he's alert and jittery. He rotates beneath George's arms, repositions himself on his back, crosses his arms on his chest like a corpse. On the wall is the row of postcards, lined up perfectly inside a band of streetlight coming in from the window. The placement, Robin sees, is intentional. George has tacked them in this arrangement so that he can look at them even at night.

James Baldwin stares down at Robin as if chiding him: "Brother, I saw this one coming."

Sleep eludes him now. There's a bright, pale flash of illumination. Lightning. He sits up as the thunder crashes, and notices then the hissing of rain. How long has it been raining? Maybe he did sleep for a while. But he's awake now.

He slides out of George's bed and tiptoes into the coolness of the apartment. They've left lights on everywhere.

A tendril of water gleams on the floor, rain sneaking in through the front window, which has been left open. He throws it open wider and sticks his head out into the slanting shower, an instant, cool caress against his bare skin. His tousled hair catches the moisture, which beads on the tops of his ears and trickles down his neck and shoulders. He melts into it, a soft wave along his flesh. Below, the street is like dark earth that has been turned over; the concrete sidewalks, empty and hushed, look like they're covered in moss. He fantasizes waking George for a naked sprint to the corner and back, a couple of urban nature boys staking their claim.

Then he turns back into the living room, and there, beneath the lamp, is the fallen answering machine. The rainwater is trickling toward it. He picks it back up, plugs it in again. The red message light blinks.

Perhaps it's penance, or remorse, or just the curiosity that accompanies insomnia, but he absolutely needs to know what Peter has said.

Play.

"I'm sorry to bother you." The voice is female, slightly strained, fighting to be heard above background noise: traffic, music, a roar that might be the wind. For just an instant he mistakes her for Rosellen, calling with a late-night request to fill a shift. Then he understands. It's his sister.

"I'm calling from Seaside Heights. Can you believe it?" Right, she's down the shore this weekend with Calvin. In his disorientation, he can't quite conjure it: Ruby in Seaside, a party town for teenagers. "Remember when Dorothy and Clark took us down here? Remember we stayed in that motel near the boardwalk? I just walked by that motel! I *think* it was the same one, with the picture of the lady diving in the water. It seems so long ago, but nothing's really changed."

Robin recalls that family vacation with a wisp of ghostly resentment: Dorothy and Clark, bickering in the car over things like which lane on the Parkway was moving fastest, or which gas station was likely to offer the lowest price per gallon, and only cheering up in the evening over cocktails at dinner. When he thinks back on it, how could he *not* have known there were problems in his parents' marriage? Years before Jackson's accident, there were already problems. But the accident brought them all to the surface.

Ruby is apologizing for the lengthy message, stretching it lengthier. ". . . I guess I just felt like talking. It's not a big deal. I left the party and didn't tell Calvin. There was this guy I used to know from Crossroads—that Catholic retreat weekend? I don't think you ever met him. He was at this party—it was so out of nowhere—and now I'm trying to find him. I *followed* him. I'm a little buzzed. I'm not sure what I'm doing—" *Blpppp.*

The machine had cut her off with a robotic slurp.

She didn't sound quite right. Ruby doesn't have much tolerance for drinking.

He digs out his Parliaments and lights one off the gas stove. Smoke fills the hollow between the counter and the cabinets. He stares at the phone. There's no way to reach her now. If he chose to indulge this flush of worry, he could call his insomniac mother; it's 2 A.M., and she might still be enthroned at this moment on her sofa, poring over the latest Book of the Month Club selection. He can picture the sheen of her cream-colored robe, the lamplight twinkling off her reading glasses, her face scrubbed of makeup. (He wonders: When Dorothy thinks of him, as she must, is she able to form such an accurate picture? The details of his routine are unknown to her; the things he did tonight are definitely beyond what she could imagine about him. She knows he's gay, she knows George is, too; but the two of them, old friends, *just like brothers,* together like they were tonight? No, Dorothy wouldn't consider it possible.)

He pushes the save button. The message light goes dark.

Tomorrow is Sunday. Ruby will probably wake with a hangover and then call in the afternoon to fill out the story. She'll be embarrassed. She'll be with Calvin again, eating breakfast at a comically late hour. She'll turn the conversation around, ask Robin about his night.

Will he tell her about this evening that began with rejection and ended up with something quite the opposite? He still feels the bruise of being dumped and the humiliation of the fight outside the club. With just a few hours' distance, he understands the finality of it. Peter is finished with him. But then there's the unfinished story: this thing with George. Ruby has known George nearly as long as he has. Will he tell his sister what has happened here? And if he doesn't, what does that say?

The first time Robin told his sister, in plain terms, about a crush on a boy, she should have been way too young to understand. She was only twelve, but she had figured out about Scott, had overheard a phone call. "Ruby, this will probably sound weird to you," Robin had stammered, one winter morning in Greenlawn, not long after Jackson died. "Scott is more than a friend."

"Does that mean you *like* him?" she asked, looking him in the eyes.

"Yeah," Robin admitted. "The way a guy likes a girl."

But Scott had moved to another town a half-hour bus ride away, and he had stopped calling, and he wouldn't come to the phone when Robin called. Robin decided he had to go see Scott and say something to his face, friendly or unkind, he didn't know which it would be. Ruby listened to all this and then told Robin she would cover for him; and so she made possible the long adventure that followed.

His time with Scott that day was brief. They were alone for a while in Scott's room; they got stoned; they kissed and groped each other and then had a fight. *Breakup sex* is what he would call it now. Robin left, knowing he probably wouldn't see Scott anymore. Afterward, wiping tears from his cheeks with the cuff of his sweat jacket, he found himself not on the bus back to Greenlawn but on a bus to New York City. He hardly remembered making the decision, but there he was, enveloped in the flurry of Port Authority on a Saturday afternoon, running from his first heartbreak.

He set out on foot downtown, along Broadway, moving from one public square to another—Times, Herald, Union, Washington—in between which were long, anonymous stretches of sidewalk. In Washington Square, he parked himself on the back of a bench, feeling less sorry for himself now that he had navigated so many city blocks and wound up in a place he knew well. He'd been in Washington Square with his mother, many times, and once with Scott, but never alone; it was a triumph just being here. The sun emerged from a bank of clouds, but he had no gloves, so his hands stayed in the pockets of his down vest. He stared at strangers moving past. In the city you saw all kinds: glamorous, exotic, trendy, scary, old, young, the kind who looked you in the eye and the kind who whizzed right by. All of them were a relief from the sameness of Greenlawn, from the hierarchy of high school, from the sadness that had overtaken his family.

Stationary for hours that afternoon, he discovered that strangers wanted to gab with him, usually bums who asked questions but then interrupted the answer with non sequiturs, and also shifty-eyed men, who wanted to sell him drugs and were sometimes hard to shake. One old white lady jabbed her cane at him, snarling, "Get your feet off the bench! People sit there!" He wished he could tell his mother about these people; she would relish the details, like the way the old lady's cane had a gold handle in the shape of a mushroom. But of course he couldn't tell her, because he was breaking her rules by being here, alone, without permission. That day, he didn't care. Jackson was dead. Scott didn't love him. What was left to lose? As long as he remained in public, he felt safe from harm, and in any case he felt strong enough to handle whatever was heading his way.

He remembers the four dark-haired Italian girls who approached his bench that afternoon. They wore Catholic-school skirts and black tights, and they surrounded him in a loose circle. He had noticed them eyeing him and gossiping with collective curiosity; now they taunted him about the sweat jacket hood he had tugged over his blue eyes. "We want to see your face," one of them said, and when he pushed back the hood they all giggled. He pulled the hood back up; one of them pushed it down again. Up again, and then back down. It was their little game, and he gave in, like a puppy agreeing to heel and accept a vigorous petting. They giggled again when he told them his name, again when he said he was from New Jersey. They went to Saint-someone high school in a Brooklyn neighborhood he'd never heard of. He tagged along with them to a diner, where they squeezed into a red vinyl both, pressing him against the wall, knocking knees with him under the table.

The oldest one, Lila, fired off questions: "Do you have a girlfriend? Do you like disco? Are you popular? Do you take a shower every day?"

He answered some truthfully, some not, creating a version of himself in bits and pieces, understanding quickly that a little bit of mystery would appeal to these boy-crazy girls. Finally, the waitress, sick of the noise they were making, told them to leave. Lila pulled a LeSportsac purse from her school book bag, and he let her pay for his éclair and coffee. She wrote her phone number down for him.

After he said good-bye to the girls at the top of a subway entrance, he turned toward Christopher Street. He had no plan for the day, but these few blocks drew him in deeper, because of all the men hanging out, even in winter. Hood up, peering into shop windows, some filled with leather clothes, some with objects that at age fourteen he couldn't identify, but which seemed to be for sex, he found himself thinking of Scott, back in New Jersey, which seemed now like the other side of the world.

"Yo! Blue eyes, come on over," called a voice from a stoop. Two guys were waving at him, older teenagers, maybe as old as twenty, and they had the kind of dark features his mother referred to as *ethnic.* He stood near them and accepted a cigarette. They laughed at him when he tried to pass himself off as eighteen. Colder now that the afternoon was turning to evening, he went along with them to a place called Julius; he'd expected an Orange Julius, the fast food chain, but it was a bar, a gay bar populated with a dozen men. He hesitated at the door, then told himself he'd just look and leave. No harm in checking it out.

He had never been in a bar of any kind and was surprised how dark it was and how smoky. Guys sitting in pairs drank beer and conversed; others stood by themselves along the walls, as if waiting for someone. He had the revelation that anyone might sit here for hours and no one would mind. That's what people do in bars, why they go. There are no expectations; there are no rules.

I'll give myself five minutes, he told himself. Just to get the sense of the place.

The two guys had seemed alike at first: Hispanic accents, dark skin, colorful winter coats opened at the neck revealing gold chains. But they were quite different. The taller, better-looking one, Juan, who did all the talking, had an exaggerated personality. He called Robin "honey" and chattered on about a "rich lover" who was going to take him on a cruise, a "Princess cruise," just like on *The Love Boat*. He was the kind of homosexual Dorothy would refer to as *flamboyant*. The quieter one, Manny, had a rough-looking face that was softened by lush eyelashes and pillowy lips. He had wiry hair on his knuckles, but his forearms were smooth and muscled. Manny leaned back on his barstool, accentuating the hefty mound in the crotch of his Levi's, and when he caught Robin staring down there, he raised an eyebrow at him suggestively. Time to go, Robin told himself, but he stayed put. Manny called him "Robby" and put his hand on the seat of Robin's pants while Robin drank from a bottle of Rolling Rock. (He associated this brand of beer with his mother's Polish cousins, carousing at family barbecues in New England, which made him remember that by now, she was probably starting to worry. He'd leave as soon as he finished the beer.) Juan slapped Manny's hand away from Robin and wagged a finger. "*Mira*, you keep off the *pollo*!" To Robin, Juan admonished: "You're jailbait, honey, and this one has a wife and baby in Spanish Harlem."

"So what?" Manny replied. "I want a boyfriend, too. A cute white boy like you, Robby." Robin downed the rest of his beer, unsure what to say, afraid of his own stiffening dick. And then, out of nowhere, the bartender, responding to a complaint from a customer about a minor in the room, ordered all three of them out. Juan got loud with the bartender, his arms spinning and gesturing as he lobbed out indignant, high-pitched fighting words, "You can't tell me what to do, motherfucker, I'm a *paying customer,*" while Robin scurried out to the street and Manny followed, laughing.

Night had fallen, and the temperature had dropped, but Robin felt encircled by light from every direction, wrapped in it. The glistening, frosty air seemed to melt around him. The indignity of being kicked out of the bar was nothing compared to the thrill of having gotten away with something adult, and the heart-quickening attention from burly, thick-browed Manny, who maybe looked a little like a shorter, stockier Clark Gable. Gently buzzed, Robin walked with them down Seventh Avenue to the subway, feeling more like a New Yorker than ever before. Manny threw an arm over his shoulders for a while, and Robin felt how tightly he was being held.

He sat between Juan and Manny on the uptown IND train. "Come party with us in the Bronx," Manny said. "Juan has cocaine at his apartment."

Cocaine: the chemical sound of it was like a cold draft on his neck, and he felt himself flinch.

"I only smoke pot," he said, in the most confident tone he could muster.

"Coca, *mota*, we got it all for you," Manny purred.

Robin nodded as if eager to go along, but he knew better. Knew that this day had to end.

At Times Square, he waited for the last possible moment, and then darted from the train without warning. His final glimpse of them was Manny's unhappy face as the doors slid shut, and Juan's gleeful giggles at Manny's expense. Robin mouthed, "Sorry," and then dashed along the platform and up the stairs.

The clamor of Times Square thumped like something already inside of him, as if the very same honking and blinking of the streets was also pulsing in his own blood. Past the porn places, he saw the marquees of Broadway theaters, theaters his mother had taken him to, as if they were the lights of his own front porch. The varied and seedy strangers all around were his own neighbors. For a few moments he was immobile with an almost religious joy. Then he realized that a dirty guy with slobber at his mouth was staring at him, and was shuffling closer, and Robin ran with all his strength back to the bus terminal.

He didn't use the words "gay bar" with Ruby that night, when he explained his day to her, because any bar at all was bad enough, especially with strangers. She was clearly upset that he'd wound up in the city, and he worried that he had revealed too much to her, that she would spill these secrets to his mother and father. But Ruby backed him up when he told his parents that he'd spent the day with Scott.

He learned then what has since proven to be solidly true: Ruby can keep a secret. Over the years, she has kept many, many secrets for him.

And yet: to explain to her about George seems like breaking some intimacy too delicate to sustain scrutiny. More time should pass. One night does not require a confession.

Robin goes back to bed. To his own bed, crisply made, the bedspread flat as paper, his two pillows placed symmetrically on either side of a corduroy covered backrest, a stuffed, squat thing with short arms, affectionately nicknamed "the husband." I'll sleep easier here, he tells himself, sleep filled with dreams. In fact he gets no rest at all. He wakes again and again, each time checking the clock, then instinctively looking toward the bedroom door, wondering if George, in his messy bed, has woken up and discovered Robin has left him alone.

Bright morning. Sudden noise: the clanging metallic ring of the phone.

Robin bolts upright with a where-am-I, what's-happening bewilderment. And then, as the phone keeps ringing, it's all there again, with the instant force of a slap on the head: What You Did Last Night.

The clock at the side of his bed reads 9:05. It's Sunday, isn't it? Who calls at nine on a Sunday?

He slides from bed without putting on clothes and trips his way through a glaringly bright living room. The machine picks up the call as he hoists the receiver from the cradle, which ignites a round of ugly high-pitched squeals, the answering-machine microphone shrieking feedback. "Hold on, wait," he mumbles, fumbling for the off switch.

"Robin?"

"Mmm-hmm."

"It's Calvin Kraft."

"Oh. Hey."

"Yeah, it's me. So, um, listen, I, uh . . ."

As Calvin hesitates, Robin tries to remember the message that Ruby left last night. She was on the boardwalk, she'd been at a party, she sounded drunk. "Is my sister with you?"

"No. That's what I'm trying to tell you."

"She called me last night. From the boardwalk."

"What time? Did you talk to her? Do you know where she is?" Calvin's eruption is plaintive, needy, so unlike him.

"*You* don't know where she is?"

"I tried to stop her, but she went off with those girls—"

"What girls?"

"—and she never came back and, fuck, man, I haven't heard from her. I thought, she probably called you—"

"I wasn't home when she called."

"Fuck. Robin, I'm sorry, but, man, it's really not my fault. You know me, you know I wouldn't *do* anything to her . . ." His voice trails away, and Robin finds himself remembering the scene in Calvin's screenplay where one of the guys gets rough with one of the girls, a repulsive little exchange rank with "bitch" and "cunt," and Carter, the guy Robin would play, honorably steps in to defend. Punches fly, solving the argument swiftly and unconvincingly.

Robin stretches the already stretched-out phone cord to the kitchen, fishes a scrap of paper and a ballpoint pen from the junk drawer, and writes down the phone number at the house where Calvin is staying, a place rented by Calvin's sister, Alice, and some of her friends. He takes down the name of the bar where Ruby was last seen, Club XS, which sounds dreadful. Apparently there was an altercation: Ruby in a slap fight with another girl, a bunch of shouting on the sidewalk. It hardly seems possible. Ruby's message mentioned some guy she was looking for; maybe that's where Ruby is now, with him, whoever he is. This also seems unlikely, Ruby abandoning her boyfriend for another guy, not telling anyone where she was going. Robin decides not to mention this guy to Calvin. Ruby will call, of course she will call, and when she does, she'll have an explanation. "Don't worry, she'll turn up," Robin assures Calvin, trying to sound unworried.

"Yeah, you're right. Of course." Calvin's voice is nearly a hush. Then he brightens: "How are you liking *Entering and Breaking*?"

"What?"

"The script I sent you. My feature."

It takes a certain amount of willpower not to just say, *Fuck you and your script, go find my sister*! "I haven't gotten that far into it."

"It's a good part for you, right?"

"Sure," he exhales heavily, trying to gain some balance in the midst of this news. "Look, call me when you hear from her, OK?"

From over his shoulder, he hears George. Robin turns and sees him, standing there in his underwear. He has long legs but a short torso, which gives him the look of someone taller than five-seven. He has a firmer midsection than Robin. Last night, while he brought himself off, George rubbed the flat, lower part of his abdomen, like a lamp from which he was coaxing a genie.

Robin lowers the piece of paper in his hand to cover his cock, now half-mast and growing.

"Did you just get up?" George asks.

"Yeah, the phone," Robin mutters, wondering if he should pretend he never left George's bed, or on the contrary, make it plainly clear.

Robin steps toward the hallway, which George is more or less blocking, and has to jockey around him to get back to his bedroom, to his clothes. George reaches out and makes a playful grab for Robin's cock, swiping the head, which pulls from Robin an involuntary gasp, the sensation so electric it might have been George's tongue instead of his fingers.

"We might have a situation," he calls out from his room, as he pulls shorts and a T-shirt from his black steamer trunk, the same one that he lives out of in his dorm room. "My sister is missing."

George comes to the doorway, and Robin summarizes Calvin's call. "Do you think I should call my mother?"

George seems to be staring past Robin, toward the bed. "I'm not really awake yet," he says. "Why don't I get us some breakfast and coffee?"

"Caffeine. Yes." Sending George from the apartment is a good idea; he'll probably go to the bagel place near campus, which will give Robin at least a half hour alone, time to get his bearings. And yet: they never "get breakfast" for each other. The gesture feels loosely romantic, the kind of thing Peter would do for him on lazy Sunday mornings.

Robin slumps on the couch, smoking his last cigarette, wishing he had asked George to buy another pack. He sips at a glass of water, wanting an aspirin. He draws his knees to his chest and squints like a cat. The sun streams through the windows; the green leaves on a single visible tree have a damp sheen on them, like oiled flesh. The early-morning storm came and went, as if something he dreamed up. Calvin's call has had the effect of snapping him into heightened alertness, but he is also aware of the dull thump of blood in his head, the effect of last night's high, still lingering in his system. The beer, the pot, the scramble from the cops. The orgasm. George.

George places the various pieces of the puzzle alongside each other, looking for clues to Ruby's whereabouts. "Calvin last saw her with a couple of girls. But Ruby's message said she was looking for this boy—"

"Someone she used to know."

"So maybe," George continues, "the girls have something to do with him. Maybe they're friends of his."

"It's just not like her."

George shrugs coolly. "She's changing. Dressing like an undertaker's daughter. Going out with a creep like Calvin, who your mother doesn't approve of. This is just one more thing."

"Why doesn't she fucking call me?" Robin hears the edge of anger in his voice, anger at Ruby's behavior, anger at Calvin for foisting this problem on him. There's even perhaps a touch of annoyance at George, at his calm detachment.

"She wouldn't necessarily call you if she's in the middle of some party weekend."

"But, come on, George. This is Ruby. We tell each other everything."

He finds himself staring into the empty coffee cup, fixating on the grounds left at the bottom, a dark constellation. He connects the dots, drawing a six-pointed star, a sailboat, a little house with the roof blown half off. He says, "In Greenlawn, my mother worked at the library with this Irish lady, Josephine, who claimed she could read tea leaves. She'd make you a cup of loose tea, then swirl the dregs around, and then she'd look into the cup with this very weird expression on her face, in a kind of trance, and she'd tell your future."

"That doesn't sound very reliable."

"Josephine supposedly predicted my parents' divorce, plus us moving to Manhattan. Maybe she saw the skyline in the tea leaves."

George reaches across the table for Robin's cup. Looking into it, he snorts, "You seem to have a pretty vague future."

"Do you see the sailboat? Maybe it means I'm going to travel."

"Well, you are. To London."

"Not by sailboat, I hope."

George takes a final swig from his own cup. He fiddles the cup clockwise, then counterclockwise, and then pronounces, "I definitely see the outline of two men engaged in sexual activity."

Robin feels his face warm up. *OK, you have to clear the air*, he thinks, though he doesn't have any idea what he might say, doesn't know how to proceed, and so instead he puts on a campy voice and says, "I feel like a cheap slut."

George manages a smile, but he seems to be waiting for something more.

Robin says, "We probably shouldn't get in the habit of that."

George nods slowly, and then pushes his chair back from the table. "Yeah, you just needed a good rebound fuck. And I needed to shake Matthias."

"You're my best friend," Robin says earnestly.

"And coworker. Speaking of which, I better get going, if I'm going to shower before work." He lifts an arm and sniffs a pit, fanning away a stench that Robin remembers burrowing into last night on the couch, licking him there.

They both laugh at the gesture, a bit too hard.

George throws away his coffee cup.

Robin watches him leave the room. He makes himself stay put, even as he imagines following George into the bathroom, stripping off his clothes, standing close to him in the shower. Letting the water cover them both.

The next couple hours, alone in the apartment, seem to lengthen eternally. Except for a run to a corner store on Baltimore Ave., where he allows himself a minute of small talk with the old-timer at the register, who seems to be getting used to Robin showing up a couple times a week for Parliaments and Diet Coke, he remains mostly on the couch, expecting a call from Ruby that doesn't come.

She's fine, he tells himself. Just because she doesn't want to phone in her whereabouts to Calvin doesn't mean she's in trouble. Maybe she's just sick of him, needs some space. George called Calvin a creep, which doesn't seem exactly fair. Yes, Calvin can be hard to deal with, but Robin knows the type well. There have been so many boys like Calvin in Robin's high school and college art classes. They're introverted and socially awkward, and they overcompensate with brash pronouncements about the only thing they know well: cult movies or comic books or the esoteric details of a science fiction writer's invented world. These boys channel their excitable and off-putting temperaments into creativity, and when their creative projects don't quite succeed, they become more defensive, more opinionated, more sure of their superiority. Robin has endured hot crushes on more than one boy like this. Alton was like that, full of facts about obscure rock bands and musicians you'd never heard of, but never actually starting that post-punk band he claimed was going to be *huge*.

There on the couch, Robin goes back to Calvin's script. He reads aloud the lines he would be saying, were he to take the part of Carter: "I'm excited by your tits. . . . Every guy who stares at your tits is like a punch in my face. . . . That top you're wearing makes your tits look great." He laughs. He's never spoken to a girl this way, crudely, about her breasts. Then his laughter catches in his throat: Does Calvin think about Ruby this way? Does he say things to her like this? Maybe that's why she's not so eager to call him back. Maybe he's a pig.

But Carter also says, "I've seen his world-famous dick," and "Do you think I'm jealous of his dick?" and "You think you can intimidate me because my cock is smaller. Think again."

Robin skips ahead to the last scene. Carter is standing in front of the bathroom mirror, holding a "straight razor" in one hand and "staring at the soft exposed flesh of his wrist." Suicide is the implication, and then the film ends. He sets the script aside, as confused by the character as Calvin seems to be about himself.

Where is Ruby? Has she gotten herself into some dodgy situation with a strange guy, or with girls who hang out at boardwalk nightclubs getting into bar brawls? He finds himself imagining a call from a hospital, "Your sister was found . . ."

A sense of menace takes hold. What if she is simply . . . gone? Disappeared. Vanished. He hears his mother scream, sees her collapse, like last time, when the news came that Jackson had flatlined, when he himself was so young and still had to find the strength to hold her up, support the weight of her grief. He sees his father weeping, his reserve breaking apart, anger melting into tears. He remembers that day all too clearly. It was his own fourteenth birthday, and they had just eaten cake and opened presents when the hospital called. It would be a perfectly cruel twist of fate if Ruby came into harm's way on Jackson's birthday, Jackson like a curse hanging over the two of them, something they can't shake, because they were there, they saw him fall. And he feels it again, that sensation: the air is being forced from his throat. Reflexively, he starts prodding at his neck, investigating his glands as if they've started to swell up. He makes himself stop. *Don't start spiraling.*

Ruby isn't dead. She hasn't disappeared, not for good. It would be too much for any of them to bear. He exhales from deep within, steadying himself, extinguishing unwelcome memories the way you snuff out a candle before leaving a room, so you don't risk burning the place down.

When someone goes missing, you either search for her, or you wait it out.

The idea of a "search" is hard to pull into focus.

But the waiting is unbearable.

At one o'clock, right on time, Dorothy calls. She sounds surprised that he's picked up. "I thought you were working today."

"No, I don't work on Sundays."

"Hmm. Your sister said something about . . ." Dorothy cuts off her sentence with a cluck. He can't quite glean the subtext, though there's something she's not saying. He hears her clattering in the kitchen: utensils scraping metal, water running, the shutting of a cupboard door. More and more, Dorothy cooks. She's come a long way from her unhappy kitchen experiments in Greenlawn, when she was forever boiling vegetables into mush or burning lasagna in the oven. Now she concocts elaborate dishes, recipes clipped from the *New York Times Magazine* and saved in three-ring binders. What does she do with all this food, when she's so often alone? It's true that she's grown plump, curvy in a way she never was, but she must be throwing food away all the time. Or giving it away. For years, an elderly couple upstairs, the Finkels, accepted Dorothy's creations, thanking her profusely with "You shouldn't have" and then inviting her in for a litany of medical complaints and grievances against their own faraway children. Then Mr. Finkel died and Mrs. Finkel was put in a home by one of those children, so Dorothy, Robin guesses, is making extra food for no one.

"I'm just chilling out," he says.

"Chilling out," she parrots, as if forced to bear the weight of this slang.

"George is at work."

"George! When am I going to see him again? How is he?"

"He's fine." *Last night, he ordered me around while I jacked off.*

The clattering stops, and Dorothy seems to turn her attention to him at last. "Something's troubling you, isn't it?"

"No, no. Just a lazy Sunday." Breezily, he adds, "I'm wishing I was down the shore with Ruby, enjoying the beach."

Dorothy lets out a just-perceptible sigh of exasperation. "I really hate the idea of her spending the weekend at a *house party*."

"It's good for her to have fun."

"I can't quite put *fun* and *beer keg* in the same sentence."

He licks his lips; his mouth is quite dry. "Did she leave you a number?"

"Mmm, yes. Are you trying to get in touch with her?"

"Actually, I wanted to talk to Calvin about this script he sent me."

"Really? I can't imagine he has anything to say. What's it about?"

"Nightlife. Friendship. My generation."

"Remember, you're a *stage* actor, Robin."

"You're right. I might have to let him down easily," Robin says, playing his part.

The phone number Dorothy recites for him is the number at Alice's house, the same number Calvin gave him; he's hit a cul-de-sac. Dorothy mentions that Calvin is supposed to drive Ruby back to the city this evening. "I'm making paella," Dorothy says. "I'm sure she'll be famished, after eating junk all weekend."

"Paella's not vegetarian, Dorothy."

"Oh, yes. *Meat is murder*, how could I forget? Well, I made gazpacho, too. She can eat that."

He wants to say something more direct, but it's just impossible. His mother can be quick to jump to dangerous conclusions, especially about Ruby. He says, rather firmly, "I don't think you should expect her too early. If she's having fun, she'll come home later."

"Oh. I see." Dorothy's voice hardens. "She's put you up to this."

"What?"

"She told you to call me, to prepare me." He can hear her smack something down onto the Formica countertop.

"No, no. Just be realistic. They might need to sober up before the long ride home."

"You don't think Calvin would drive under the influence?"

"No—"

"I'll absolutely strangle him."

"Stop! All I'm saying is, they might have a mimosa or two at brunch, and then need to sober up before the ride home."

"It's a good thing I didn't put the paella in the oven." For a few moments he hears breath moving heavily from her nostrils. Then she delicately sniffles, as if fighting back tears. "There was a plan," she says. "Ruby was going to see your father and visit the grave. I was thinking about joining them, but she said you had a shift at the restaurant today. And I thought, well, I'd rather not do it if you weren't going to be there."

So that's it. Yes, it's true, Ruby had tried to wrangle them all to spend some time at Jackson's grave, "as a family," was how she'd put it, which had infuriated Robin because it sounded like a guilt trip at best and a willful distortion of reality at worst. They weren't a family, not since the divorce, perhaps not since Jackson died, when the fracturing and splintering accelerated between Clark and Dorothy. He'd told Ruby bluntly that he couldn't handle it: neither the grave nor the memories it would stir up, and certainly not the idea of the four of them together.

Dorothy says, "I wanted to be with at least one of my children this weekend."

"I know, Dorothy. I know what day it is. June 16th."

"And what year," she adds.

It takes him a moment to understand what she means, and then he computes: Jackson had been ten in '77. Softly, he mutters, "Wow. I'd lost track—"

"Yes," she interjects, "your brother would have been eighteen today."

"He'd be going to college this fall."

"Old enough to vote. Old enough for the government to take his Social Security number for their Army records." She falls silent; he can think of nothing to say, because all he can think is Ruby, Ruby, Ruby.

"Why don't I call again later, Dorothy?"

She clears her throat, seems to pull herself together. "If you speak to your sister, tell her I'm going visit the cemetery on my own, with or without her. If she *deigns* to call me sooner rather than later, perhaps I won't have to read her mind."

He agrees. He gets off the phone and calls the number at Alice's house, and talks to Calvin. There's still no word from her.

His mind expands to a vision of Jackson as an eighteen-year-old. Jackson would have graduated from high school, would be living at home, getting ready for college. Maybe he'd be going somewhere on athletic scholarship. Even at age ten, he had been great at sports, baseball especially. By eighteen he'd have transformed into a sturdy, all-American jock, a state champion, the pride of Greenlawn. And in a startling flash Robin sees that the "home" he has been picturing here is Greenlawn, not Manhattan. Jackson alive means all of them still together, Clark and Dorothy still married. No divorce, no move to Manhattan: the life he would have lived.

On his own eighteenth birthday, he had been a college freshman, home from Carnegie Mellon on winter break. He'd dyed his hair platinum for the occasion. Dorothy set up a dinner party. He remembers being nervous, because they never made a big deal about his birthday, since it was also the anniversary of Jackson's death. But Dorothy filled the apartment with some of his pals from high school and college. George was there, and Alton and his girlfriend, plus a few of her own friends, chatty women she'd known since her days at Smith or from her single-girl years in New York, who had reemerged after the move to Manhattan and were now part of Robin's life. They drank champagne, opened gifts, ate chocolate soufflé for dessert.

His night ended in a cab, with Marco, a South American guy, a friend of a friend who had tagged along to the dinner party and flirted with everyone all night. He was lean, his eyes the color of caramel, his dark hair thick and wavy, his smile devilish. Marco directed the cab to a club on White Street, but the drinking age had gone up from eighteen to nineteen just ten days earlier, and Robin couldn't get past the bouncer. So on the early hours of the morning, Robin found himself in a studio in a high-rise at the edge of Tribeca, making out with a guy who whispered in his ear, "I want to dominate you." Scared, he still said "OK," because Marco was probably the sexiest guy he had ever been with. Marco tied Robin's arms to the bedposts during sex, but loose enough that Robin could twist around (and, he hoped, escape, if it came to that) and take in a view out the picture windows, a view across the Hudson River, looking back on New Jersey, the place where that life he used to live was being lived by other people. At eighteen, it seemed to him that he had already become the person he was going to be always. Now the memory of that night is tainted with something else, with the sex they had, and what sex has come to mean. Because who knows if Marco was healthy or not. Who knows where Marco is today.

The phone rings again. *Finally!*

But no. Not Ruby. George.

"The place is dead," George says. "It's too nice out, no one wants a restaurant."

"Are you staying through dinner?"

"I could, but—" There's a moment of humming silence. "I guess I'd rather come home."

Robin lets this hang in the air. He hears the emphasis on "rather," the suggestion it contains. Will it be that from now on, every time they're both in the apartment, they'll end up naked? It can't be, it's too much. But if they're both into it . . .

"You just got real quiet," George says.

"Sorry. The Ruby situation is stressing me out."

"She hasn't turned up yet?"

"No."

"That seems bad."

"I called Dorothy, but I just couldn't tell her. It's Jackson's birthday today."

"Oh, boy."

At once, Robin finds himself expressing an idea only just making itself known to him: "What do you think about a road trip?"

"This doesn't have anything to do with Peter, does it?"

"No. Just you and me. Seaside Heights is just a few hours away, right?"

"Are you talking about tonight?"

"As soon as you get home."

After the briefest hesitation, George says, "You wanna drag me to the Jersey Shore, huh?"

"Believe me, I don't like the idea, either, but—"

George finishes for him. "Gotta do what you gotta do."

Robin hangs up the phone, and the air seems freshly voltaged. The time for waiting has passed. He knows immediately what to do next: pack a bag with overnight clothes, pull a couple bottles of Diet Coke from the fridge, fold his tips into his money clip. He makes a list of the relevant phone numbers, scavenges for dimes and nickels in case they need to use a phone booth. He finds a road map in a drawer.

He goes into George's room to grab some clean clothes to pack for him, too, in case they wind up staying overnight somewhere.

The bed is unmade, still. He can picture everything they did, unfolding all over again. Next to the bed is the K-Y Jelly. He replaces the cap, wipes it off, carries it back to his room, and finds his condoms. Before he can change his mind, he packs all of it with their stuff.

The last thing he does is find the letter from the university, in the pocket of his work pants. He smoothes it out. Rereads it. *Congratulations . . . London . . . highly competitive . . . a true challenge.* He understands that he hasn't given them his answer yet. He hasn't confirmed that he's actually going to do this. Why is he putting it off?

He leaves the letter resting in a beam of sunlight, faceup on his desk. It seems to pulse with its own power. When he gets back from this trip, when he finds his sister—he will find her, he must, he absolutely must—he'll know what his answer is.

He's clenching his jaw, he realizes, as if he's primed for a fight. A fight with whom? When he tries to envision his opponent, he sees only himself: two nights ago, at the restaurant, framed in the mirrored wall, sweating through his white shirt, doubled over a bottle of wine he is struggling to open, while everyone stares, waiting to see if this time he'll get it right.

Part Two

Down the Shore

Through dark glasses, Ruby watches a girl in a hot-pink bikini—crimped hair, bony body, viper face—rush through the living room, laughing and shrieking as she moves toward the front door. There's a guy in pursuit—burly but agile, dodging bodies, furniture, outstretched legs. "You're dead, you're *so fuckin'* dead," he shouts, through a big, sloppy grin. His yellow tank top is soaked, doused in beer. Ruby can smell it as he flies by. Then more flesh—another girl, another bit of skimpy summer clothing. She holds high a plastic cup, sloshing beer, ready to dump it on one of them. Voices from around the room cheer them on. One, two, three, they escape through the screened door, sucked into the afternoon sun. One of the girls shrieks from the front yard. The other laughs loudly. The all-weekend party is hitting an early peak.

God—tell me, please, how I wound up here.

But she knows how it happened. Calvin wanted to. She came along. Same as always.

Remind me, God, why I said yes.

She sits on a lumpy love seat, squished between the sofa's hard, upholstered arm and her fidgety boyfriend. Calvin is carrying on a loud conversation about what else?—movies—with the guy on the other side. Calvin's a film student at Columbia and knows more about every movie ever made than anyone in the whole wide world. Ruby's heard it all before. She's struck by how out of place his snooty urban attitudes seem here, at this frivolous beach party. Maybe he senses this, too, maybe only half-consciously, which is why he's getting louder. It's like biting a hangnail. You keep biting until you're nipping at the skin but you can't stop. She wishes her nails looked better. The black paint is chipping off. She studies the arm of the couch. The upholstery is a ragged, pilly, green-and-white plaid. The white part is discolored to a popcorny shade, and the green part, where her elbow wants to rest, is marked by a hard, flattened splat of chewing gum. She becomes transfixed by that gray wad, wishing she could have witnessed the moment when it was left here. Just to see the person who did it, the *kind* of person who does something as vulgar as that. Was it deliberate vandalism? Or something casual: *Oops, meant to drop it in an ashtray, now it's stuck, might as well leave it.*

This beach house is a weird melding of things that have been neglected and things that someone spent money on. The furniture, which probably came with the lease, is battered and mismatched, but sprinkled throughout are the current renters' state-of-the-art stereo system and lots of fancy knickknacks. She sees the kinds of things that rich kids—one of them being Alice, Calvin's younger sister—bring to even the most downscale beach house. A huge, vintage poster of *Casablanca* on the wall, expensively framed by bright white matte board. A polished silver martini shaker, possibly an antique, coated in condensation. A big spray of long-stemmed pink roses in a vase on an end table. Where did anyone get roses? Near this she sees two preppie-looking guys in a beer-chugging contest, egged on by the group circling around them. Ruby expects one of their elbows will send that bouquet crashing onto the dirty, low-pile carpet. She'd get a kick out of that—except, for all she knows, she's sleeping on that carpet tonight.

She sits in a wash of afternoon light, so bright that she's left her cat-eye sunglasses on. Sunglasses in the middle of the summer shouldn't necessarily draw stares, but she's already overheard one girl say to another, "Maybe she's blind." What a bitch. *Maybe I'll just leave my shades on for the whole weekend.*

In a house full of tanned and sunburned bodies clad in neon swimwear, she knows that she stands out. The black dye in her hair framing her frosty skin, her inky black Smiths T-shirt and black miniskirt up against the bare white of her arms and legs, her rubber-soled boots. The girls at this party are of the type who've sneered at and gossiped about her all her life, once because she was a quiet goody-goody too eager to please, and later because she reinvented herself as a cool outsider who didn't seem to notice them at all. Now they look at her and then look away. Most of them are younger than her—most of them are probably still in high school, or just recently graduated. High school is only a year in her past, but it seems like something she endured a long time ago.

Until she determines a good reason to get up, she's staying put on the couch, no matter how disgusting it is. Her hand, resting in her lap, is clutching a plastic cup of beer, which she has no taste for. The cup is half head—she has no idea how to properly fill up from a keg. The first gulp had the airiness of cotton candy and the sourness of French bread. When she licked off the foam, she tasted her own dark lipstick. The keg is on the front porch. She should have found the kitchen and poured herself a Diet Coke.

God, please get me out of here quickly.

This is not a prayer, but the leftover habit of prayer, still holding on two years after she decided she was an atheist. She waited until her seventeenth birthday to announce that she'd no longer be attending mass—she'd been going every Sunday since Jackson's accident. She didn't explain herself, didn't need to. Her mother, her brother, her father—not exactly churchgoing people. Nana was the only one upset, but she didn't live nearby, so Ruby could just tuck that guilt away. Now "God" is just a placeholder. A way to contain a thought when the feelings are threatening to spill over—as they are now, with her annoyance at Calvin coming to a boil.

Calvin is raising his voice, so loud it's starting to sound like he's in an argument. Only thirty minutes at the party, already making enemies. The current topic seems to be that new movie, *St. Elmo's Fire*, which Calvin has called "a perfect example of Hollywood trying to crush youthful rebellion," and which the other guy is arguing "speaks for our generation."

Calvin says, "Those characters would never be friends with each other in real life. They take one from every walk of life and then put them all through the same pseudo-romantic plot machinations."

Ruby pipes up, "It's not romantic. Half the guys in that movie are stalkers."

"Exactly my point," Calvin shouts, though that didn't sound like his point to Ruby. "The quote-unquote bohemian character, the writer who keeps questioning the meaning of life, he's supposed to be in love with the boring girl in pearls. If you ask me, he should have been in love with her boyfriend."

"Man, that's just weird," the other guy says.

"It should be weird! It should be like life, which is messy and unpredictable!"

He's getting worked up, his body jerking and shifting and creating vibrations that Ruby feels in her ribs, her hips, her arm. She gulps her beer to avoid a spill. Already she feels the alcohol doing its work, warming her up. She feels a trickle of sweat slide toward her elbow.

"Look, man," the guy is shouting to Calvin above a synth-pop song that Ruby recognizes as the theme to *St. Elmo's Fire* ("Wanna be a man in motion, all I need is a pair of wheels")—the likely trigger for this entire pointless conversation—"I'm not saying I *like* this reality, okay? But after college, man, life is gonna *force* us to make tough choices."

"*That*—" Calvin cries, rising up off the couch a few inches, "is exactly the brainwashing *bull*shit I'm talking about! This movie makes you think your only real option is to *fucking* settle down." His arm goes wide for emphasis, and for a split second Ruby sees a twinkle of sunlight on the silver bracelet at his wrist. Then—*wham*—his elbow smashes into her beer cup just as she's taking a sip.

The cup crunches into a ring around her nose. Alcohol floods her sinuses, rushes down her throat. She gags and spits, shakes her head. It's like being jabbed inside her brain by two fat, wet fingers. Beer splatters her glasses, blurring her vision. The flattened cup lands in her lap. Her skirt is soaked.

"What happened?" Calvin asks, almost scolding her.

"Your arm happened," she says, rising to her feet, coughing, flinging droplets from her hands.

"Hey! How about a towel?" he calls out to no one in particular, to the room at large. She recognizes the tone of his voice, rank with the confidence of someone whose needs have always been attended to, by parents, by his sister, by tutors and hired help.

She removes her sunglasses. Everything sharpens, becomes more defined, as if up until now it had all been a grainy movie on a far-off screen. Faces turn in her direction. A guy staggering nearby gets a look at her and says, "Nasty!" All of a sudden she is nine instead of nineteen. Small, confused, angry. These kids all around her, most of whom are younger than her, seem cool and worldly compared to the public mess she is.

She wipes wet snot from her nose and looks up at Calvin, nearly a foot taller than she is. Calvin, who has more or less ignored her since they got here, who hasn't yet introduced her to his sister, who made her fill her own cup from the keg, the very same cup he's just rammed in her face. He reaches his hand around her back and rubs her shoulder in little circles, asking, "Are you okay?"

She finally hears genuine concern in his voice, but he still hasn't found her a towel. She doesn't even know where the bathroom is, because they haven't gotten past the couch since they arrived.

Another guy steps up, a solid, jocky man-boy with a button nose, thick neck, and dark, wavy hair. "I got ya," he says. He yanks his football jersey up and over his head. "Use this."

"Look, she's with me. I'll take care of it," Calvin says.

She takes the shirt and runs it across her cheeks and neck, dabbing at the excess, but she's so wet it doesn't really help. Her gaze lands on the guy's bare torso, rippled with dark curls, as muscular a body as she's ever seen this close up. She feels heat flare in her neck—she imagines he can see her blush. "Thanks," she says. "Where's the bathroom?"

"Through the kitchen," Calvin interjects, a long arm pointing through the crowd. "That's my guess."

"Stay here," she tells Calvin.

Shirtless Guy steps closer. "Want me to show you, baby?"

He wobbles a bit, clearly buzzed, but he has her attention. His lips are red as punch and probably taste like wine. She imagines saying yes—yes, show me the way—and once there, pulling him in with her, closing the door and kissing him on the lips. He's a fantastic kisser, experienced, sensitive, the kind of guy who holds your head carefully in his palms while his tongue spreads your lips, the kind of guy with soft curls on his chest, soft like the fur on a big, gentle dog.

But Calvin's standing between them. Calvin whose chest is smooth as a girl's, a baby-soft surface too much like her own.

Last night, back in Manhattan, getting ready for the weekend but already regretting it, she found herself rehearsing a breakup speech. It had been months since she first understood that something was off. Something physical. She had started pulling away from his kisses—his tongue too hard, like a lollipop in her mouth, his lips too dry, like bread crust. She'd been offering instead her neck, her bare shoulder, any patch of flesh to satisfy him while she looked away and fretted. Last night, she'd looked into the bathroom mirror and mouthed the words, "I don't need a boyfriend, I need a lover." It was a word her brother used about the guy he was dating. Peter was Robin's *lover*.

They were *in love*, they were having a *love affair.* She liked the sound of "affair," the way it held the word "air" inside it—lovers carried upon the air in a private chamber for two, whisked away to somewhere exotic. Calvin was the opposite of that, Calvin was earthbound and too familiar.

She pushes past the stained sofa, past a TV cabinet covered by a plastic tablecloth dotted with puddles of beer and melting ice. Into a dining room, where a noisy drinking game is in full force around a circular wooden table. Then a crowded kitchen. She has to knock into people to get past, muttering, "Excuse you, excuse you."

From behind her she overhears two girls she's just blazed past:

"That goth chick just totaled her beer."

"Do you know her?"

"I think her boyfriend is Alice's brother."

"Alice has a brother?"

"Yeah, that tall freak?"

She steps into a dark hallway, mostly empty, no windows. She tries a door on either side—a linen closet with nothing on its shelves except frayed contact paper, then a bedroom with overnight bags piled chaotically along the walls.

She opens another door. Another bedroom. A handful of guys and girls are huddled over a small mound of what looks like cocaine. A half-dozen faces pivot toward her, like button-eyed lemurs in the Central Park Zoo. "Oh, sorry." She pulls the door shut again.

At the end of the hall, a guy and a girl are making out in front of what must be the bathroom door. She takes her place behind them, leans against the wall, waits for her turn. She wills herself not to cry, she can feel something welling up. *I'm stronger than this,* she thinks. She's sticky all over.

She blames Calvin for this mess, but really it's herself she's angry at. Calvin told her Alice was renting a house down the shore, and that she was having "a few friends" over for "a little party." A perfect way for Ruby and him to escape the June humidity for the weekend, he said. But hadn't she pictured exactly what this party would look like—pictured herself in the midst of not *a few friends* but a big crowd? She knows the Jersey Shore. Her family spent the occasional summer weekend in towns like Seaside Heights, where they are now, and Wildwood. Boardwalks and packed beaches. Motel rooms with icy air conditioning that carried the whiff of mildew. She used to gaze out the window of their Plymouth at teenagers draped over the porches of rental houses. Longhaired guys air-guitaring to amplified music, girls in bikini tops and cut-off denim shorts, all of them glugging from plastic cups like the one that just smashed her in the face. Her mother disapproved of these people, which was enough of a reason, as a young girl, to be fascinated by them. But she hasn't been that girl for a long time.

Still, she let herself be persuaded by Calvin. Pressured by his constant need to be told he was right. Always right.

When she first started dating Calvin, she liked that he too felt alienated from other teenagers, their so-called *peers*. He was the tall guy in the ratty overcoat, hiding his Nordic bone structure and gray eyes behind messy, greasy, white-blond hair. The one who smoked British cigarettes while arguing over coffee at midnight after a film at the Bleecker Street Cinema. He got easily upset about politics—nuclear winter, Third World intervention, anything to do with Ronald Reagan—and he said the way to dissent was not at the voting booth but through "cultural production." He reminded her a bit of her brother in his outspokenness, though Robin had a daring side that Calvin only imagined he possessed. He railed against "the new morality" but didn't seem especially interested in sex, and this was fine with Ruby. She had made it clear she wasn't ready to go *all the way*, thankful that in this one area, he didn't put pressure on her. She wasn't really sure why. She might even give over to her suspicion that he might be gay, if he weren't so fixated on her breasts.

At Columbia he'd made a couple of short films—"critiquing the seduction of advertising," he said. She'd starred in a scene for him, sitting on a toilet seat under a single high-watt clamp-light in only her bra and tights, brushing her hair while reciting Foucault. She'd had fun doing it—the whole shoot felt stupid and glamorous—but she couldn't really defend the film when students in Calvin's workshop accused him of being pretentious. (And maybe the criticism made an impact. Calvin was now working on a more traditional script, set in the world of downtown nightlife. He hadn't yet shown it to her, though he'd mailed her brother a copy. She wasn't sure if she felt insulted by that or not.) She never pointed out to him the contradiction of a so-called anticapitalist living off the dividends of his family's stock portfolio. The problem with Calvin, she had finally figured out, was that underneath it all he was just a spoiled boy. Unable to pick up after himself, used to having things done for him, always *expecting*. Expecting her to agree with him when he got worked up about a particular topic—and if she disagreed, expecting that she'd eventually be persuaded, or least stymied, by his arguments. It had begun to wear her out. Spending time with your boyfriend isn't supposed to feel like a battle.

And so last night, she had rehearsed that sentence about needing a lover, but she didn't say the words out loud. Didn't want to hurt his feelings. She told herself a weekend down the shore might be a fun vacation. She could ignore the party and play in the surf, like she used to with her brothers when she was little, salt water on her lips, her skin turning pink in the sun.

And that's what they did, for a little while this morning. She and Calvin went to the beach first. Calvin found parking near the boardwalk in one of those lots where an old retiree in a lawn chair collects the money and keeps an eye on the cars while deepening his lifelong leathery tan. They paid for their beach badges at a wooden stall that reminded her of the one Lucy sat in, in the *Peanuts* cartoons, with her sign announcing "The Psychiatrist is In. Five Cents." On the sand, they found a spot amid the endless sprawl of bodies—bodies on blankets, in fold-up chairs, under umbrellas or exposed to the sun, baking their oily flesh. Kids ran in every direction, radios blared the local "hits" station, and the occasional piece of garbage—a soda cup or a Doritos bag—tumbled along the sand, sometimes chased by a conscientious bather but often just carried by on the breeze, ignored by all as someone else's problem. Seagulls whined, circling above garbage pails stuffed with scraps from lunches.

She stripped down to a bikini, black and relatively modest, bought just for this weekend. Calvin told her she looked like Bettie Page. He peeled off his jeans to reveal old, plaid Bermuda shorts underneath. He left his long-sleeved shirt on and sat up, knees bent, a book balanced there. *Eros and Civilization.* She knew Calvin wouldn't go in the water, so she wandered in by herself. She was cautious, afraid of getting knocked over by a wave—aware of her childhood fear of riptides, of a sudden injury. She kept herself in proximity to a family, a young father and mother wrangling a handful of kids diving in and out of the crashing waves. But when she looked back she saw that Calvin had indeed kept her in his sights, peering out over the top of his book.

When she got back to the blanket, she asked him to rub sunblock on her, but he said he didn't have any, even though she was sure he'd said earlier that he'd packed some, and then they both sulked for a bit. She lay on her back, feeling the sun heating the exposed flesh between her bikini top and bottom. In the sky above, a flock of sea birds flew by in V-formation. An unseasonal migration. A sign that everything shifts and moves, nothing stays in place. She swatted the thought away, squashing the urge to attach meaning—a leftover from the influence of her Catholic Nana, who found "signs and wonders" everywhere, proof of God's intentions, answers to her prayers. A lot of superstition, or so it seemed now, though back then she saw life that way, too. So she closed her eyes and pretended that she was somewhere more exotic, and that she wasn't with Calvin. She thought about how she'd have to wait out the rest of the weekend before she broke up with him.

And now, in the hallway, she wonders again why she didn't just get it over with the night before in New York. Now, instead, her skin feels sunburned and her clothes are covered with beer, and how is she going to get through the rest of this hellish party? Why did she wait? When has waiting ever solved anything?

"Ruby! Right? It's you? Oh, my God." She turns around to see a flat-chested girl in a pale orange bikini, two tiny triangles of fabric, as if a single slice of Kraft American cheese had been cut in half along the diagonal. Her body is long and lean. She's nearly as tall as Calvin and has his same thin-boned features. Same shocking whiteness to her hair, though her hair looks clean. So of course this must be Alice. She exclaims, "I can't believe we haven't met before!"

"I've been here for half an hour," Ruby says dryly—wondering where Alice has been all this time. "I'm covered in beer."

"I heard my brother just spazzed out on you. It's the talk of the party." Alice holds out to Ruby a brandy snifter with an inch of amber jiggling in its bulb.

"Spaz" suits Calvin, though Ruby could never get away with calling him that. She takes the snifter, which might be leaded crystal—another unlikely object that Alice has brought along for the summer.

"Oh, my God," Alice repeats. "Come with me." She pivots and moves down the hall, talking over her shoulder in a jittery stream. "Are you having fun? Do you like the house? We rented last year but closer to the ocean, but it's totally crazy there, so we decided to rent on this side of Central, but you know it's too many families over here, so someone's always calling the cops on us. Nightmare!" She reaches a door and pauses before entering, as if to impart secret rules to Ruby before they step inside. "We're keeping this room off limits except for me and Cicely and Dorian. They're the other renters. Have you met them? Cicely is gorgeous, with the biggest breasts you've ever seen—she's probably going to get a reduction, I mean, *I* would if it were me, but I'm as flat as they come, and between you and me I like it that way. I'm a perfect size two. And Dorian's just a lush, but she's sweet. I've known her for years, we go to Dalton—I mean we *went,* we're graduates now! Free! We have a bathroom off my bedroom that's strictly *entre nous. Comprendéz*? I'm not letting all these trashy people, whoever they are, puke in my toilet. Plus, I have like $150 worth of Estée Lauder cosmetics in there, so—"

She pushes open the door, and they enter the room with the coke mirror. "Help yourself," Alice says. She gestures toward the same group of faces Ruby had barged in on just moments ago. "Attention, all you beautiful people. This is Ruby. She's from Manhattan, too."

Ruby waves feebly toward the group, three guys and two girls, a wild-eyed bunch dressed several notches less trashy than the beach bums in the living room and kitchen. The inner circle. She identifies gorgeous Cicely, on the bed in a black-satin Chinese robe, which hangs open, highlighting her remarkable cleavage. She has the kind of trendy, teased-up hair—curly all over, with ironed-straight bangs over her forehead—that defies both gravity and taste. She smiles sweetly and waves at Ruby. Sprawled next to her is a sweaty, red-faced guy wearing a linen blazer over a tank top, wiping a frantic finger across his gums. This guy says, "Fuckin' welcome and shit."

There's a guy next to him wearing only a pink oxford shirt, unbuttoned, a pair of white briefs, and a paisley-patterned necktie wrapped around his forehead.

Necktie Guy sits up straight, legs dangling off the edge of the mattress, thighs spread. He checks Ruby out from head to toe. "Fantastic legs," he remarks. He then jabs a rolled bill into his right nostril and, in a single, seamless gesture, vacuums up an inch of white from the mirror.

The third girl—this must be Dorian—is the crimped-haired brunette in the pink bikini who Ruby saw shrieking through the living room. Dorian whacks Necktie Guy on the arm—it's not clear to Ruby if the swat is because he took more than his share of the coke, or because he paid her a compliment. Maybe the latter. Dorian addresses Ruby through a sneer: "What brought you and your *fantastic legs* to our party?"

"I came with Calvin."

"Calvino?" says Necktie Guy. "Where is he?"

"I left him in the front room," Ruby says, "after he totaled his beer all over me."

"That explains the wet look," Dorian says. "For sure."

Ruby forces a smile, as if the spill were merely a bother and not a public humiliation. As if Dorian wasn't being rude but just clever. In her gesture is an attempt to conjure the blasé sophistication she knows runs through the veins of this crowd. Since moving to Manhattan, she's been surrounded by kids like these. Adopting their nonchalant manner is a way to blend in, especially when you don't have the money they do. Besides, she *does* have nice legs—her mother says her legs are her best feature—but she doesn't need any coke-wired guy getting all worked up about them. Not in front of his girlfriend. Not here, not now.

But Dorian isn't done with her yet. "*Calvin*," she says, rolling her eyes. "He's so tedious."

"*You're* tedious, Dorian, especially on coke," says Necktie Guy. "You should stick to drinking." This sounds like an insult, but Dorian lifts her mouth to his and they commence a particularly wet tongue kiss.

"Is Calvin your boyfriend?" This comes from the third boy in the room, speaking from the corner, where a sunny window behind him casts him in silhouette.

Ruby senses that this guy been silently watching her all this time. She stares back toward him, wanting a look. After she says yes, he drops his gaze.

From the bed, Cicely points a finger at Ruby and exclaims, "Oh, my God! You're the virgin!"

Dorian breaks out of her kiss and exclaims, "You *are*!"

"Well, I mean, *God*—" Ruby stammers, feeling every bugged-out eye in the room home in on her. "I guess someone's been talking to Calvin."

Alice says, "Calvin tells me *everything*." She is standing at a wall-mounted mirror examining a tiny blemish on her face. She meets Ruby's eyes in the glass, her face fractured by a hairline crack running down the center. "We were just involved in this entire *discourse* about how there were no virgins at this party."

Linen Blazer says, "And then a fucking virgin walks in and shit."

Ruby raises the brandy snifter as if to toast them all—another bit of nonchalant fakery—then gulps down the contents. Her tongue swells and her throat constricts. She really is an inexperienced drinker.

"Leave her alone." It's the boy silhouetted in the corner again.

He stands suddenly, and she gets a quick look at him. His hair sticks out on top and runs below his ears, nearly as long as hers and dyed the same black. His sleeveless, scarlet T-shirt bears the logo of a band she likes, the Clash. He wears tight, knee-length shorts cut from black jeans. He wears black socks and black boots. Between shorts and socks is a strip of pale skin. Then he scurries to the bathroom and slams the door behind him. His gestures are jittery—he's probably been doing coke with the rest of them.

"Ruby!" It's Necktie Guy, raising his voice to command her attention. "You mean to tell me that Calvin hasn't—"

Dorian interrupts him. "I wouldn't give my cherry to Calvin."

"Neither would I," says Necktie Guy, through a burst of satirical laughter.

"Ewww—" Dorian whines.

"What's so bad about Calvin?" Alice asks.

"Oh, you know, he's just so . . . *Calvin,*" Cicely says. Snuggling up to the guy in the linen blazer, she says, "I couldn't *wait* to get rid of my virginity."

He throws an arm around her and says, "A big fuckin' thank-you for that."

"I'm so sure you're fucking *welcome*, Nick."

Alice, frowning into the mirror, says, "I sometimes wish I had my virginity again. I gave it away like a hundred years ago—"

"To my brother," Dorian screeches. "Slut!"

"That's right. I lost my virginity to your brother, and you're like totally insulting mine. In front of Ruby."

Ruby feels like a soft, small toy batted around by enormous paws in a room filled with cats. They're only playing, but at any moment they might pounce, their sharp claws piercing her skin. Her eyes dart to the bathroom door. Why didn't she go in there while she had a chance? She places the empty snifter on a dresser and wipes her beer-sticky hands on her shirt.

"Refill?" Alice asks.

"What I really could use is something clean to wear."

"Oh, my God, yes, yes, yes!" Alice exclaims, tearing herself away from her reflection and throwing open a closet door. So many clothes!

Cicely exclaims, "Awesome," as she rolls her curvaceous figure off the bed and joins Alice at the closet. Ruby steps gingerly between them as they pull hangers from the rack and hold the garments up in front of her.

"This would look soooo cute on you," Cicely coos, pressing a shiny, violet, one-piece swimsuit against Ruby, "but it's cut for my size. It'll just *hang* off your little shoulders."

"I have a bag in Calvin's car," Ruby says, "I should just get it."

"You need something for tonight," Alice says, though Ruby has no idea what *tonight* promises. Alice pairs a spaghetti-strapped top with bright white pants many inches too long for Ruby. "You really *need* something like this."

"I mostly just wear black," Ruby offers.

"I had no idea," Alice says, airing a fuchsia-and-turquoise shirtdress with an attached silver belt. "You need more of a nightclub look. This vampire thing you've got going on, I mean . . ." She shakes her head.

"I've got it," Cicely announces, waving a narrow yellow tank top and a pair of madras shorts.

"Hey, those are *mine*." This reprimand comes from Dorian, scowling from across the room, as she pours champagne into a plastic beer cup. "She can't wear my clothes, she smells like a keg."

"She'll shower," Cicely says.

"Dodo," Alice says to Dorian, her voice cooing with persuasion, "you're the only one who's Ruby's size."

"What if I planned on, like, wearing it?"

The sourness in Dorian's voice is obvious to Ruby, but Alice pays no mind. She presses the clothes into Ruby's hands. Ruby holds them in front of her body and takes a quick look in the mirror. She can see how they will fit her. The shirt feels expensive to the touch, with the kind of fine stitching that indicates good tailoring; its softness will feel good against her sunburned skin. This is exactly the kind of stuff her mother is always buying for her—and always returning when Ruby refuses to wear it.

Dorian shouts, "Like, am I talking to deaf people?"

"I hear you loud and clear," Ruby says to Dorian, holding her stare, thinking, I'll just wear her ugly preppie clothes to spite her. She's not sure how this girl became her instant nemesis, but there's no mistaking it.

"*Put them on*," Alice insists. She shoots a daggered look to Dorian.

"Oh, like I even care," Dorian says, raising her middle finger and then downing the champagne. She tosses the empty cup across the room and flops down on the bed between the two boys, exhorting, "Let the virgin wear my whore's clothes."

"You're such a bitch." It's him again, the black-haired boy, standing in the bathroom doorway, looking at her with such intense sympathy she can't hold his stare. How long has he been watching?

She steps toward him, flapping Dorian's clothes. "I need to—"

He nods, but he's blocking her passage. His eyes, intriguingly, are rimmed with black liner. His face is strangely familiar—is he a friend of Calvin's she's met before? Maybe at that awful Barnard-Columbia mixer. The memory is buried just below an opaque surface, poking upward for air.

She takes a step closer. "Can you let me by?"

He turns sideways, forcing her to squeeze past. She sees a thin, crescent scar bisecting the childlike swell of his upper lip.

Nearly face-to-face, he whispers: "I can't believe it's you."

She says, "I was trying to remember where—"

He says, "Don't let them make you over." She lets out a little chuckle, meant to neutralize. He touches her shoulder. "I'm not joking. You're perfect."

"What?" She can't believe this guy's nerve, using a line like that—just one more *thwack* from the cat's paw. These people are unbelievable. But his eyes, slightly forlorn even in their cocaine alertness, beseech her to pay attention.

He says, "I'm sorry about this." Then he tilts his head, dreamily, his eyelids half closing. He leans in. He wants to kiss her.

She pulls back, her shoulders hitting the door frame. She feels his breath as his mouth approaches. He makes contact. Lips, no tongue. She's aware of the delicate ridge where the scar interrupts the flesh. He tastes clean, like mouthwash.

She understands that she is letting herself accept this. She feels his breath move into her. She feels herself giving in—her throat flutters warmly.

Calvin doesn't kiss this way, to romance her, as if in slow motion. Maybe if he did, she wouldn't be doing this now.

"Christopher! Let the de-virginizing begin." A clownish hoot from the room. It's that guy with the stupid necktie on his head.

Ruby breaks from the kiss, pushes the boy away, slides behind the bathroom door, pushes the lock on the knob. She leans against the wall and catches her breath.

God, what was that?

She flicks a switch and starts the hum of a fan. Blown air hits the wet circle where he kissed her. Blood pulses in her head—liquor, nerves, excitement. Her thighs are sticky from the spill. She can smell her own body odor beneath the yeasty stench of beer and the floral waft from an air freshener on the toilet tank. The walls are papered in a metallic pattern, chrome and cobalt, abstractions of butterflies and snails. In that reflective surface she sees a blurred, schismed version of herself—a soiled, frazzled girl working through an alcohol buzz, clutching borrowed clothes.

She starts the water, testing hot and cold on her open palm. Pulls her shirt over her head, shimmies out of her skirt. She pauses in front of the mirror, staring at herself in black bra and panties, at her bare legs and thick-soled black shoes. She doesn't look like a virgin. That's why they all took so much pleasure in the rumor. Calvin's girlfriend, the unlikely virgin. But Calvin believes it, and that's what's important—he accepts that this is the reason why their sex life never gets past kissing and hand jobs.

Someone in that room is going to tell him that she was just kissing this boy. Maybe that's a good thing. It'll prepare Calvin for what she has to say to him when they get home.

The kiss didn't mean anything. It was just his intensity. And his style—the only person at this party who looks like someone she'd actually want to hang out with. And those eyes, the wounded look he was giving her. *And I'm in a daring mood. And I know him, don't I? But from where?*

The pounding shower unknots her shoulders. Who is he, who is he, who is he? She almost has it, pushing up through memory. Can picture him against a wall—a blank, institutional cement wall. His hair isn't black. Neither is hers. This was years ago. Long before Calvin. Before college. Those first couple years of high school, St. Vincent's.

In an instant she knows. It's Chris Cleary.

"Oh, my God," she says out loud. "Oh my God, oh my God, oh my God." Even under the hot water she feels the chill of goose bumps.

How could she not have recognized him right away?

But he looks like a different person now. The hair, the clothes. The shape of his face seems changed—longer, more narrow. That scar on his lip—that's new.

They met at a Catholic program called Crossroads. Teenagers from parishes all over the city and beyond. A weekend away at a seminary in the country. The girls in one dorm and the boys in the other. Communal meals in a cafeteria, mass in the "multipurpose room." There were blindfolded trust exercises. And "talks" about forgiveness, about God's love.

They held hands during Shared Prayer. They sang songs from *Godspell—"All good gifts around us are sent from heaven above . . ."* In a room lit by candles he told her he'd been messing with drugs. She told him she felt guilty for her little brother's death. They talked about *not giving in to peer pressure,* and they cried together, because Jesus understood.

They went for a walk in the woods, held hands, and they kissed, quickly and anxiously, because they were breaking the rules.

It's all there now, all of it, returning.

After the weekend, there were phone calls. For several weeks, they spent hours on the phone—her mother scolding her for tying up the line, her brother teasing her about her *new boyfriend*, offering to cover if she wanted to meet Chris on the weekend without Dorothy knowing. But they didn't meet. He lived out on Long Island. Neither had a driver's license. Their phone calls, carried on in quiet, confessional voices, in rooms with the lights turned off, were their own covert meetings.

They had talked about everything, so easily. They had so many things in common: life as the middle child in the inescapable shadow of a favored older sibling. The need to tiptoe around unhappy parents—hers newly divorced, his married but hardly speaking. The knowledge that there was some other life out there, years in the distance, and if you just hung on long enough maybe you'd get to see it. Secrets to be shared. Chris: "I put modeling glue in a paper bag, with the cap off, and then I inhaled and my brain just went crazy." Ruby:

"It's so easy to shoplift. They never even notice me. And everything just fits under my sweatshirt." She stole a Stephen King novel, *Firestarter,* and she was going to mail it to him.

Jesus will forgive us, they told each other.

Then one day the phone calls stopped. She guessed that maybe he moved, because his line was disconnected. But she never knew. He never called. She was crushed. She prayed, *Jesus, help me find Chris.* He was Chris in those days, not Christopher like they call him now. Chris Cleary.

She needs to let him know she remembers. He's out there, in the room with those cruel-cat people, snorting poison. She needs to get him away from them. But first she has to get herself made up. All these pricey cosmetics to choose from. Alice won't mind. None of the lipstick is dark enough, and in this borrowed yellow shirt, these ridiculous plaid shorts, which are too long, nearly to her knees, she looks not like herself at all, not like the person she's turned herself into, but like the Catholic schoolgirl she once was. Is it better that way, better for Chris to see her like she was?

There's a knock on the bathroom door—Calvin, calling her name, jiggling the knob.

She says loudly, "I'm changing."

"Are you okay?"

"Alice gave me clothes. I'm fine."

"I had no idea where you—"

"I'm fine. Will you get me a beer?"

"Open the door, Ruby."

He clears his throat loudly—the telltale signal for a kind of impatience that Calvin falls into when Ruby doesn't answer him the way he expects. Usually this leaves her stabbed with guilt, but she doesn't care now. Chris Cleary is out there.

She checks the mirror once more.

Calvin is standing right outside the door, chewing on a fingernail, bouncing on his toes. He blinks, taking in her changed appearance. "What's going on here? I heard about you and that guy—"

She looks past him, into the room, but doesn't see the one she wants to see.

Alice is pushing Calvin out of the way. "Let's see, let's see. Oh, my God. We *so* got it right, you're totally bitchin' now. Oh, yes, yes, yes. This is so fun, I want to do it again, can we keep changing your outfit all night, please? We have ten million outfits, you have to try them all." Her speech is even more rapid-fire than before. More coked up.

Cicely calls out to Dorian, "Look, Dodo, she's all dressed up like one of us," but Dorian is sandwiched on the bed between Necktie Guy and Linen Blazer. The boys fumble messily, a hand inside her blouse, a face nuzzling her collarbone. Necktie Guy is thrusting at the hips. Ruby sees his white briefs humping Dorian's exposed thigh—no, he's actually humping the other guy's thigh, which is mashed into Dorian's. One of the boys' hands is snapping at the elastic of her pink bikini bottom.

Ruby sees that Calvin is staring at the bed, too. "Ben? Um, you guys are grossing us all out." They ignore him.

Alice turns Ruby this way and that, running hands across her back to smooth wrinkles, pinching at the waistline of the shorts. She says, "It's big at the waist, maybe we have some safety pins or something. God, you're a skinny little virgin."

"Alice!" Calvin protests. "What the hell?"

Alice flaps her hand at him. "Ruby and I are friends now."

Ruby catches Calvin's gaze, shrugs her shoulders. Out of my hands.

"Let go of her, Malice," Calvin barks at his sister. "Come here, Ruby. I'm sorry I spilled on you. Don't go kissing other guys." His arms pull her close, and he sniffs her hair.

For just a moment she thinks, I guess I'll stay here with Calvin wrapped around me, and we'll get through this stupid weekend together—a thought with so little gravity that she feels herself float free of it, released from him like smoke from a cigarette.

She hears a blast of pop music from the house, a honeyed male vocalist insisting, *"I wanna be your lover, lover, loverboy."*

Beyond the bedroom doorframe, a parade of partygoers crowds the hallway, as if in an adjacent universe. Where did he go? Chris Cleary from East Meadow, Long Island. Chris Cleary from the Crossroads youth retreat weekend. Chris Cleary in your new black hair, where in God's name are you?

It's as if he had never been there, as if he'd been an apparition she'd conjured out of her need to give her life some greater purpose.

Chris is nowhere to be found. Apparently he left the house while she was in the shower, after Calvin came into the bedroom and Alice or someone else told him what happened.

Ruby has gleaned this disappointing information from Necktie Guy, whose name, it turns out, is Benjamin Dinkelberg, and who knows "Christopher" from Princeton, where they all go to school. The necktie is no longer wrapped around his head. She imagines it tangled in the bedsheets, loosened during his ménage à trois.

He's taken to calling her Princess. "You're a princess in a temple of whores," he told her, after emerging from the bedroom for a smoke and finding her here, on the back porch, leaning against the splintering railing and staring quietly at the raucous backyard. She's barefoot now—too hot to put her boots back on, and anyway she did her toenails in black polish before she came down the shore, so why not show it off?

She asked Benjamin about Chris, and he reported that Chris was seen leaving the party on foot, in a hurry. "Are you *hot* for Christopher?" Benjamin wanted to know. "Are you warm for his form? There's a certain kind of damaged chick—you might be the type—that finds an *enigma* like him irresistible."

"Did he say where he went?"

"As his former roommate, I can report that he has a small penis," Benjamin said. "I myself am above average."

"You're an average idiot," Ruby told him, as he smiled in a way that said he didn't care.

The sun is setting, the sky glazed in pink and tangerine. The porch looks out onto a grid of backyards, most of which are crowded with kids her age doing variations of the things going on here. To the left, the smell of reefer and the music of the Grateful Dead. To the right, a gang of jocks and frat boys doing beer funnels. People flow between the yards.

Barbecue smoke paints the air, hot dogs blackening on the grill like corpse fingers. There's nothing for her to eat here, but she barely has an appetite anyway, with the rancid smell of vomit rising up from the alley alongside between the houses—the designated place to puke.

"I love summer," Benjamin says. "I love the humidity and all the exposed flesh and everyone dropping their inhibitions, girls especially. I love bikinis. I love a chick's stomach. And when they shake water out of their wet hair, I love that. I love the way your hair looked when you came out of the shower. Much sexier. I love the days being so long. Winter sucks, the whole turning-back-the-clocks concept, and the fucking cold. Last winter I got a backache from tensing up because of the cold air. I went to a physical therapist, like I'm some kind of middle-aged man, can you believe it? I'm from Florida, we don't have winter, you know? It's stupid to live in these cold places. Do you see my point, Princess?"

Ruby nods. It doesn't matter if she says yes or no, Benjamin is talking for the sake of talking, his voice an apparatus running on cocaine.

"Ruby?"

It's Calvin, pushing open the back door. He looks at her with a droopy-eyed expression that could be worry, or is perhaps just the result of too much beer. "Come on a booze run with me. I'm going to the store with this guy."

Behind him is the curly-haired jock who helped Ruby wipe up earlier in the day. He waves at her like they're old friends and announces, in his own tipsy slur, "I'm legal, so I'm buying."

"I'll wait here," Ruby says.

Calvin looks from Ruby to Benjamin, and there's something very unsure in his eyes. "Whatever you do," he says, pointing a finger to Benjamin, "don't listen to anything this hose-bag says."

"What would I possibly say to your girlfriend that she wouldn't want to hear?" Benjamin is so smarmy, it makes her wonder. What secret is being held here?

"Ruby," Calvin says, almost a whine. *Do me a favor,* she wants to say, *and go.*

The jock places a meaty hand on Calvin's shoulder and says, "This is a mission for men."

Calvin turns to the guy and breaks into a smile—it's almost sweet to see—as if he's been granted some great and unexpected honor among his gender.

"I'll be right here," she says. *Unless Chris returns, and then . . .*

"Right here," Calvin says, pointing his finger down emphatically, as if she mustn't leave this little dirty wooden porch. He backs away with his new friend—making room for Dorian, who stumbles onto the porch waving a cigarette that she doesn't seem to be smoking.

Dorian looks at Benjamin, then throws a hard stare at Ruby.

"How nice to see you again," Ruby says. She's pretty sure this will provoke Dorian, and she's surprised to discover she doesn't care. Why did she agree to wear this awful girl's clothes? It's like she has donned a uniform making her Dorian's employee.

Dorian turns her gaze back to Benjamin and says, "You can't fuck her."

Benjamin flashes Dorian a delighted smile. "Do blow jobs count?"

The cigarette flutters through the air, but Dorian—so drunk that she can't keep her balance—is unable to form a response. She points a finger at Ruby and dramatically says, "You don't fool me," and then she's gone, swerving back into the house like a shopping cart with a loose wheel.

Ruby and Benjamin glance at each other and share a laugh at Dorian's expense. For a brief moment, she forgets her dislike of this guy. Then he opens his mouth again. "What I'm wondering, Princess, is, who are you saving it for, huh? I'm referring to the Big V."

"Do we have to talk about this?"

"Are you some kind of Puritan, dressed all in black?"

She turns back to the yard, squinting into the sun. "Once it was a religious belief. But now I'm just used to the idea."

"Are you going to give it to Mr. Right when he comes along?"

"I've waited this long, it might as well be right."

"And how will you know exactly?"

"I'll feel it. Like an answer to a question I've been carrying around." She looks at him, wanting this to be the last word. He frowns. Maybe her answer didn't convince him. She's not sure she's convinced herself. But how could she tell him the truth—that the next time she has sex, it has to be someone who won't rush through it, won't hurt her with his clumsiness, won't say, *Let's just get it over with*?

Alice reappears, carrying a tray of Dixie cups. "Jell-O shots, Jell-O shots," she announces. She hands one to Benjamin, then holds the tray out to Ruby. Ruby tries to refuse, but Alice insists, "You have to take one before they get scarfed down by the townies." She waves an arm over the backyard.

There's a song coming from inside the house that Ruby has heard before—in a store, in the background somewhere, who knows—one of those songs she hears a lot lately. It's this pretty clichéd rock and roll song about a boy, a girl and a guitar. She hates this song and every song like it, but it's catchy, and she finds that she actually knows the words: "*Those were the best days of my life, back in the summer of '69.*" Her life is not going to be like that, a slide downhill after some fabled glorious youth.

"What's that look on your face?" Alice says. "Loosen up!"

Ruby reaches out and takes a cup in each hand and throws back one, then another blob of colored gelatin. The faintest taste of liquor passes coldly across her tongue. "Happy?" she asks Alice, but Alice is already moving down the steps into the yard, where she's swarmed by the crowd.

"Maybe you're a lesbian," Benjamin says. "D'you ever think of that?"

Ruby crumples the cups in her hand and throws them at him. "Maybe you're mentally retarded. Ever think of that?"

The insult just rolls off him. "I'm from Florida, we Christmased in Key West every year—I know from lesbians. They're not all diesel-truck drivers. Some are cool customers like you."

"My brother's gay," Ruby says angrily. She's surprised to hear herself say it; she doesn't blurt this out to strangers. Benjamin has probably already heard it—Calvin would have told Alice about Robin, Alice would have told Dorian, who probably told Benjamin, and probably not in very nice terms: "Calvin's girlfriend's brother is a fag, can you believe that? Isn't that sick?"

Benjamin says, "Why don't they just stop having sex altogether? Death, my Princess, is stalking the faggots."

"Straight people get it, too," she snaps. "In Haiti it's men and women both."

"In Haiti the men fuck the women up the rear. That's the problem. The body is rebelling against this invasion to the system." Benjamin reaches into his pocket—since leaving the bedroom, he's put his pants on—and he retrieves a box of Dunhills. He lights one and puffs on it like an amateur, pulling the cigarette away from his face and spitting out smoke without inhaling. Ruby knows what a real smoker looks like. Her mother and her brother smoke constantly. "There's a very fantastic article about it in *Rolling Stone,*" Benjamin says. "It's almost mystical, this plague. Like a cosmic cleansing mechanism."

"It's not cosmic, it's medical," Ruby tells Benjamin. "You should learn something about the science." She knows about these terminal cases, the young men dying in New York hospitals as if they're at the end of their lives, their bodies unable to fight. There's a man in her apartment building with a purple splotch on his handsome face. In the elevator, he caught her staring, and before she could look away in embarrassment, he started up a conversation about the building's garbage collection, and they chatted, like all was normal, for five flights down.

She worries for her brother. He took an AIDS test last year, right after they became available. He was negative. But still—he's told her about a lot of sex in the past. So she can't help but worry. She has asked him if he used poppers—they say that poppers have something to do with it, with immune system damage—and he said only a couple of times. He and Peter are monogamous, he said, and they're using rubbers, which is what doctors say you should do now. He told her, you're lucky you're not fucking your way through college. She told him that she didn't feel lucky. She felt apart from people because of it.

"You know," Benjamin says, "there's talk about Calvino being a little, um, *susceptible*. To, you know, *tendencies.* Alice says Calvino used to wear their mother's lipstick."

"Maybe you haven't noticed, lots of guys wear makeup now," Ruby says. "It's fashionable." Chris was wearing eyeliner, she thinks. But she hates hearing this about Calvin. What does it say about her, to be dating someone who could be in the closet?

Alice comes skipping up the stairs, her tray now empty but for one last shot. "Right, Alice? Calvin wore your mother's lipstick?"

"Shut up," she says, but her voice lacks force, and she turns to Ruby, jabbing the edge of the tray into her chest. "Why don't you give Calvin some action, so people will just shut up?"

Ruby's stomach tightens again as she considers the sticky, dense world she's been lured into—she's not a toy for cats but a winged insect snagged in a spiderweb. She wants to make herself weightier, heavy enough to break through the cords they're trying to tighten around her. She nudges the tray away. "Mind your own business, OK?"

Alice presses her lips together, and Ruby wonders if she's gone too far. She doesn't want to make an enemy here. But she's fed up.

"Ladies, ladies," Benjamin says.

Alice downs the last Jell-O shot, and then the injury or anger or whatever it was vanishes, smothered in a toothy smile that takes over the lower half of her thin face. She throws an arm over Ruby's shoulder and says in a too-emphatic voice, "I know we'll be great friends if we just keep drinking!" And she slips back into the house, and Ruby lets go the breath she was holding.

Benjamin relights his cigarette—which apparently went out because he wasn't smoking it right—and Ruby studies his face as the light casts a perfect magic-hour glow upon him. Benjamin is one of those people you could never be friends with no matter how much you drank. She takes a guess that of everyone here, he comes from the wealthiest family—maybe from the most uptight, emotionally frigid family, too. A rich kid, always suspicious of everyone he meets, because he has more than they do—more money, more *things*, has probably traveled more and been schooled more rigorously. Even with his drug-induced twitchiness, he's not bad looking. He was probably a cute little boy. Now he's a horrible, handsome young man. A user. It was unfair, how the sun cast the same light on the good as it did on the bad, on kind people as well as cruel. She still finds herself wishing for cosmic justice—if there is a God, why doesn't he punish those who truly deserve it?

She looks westward into the sun, hovering between some distant, inland hills and the town's water tower. It's a solid, fiery ball. And she thinks of all those Friday evenings, after they moved into Manhattan, when she and Robin were driven by their mother across the George Washington Bridge to the house in Greenlawn where her father still lived. The fireball in the sky is the very image of *joint custody*, of every-other-weekend, of sinking into the tan upholstery of the Nissan Maxima as her mother and her brother gabbed up front, smoking their cigarettes.

The house on Bergen Ave. still retained touches of their mother's decorating style—arty black-and-white photos hung on the living room walls in pricey frames—though after the divorce, Dorothy never again stepped inside. She never made this refusal explicit, she just held back at the front door, and the rest of them came to understand that she would not cross that threshold. When she dropped them off, money went from Clark's hands to Dorothy's on the stoop, and then she drove away. The scenario changed over time: Dorothy staying in Manhattan, and Ruby, after she got her driver's license, taking on driving duty. Their father couldn't cook much more than hamburgers and macaroni and cheese, SpaghettiOs in a can, or frozen fish sticks, so she and Robin would stop at the A&P and concoct a menu: meatloaf or tuna casserole or pan-fried chicken breasts glazed with apricot jam. Clark loved it, he always thanked them, said they were better cooks than their mother had ever been (information that they passed on to Dorothy, who fumed in response but then bought cookbooks and became more skilled in the small kitchen of their Upper West Side apartment than she had ever been in the suburbs). In New Jersey, Ruby and Robin would pass hours of the weekend in silence with their father, but it was a gentle silence, not the tension of unhappiness that once ruled the house. After dinner, they watched movies on HBO or Cinemax. Their father paid extra for the good cable channels; in Manhattan their mother didn't even get the basic package that would have removed the static from the screen. That's what the setting sun conjures up—years of adjusting to separation. Separated parents, separate homes, a dividing line between her old life and her new.

She learned to sleep well in her old room, still appointed as when she was a little girl—the tramped-down russet carpet, the closet door with its mousy squeak, that ceramic bedside lamp in the shape of a ballerina, its hollow pedestal once a hiding place for little things she shoplifted—though it wasn't easy at first. The house had a negative charge buzzing through it. Not just the divorce but the terrible time leading up to it. And before that, the time of Jackson in the hospital, in his dark, damaged sleep.

Tomorrow's his birthday. Jackson's. She's been thinking about it for weeks. Thinking about going to the grave, and how frightening the idea was to her, because of what happened the last time she was there. She'd had the idea, a week or two ago, that she'd be able to deal with the cemetery if she could get all of them to go with her, her mother and father, showing up at the grave at the same time, and maybe Robin, too, if he could get a train from Philadelphia. They could all be there together to mark Jackson's birthday. But Robin said he had to work, and her father said that he didn't know if he and Annie, this woman he'd been dating lately, had made plans already. He had managed to slip into their conversation that Sunday was also Father's Day—she hadn't remembered, and felt bad about it, though, really, Father's Day strikes her as a fake holiday, a Hallmark holiday, not an important memorial like Jackson's birthday. (Plus, wasn't it creepy that the person her father had planned to spend his Father's Day with was Annie, his much-younger girlfriend?) Her mother hadn't been open to the idea of the group outing to the cemetery, either. She said that she had her day planned out, and she wasn't feeling very flexible about the schedule—she wanted to be at the grave early enough to allow her to get back to Manhattan and cook dinner. Of course, she was just avoiding Clark, still holding on to all the unfinished business surrounding the divorce, even though they'd actually been civil to each other lately—they even managed to share a few laughs at Uncle Stan's wedding last weekend. Still, the plan fell apart, because everyone in her family was basically self-absorbed or petty or both, and Ruby wound up feeling that she had expended way too much energy on the plan, and gotten nothing back from any of them, which was typical. Calvin tried to be nice about it, told her they could stop at the cemetery on the drive back from the shore tomorrow, but she wasn't sure she wanted to go with Calvin. He didn't know Jackson. It wouldn't mean anything to him. Plus, he'll probably have some critique of the whole concept of a cemetery, the way the funeral industry is essentially capitalist exploitation of grief, which of course, it kind of is, but who wants to hear that when you're standing in front of your dead brother's tombstone? What if she started praying and Calvin challenged her about it? It would be better not to be there at all than to be there with someone who misunderstood.

She makes a decision.

She turns to Benjamin and says, "I'm going for a walk. If Calvin asks, tell him that."

"Are you going to the boardwalk?" Benjamin asks, exhaling smoke past her shoulder. "We should *all* go!"

"No, *we* shouldn't."

"Oh, the Princess needs her personal space?" He winks at her, as if cementing a pact between them.

So she assumes, though she can't be sure it's true, that Benjamin has guessed that she's going to look for Chris.

The beach is only a few blocks away. Ruby walks eastward, away from the now-set sun, her boots slung over the strap of her handbag, a thermos in her hand filled with something called a New Jersey Iced Tea—lemonade, Coca-Cola, rum, and vodka—mixed by the girl playing bartender back at the house. She passes a church called Our Lady of Perpetual Help. She thinks of the fact of the ocean, and how they take it for granted as a place of recreation, though it's more powerful than any of them. She felt that briefly today when she was jumping around in the crashing waves by herself. She thinks of sailors lost at sea, of capsized boats, of swimmers carried away. The ocean is perpetual, and the tides, and drowning. But so is love, and desire. She is staring at the church, a brick building with a strip of dehydrated lawn surrounding it. She ignores the pull she feels to enter, kneel, and pray to God that she finds Chris. She keeps walking. She walks another block and comes upon Waterworks, a giant waterslide occupying an entire block in the middle of this neighborhood, emitting splashes and shrieks from every direction. This is what people do, we take the forces of nature and we corral them into amusements. We're always trying to control everything. She hears her thoughts cascading and realizes she's definitely buzzed. Waterworks is situated catty-corner from the borough hall and the police station. Could she get arrested here, for being underage and under the influence? No, not with wasted teenagers everywhere. But she keeps her head down anyway.

Twilight settles upon streets dense with cruising traffic. With every step the noise of the night swells up. She dodges cars turning in and out of liquor store parking lots. Gangs of happy-hour drunks stumble serpentine along the sidewalk. Everyone seems so young, so inconsequential, and yet she doesn't feel safe, on her own like this. Catcalls fly out from guys on porches and hotel balconies. She guesses she's an easy mark, a single girl in preppie shorts, barefoot, unsteady on her feet.

Someone yells from a second-floor motel balcony, "Show us your tits." She hears the same thing a half block later from a different group of boys. She drops her head and walks faster, away from the harassment. Calls of "prude" trail her like the barking of provoked dogs. If it happens again, she thinks she might just do it. Drop everything, yank up her shirt and bra, give them a glimpse of her B-cup breasts, gleaming white in the darkening night air. She'd yell back at them, "Satisfied?" An Amazon, a Bond Girl, Bettie Page.

She sips from the thermos, wipes a splash from her chin. Just forget about those guys. *Fuck* those guys. That's what she'll yell next time they shout at her. *Fuck you. Show me your prick.* The strong drink stimulates courage, or the concept of courage anyway. But then she rounds a corner and comes upon a tall motel taking up half the block. Its sign bears the lofty name Skyview Manor, but there's nothing posh about the four floors of long balconies jammed to the railing with riotous teens, like a hundred-eyed creature from a monster movie. If anyone gives her serious trouble, she'll run back to the police station. Until then she's keeping her course. She has no idea where Chris is, but the closer she gets to the ocean, the more urgent it seems that she'll find him. Maybe then she'll have the answer to the question that nagged at her all day long. *Why am I here?*

She turns a corner and comes upon another motel, the last block before the boardwalk, lit up in white light. This one looks more typical of Seaside Heights—a two-story building, a parking lot, a vending machine near a sign marked OFFICE. There's a fenced-in pool running the length of the place and a big sign bearing its name, The Surfside. The picture on the sign stops her in her tracks—an illustration of a woman in a swimsuit, her body bent in half, diving into the water. Ruby has been here before. That family vacation, all those years ago. She was only eight, maybe nine, and she shared a room with her brothers. It felt like an adventure, like being on their own, though Dorothy and Clark were just on the other side of the wall. Jackson wanted to build a fort, so she and Robin stretched sheets and blankets between the twin beds, and brought the desk lamp underneath, and the phone, too—whatever they could move from all corners of the room into their "underground hideout." Robin decided this should be the Batcave. Robin was Batman, Ruby was Batgirl, and Jackson was Robin the Boy Wonder (which was confusing to him, only six years old and asked to play the character with his older brother's name). Robin fashioned capes for them out of pillowcases and they ran around the room fighting crime. Then they started over, playing criminals this time. Ruby called Catwoman, but Robin wanted to be Catwoman, too, so she agreed to be Catgirl, a criminal not part of the TV show but fine for pretend. She and Robin hissed to each other in cat-voices—"We're going to commit the *purrfect* crime"—while Jackson, as the Penguin, waddled around making honking noises. Eventually the door swung open and their father barged in, annoyed. "Aw, come on, guys! Clean up this mess." He wore his bathrobe, bare chest showing at the collar, hairy legs visible below. After lights out, she and Robin giggled about it—*Daddy wasn't wearing pajamas!*

This was the very place, wasn't it? The Surfside Motel. She remembers her mother lounging by the pool, even though the beach was just a block away, reading the *New Yorker*. She remembers that they only stayed one night before they moved to another place—too many teenagers, making way more noise than she and her brothers ever could. Ruby strides past the pool, full of girls and boys splashing around, toward a phone booth near the vending machines. She pulls a few dimes from her purse, flips through her address book, and finds her brother's new phone number in Philly. It's Saturday night. He's probably working at the restaurant, or maybe he and George are out for the night. (He's only been in Philly for a month. Does he have friends? Where do they go when they go out? Do they use fake IDs and go to gay bars? Do they have parties?) The phone rings, then the machine picks up. Dorothy bought him an answering machine when he moved in with George, afraid that she'd lose him in the wilds of West Philly—after the news of the police bombing, she'd called the neighborhood a "war zone." Ruby had argued that Dorothy didn't understand politics at all; Dorothy said Ruby had no idea what it was to be a mother. Another standoff.

Robin and George have recorded a funny outgoing message together: "It's Robin. And George. We're out recruiting for our secret club. If you leave a message, we might let you join." When she hears the beep she fumbles with what she wants to say. It's harder to form words than she'd expected. (What was in those Jell-O shots?) She mentions Seaside, the motel, the party, Chris. "I'm trying to find him. I *followed* him. I'm a little buzzed." At some point she realizes the machine has already cut her off. There'd been a time limit, without warning. She thinks about calling back, changes her mind. Keep to the mission.

She's remembering more and more of Chris, things he told her during those phone calls after the retreat weekend. His father was an engineer at an aircraft company. His mother was a college English professor. Ruby remembers Chris's descriptions of how brilliant his mother was, but also how unbearably skinny she had been. How he never used to see her eat anything of substance. His older sister was a curvy beauty, a good student with good looks planning on earning scholarship money by entering the Miss New York pageant. Brainy and bubbly and blond. There was a younger sister, too. Chris told her that his bedroom ceiling was hung with model airplanes, rockets, spaceships. Tiny components pieced together by hand. The satisfaction of assembling something intricate. And then, the discovery of inhaling glue. He'd seen a psychiatrist after his sister found him passed out on the stairs, eyes rolling back in his head. He laughed bitterly when he related the catch-22 that emerged during his treatment: the shrink said a "creative outlet" was important, but since his beloved models provided the means to getting high, they were forbidden. The solution was painting and drawing, but the images he came up with frightened everyone—space creatures devouring children on barren planets, blood bursting out of human ears, noses, assholes. He told Ruby he used to squat over a mirror to get a look at his own asshole, in order to be able to draw one correctly.

His confessions made her uneasy, and then made her bold. She, too, held her privates open in front of a mirror, wanting to see the parts she contained. After reading a sex-soaked paperback found in Dorothy's bedroom, she tried out different textures down there, not just her fingertips, but stuffed animals and a hairbrush and a powder puff stolen from her mother's makeup table, which tickled to the point of ecstasy. She nicknamed the most tender spot her "clint," because she wasn't sure how to pronounce its real name (*clit*oris or cli*to*ris?). She told him she gave it a man's name because it felt like a stranger living there inside her. A sensitive, secret self.

It was Chris's mother who brought him to Jesus. Chris's shrink had taken one look at Mrs. Cleary and decided all was not well with this bone-thin woman. She had been seeing a therapist, too, and attending a regular support group, and letting a nutritionist put her on a regimen. The Save Your Life Diet, Chris called it. He told Ruby that before, he never hugged his mom because she was so hard and brittle—"Can you imagine that, thinking you could snap your own mother's bones?" But she put on flesh and grew softer, and the first time she held him against her newly cushioned body, he wept. His mother hushed him, "Don't cry, I'm getting better." She told him the change was not only in her body but also in her soul. It wasn't just the doctors, it was prayer that had made the difference. So the Cleary family went back to church—sober Chris, fleshy Mom, and the rest of them. Chris told Ruby he would stare at a painting of the crucifixion—Jesus' suffering like an image he himself might have sketched in oil crayons, Jesus with long hair like a rock star and a body as starved as the one his mother had just conquered. Chris would stare and then go home and read the New Testament, looking for anything that spoke of the pain, the actual bodily suffering. He went to their priest trying to understand the meaning of a single idea—that this man who walked the earth so long ago had *suffered in order to end our suffering.* It didn't make sense. The priest told him about a teen retreat called Crossroads.

Ruby remembers all of this. She remembers, too, the jealousy she felt. Chris lived in a house where healing had been possible. (And now? Who was Chris Cleary now? What did he believe in, if anything?) In her own home, pain only rooted deeper over time. Her mother did not go to church, did not forgo her bottles of wine to drink from the cup of Christ, had no miraculous transformation. Dorothy didn't even drive Ruby to church on Sundays, not even in the winter when the sidewalks were treacherous with ice, and slush seeped into her boots.

Ruby believed all on her own, until she stopped believing. That's what she tells herself, and others, too: She no longer believes in God, as she did back then, when the circumstances of her life brought her face-to-face with the kind of pain only God seemed fit to remove. Because He didn't remove it, and it deepened: an injured brother became a dead brother, a troubled home a broken one. She'd been uprooted from a quiet town and dropped into a dangerous city. So for a couple years now, she has resisted anything that smacks of the divine. It's all superstition, placebo. Rhetoric about things that are *meant to be* is just a way to rationalize a power structure, one that keeps people in their place, especially women. But given all that—how is she supposed to explain why crossing paths with Chris feels so preordained, so fated?

She joins the throng filing up a wooden ramp to the wide wooden boardwalk. Flares of color. Strobing surfaces. Bulbs flashing the entrance to the Casino Pier. Barkers in front of wheels of fortune calling out, "Round and round she goes, and where she stops nobody knows." The buzzing and whirring of games of chance. She sees Whack-A-Mole and Skee-Ball and the one where you squirt water into the open mouth of a clown, which somehow triggers an inflating balloon coming out of the top of the clown's head. First one to pop the balloon is the winner. The prizes are enormous stuffed animals, blacklight posters, mirrors painted with beer labels and rock album art. There's the smell of fried food in the air, pizza and hamburgers and Italian sausage smothered in onions. Music and sound effects compete for attention. She hears *"Everybody wants to rule the world"* emanating from a blazing blur in neon pink—an enormous disk, tilted on its side, spinning seated, screaming people high into the sky and back down again.

Past the glowing, screaming arcades she sees the ocean. She sits on a bench and puts her boots back on and looks out over the beach, which is mostly empty now. The water is bisected by a wide white stripe. The black waves are capped in glowing foam.

She looks up—a fat full moon is on the rise, big and nearly as bright as the sun. So beautiful. It gives her a moment's peace. If only it were a spotlight that could pinpoint Chris in its beam and lead her directly to him.

At first she feels the power of moving solo through a mob. The power of invisibility, of sliding under the radar. Couples, families, groups of friends pass by, absorbed in their own good times. Then she gets slammed by a fast-moving shoulder. She gets jostled again moments later. When she calls out "Watch where you're going," a burly guy shouts back, "Eat me." His girlfriend stops, stares Ruby down. "What did you say, freak?" A menacing girl is worse than a bullying guy, more likely to hit another girl. This one is a terror—enormous mane of hair, weighty gold jewelry, animal-print shirt, and matching leggings. Ruby hates the way girls look these days—garish eye shadow, shoulder pads sewn into flimsy cotton T-shirts, athletic jackets that match the ones their boyfriends wear. Do they know they seem like clowns—goofy from a distance, aggressive and scary close up? She wishes she could squirt water into this girl's mouth until her head exploded. She can't shake the feeling that the eighties are turning into a mean decade. People are pushy in a way they didn't use to be. Or maybe she's just older, more like an adult than she's ever been and learning the very adult pressure to take from the world what you want, the hell with everyone else.

It becomes clear that her presence is not going completely unnoticed. There are other solo observers here—all men. They catch sight of her and smile. Unwelcome smiles. One of them, early twenties, sports a white, ribbed "Guinea T-shirt," a slender gold chain, and the short-on-the-sides-long-in-the-back haircut favored by South Jersey boys. He locks eyes on her and breaks into a toothy grin. When he starts to move toward her, signaling for her attention, she darts away, heading not deeper onto the Casino Pier but parallel to the ocean, along the diagonal wooden slats of the boardwalk. In the middle is a bathroom, a moist, smelly concrete chamber. Sitting on the toilet in a locked stall, waiting him out, she feels for the first time all night the risk of what she's doing. It's not like her at all, taking this kind of chance, on her own. She guzzles from her thermos, wanting to regain that fearlessness she felt less than an hour ago, when she set out from the party.

"Women are not meant to be alone," her mother had said one night, preparing for a date with a man she'd admitted she wasn't all that fond of. The message seemed to be that any man was better than no man. Dorothy remains unmarried but, not yet fifty, still pursues her prospects. Last week she took a man she hardly knew to her brother's wedding, mostly, Ruby thinks, because she didn't want to face Clark without a date. Ruby sees now that only men appear on the boardwalk without company, not women. Certainly not *young* women.

That last chug of booze might have been a mistake. She feels the wobble in her walk as she exits the restroom. She's had so little to eat today. Breakfast in Manhattan, hours and hours ago with Calvin. A couple mouthfuls of potato salad in the kitchen at Alice's house, scooped up on a hotdog bun. She needs to eat, feels a craving for something sweet. Cotton candy and a root beer. The airy tastes of a beach vacation.

She enters the glass door of one of the restaurants that run the length of the boardwalk. This one is called Lucky Leo's, and it's crowded. Waiting her turn at the end of a long line, she tries not to make eye contact with anyone, but at the same time she needs to look around for Chris. She sees on the menu something she hasn't had in years: zeppoles, balls of fried dough coated in powdered sugar. She buys a bag, plus the root beer she'd been craving, pays with a couple of singles dredged from the bottom of her purse. She sits at the edge of a table occupied by a harried family—young parents trying to soothe cranky children with French fries.

If she really knew Chris, she could deduce where he'd gone. The boardwalk had seemed the obvious choice, the town's almighty magnet. Chris might indeed be nearby, drinking a beer under an awning, taking in the swirling decadence. Or he might have known better. Might have understood just how lonely being alone in an amusement park would feel. To *deduce,* she has to work with the little of him she witnessed. He saw her, kissed her, doused her in cryptic comments, then vanished after Calvin appeared. He was trying to lure her out after him, away from Calvin, away from that crowd—she feels certain of that. But how could he know that she would follow? How could he reasonably expect her to find him?

The children at the end of the table are crying and whining. Dad declares the evening over. As soon as they leave, their seats are occupied again. Two girls about her age sit down across from each other. They are dressed in black. The more petite of the two wears a miniskirt like the one Ruby shed earlier at the house. The girl's long, flat face reminds Ruby of the head of a snake. She is transfixed by her right index finger—its black-painted nail has had a chunk torn from it. "Joanne," she says to her friend, "should I just bite it off?"

Ruby winces.

Joanne, the larger of the two, rifles methodically through an enormous black vinyl purse, commanding, "Don't do that! I have an emery board in here." Her heavy New Jersey accent turns emery into *amree*, board into *bawd*. Her pretty, feline eyes are ringed in dark eye shadow. Her entire face, moon-shaped and powdered, is like that of a white lynx.

"I have a nail file," Ruby says, and opens her own purse to fish it out. The girls notice her for the first time. She offers them a hopeful smile. They're the first people she's seen all day who in any way resemble her, at least in the way they dress—though she realizes, in Dorian's clothes she doesn't quite look like herself.

"She tore it on the Himalaya," Joanne explains, gesturing toward her friend.

The girl with the ripped nail explains, "You know that safety bar that comes down? It had this little *thing* sticking out, and I got caught on it. It hurts like a bastard." She puts her finger in her mouth for a second, and then flicks it in the air as if to shake the pain away. "I should sue."

"You can't sue for a fingernail, Wendy." Joanne looks to Ruby for confirmation. "Am I right or am I left?"

"Right," Ruby says, smiling.

"Did you go on the Himalaya?" Wendy asks her. "It's my favorite."

"I didn't go on anything."

"Nothing?"

"I just play the games," Joanne says. "Last time I won everything I played. It was crazy! I couldn't even carry it all. These stuffed animals and things, I gave 'em all to my nephew. But I can't win *nothin'* today. And tomorrow's my birthday!"

"Oh!" Ruby says. "Happy birthday."

"It's all rigged, Joanne," says Wendy.

"Then how come last time I won practically every booth?"

Ruby says, "You were on a winning streak."

"Right?" Joanne slurps from a straw, seeming to disappear into thought. The cup has an illustration of a snowman on it, and the words RICH AND CREAMY! Ruby wishes she'd had a milkshake instead of the zeppoles, which already feel like they're expanding in her stomach, gaining mass. A vanilla milkshake seems in this moment like a great comfort.

The girls begin a conversation that Ruby can't help but listen in on, even though their attention has returned to each other. They're headed to a club, a place called Club Excess—Wendy is ready to go now, Joanne hasn't quite given up on the boardwalk, on wanting to win something for her birthday. "Look. We have to get there before eleven," Wendy says, flashing her watch, square black face with bright green digits.

Ruby squints to read the time.

"Ten thirty-five," Wendy tells her. "Have you been to Club Excess?"

"I don't really know this area," Ruby says.

"It's the only club in Seaside that plays new wave."

Ruby says, "I like new wave," and Wendy immediately barrages her with the names of bands. "Do you like Siouxsie and the Banshees? Depeche Mode? OMD? The Smiths?" Ruby nods and nods again. They all agree that they liked INXS better before they sold out.

Joanne says, "Tonight is Ladies' Night. No cover for girls before eleven. Are you here with your girlfriends? Do you want to bring them along?"

"No, I came down here with my boyfriend." A pinch of guilt catches in Ruby's throat. She pictures Calvin back at the house, glowering in a corner, while Benjamin gossips that she went out looking for Chris, and Alice says mean things about her. Can she blame them? What kind of girl kisses a guy behind her boyfriend's back, then disappears without explanation? All along she's imagined that *Calvin* is wrong for *her*, but maybe it's the other way around.

Joanne asks, "Are you waiting for him?"

She shakes her head. "I'm going to break up with him." She hasn't spoken these words out loud until now, but she finds them very easy to say. She adds, "Actually, I'm trying to find this other guy." She tells them about seeing Chris at the party, how he kissed her before she remembered who he was, how she set out into the night, tracking him blindly. She describes what he looks like, his clothes, asks if they've seen him.

"He sounds cute," Joanne says.

"Totally," Wendy adds. "Maybe he went to Excess. You should come!"

"Maybe I should hang out here. What if he shows up?"

Wendy purses her lips, which has the effect of elongating her snake-like face even more. "I wouldn't stay here by myself. Every summer, like five or six girls get raped."

She hands the nail file back to Ruby, who imagines stabbing it into the neck of the creepy guy who had sent her fleeing to the ladies' room. "Watch out, rapists," she says softly.

"We can help you look for him," Joanne says. "It'll be fun."

Wendy nods along with Joanne. Ruby looks at them and thinks of her mother—of Dorothy's disapproval at the idea of Ruby tagging along with *Jersey girls* to a bar down the shore to look for a boy she hardly knows.

"Why not?" Ruby says. She pushes her thermos toward them. "Here, help me finish this."

Ruby's fake ID makes the claim that she's twenty-two and a student at the Fashion Institute of Technology. It's still legal for her to drink in New York, but it's only a matter of time until the age gets raised there, like it is here, in New Jersey, to twenty-one. All those Mothers Against Drunk Driving are slowly but surely making their case to legislators. She bought the ID last year at a place Robin knew about in Times Square called Playland. When he came home for Thanksgiving, he took her there—a crammed, scuzzy arcade just down from the dirty movie theaters on 42nd Street. He warned her, "Every bartender on the East Coast knows about Playland, but for some of them, it's good enough. They just want you to show *something*." She had parroted Robin's words to Calvin after he mocked the crude, laminated card she showed him. But eventually Calvin went to Times Square for one of his own.

Wendy uses her sister's cast-off driver's license. "We look alike, so it works," she says. Joanne, it turns out, is twenty-four, which is a surprise. She certainly doesn't act five years older than Ruby.

"You'll be fine," Wendy assures her. "Just flirt with the door guy."

They wait outside of Club XS—not "Excess," just the letters—behind two fair-haired girls in bikini tops and cut-offs, who are sent away by a bouncer with a ZZ Top beard because they don't have ID. The bouncer frowns when he sees what Ruby has presented him. He stares her up and down. It's probably in her favor that she's wearing Dorian's clean, preppie clothes—she doesn't look like someone who'll cause trouble—and that she's with an older girl like Joanne, though what seems to tip the balance is Ruby saying, in her sultriest voice, "I had so much fun here last time, I totally had to come back."

"You better behave yourself," he says, and lets her past.

She's only been in one nightclub in Manhattan—the Palladium, a huge place so saturated with attitude and high fashion that she was reduced to slinking around like a child at a grown-ups' party. Walking into XS isn't like that at all. The entry, where she pays the price of admission, is dark, and she has to push aside a black curtain, beyond which a big room opens up: two floors, one with a balcony looking down on the other. A DJ hovers over the dance floor from the upper level. She follows Joanne and Wendy into the crowded room thick with cigarette smoke and the smell of spilled beer. The bar is a kind of horseshoe off to one side, surrounded by a field of impatient faces. It's a mostly new-wave crowd, though she sees plenty of the same people she saw on the boardwalk: the guys with the thick necks, the girls with their boobs pushed up and out. If Chris is here, it won't take long to find him.

The dance floor is already full. A lighting board on the ceiling spits colored beams across gyrating bodies. The density of the crowd is overwhelming, the vibe not very friendly, but the music is good, and she feels some sense of relief to be with these two girls, who are treating her like someone they've known for more than just the last hour.

Joanne buys her a drink called Sex on the Beach, sweet and strong. They clink glasses. "Here's to Ladies' Night," Joanne says, lifting her arms in the air with a whoop. The liquid slips down Ruby's throat way too fast.

Wendy yanks her by the elbow, nodding toward the bathroom, where she reapplies her makeup and warns her about Joanne. "We can't let her drink too much. She has to drive me home, and she can't handle her liquor. You don't have a car, do you?"

Ruby shakes her head. "Even if I did, I'm not sure I can handle my liquor, either."

"Great." Wendy's face elongates once again, her lips puckered, her chin poking upward. "Won't be the first time I had to sleep on the beach."

"You can probably stay with me at Alice's."

"Really?" Wendy's face brightens. "Good, because I hate getting sand in my panties."

Ruby realizes she has no idea how the sleeping arrangements at Alice's are supposed to work. Calvin had promised her a room to sleep in—a promise he can't possibly keep. She'd only noticed a couple of bedrooms in the house, and by now there are probably people *doing it* in each of them, or passed out from drinking. There may not even be a clean stretch of carpeting to claim, with all the beer spills and crushed potato chips and sand dragged in from outside.

Wendy asks her where she is from and seems stunned by the news that Ruby lives on the Upper West Side of Manhattan, that she goes to Barnard. "I could tell you went to college," Wendy says, in a tone that seems to indicate some regret.

"I haven't decided on a major. I'm taking a lot of women's studies classes."

"I'm getting my cosmetology license," Wendy says.

"Really? That's so great."

Wendy frowns. "Actually, it is."

"No, I mean it," Ruby says, wanting to close whatever gap this conversation has opened. "What am I going to do with a liberal arts degree?"

"I have a cousin who works on commercials in Hollywood. She can get me a job doing makeup for TV stars." Wendy pulls a tube of lipstick from her purse and stands in front of the mirror. She expertly swipes a bloodred streak once, twice, three times. Then she sticks her index finger in her mouth and pulls it out through closed lips, explaining, "Keeps it off my teeth."

"Can I?" Ruby asks.

Wendy hands her the tube. "Vampire's Kiss."

Back in the bar, Joanne squeals, "Where have you been?" and drags them onto the dance floor. Ruby sucks down her fruity cocktail and drops the glass on a table, where it falls on its side and sends ice across the tabletop. "Sorry," she yells at the girls who are sitting there. I'm a little drunk, she thinks. I'm not myself.

Under the shifting lighting, among the bodies, Ruby forgets she's a sometimes-awkward dancer and lets herself sway, her fists out in front as if gripping a grocery cart. It doesn't take long for her arms to limber up, for her feet to come unglued and find the beat. She used to dance with Robin at home, in the kitchen, listening to his favorite pop radio station, teasing him that his taste was corny but having fun anyway. She pirouettes, and her purse, weighed down by the thermos, bangs her hipbone. She drops the purse on the dance floor, as Joanne has done with her own bag.

"You're so cute!" Joanne shouts to her between pulls on her cocktail straw. Wendy leans toward Joanne's ear, no doubt warning her about her drinking, but Joanne waves her off. "We just got here! Cut loose, baby!" The message isn't much different from Alice's "Loosen up," but the intent is a world apart.

Ruby loses herself in the music, singing along when she knows the words, rolling her head with her eyes closed when she doesn't. The last blast of liquor has ignited a kind of aura around her, a warm force field of light and sound. One song shifts into another—this is one she adores, A Flock of Seagulls' "Space Age Love Song." It progresses at the same dreamy, yearning pace as the alcohol in her blood. It's exactly the right rhythm, exactly the right song, she can forget everything and simply ride a wave of sonic longing. *I saw your eyes, and it made me smile, and in a little while, I was falling in love.* The long unlikely day compresses itself into a contained, knowable moment, outside time—gone are the hostilities at Alice's house and the anxiety of being alone on the boardwalk amid thousands of strange faces. Here now is something private and nearly abstract, outside of logic but complete, whole. Like a dream. She forgets about her search, forgets her driving need for meaning. Maybe all that this weekend is "meant to be" is an escapade, a chance to meet new friends, to *cut loose.* Maybe the only reason she's been brought here is to wind up on this dance floor, in this little square all of her own.

She opens her eyes. Looks around. And then she sees them, and the trance is shattered.

Alice. Dorian. Cicely. Benjamin, with that fucking necktie wrapped around his head again! That other guy, Fuckin'-Nick-and-Shit. They are several yards away, elbowing a path to the floor. Their antics are too big, every gesture demanding extra space from the strangers in their way. They don't know this is a sanctuary you have to give yourself over to slowly. They are behaving like this is just one more place to claim for their own.

She almost stops dancing. Thinks of fleeing. Then Benjamin notices her. His eyes move from recognition to excitement and then narrow into a particular expression, a *gotcha.* In his gaze she feels accused—for ditching Calvin (who must be with them, maybe up at the bar, ordering drinks), and also for something greater. For being here without them. Replacing them with other people. She was supposed to belong to them, to be their toy. But, see, she has discarded them.

Benjamin continues to appraise her as he shuffles closer. He looks down at her *fantastic* legs and leers.

When their eyes meet, she mouths, "What?" with just enough challenge to let him know this is not *his* moment.

He slithers over, arms in front, crotch thrusting, enveloping her like a crab, snapping her up in his pincers.

The benefit of having consumed so much alcohol is that she can let this happen without losing her nerve. Without letting him win, either. She can swivel around and shake her ass and act like she doesn't owe him any explanation at all. He can move in too close and she can handle it.

She sees Wendy and Joanne looking her way, gossiping behind their drinks.

Now Alice is near, pointing at Ruby and shouting—"I am so totally sure!"—so tall and so pale she's like a translucent apparition. Dorian is right behind her, wide-eyed and slack-jawed. Ruby cocks her head away from them, lifts her eyebrows. A challenge. She has decided to enjoy this. She is going to astonish them all.

Hands in the air, she backs up into Benjamin, who's got her by the hips, his own hips gyrating across her ass, thrusting like she saw him do on the bed with Dorian. Humping like a puppy—it makes her laugh, him thinking he's got something on her when in fact she's *letting him* do this, she's the one in charge, and in a minute she's going to walk away and not look back.

She's never had a moment like this before in her life.

The music switches: *Would I lie to you, would I lie to you, honey?*

Dorian pushes past Alice and plants herself directly in front of Ruby. Dorian is standing in place, but having trouble staying upright, her face is a drunken smear around a furious set of eyes. Ruby sees indignation inside that fury, directed at her. Because she's dancing with Benjamin?

Dorian points a finger at her. She shouts, "That's my—" and Ruby expects "boyfriend," but Dorian screeches, "clothes!" And then she lunges.

Ruby's sensation of control shatters like window glass, shards raining down. Time roars back, asserting its power—igniting a sequence of rapid, raging action that she can barely keep up with. Dorian is clawing Ruby's shirt and shorts—her own clothes—as though she'd rather tear them to shreds than see Ruby in them one more minute. Ruby tumbles backward into Benjamin and then the three of them are going down, Benjamin collapsing from unsteady feet, Ruby bracing herself as

Dorian swipes blindly and tumbles onto her. Ruby feels a fingernail score her neck. She swats blindly, defending against Dorian, who unleashes a spray of invective, "Fucking virgin in my clothes, fucking bitch," dousing Ruby in spittle. Ruby grunts as she hits the floor. Her hip slams down on the metal thermos. She remembers that nail file in her purse and wishes she could stick it through Dorian's skin.

Benjamin is yelling from beneath them; it just sounds like noise. And then there's someone else descending into the huddle, trying to pull Dorian off Ruby but losing her footing and falling into the mess as well. It's Joanne.

The fierceness on Joanne's face is a revelation. She's a lioness, Ruby her cub. Joanne's fingers snatch at Dorian's hair. Dorian's scream is like an arrow piercing Ruby's ear.

Then someone is yanking Ruby from the dog pile—ungentle hands taking her up and away. A force so sudden she's not even sure what's happening, who's behind it.

"You're outta here," shouts a man she's never seen before. She blinks to clear her vision, steadies herself on her feet, but he's got her by the arm and is pulling. He's got Dorian in his grasp, too. Dorian is wiping her face with such a frenzy she looks like she might erase her own features. A moan escapes from her.

The bouncer shoves Dorian in front of him and pulls Ruby behind, and like this he wrangles them through the crowd. Faces painted black-and-white gawk at her. There among them is Calvin—he registers Ruby's presence, and she has to look away. She wants to tell him, this isn't my fault. But she's pulled quickly past him and out the front door.

The air is cold against her clammy skin. She touches a finger to her neck, there's a spot of blood there from Dorian's assault. She waves her hand at Dorian. "You did this!"

The bouncer slaps her arm down roughly.

The sidewalk in front of the club fills with raised voices and accusations, as a second bouncer, the one with the enormous beard, emerges with Joanne in his grasp—she looks absolutely intent on doing damage to anything in her path. She spots Dorian and yells, "Come on, bitch, finish what you started."

"I don't even know you," Dorian slurs. With an arm flapping at Ruby, she says, "It's *this* one."

"What did I ever do to you?" Ruby shouts.

"You don't fool me," Dorian hisses.

She said something like this earlier, too, Ruby realizes. If she wasn't so furious, if she wasn't the center of all this unwelcome attention, she would ask Dorian what the hell she means.

The rest of them are there—Alice and her gang circling around, Benjamin looking completely entertained, Wendy getting as close to Joanne as the bouncer will allow and urging, "Take a pill, Joanne, take a big fat chill pill."

And Calvin is there. He's trying to get the bouncers' attention, as if he alone can negotiate this mess. "Step back, kid," the bearded one commands.

Calvin points to Ruby. "That's my girlfriend." She looks away from him as if from an accusation.

It won't be hard to break up with him now, she thinks. He'll welcome it. I've shamed him.

She's not going to let herself cry, though she feels tears forming, intent on release. A wall of swelling, swirling pressure behind her eyes, in her nose, her throat. Her skin throbs in half a dozen spots. She again touches the scratch on her neck. She looks to her purse for a tissue—but she doesn't have her purse.

The big bouncer who pulled Ruby off the dance floor is shouting, "I will call the cops, unless all-a yous calm the fuck down!"

"Call the cops on this one," Joanne shouts, pointing at Dorian.

Ruby thinks it must be clear to everyone that Dorian is to blame for the melee—she's the drunkest, looks the craziest—but Joanne's roaring cat-face has ignited a rally behind Dorian.

"You're making it worse," Alice snaps at Joanne.

"Now *you* wanna start with me?"

"Does anyone even *know* her?" Alice asks.

"I know her," Ruby says.

"You do?"

"Dorian was scratching my eyes out," Ruby says, "and none of you did anything about it!" From somewhere she's found this rage. Alice must sense it, too—she turns away without another word—and Ruby realizes she's disappointed her, that Alice will never really accept her as Calvin's girlfriend after this.

"I want my clothes back!" Dorian shrieks.

"What am I supposed to do?" Ruby yells. "Take them off? Right here?"

Ruby sees Calvin stand taller, wanting to be taken seriously. He calls out to the bouncers again. "Excuse me, guys? Mister? I think we can handle it ourselves from here."

"Here's how it's gonna work, kid," the bouncer says. "I want to see these girls leave separately. I want one to leave, then the other, and I don't want them within ten feet of each other until all-a yous are far away from this establishment. Because I *will* call the cops, and trust me, they ain't happy about drunk chicks disturbing the peace."

"I understand," Calvin says. "Alice, take Dorian."

"I don't want *that virgin* in my house," Dorian says.

"She's coming with us," Wendy calls out.

"I don't have my bag," Ruby says.

"It's in my car, over there," Calvin says. He steps closer to Ruby and lowers his voice. "Do you really know these two?"

She nods, sucks wetness up her runny nose. Her tears have retreated back to their source. She tells him, "I'm not going back to Alice's."

"Sure. We can drive home tonight. Or get a room somewhere."

"I'm not going with you."

Calvin stares at her, confusion on his face. She wants simply to tell him, it's over. It was over before this weekend and it's definitely over now. Say it kindly, and firmly. But it's the wrong place, the wrong time, everyone is here, the bouncer is repeating his orders. Alice calls her brother's name, waiting for instruction. He waves Alice away, and she files out with her entourage: a deflated Dorian, leaning on Cicely for balance, Benjamin fake-puffing on a cigarette, Nick and some other guys and girls from the party who have been audience to the entire spectacle. The last thing Ruby hears is Dorian telling Benjamin, "You're a shit-stirrer. That's what you are." Benjamin just laughs.

Then they're gone. All but Calvin. "I'm waiting here with you."

"My purse is in the club."

Calvin looks at the bouncer, who says, "You can send one person back in. Not her—" pointing to Ruby, "or her—" Joanne.

Wendy says, "*I'll* go," and scurries away, flashing a hand-stamp to the guy at the door, a new guy who must have taken over during the chaos. Ruby wonders if she can trust Wendy to come right back, to not get distracted. She realizes she has no choice.

Everyone waiting in line has been watching. Between the streetlights and the full moon, the whole scene could be taking place in the bright middle of the day. She's given them quite a show. She scans the gawking faces of strangers greedily lapping this up.

And then she sees Chris.

Chris Cleary, sitting on the hood of a parked car, not even half a block away, arms at his side, legs dangling. His eyes are on her.

She has to look twice, because she might be mistaken. This might be some other boy in pegged black pants, an old pinstripe blazer, a red T-shirt, some other new-wave clubgoer. How long has he been there, watching?

He lifts a finger to his lips. *Shhh*, he's telling her.

Calvin hasn't seen him. He's in the midst of a transaction with the bearded bouncer. Slipping him money. Sealing his man-of-the-moment status.

Joanne—finally set free from the bouncer's grip—shakes her hair, smoothes out her clothes, makes her way to Ruby. "Was that him?" she asks.

"Who?"

"The one you were dancing with. With the tie? Was that *him*?"

"No." Ruby has to smile, it's so absurd. "That was so not him."

"Look, you can totally stay with us tonight." Joanne's voice, post-uproar, is startlingly composed.

Calvin steps between them. "Rubes, you're not thinking straight. You're drunk, right? Where have you been?"

"I'm not going anywhere near Dorian or your sister or any of those people."

"Okay, sure, I get it. But come on," he pleads. "I can't let you go with these girls. I'm responsible for you. Your overnight bag is in my car." He touches her arm, pulls her toward him. He seems to want to hug her. She won't, she can't. It feels cruel to withhold this affection. He helped her out, he's still her boyfriend. But he's guilty by association: his manipulative sister, evil Dorian, Benjamin the *shit-stirrer*.

And Chris is here. Hiding in plain sight.

"I'll get my bag from you tomorrow," she says. "I need some personal space."

Calvin swears, slams one fist into the other palm and spins around—he nearly bumps into Wendy, who has reappeared with Ruby's purse—and then he starts to walk away, down the street. He takes no notice of Chris, still on the hood of that other car, observing Calvin with a serene detachment that she finds breathtaking.

That's when she knows without a doubt that he's waiting for her. For the right moment. This thing she's been looking for all night—it's close at hand.

Calvin turns suddenly and strides back toward her. He's seething.

"I said I'll call you *tomorrow*," she tells him.

"I don't get it, Rubes. I don't fucking get it."

Joanne jockeys back into position. "Um, Alvin? Do you speak English? Because I think Ruby's being pretty clear? She needs some *space*."

"Jesus Christ! Who is this tramp?"

"Who the fuck are *you*?"

Their raised voices have alerted the bouncers, who begin a new, snarling approach. "Just go, Calvin," Ruby says.

He turns and continues down the block, and this time he doesn't turn back.

She's free now.

She looks over at Chris, also watching Calvin disappear. After a moment, Chris hops off the hood, which is when she begins to make her way over to him.

Joanne and Wendy call her name, their voices overlapping. Ruby gestures over her shoulder—*Wait*—and takes another step toward Chris. Then another.

She can't take her eyes off him. What she sees is the young man he is now—a wiry frame draped in outsider's black, his hair jagged and mussed, his face worldly and strained—layered on top of the boy he was back then, the tender stranger who clasped her hand while they prayed aloud amid incense and votive light, who whispered to her over the phone from his bedroom beneath his model airplanes. Layered like transparencies are all the pictures she created from the stories he told her about his life: The time he wore a four-inch silver cross around his neck and endured the taunts of kids at the mall who called him Jesus Freak. The time he painted his nails in the bathroom, gulping up the fumes—as close as he let himself get to the stimulants that had been forbidden to him. The time he put his hand down his pants and rubbed until he had an orgasm, while she, on the other end of their phone call, pressed down on her *clint* and let him hear her earliest attempts at pleasure.

Their conversations had grappled with the question of sex. They talked about being each other's first, and only. Would God forgive them if they did it? The real sin was in sleeping around, wasn't it? Treating your God-given body like something dispensable? (Though Jesus loved even the prostitutes seeking forgiveness.) Wouldn't God understand sex done in the name of love?

They made plans.

But everything ended without warning, his phone disconnected.

There were no more conversations. She'd been abandoned—the displacement that follows a catastrophe.

She had always blamed him. He could have found her, if he'd tried.

She had dammed up the memories. Maybe that's why she didn't recognize him at first. He'd been banished to some unreachable part of her mind. Until this deluge, tonight.

He meets her with arms outstretched. Their hands touch. Cold fingers braid together.

"You figured it out," he says.

"I didn't recognize you at first."

"It's unbelievable. On this weekend of all weekends."

"I've been walking around looking for you."

He shakes his head. "You can't imagine—"

"What?"

"I'd done all this blow. I needed to come down before I saw you."

"Meanwhile, I drank too much, and got into a bar fight. Did you see that?" She lets herself smile, now that this tumult is behind her. She wonders how it is that she no longer feels drunk. Adrenaline maybe. Her body seems to throb all over.

He traces a finger along the scratch on her neck. "You should clean this. Come with me?"

"You have a car? You're all right to drive?" He nods. She says, "Okay."

She thinks, *This is the bravest moment of my life*.

He holds her hand as he walks her back to Wendy and Joanne. She takes their phone numbers and gives them her mother's in Manhattan. Walking away with Chris, she shivers again, this time not from the cold but from the prospect of all this unmarked space ahead of her, the emptiness she's thrusting herself into. She might be anywhere in a few hours. She might be anyone.

His car is parked in a lot down the street, another lot overseen by an old man in a lawn chair. They stop first at a 7-Eleven and buy bottles of water and potato chips—she wants to tame the effects of all that alcohol. What was she thinking, guzzling so much? He offers her aspirin from a huge bottle in the glove box, and then he stands outside his car—a vintage BMW—while she changes in the backseat. He gives her a T-shirt and she removes the yellow top, now soiled and clammy. She shimmies out of the madras shorts and into Chris's extra pair of black jeans, her underwear sliding on the leather upholstery. The night is cooler than expected, and her legs have goose bumps. Wearing Chris's jeans was his idea. As she slips from the back seat, she notices a Bible on the floor of the car. The paperback cover reads *Good News for Modern Man*.

Chris is bent over the trunk. She sees him stash a notebook, the spiral-bound type she uses for school, covered in cartoonish doodles.

They marvel at the fact that they have almost the same size waist. She cuffs the legs to keep from tripping. He offers to slice off the extra material—he has a Swiss Army knife in the car—but she says no, don't ruin them on my account. "They're just clothes," he says, which makes her laugh, because there's been so much fuss about clothes that taking off Dorian's is like shedding a layer of skin. She considers for a moment how she'll return them, and then, with a small, victorious smile, she drops the shorts and shirt onto the ground and leaves them there.

"All done," she says.

They drive through the grid of streets, down the main boulevard where the clubs are, past the big waterslide, past motels and rental houses. Outside the window the glimmering town goes about its business. This place she's been rescued from. Music plays from the tape deck, Depeche Mode, which is absolutely perfect, because she recently bought this album herself and has been listening to it over and over. She sings along to "Blasphemous Rumours," with those twisted lyrics about God's sick sense of humor. She asks Chris how this song squares with the *Good News* in the back seat, and he says that the way he sees it, Jesus was a healer and holy man, and that's all that matters. God in the Bible is angry and vengeful, is too much of a mystery to make sense of. She tells him about the paper she wrote for her religion seminar where she posed the theory that Mary was a teenage girl who had been raped and who made up the story of virgin birth to save herself from being cast out, or worse. Her professor said that it was too speculative, not well-researched. Chris says people in authority are afraid of the truth. He says, "I'd like to read that paper."

Of every enthralling aspect of this reunion, none is better than the revelation that in the intervening years they've become the same type of nineteen-year-old. They've slid into the same pocket of style and taste. They've come to question the religion that once drew them together.

"I can't believe this," she says.

He lets go of the stick shift and takes her hand, his fingers warm now. As he maneuvers through traffic, he has to release his hold on her in order to shift gears, but each time he returns. The car fills with calmness. This is what happiness is, right? Not the intrusion of some wonderful new thing, but a confirmation of what was already there, lying in wait for recognition.

They've passed through the touristy hubbub, the busy downtown, the streams of people moving from the boardwalk, now shutting down. They pass into a neighborhood that is a cleaner, quieter version of the one they've left. The rental properties here are larger and better taken care of. Lights are on in windows, but no parties are illuminated inside. A short while later the residential area thins out. A sign at the end of the road reads ISLAND BEACH STATE PARK. She sees a ranger's booth guarding a long stretch of undeveloped shoreline—dunes, scrub grass, pale sand drifting out from the shoulder onto the paved road. A chain pulled across the entry gleams in the moonlight. A sign reads NO TRESPASSING.

"You're not worried," he says.

"Should I be?" She smiles as if he's made a joke, but she sees that his face is serious.

"You don't know me," he says. "I mean, in years."

A stab of panic: Maybe I'm a fool. This isn't like me. Unless, of course, it *is* me, and everything else in my life has been false. She says, almost shyly, "You're probably the only person I was ever really honest with."

"But why trust me *now*?"

"Are you trying to spook me?"

He shakes his head, clasps her hand tighter. "I just want you to be sure. I don't have a plan, okay? Not anymore. I don't have a plan for tonight, or tomorrow, or two days from now. We're just making this up as we go. OK?"

She nods. She's never felt so awed by her own life.

He parks on a side street. They get out and step over the chain, past the sign. It's a long walk down the paved road before they find a passage through the dune scrub and onto the beach. She holds on to him, feeling the lingering unsteadiness of the booze. She doesn't feel drunk at all, just worn down. Needing to rest. On the sand, they take off their boots and sit on a blanket that Chris has carried from his car. She asks him why he stopped calling, all those years ago. He tells her that his parents divorced, he moved to San Diego for a while with his mother when she took a different teaching position. He got into trouble with drugs again, almost dropped out of high school, but pulled himself back together. His mother is teaching now at Princeton, that's how he managed to get in. If he wasn't trying to please her he wouldn't stay, because it's a place full of conformists and snobs.

She shivers, and he looks at her with alarm. "Am I saying too much?" he asks. "Am I freaking you out?"

"No, I'm just cold." She curls into him and closes her eyes.

She opens them with a start. "Was I asleep?"

"A few minutes. I kept my eyes on you."

The ocean roars. Waves crash in a mighty whoosh, then sizzle as the current pulls back to the depths.

The moon has shifted from its earlier zenith and has begun its descent over their shoulders, behind them.

"Did you see it rise?" she asks. "It was so big it looked fake."

He breaks into a big smile. "You saw it, too?"

She nods.

"Yes!" he exclaims, like a game show contestant who's guessed the correct answer. "I watched it rise, thinking of you, hoping you were watching, too."

"You're so corny."

"Don't say that." He shakes his head adamantly, speaks quickly. "Don't be cynical. You have no idea. Really."

"I didn't mean to—"

They fall silent. She feels the altered mood, feels it in her chest, heartbeat increasing. She's done something wrong, she's spoiled the perfect moment, she's going to ruin everything.

On the towel, he shifts his weight away from her. It scares her to think she's offended him so easily. She lifts her leg and drops it over his. The brush of denim on denim is like a compressed echo of the crashing surf. She rests there until she hears him exhale, until she's sure he hasn't totally closed up.

"Say something," she tells him.

"Like what?" There's a sulkiness in his voice.

"I want to get to know you," she says.

He clears his throat. "You can ask me whatever you want."

She hears this as an offering, a willingness to bare himself to her. Calvin has never said anything remotely like this. The sum of Calvin's entire bearing seems to be, *don't ask. If I don't offer, I don't want to talk about it.*

"How well do you know Calvin?" she asks him.

He snickers, a bitter little sound. "That's what you want to ask me about? Calvin?"

"I'm trying to put all these pieces together."

"Yeah, it's strange." He grabs a fistful of sand and sprinkles it across their feet. "I dated Alice for a little while. And then she tried to pass me off on her friends. They do that, work their way through guys."

Ruby steadies her breath, working to banish the image of Chris with these girls. She doesn't want to think of him entangled in their awful world.

He says, "I think I was supposed to be on Dorian's menu this weekend."

"She's a nightmare."

"Everyone knows she's a fucking alkie. Who knows what she'd be like if she stopped?"

"I thought she was with Benjamin."

He snorts. "Trisexual Benjamin. Give him enough coke, he'll try to fuck anything."

"Really? He said the most evil things to me about gay people."

"You have to be a code-breaker with that one. We were roommates last semester. I've heard his farts, I've heard him jerk off at night." He glances at her. "Sorry. That's gross. I just—like, I've seen him crying on the phone to his father, you know?"

She pictures Benjamin crying—it isn't actually hard to imagine. All that bluster covers a core of softness. Weakness, even.

Chris speaks about Benjamin and Dorian, the drugs and drinking, their moods that swing depending on what they've imbibed. As he talks, Ruby can't help but think about Calvin. Where is he? He must be worried about her. She knows that he does care about her, even if he's rarely careful with her. It was wrong to walk away from him, but how could she go back to that party? How could she not follow Chris?

She waits for a break in his story. Then she asks, "Why was it so important that we were both looking at the moon?"

"Um, OK. Let me try to explain." She doesn't attempt to fill the silence. Lulls in conversation with Calvin seem like punishment: her failure to keep him interested. But with Chris it's OK. With Chris everything is different.

He says, "Here's how it went. After I saw you at the house, I was pretty freaked out. So I left, just started walking, not sure where, just needed to get away from all of them, needed to walk off the coke. I already said that. OK. So . . . I found a diner, drank a bunch of milk and ate pancakes with butter even though the cocaine had kind of taken away my appetite. I wanted to get it out of my system. Then it was dark and I went to the beach. I was under the pier, all by myself, my feet were wet, and I was getting cold, and I was feeling terrible."

"Why didn't you come back to the house?"

He takes in a long gulp of air, releases it. "I'm not sure you can handle this."

"Of course I can."

"I came down here this weekend—" his voice is pitching higher, there's a warble in his throat "—thinking I was going to kill myself."

The night drops into silence.

She can't find words.

He spins to face her. "I've been feeling like shit for a long time, Ruby. Really unhappy, that's the only way I can explain it. Partying way too much. Being a fuck-up. I've been making my mom miserable. I decided to get away from home. I didn't want to make a mess, you know, cut my wrists in my mother's bathroom or whatever, bleed all over the place."

She thinks of the Swiss Army knife in his car, the New Testament in the back seat, enough aspirin to choke a horse. The notebook he shoved into the trunk before she could see it. Is that where he wrote his suicide note?

"I thought I could put rocks in my pockets and walk out into the ocean."

"Like Virginia Woolf."

"Yeah! Have you read Virginia Woolf?" His eyes light up for a moment.

"Yes. I wrote a paper about her, too. *The Waves.*"

"I thought, I could have one painful flood of water in my lungs and then I'd be shark food. Over and done, no mess. I'd leave a note and everyone would know what happened. That's why I did so much coke. For courage."

"Chris," she says. She holds his hand between both of hers. Can think of nothing else to say.

He says, "I stopped believing that God could save me a long time ago. In San Diego, I had a bad car accident."

The scar on his lip—a little shadow in the moonlight.

"A lot of shit happened to me, and I thought, fuck this God stuff. But truthfully, I never stopped praying. And as I was driving down here, I said a prayer over and over. I said, *God, give me one sign.* It's the most selfish way to pray. Expecting that the Supreme Being will swoop in and take care of my life. If you read the Old Testament, you realize God has other things on his mind. Like, the whole human race, and the fate of nations. But I thought, fuck it—I don't want to live if there's no reason. I mean, I don't know where you're at with your faith, but . . ."

"Sort of like what you're talking about. Prayers just pop into my head." One pops in now—*God, don't take him away from me.*

"So, like, that was when *you* walked into that room," he says. "I thought my mind was playing tricks on me. I thought it was the drugs. I went into the bathroom and splashed all this water on my face. I even brushed my teeth. Then it dawned on me: *You* were the sign, the sign I asked for."

"Chris—"

He cuts her off. "But maybe you were a sign that I should go ahead with it."

"Chris—" Now it seems that she *must* speak, must slow him down.

"No, listen. You were there, like some kind of reminder to me of a time when I was more hopeful. But you were changed, too. You were being turned into another girl like Alice or Cicely, just another soulless person."

"No, I wasn't—" Why won't he let her say something?

"I know that now. But I couldn't tell. And then someone made that comment, that you were a virgin. And I thought, wow. Ruby MacKenzie stayed true. She kept to her word all these years. Like you were still waiting for me to be the one. Remember how we talked about that? That's why I kissed you."

She jumps to her feet and wraps her arms around herself, feeling how cool the night is, how the ocean carries a chill from some faraway place. She wonders if it's an indication of a storm. "Is it supposed to rain?" she calls over her shoulder to him.

"I didn't check the weather report. I wasn't really thinking past this weekend."

The bright stripe of moonlight on the water's dark surface breaks apart and comes together, breaks and rejoins.

Should she tell him? Tell him the truth? The dilemma churns away inside her, sets her teeth chattering. She senses that behind her, Chris has risen to his feet, is closing the gap between them. She commands herself: Don't walk away. He's being honest. Be honest with him. She turns around, he's right there.

He pries her arms loose, takes her hands. He steadies her as he speaks. "When I came out from under the pier, I saw the moon. I had this feeling that you were looking at it, too. That's why I didn't go through with it. I went back to the house instead." He explains how he returned to the party, where Benjamin told him that she went for a walk. He knew then that what he'd sensed was right, that there was this connection between them still. He drove around for a while, hoping to find her, refusing to let go of this vision. He was working up the nerve to go into the club, and then there she was, getting dragged out by the bouncers.

The moon floats over his shoulder, descending. Half his face is pale with reflected light, the other a gray shadow.

He is quiet again, and she thinks, this is the story he had to tell me, he's gotten through it. Now it's my turn.

I'll say it fast. Tell him it was just once, it went by in a blur, it only lasted long enough for the pain to shoot through me, up from between my legs into the rest of my body, only until I found my voice and could tell Brandon to stop. It hardly even happened. It's never *counted.*

He touches her face, runs a thumb beneath her eye. Is she crying? She blinks. Her eyes are wet.

"Chris, I'm not a sign. I'm not even—"

"What?"

A virgin. The words don't come out. She's never said them to anyone, not since she told her mother about that quick in-and-out from Brandon Richards, those minutes of discomfort and the blood that followed. Her mother hugged her tightly, insisting, "If you don't want it to count, just forget it. It has to *matter* to you. You haven't lost anything."

She can see Dorothy's face, meant to reassure her, though now, years later, it reveals itself as a mask of falsehood, the imposition of wishful thinking. It was bad advice, to establish this lie of virginity. It's been a bad idea to keep it going.

"I'm not—" she repeats.

Chris is waiting.

She can't say it. He needs it to be true.

"I'm not a believer," she finishes. "I stopped believing in God a long time ago. How can *I* be a sign?"

He stares into her eyes and again she's afraid, afraid of what will happen if this elaborate image of her he's constructed now crumbles.

But he smiles. "Oh, I forgot! I won you something. When I was looking for you on the boardwalk, I played one game, Whack-A-Mole, and I won." He squeezes a hand into his pocket and pulls out a toy ring with a big fake red stone on it. "It's a ruby."

She shakes her head as he takes her hand. "Don't make me a hero, Chris."

"You don't have to be perfect. That's not what I meant. You just have to be you." He slides it onto her ring finger, and she lets him.

It fits. It won't fall off. Now she is crying. His skinny arms are cradling her. He's kissing the top of her head, lifting her face to him. She looks up into his eyes and there's this click, this moment of broken pieces being snapped back together. She knows that this is the beginning of a night of kisses, and more. He isn't pushing for it, but she's ready, she knows where it will go, she's ready. But there's still this reserve, this pressure, behind her tears, behind the kisses. She pulls away from him.

"What?" he asks her.

"Are you still thinking about doing it?"

His eyes flutter. He shakes his head. At last, he speaks. "I'm thinking I'm going to fall in love with you."

As she moves in to kiss him once again, she hears her own mind working. She hears the thought take form, *God, stay with me.* It is not belief, but the memory of that time when she did believe, which is, she understands, the hope for belief's return.

Part Three

The Garden State

Feet pressed against the dashboard, gaze fixed on the landscape through the windshield, Robin feels the heightened awareness that comes from making your way *toward* something: toward his sister, yes, he hopes, but also toward some larger thing that he can't quite define or see. It's as if he and George, moving along a rural New Jersey highway in George's battered Cadillac, are filaments being pulled magnetically toward some stronger, steely force, some complex machine, the great and powerful Oz.

But of course Seaside Heights will not greet them like the Emerald City. It will be like high school, minus teachers and rules, plus alcohol, plus the anything-goes attitude of summer. He thinks of the time he and Ruby went to Coney Island and squealed through the ups and downs of a roller coaster, and afterward the guy from the car behind them made some comment about "the two girls who wouldn't shut up" while the guy's friend lisped out "that wuth thsssoooo thhsscary." What can you do? If you say, "Fuck off," they say, "Wanna make something of it?" You think you're on vacation, but some things follow wherever you go.

It's not that he expects intimidation when they get there. This anticipation feels bigger: more like confronting a monster than dealing with a bully. It has something to do with Jackson's birthday; if today was any other day, he might have waited longer before getting on the road. Whatever trouble Ruby has stirred up has the power to set ghosts into motion.

George hasn't said much. As he steers them along Route 70, a winding road cutting through a lush South Jersey landscape, his face is unreadable, his eyeglasses reflecting the bluish white hue of the late-day sky. The car's air conditioning is unpredictable, so the windows are down, those that work, anyway, and hot blasts of wind carry in the smells of Robin's childhood: cut grass, car exhaust, tar released from softened asphalt. All the foliage is familiar, too: elm trees with patchy green bark like Army-issue camouflage; round azalea bushes, their red and purple blossoms now browned and littering the ground; spindly dogwoods, refusing to let go of wilting pink flowers. This part of the state is another world from the congested suburbia where they grew up. It's rural, quaint, stopped in time. They pass the Evergreen Dairy Barn, with its sign for "soft serve custard," looking as if the same coat of paint has been peeling from its walls since the 1950s. Farther along is The Hub Cap Place, a nearly dilapidated shack announced by a hand-lettered sign and a fence covered with cast-off car parts. The occasional road marker points the way to towns called Chairville, Leisuretown, and Mount Misery, names that suggest histories Robin can't quite put together.

"Look at that one," George says, pointing to a sign marked with only an arrow and the word RETREAT.

"We've been warned," Robin says, and then adds, with heroic emphasis, "Onward!"

"What are we going to do when we find her?" George asks.

"I guess that depends what condition we find her in."

They are both quiet for a while after that.

He isn't sure what George is thinking. But his own mind is full of grim scenarios stronger than any attempt he makes to push them away: rape, kidnapping, his sister drugged and abused, gone for good. He doesn't even have images to go with these fears, just the ugly words and the anxious intensity attached to them. He rubs his eyes. He feels a dull pounding behind them.

George turns on the radio and rolls up his windows so he can hear the music. He can still pick up the Philly R&B station he likes. An Aretha Franklin song is ending, and the smooth-voiced DJ comes on to introduce something by Nat King Cole. Rosellen plays this music at the restaurant, and to Robin it conjures up the sensation of being at mid-shift, sipping Diet Coke by the bar during a lull in the orders and becoming aware, in the momentary calm, of the soundtrack that's been playing all along. "I feel like I should be checking in with the kitchen right about now," he says. "Or visiting Table 3. *How's everyone doing here?*"

"Or not."

"What's that mean?"

"You check your tables too much. You hover over them."

"Seriously?" Robin pivots toward him, and George nods.

Instantly he revisits a string of recent customer interactions that all seem like evidence of hovering, of *too much.* "George, I can't pay *less* attention to them. I'm on probation."

"Probation is nothing, it's just an expression."

"Easy for you to say."

"Someone on probation just means they've been *caught.* Like you got caught with that wine bottle."

"You have to remind me?"

"Well, people are still talking about it." George relates a conversation he heard between Malik and the hostess.

"I don't really want to know," Robin says, feeling his mood turn sour.

But George keeps going. "I was thinking, it's kind of like when Cesar said you were uptight. People can read that on you, man. You gotta figure out how to get into Rosellen's vibe more. When folks come for Southern cooking, they want a laid-back experience. Why don't you do like I do?"

"You're not *Southern,* George. You're not even that black."

"I'm not *what*?"

"I mean, compared to everyone else who works there. You're from the suburbs. You've got a scholarship to Penn. You only sleep with white guys." The car seems to be slowing down, and for a moment Robin thinks George is going to pull off the road. He suspects he's gone too far, but he can't stop. It's one of those moments when you probably should just shut up and apologize, but you keep digging in. He says, "Come on, we grew up in the same town."

"Except I grew up in the black part of Greenlawn. In my black skin."

"Marble Road isn't West Philly."

A vein seems to pulse in George's neck. "How many black families lived on *your* block? How many black friends did your parents have?"

"My family isn't racist. They've practically adopted you."

"Like a stray from the Humane Society?"

"What are you talking about? You're my best friend."

"If I was your *boyfriend* we'd see how racist they really were."

Robin almost says, *But you're not,* which seems exactly the wrong thing, though he doesn't understand why. George turns up the music, too loud. He accelerates again, and Robin feels pushed back into his seat. The conversation is over, but the hostility buzzes in the air like a persistent mosquito. Melancholy settles around Robin like a net, barely keeping their harsh words at bay.

The radio shifts to James Brown panting to a crackling beat—the lyrics all sexual innuendo.

A half mile down the road, George swerves suddenly into a tiny gas station that looks like an abandoned farmhouse, except for the two pumps advertising a brand Robin's never heard of.

A stern, pale-faced woman in a kerchief takes her time moving across the gravel, scrutinizing the Cadillac as she approaches. She peers into the backseat, as if there's something half-hidden there. Over James Brown singing from the back of his throat, she asks, "What're you boys doing out this way?"

George just glares at her, so Robin leans across him and answers, "We're driving down the shore. From Philly."

George says, "Did you just call me *boy*?"

The woman emits a stunned little grunt.

"Because I don't have to buy my gas here."

She says, "Mm-hmm," as if confirming a suspicion, and then backs away, her lips tight.

George twists the key in the ignition and within moments is tearing back onto the road, tires shrieking a protest. Robin looks at him, astonished.

A couple minutes later, a police car appears behind them and stays there for a mile, a couple car-lengths back, like a hawk tailing its prey.

"Jesus Christ!" George exclaims. "Are we in South Jersey or South Carolina?"

"You think that lady called the cops?"

"Apparently I was black enough for *her*."

The squad car pulls alongside, the cop at the wheel peering at them, all scrutiny. Gradually he moves past before at last speeding away. Robin takes a deep breath, but George remains on alert, his fingers so tight on the steering wheel his knuckles blanch.

The miles roll by, marked by the whoosh of the road and the radio.

Robin rests his cheek against the window, wishing he could roll it down, wanting to smoke, mystified. It all happened so quickly.

A song comes on that he recognizes, "Let's Stay Together." It's not the version on the Tina Turner record that he bought last year but a man with a sort of high-pitched voice. Marvin Gaye? Teddy Pendergrass? There's a whole era of music, late sixties to early seventies, that he doesn't know much about. He hadn't actually known that Tina's version was a remake. It's a little deflating to find out that a song you're into, that has the crackle of something new, is a retread of something else; what felt like a discovery becomes tarnished. This is the kind of observation he would have made to Peter as they drove around Pittsburgh, popping tapes in the cassette player, sharing with each other their favorites, keeping a running commentary. At this very moment Peter is likely driving in the exact opposite direction, back toward Pittsburgh, and that kid Douglas might be with him, playing his own mix for Peter. Change is already in motion: Douglas will move on in, share Peter's bed, make breakfast for him before his first class of the day. He'll become for Peter a safe, young, trouble-free boyfriend. The anti-Robin. The remake.

The song gets taken over by static. They've fallen out of range. He decides he prefers the original version better, the way Al Green sounds both needy and absolutely sure of himself at the same time. *Al Green.* He's remembered! How does he even know that? Because it's something George taught him.

He looks to George, who stares straight ahead, unflinching. Robin says, "OK, not to make excuses, but I just got dumped by my boyfriend, and then my sister goes AWOL, and so to get criticized by you about my job, which was your idea to begin with . . . I'm a little touchy today."

"Don't take it out on me."

"Well, you're not exactly *relaxed,* either."

After what seems like five minutes, but is probably thirty seconds, George finally looks at him. "It's like this," he says, pushing his glasses up, a gesture Robin has seen him do a hundred times: logical George, ready to present his case. "If I was any blacker, that cop would have pulled us over. And if I was any less black I'd get my ass whooped in West Philly, living with a gay white boy like you."

"OK, I probably shouldn't have," Robin begins. "I'm not sure why I . . ." *Just apologize.* "I'm sorry I was talking shit back there."

"And if you're not into working at Rosellen's, you shouldn't stay. If you're not into living with me, ditto."

"Do you want me to move out?" Robin asks, alarmed.

"No."

"Because I like living with you, even if it sometimes sucks for me in that neighborhood. Maybe if I could get another job . . ."

"If you quit, you'd probably just go back to Pittsburgh and throw yourself at that hairy white boy. Which would be a mistake."

"You sound pretty sure about that."

"I have a prediction," George says.

"What?"

"I predict you're going to be over him really soon."

Robin smiles, against his will, really, and then, for whatever reason, neither of them says anything else, and the silence settles in, and it seems like the worst has passed. Robin keeps thinking he should say more, explain something, clarify, but letting George have the last word feels intuitively right.

On George's face, in the set of his mouth, perhaps, and in his eyes, shining behind glass, Robin sees the best friend he knows so well and, truly, loves so much. The rock-solid George of so many years, peeking out from the new George, who is someone changing and less predictable. This George is deciding who he wants to be and how he wants to see the world. It is this new George he was trying to wound with words, this new George who'd rightfully gotten angry in return.

Without warning Robin is overtaken by a fluttering of heat rising up through him. It opens like a tiny bud on a branch, in the air after a storm. There is pulsing energy inside this feeling, and he understands that it's this new George who makes him feel this way. The more confident one. The one who wanted to take control. The one he had really exciting sex with, who read the tea leaves this morning and saw more in their future. This morning, George called it a rebound fuck, but *rebound* doesn't cover it. This is something else. You can learn a lot from someone like this, someone who isn't afraid of who he is.

Unpopulated countryside gives way to the loose density of coastal towns, their names identified on water towers that loom above the landscape like giant eggs. On Route 37, in the town of Toms River ("Where's the apostrophe?" George wonders out loud), the traffic thickens. It's even heavier in the outbound direction, as a congested stream of weekenders heads back home. These are the folks who leave the shore at four o'clock to beat the evening rush and wind up creating an afternoon rush of their own.

The highway funnels eastward onto a drawbridge that arcs over the bay. Robin has a memory of stopping near the top of this bridge, as a kid, marveling as the road snapped up in front of them. He'd been in the backseat, licking at dripping ice cream, a braided swirl of vanilla and orange sherbet, while Jackson leaned across him to gawk at the boats cutting through the passage below and Ruby wanted to know if cars ever fell into the gap. It all comes back to him: the summer heat, the sweet melting cone, the road splitting open and stopping the world for a moment. From that long ago day to this one seems like a journey of loss: not just of his brother, of his family's cohesiveness, but of wonder, of awe. When was the last time he even enjoyed ice cream without guilt? (Probably before his fellow actors started bombarding him with cautionary edicts like, "If you want to do film roles, the camera adds ten pounds." And this was also when he started getting more self-conscious about being naked in front of other guys, worrying about his body, fretting over little folds of excess flesh pinched between his fingers.)

Today the bridge lies flat. Up and over they go, down the other side to the coastal island, into the town of Seaside Heights.

He guides George through the grid of streets, windows lowered, salt air on the breeze. It's a comforting smell, a childhood smell. For a moment, it blankets his apprehension about Ruby with something benign: this is where people have fun in the water and thrills on the boardwalk, where sexy strangers wear skimpy clothes. How can something go wrong here? They locate a parking spot in a lot at the end of the boardwalk. Robin steps from the car and stretches. A breeze rises over the sparsely grassed dunes. All around is a parade of tanned, exposed flesh, pink and bronze and deep olive, bimbos and himbos: girls in bikinis and short-shorts, bare shoulders and cleavage; boys in tank tops and mesh, boys shirtless, boys in snug swim suits, baskets bouncing as they walk. One buff, barefoot dude in OP shorts goes stumbling past, smelling of beer, chasing after a girl and shouting, "Whaddaya want outta me?" Robin catches George's eye over the roof of the car, and George smirks, saying, "Don't answer him," and then Robin puts on his sunglasses and they both laugh.

As they walk to the boardwalk, Robin almost misses sight of Calvin, pacing anxiously at the side of a boxy white building, moving in and out of shadow. He is so disheveled he might be some kind of boardwalk bum, sniffing around the Dumpsters for cast-off pizza crust. His face has the pallor of the undead. His hair never looks clean, but it's almost repulsive now, matted down on one side and clumped up in other places. His black trench coat, a kind of anti-fashion statement in Manhattan, is a complete anomaly in Seaside Heights, a red flag: avoid this unstable person. Fresh anger ripples through Robin: of *course* Ruby wouldn't stick with this guy, he doesn't take care of himself and doesn't look like someone who would take care of his girlfriend, either. He thinks of the attention Ruby has always given to her own appearance, all that time she spent locked into the bathroom they shared in Manhattan, emerging with glossy hair, makeup just so. Even in her recent funereal fashion, she's precise, exact. Like him, she's inherited their mother's vanity, her need to keep up appearances.

"Man, am I glad to see you," Calvin says, extending his hand to Robin, then to George. His grip is too tight, like he's clasping a tree branch to hoist himself out of rushing water. When Robin takes out his Parliaments, Calvin grabs for the pack, saying, "I need one of those." Blowing smoke, he asks them, "So what's the plan?"

George says, "You're the last one who saw Ruby. Why don't you tell *us*?" He stands a step apart from them on the wooden boardwalk, arms crossed over his T-shirt, eyes assessing.

Calvin's eyes dart to Robin, as if to confirm that George's "us" speaks for both of them. It occurs to Robin that Calvin and George have only met once before, in New York around Christmastime last year, when Dorothy invited them all to dinner, and they bonded over how depressing Ronald Reagan's reelection had been. Calvin probably has no idea what to make of George now. "It's not my fault we're in this mess," Calvin pleads, sounding suddenly vulnerable, in over his head.

"You left Ruby at a nightclub," George says.

"What, I'm supposed to drag her down the street while she's telling me, 'I'm not going with you'?"

Robin says, "Couldn't you have *persuaded* her?"

"Man, maybe you know how to make your sister do something she doesn't want to, but I haven't fucking figured that one out."

It's true that Ruby isn't as malleable as she once was. With every passing year, she more readily goes her own way. But he can't just absolve Calvin of responsibility. "We need more to go on, Calvin."

"I barely slept last night. And today I drove around with a total hangover, went up and down the boardwalk like three times. What a fucking capitalist nightmare this place is. People just pissing their money away on cheap thrills and junk prizes made in Hong Kong. I finally just passed out on the sand, I have no idea for how long. And then," he adds, lifting his voice, "I got hassled by the fascist beach patrol."

George asks, "Did you tell them you were looking for Ruby?"

"Yeah, and they said, 'Happens every day.'"

"And you let it drop?"

"What was I supposed to do?" he shouts. His arms sweep wide, and his cigarette flies from his fingers, sending sparks skidding along the wooden planks.

Robin catches passersby staring their way. What a sight the three of them must be. "Why don't we sit down, eat something, and figure out the next move?"

They step into a place advertising "giant slices" of pizza. It's called the Saw Mill, and its painted sign features a 3-D illustration ripped from *The Perils of Pauline*: a villain in top hat, cape, and curled moustache leering over a busty damsel who is tied to a log, her mouth open in a scream as she is sent downriver. What this has to do with pizza isn't at all clear, and as an omen, Robin thinks, it's about as bad as it gets.

Bon Jovi blares over the bleeps and whistles of pinball and video games.

Calvin asks the Italian guy behind the counter if they take credit cards. "For a slice?" the guy asks. "Ten-dollar minimum."

Calvin turns to Robin. "Swing me?" Robin hands him a few bucks, sighing. It's always the rich kids whose wallets are empty.

Robin and George sit side by side, their thighs slapping beneath the table, neither of them pulling away. Robin realizes he'd been harboring the hope that by the time they got to Seaside, Ruby would have already reappeared, crisis averted, and that he and George could then . . . what? Get a room? Go back home and have sex again? Roll around in the waves, a gay version of *From Here To Eternity*? He sucks his icy Diet Coke through a straw, telling himself to concentrate.

George takes charge, leading Calvin methodically through the events of the last day. Does Calvin carry a picture of Ruby with him? He shakes his head no. Robin pats his own pocket, remembering the laminated photo in his money clip. Ruby was twelve when it was taken;

why didn't he remember to bring something more recent, something they might show to people? To the police, if it comes to that. It's hard to be angry with Calvin when he himself is so poorly prepared.

One thing in particular from Calvin's story stands out: Chris, the guy who had apparently been kissing Ruby at the party. He seems like the answer to wherever she is.

"I barely know him," Calvin says. "He dated Alice for, like, two whole weeks. He's a fucking cokehead. I hang out sometimes with Benjamin, Chris's roommate. There's always a lot of coke around."

"Was Ruby doing coke?" Robin asks.

"Not that I saw."

"Were *you*?" George asks.

"I hate that stuff," Calvin says. He lowers his voice and locks eyes with Robin. "Personally, it makes my dick go limp."

"I've had that happen," Robin replies.

"What's the point of a drug that messes with your manhood?"

"Exactly." They share a chuckle, and Robin pulls out his cigarettes, offering another to Calvin. As they light up, he realizes George is looking back and forth between them with obvious impatience on his face.

George says, "When the food comes, would you two put those out?"

Robin fans the air with his hand. "Sorry."

"If the club is the last place she was seen, that's where we should start," George says. "Unless they're not open on Sundays."

"Everything's open here on Sunday," Calvin says. "Trust me. I've been all over this place."

Robin thinks, Ruby might have gone to church today. For years, she always went to church on Jackson's birthday, sometimes with Nana, and sometimes he went along, too. She would light votive candles around the apartment and lead them in prayers at the dinner table. She even helped start a youth group at the Catholic church on 71st Street; she tried to get Robin to join, but he told her one member of the God Squad in their family was plenty. Churches have never struck him as particularly welcoming, though he understands why people want something to belong to, why they want to pray to a Big Daddy in the sky. A couple of years ago, Ruby pulled back from all of that, but he wonders: Can you simply turn it off? It's like breaking up with a boyfriend: just because it's over, doesn't mean you don't feel the need to dial his number just to see if he's home.

* * *

A block from the boardwalk, Robin stops at a phone booth. Between the three of them, they cough up enough coins to make a long-distance call. He dials his home number, glancing through the scratched glass at George, who is looking back at him with just the faintest hint of a smile, almost as if he knows at this moment that Robin is listening to the goofy outgoing message they recorded together. He punches in the message code, which is 1964, the year they were born. The electronic voice warbles: "Two messages."

The first is Ruby's from last night. He listens to it again, hoping for some new insight, like when he reads a play for a third or fourth time and finally grasps some truth about his character. He wonders about the motel she mentioned, with the diving woman on the sign. Maybe he could find that; it can't be far from here. For all he knows, she might have been calling from this very phone booth. Now her voice is saying, ". . . I'm trying to find him. I followed him. I'm a little buzzed." This boy, Chris. He must be the key. Even though Calvin didn't see him at the club, Ruby might have made a plan to meet up with Chris later. Her final words, "I'm not sure what I'm doing," are cut off so abruptly it's as if a hand had reached into the phone booth and covered her mouth. The image suspends his breath, and then the second message begins, and it's Peter:

"Hi. I'm about to drive back to Pittsburgh, and, kind of against my better judgment, I'm calling. But you're not there now, and I need to get on the road, so . . . Honestly, I thought I'd hear from you first. Don't you think you owe me an apology? For acting like a complete bully? I know you were upset, but Douglas isn't—you blew that out of proportion. We could have talked through this, but . . . maybe when you get back to Pittsburgh, we'll see if—" *Blpppp.*

If what? We'll see if we can be boyfriends? If we still miss each other? If you test negative for AIDS like three or four more times . . . ?

They've got to get an answering machine that allows for longer messages.

Robin's finger hovers over the keypad. Will it be "3" for save, or "2" for erase?

He presses "3," then slams down the phone.

They continue on foot to Club XS, Calvin a half stride ahead of them, his long legs setting the pace. The building is two stories tall, cement, with blacked-out windows along the sidewalk.

Calvin swings open the front door, and they are blasted with air-conditioned cold. Eyes adjusting to darkness, they follow the sound of Madonna singing *You've got to prove your love to me* through a black curtain to a vast, nearly empty dance floor. Robin loves this song, but in this cavernous setting it sounds robotic, the siren call of a machine forcing fun on the masses. Four women, their skin leathery, their hair permed, shake their asses at the center. At a horseshoe-shaped bar, under a wide banner promoting "Sex on the Beach Shots $1," a couple of very loud girls in tank tops, too much makeup, and short denim skirts are flirting with a couple of silent, thick-necked guys in baseball caps. Everyone looks a little baked, by the sun, the long weekend, the cheap shots of Sex on the Beach.

Something about the decor here reminds Robin of a place he took Ruby and Calvin to when they visited him in Pittsburgh. They were taking a chance, hoping their fake IDs would work. For Robin, it was an acting exercise, as he successfully channeled the nonchalance of someone older. Ruby had been intimidated. She ordered a club soda, even though Robin and Calvin had no trouble being served vodka, and she kept tugging at the hem of her skirt, worried that in her attempt to appear of-age she wound up looking cheap. She had only just begun to commit to her new style, the skirts and boots, the ink-black hair and frosted makeup, and she was behaving like a guest who wants to leave a party soon after arriving, convinced she has dressed wrong and is attracting too much attention. He had tried to ease her mind, telling her if anyone stared, just smile and look away. The key to dealing with unwanted flirtation was to absorb it, but not to look back. Remembering that night, when Calvin was dressed sharp and had a fresh haircut, Robin realizes what bad shape he's in now. Ruby's disappearance has really wrecked him; that, or maybe he's caught in some larger downward spiral, slipping loose from the orderly world.

Robin approaches the bartender, who looks both fleshy and muscular at once. He's got gel in his hair and gold at his neck. You can smell the cologne from far away. He lays down two cocktail napkins, at which point Robin realizes George is hanging back several paces. He's the only black person in the club; it's possible they haven't seen any black people since they drove into Seaside. He's also the only one of the three of them of legal drinking age. "Actually, I'm looking for information," Robin says.

"There's a phone booth in the corner," the bartender says, smirking. "Try 4-1-1."

"No, I'm looking for my sister, she was here last night."

"I didn't touch her!" He barks out a laugh, then shuts it off impatiently. "Beer? Shot? What? You guys even legal?"

"Yeah, we're legal," Robin says. He hands over his ID.

The bartender glances at it for a split second and hands it back to him. "You shouldn't even be here."

"What are you talking about? That's my college ID."

"You bought this at Playland in Times Square. You think I'm new at this?"

George pushes up next to Robin. "Were you working here last night?"

"Oh, you brought Beverly Hills Cop along with you."

"Excuse me?" George says.

"Joke, little man. Joke." He slides down to the other end of the bar to take an order.

"Hey!" Robin calls out.

"This guy's a dick," George says. He turns and walks back toward the door they came in, moving through the black curtain.

Robin calls his name, to no avail.

"Let him go," Calvin advises.

Robin nods. He can't give up on this place yet, asshole bartender or not. He recalls an exercise he was given in acting class: Get the attention of someone ignoring you. The instructor offered three options: go big to intimidate, go small to elicit pity, or become like the person you need to impress.

So he deepens his voice and calls out, "I hear she was a fucking bitch to deal with. You should try being her brother." The bartender looks back toward him. Robin pulls out his money clip, bulging with bills. "Man, I gotta clear this up before my mom gets on my case. Anyone here who can help?"

"Hang on, I'll call the office." The bartender picks up a phone mounted on the wall and mutters a few sentences. Then he tells Robin. "Mick is coming downstairs. He was at the door last night."

"Thanks, man." Robin begrudgingly leaves a couple singles on the bar.

A minute later, a big guy appears from the dark reaches of the club.

Robin extends his hand, and the guy grabs it so that only their thumbs interlock, like they're old pals bumping into each other at a rock concert. *"Qué pasa?"* he says, though he doesn't look like he has a drop of Spanish blood in him. He looks more like an Amish farmer, his pale face obscured by a broad, fuzzy beard. His eyes are small, the pupils large, as if he never leaves the club during daylight. Robin can see that the guy is probably only a couple years older than he is, a young face disappearing into hairy manhood.

Calvin says, "Hey, man."

The bouncer takes notice of him. "Oh, you. *That's* what this is about."

Calvin says, "His sister, my girlfriend, was one of the girls who got kicked out—black hair, blue eyes, kind of pale?"

"Oh, yeah. The foxy preppie chick. I had to get in there and fuckin' break shit up, 'cause that other one, the really wasted twat, was wiping the floor with her. Another minute and somebody was gonna get hurt." Pointing at Calvin, he tells Robin, "This guy was the only one making any sense."

Robin is still absorbing Ruby as a "foxy preppie chick"; there's hardly room to imagine her in the midst of a scuffle, much less Calvin stepping in as a sensible hero.

Calvin says, "The last I saw of her was when she left with two other girls. A fat one and a skinny one."

But the bouncer shakes his head, his beard floating in front of him like seaweed on the surf. "Nah, I'm pretty sure those two chicks went one way, and your girlfriend went the other way with some guy."

"A skinny, coked-out guy?" Calvin asks. "Dressed in black?"

"It was new-wave night. Lots of guys fit that description. But yeah, he was skinny. They went—" He points toward what Robin guesses is the south side of town.

"Are you sure?" Robin asks.

"That's what they pay me for," he says, with obvious pride. "I don't miss anything."

"That fucker," Calvin says, stamping his foot on the floor and twirling around. Even in the low light of the bar, Robin can see the frustration on his face. And who can blame him, betrayed like that? Maybe the beach patrol was right when they told Calvin that stuff like this happens all the time. Even so, it's not like Ruby. He tries to imagine the kind of guy who could get Ruby to go off with him. When he tries to picture Chris, what forms in his mind is a picture of Douglas.

Outside the club, there's no sign of George at first; then Robin spots him across the street, waving them over.

Robin starts an apology, something about the bartender and his insults, but George stops him. "Wasn't your fault," he says. "I have an idea. Let's check out this parking lot." He points farther down the street, to a sign announcing, PARK HERE FOR CLUB XS, BAMBOO BAR, YAKETY YAK'S.

The lot is presided over by an old man sitting on a folding lawn chair. He wears dark glasses and a baseball cap and keeps his hands folded over a fanny pack at his waist while Robin asks him questions. Turns out this guy wasn't on duty last night, but his son was, and if they leave a number, he'll have him call.

The old guy looks past Robin's shoulder. His eyes are on George and Calvin, who are wandering around the cars at the perimeter of the lot. "Hey!" he shouts. "Get away from the vehicles!"

When Robin joins them he sees that they've huddled together over a discovery: a mound of clothing that includes a woman's shirt, yellow and damp, and a pair of boxy madras shorts, smudged with dirt.

"She had those on!" Calvin exclaims.

"They don't look like Ruby."

"She borrowed them from Alice. I spilled a beer on her," he says, his face going slack, "so she had to change."

For the first time since leaving Philly, Robin feels what must be dread: a chill along his skin, a tightness in his throat, sour as bile. "We don't know what it means," he says quickly. "She might have just changed when she got to the car." He finds George's gaze and holds it, wanting some measure of George's customary calmness to transfer to him.

But George seems rattled, too. "If she was just changing her clothes, why would she dump these on the ground?"

"I don't even want to say what I'm thinking," Calvin mutters.

It's what they're all thinking, Robin knows, understanding, too, that it's time to go to the police. He's been resisting. To tell the cops means giving in to his worst fears. And it probably means telling his mother what's going on, too. He had wanted to spare her the anxiety of a missing child. Especially today.

But he knows he's in over his head. "Calvin, let's go to your sister's house. I want to use the phone there to call the cops."

Calvin nods. He picks up the cast-off clothes and tucks them under his arm.

George suddenly grabs hold of him. "It'll work out," he says and surprises Robin with an arm around his shoulder and a comforting kiss planted on his forehead. It feels very public: Calvin is looking back at them, another car is moving slowly past toward a parking spot, and the old guy in the baseball cap is now standing up and waving his arms in the air. "You're all trespassing," he yells. "Move along!"

Then it finally hits him that the person he needs to call is his father.

They don't talk much these days, and Robin isn't sure he knows how to talk to him, not about anything deep. Clark's expectations have always seemed at odds with what Robin wanted for his own life. While Jackson was alive, the burden of being the right kind of son was alleviated for Robin. He had a brother who could play sports, who liked to roughhouse and tease, who wanted a father's advice (as opposed to a mother's, which is where Robin always turned). During those months when Jackson was in the hospital, in a coma, his father dealt with the pall of uncertainty that hung over all of them by knocking out the dining room wall and beginning construction on a new room, built to be the bedroom of a handicapped child. No one used that word, handicapped, but phrases like "diminished motor skills" and "permanent damage" were spoken quietly, and Robin would rehearse the scenarios in his mind, the various ways that Jackson, once the fastest sprinter in his elementary school and the most reckless tree-climber of any kid in the neighborhood, would return to them in some frightening, diminished version of himself. But Jackson didn't return.

Inevitably there was an argument between his parents about what to do with the room. Robin listened as they went back and forth. Dorothy had assumed it would make sense as a breakfast nook or a pantry, some expansion of their kitchen, which had never been quite large enough. Instead, Clark announced, "It's going to be my office."

"But you have one at your job."

"I'm claiming a little personal space."

"Space for what?" Dorothy demanded.

"For myself."

Personal space struck Robin as an odd fit with his father's personality. Clark had always been pragmatic, social, and not one for self-analysis. Now he installed a couch that took up an entire wall. It was wide and plush, and it cost, his mother complained to Robin, "a pretty penny." He would work late at the office, as a sales manager for a Japanese company, in their battery department, a job that Robin never understood. (Battery sales? You just buy them at the store, right?) At night, Clark would close himself into this room. Robin would spy him through the partly opened door, reclining on the couch, some technical manual splayed on his chest. He became a ghost presence, sealed off from the rest of them.

After the divorce, Robin and Ruby's weekend visits to Greenlawn had the atmosphere of time spent with a distant relative, more a chaperone than a parent. They shopped for groceries, cooked for their father, ate together in front of the TV. Then they went to their bedrooms to do homework or talk on the phone while Clark retired to his office. It was a kind of limbo. Life as aftermath.

Right before Robin went away to Pittsburgh for college, Clark pulled him aside and said, "I hope we can be close again one day," and Robin, at a loss to think of when they were ever close in the past, simply said, "Yeah, sure." He didn't really have a sense of what a close relationship with his father would even look like. But eventually, he decided he might test things out. During a phone call, when Clark asked Robin if he had a girlfriend at college, Robin said, "Dad, I don't think I'm going to have any girlfriends." Clark seemed taken aback, and managed to say, "Time will tell," to which Robin replied, "I'm telling you now, I don't think so." And that was that. The idea of a renewed relationship seemed to be sucked away into the vacuum of this unspeakable subject. Clark wasn't invited to the dinner party Dorothy threw for Robin's eighteenth birthday, and Clark in turn didn't find a way to make it to Pittsburgh to see Robin onstage in *Cat on a Hot Tin Roof*. Clark was contributing to his tuition. But that was the extent of it.

So when Robin stops at yet another phone booth and places a collect call to Greenlawn, he doesn't at all know what to expect.

"Dad?"

"Oh, hello there." He sounds a bit groggy.

"Did I wake you?"

"We got the news on. They've got that hijacking happening over there. Terrible stuff."

"I didn't know you were much of a news watcher."

"Well, Annie's gotten me into it. She's a real newshound."

In the background, Robin hears a woman's voice playfully interjecting, "Learn a little about the world, why don't you?"

Before Robin can ask who Annie is, Clark says, "This is what happens when you date a younger woman, she keeps you on your toes," and then Annie says something else that Robin can't make out, though there's an unmistakable intimacy in her tone.

He feels swarmed by conflicting reactions: startled that his father is dating someone, perplexed by the offhand way in which this is being announced, and vaguely bothered by the idea of a "younger woman." Exactly how *young*?

As if registering the break in the conversation, Clark says, "So, tell me, what the heck's going on? Your mother called me—"

"She called *you*?" This is not a common occurrence.

"She was in Paramus," and here his voice drops tentatively, "at the grave."

"Right, because today . . . is the day."

"And she wanted to know, did I hear from your sister, because there was some talk of Ruby going to the cemetery, too." Clark breathes heavily, and in a noticeably shakier voice, he says, "I gotta tell you, Robin, I couldn't do it. Just couldn't get myself there. That tombstone and the ground and . . ."

This, too, catches Robin off guard. The nakedness of it. "That's OK, Dad. I mean, I don't like going there, either."

"Well, sure. The memories." Clark recedes, and Robin decides to just wait to let him recover. "So, no word from your sister?"

OK. Here you go. "That's why I'm calling you. I'm in Seaside Heights—"

"*You* are?"

"I'm with Calvin."

"Calvin. Yeah, doesn't sound like she's too happy with him."

"Ruby said that?"

"Dorothy did. Your sister doesn't tell me anything."

Robin says, "Well, he called me, because she left this party, and she didn't come home, and he hasn't seen Ruby since around midnight last night."

"Midnight? Yesterday?" There's a shuffle on the end of the line; his father is standing up, moving away from the TV.

"We're trying to figure out where she went. We've been, sorta, retracing her steps."

"You talk to the police?"

"That's probably what I should do. She might have gone off with this guy—"

"What guy?"

"A boy from the party."

Clark raises his voice. "I don't understand why you waited this long—"

"Well, I used to disappear on you and Mom, and I always turned up." Robin immediately understands that this was not the right thing to say; he meant it as a bit of levity. In the silence that follows, the gravity of the situation tugs at him, and he feels suddenly ashamed. He's been handling this all wrong, ever since Calvin's first phone call this morning. He's been taking it on himself, instead of getting help. He isn't up to this responsibility. *You've made it all worse.*

Clark says quietly, "Go to the police. Or call them. Have them meet you."

"OK," Robin says.

"And then call me again. I'll deal with your mother."

"OK."

"Call me soon, whatever you find out," Clark says.

It's only then that Robin remembers that today is Father's Day, but it's too late to say anything, because Clark has hung up.

When she looks up to the black sky, she can no longer find the moon. She has lost all sense of time since they left the beach. By now it must be Sunday, a new day on the calendar, though she feels herself deep in the middle of the same endless night, as if floating far out in the dark ocean, all civilization—life as she knows it—left behind.

Chris, at the wheel of the BMW, brakes suddenly, shouts "Holy fuck," and Ruby is yanked back into the moment. A dumbstruck boy stares through the windshield, red-rimmed eyes and slack jaw. A startled drunk, awash in their headlights. He mutters something she can't hear through the glass and gives them the finger. Chris steers around as the guy stumbles away, another Seaside Heights party casualty trying to find his way to bed. A reminder that they are nearly back at the center of town, at the boardwalk.

"I think it's just a few more blocks up ahead," Ruby says.

It was her idea to go to the Surfside Motel. Earlier tonight, the sign out front advertised vacancies. It seemed worth a try.

But now, nearly there, the suggestion seems almost sacrilegious. To walk through the door with Chris, when her memories of the place were of her family on vacation—all five of them, all those years ago, intact—she might as well be taking him back to Greenlawn to have sex in her parents' bed.

As they approach the front desk she can tell right away something is off. The small lobby smells too strongly of cigarettes, and beneath that, the musty wetness of mildew. A stoned-looking guy—he'd be right at home at the Deadhead party next to Alice's—stands behind the desk staring at a small television with a horror movie on it. A man with a chainsaw pursues a screaming girl until she hurls herself from an open window to the ground far below. The Deadhead asks them if they want to look at the room before they pay. Chris says, "I'm sure it's fine," but there is something in the way the guy pauses, as if to allow them a chance to reconsider, that makes Ruby speak up.

"Actually, I'd like to see it."

He leads them down a corridor, a tunnel of dingy yellow light. There is noise from behind doors—music, laughter, gleeful screams. It's like the party at Alice's all over again. The guy stops and swings open a door, and her gaze immediately lands on an air conditioner across the room, missing a cover, its mechanical guts exposed, duct tape fixing its edges to a grimy window. A stained couch has a slash in it, revealing the foamy stuffing. One of the pillows on the bed doesn't have a case. The other has a cream-colored stain the size of a dinner plate. "The bathroom's through there," the guy says, though she doesn't make a move. What would be the point? Reflexively, she turns back to the guy at the door, as if to gauge how he is reacting to her. He pulls some kind of rag out of his back pocket—she had seen him grab it as he left the front desk, and now she knows why. He swats at the wall. She sees a dark, narrow spot go scurrying down toward the floor.

"Was that a roach?" she asks.

"Water beetle," he says. He pulls a pack of cigarettes out of his pocket and lights one.

She looks at Chris, incredulous. She can't read his face. Blank. She wants him to be outraged.

Ruby says, "I stayed here when I was a little kid, and it wasn't like this."

The Deadhead says, "There's one more empty room, if you wanna check it out."

"But this is the better one, right?" Ruby asks. "Or you would have shown us that one first?"

The guy laughs. "Not necessarily."

Without another word she turns around, steps past both of them and walks steadily down the hall. The idea that in *that* place she might have—she can't even complete the thought.

Back on the street, there's an electric feel to the air, the threat of a storm. The wind has picked up, and clouds have moved in. She waits near the car, and Chris is there a moment later, nuzzling his face into her neck. Pulling her head away from him, she says, "There was *no way*."

"I'm sorry," he says. "I would have taken it without looking."

He pulls her against his chest. She isn't quite ready for a hug. Her face winds up in the moist, metallic heat of his armpit. Why do guys' bodies smell so much stronger than girls'? What's churning away inside them that women don't have? Is it elemental, like testosterone? Or emotional, all the ways they hold everything back, feelings that rot beneath the skin—

Chris says, "We could go back to the beach and sleep—"

"It might rain," she says, looking up. Rough-edged clouds are advancing, a scruffy gray blanket yanked across the black sky.

"I'm really exhausted," she says.

"We'll find somewhere else," he says. "Didn't we see someplace back by the state beach?"

So they drive back the couple miles they've just traveled to a motel they've already passed twice tonight. Island Beach Motor Lodge. The man at this desk is a little bit older, and better dressed. He isn't smoking or watching TV. A love song plays on a radio. He stands with both hands behind the desk, fingers tapping anxiously against some unseen surface as he listens to their request and asks for Chris's ID. "Can't rent to you if you're under twenty-one. I suggest that you go up to the Heights."

"We were just in the Heights," Chris says. "Come on, man. We're looking for someplace clean."

The man eyes Ruby up and down. "Rules are rules."

It comes to her, what she needs to do—she twists the fake ruby into her palm so that only the metal band shows. Then she steps forward and rests her hand on the desk, saying, "I know you probably get a lot of irresponsible people showing up in the middle of the night. But honestly, I went to the place in Seaside Heights where we were supposed to stay, and it was gross. Like, cockroaches and broken furniture and worse. Maybe for high school kids, that's all they need because they're just here to party. But we're on our honeymoon, and we're looking for something nice."

"Your honeymoon?" His eyes shift back to Chris, who throws an arm around Ruby.

"Um, yeah. Mister and missus," Chris stutters.

The man blows air through his lips, a flapping, exasperated noise. "Hold on."

As he picks up a phone and presses a button, Ruby adds, "And we can put down an extra deposit, for cleaning, or security, or whatever, if that would make things nice."

An older man walks through the door in a bathrobe a few minutes later. He looks like he could be the first one's father. He looks, in fact, like he could be *her* father. Same thick white hair—Clark is not even fifty but he's gone totally silver—same gangly body. OK, the face is different on this man—the nose is smaller, the eyes not so blue. But still. The resemblance makes it painfully simple to imagine what she looks like through his eyes. She hasn't fixed herself up in hours. She's wearing Chris's clothes. His pale skin looks almost green in the fluorescent light. Maybe she should have stayed in Dorian's preppie clothes. She might pass inspection now.

"Where are your bags?"

"We don't—" Chris starts to say.

"Look, this is a family operation, and we don't go for—"

"We don't need them right now," Ruby interrupts. In the last half hour, she has begun to understand the implications of what Chris meant by not having a plan. She didn't expect that "making it up as we go along" would meant that she would have to take charge. "Bags are in the car," she says.

The man takes another look at her, scrutinizing.

Chris says, "How much? I've got a lot of cash."

"I want a credit card."

Chris looks at her. He lowers his voice. "Do you?"

"Yeah, my father—for emergencies."

"Mine is maxed out," he says, adding quickly, "I have to pay for it myself."

She digs into her purse and finds the MasterCard behind her driver's license—an ugly photo of her in a gray sweatshirt, her hair pulled back so severely she looks like the new inmate at a women's prison. (All those years she spent never wearing makeup!) She feels a pang of reluctance as she hands over the plastic, knowing that her father will see the statement at the end of the month. She'll have to lie, say she's here with some girlfriends. Clark knows she's in Seaside. He'll understand that she has to sleep somewhere. Of course, he'll suspect she's with Calvin.

Is it better to let him think that? She'll pay him back. And if she can't afford it, what's he going to do? Cut off her tuition? Let him. She wouldn't miss college. She could leave Manhattan. She could move in with Chris.

She realizes that she doesn't even know where he lives.

Standing at the threshold, Ruby pauses. She lets Chris enter ahead of her, watches as he flicks on lights. The room offers no surprises—two full-sized beds covered in mismatched patterned bedspreads, a nightstand between them. A lamp glows there, and above it she sees a faded, framed print of a lighthouse sending its beam across a stormy sea. (She's seen this lighthouse before, it's somewhere on the Jersey Shore. Barnegat? Sandy Hook? The names come back to her from other family vacations. Other moments when Jackson was alive . . .)

Thick vertical drapes block out the windows, and when Chris pulls them open she can see, even from the doorway, that they weren't given a room with an ocean view. All that is visible is the parking lot where they've left Chris's car and beyond that the grid of streets. Speckles of rain are landing on the plate glass. A thick, soft smell floats out toward her—she recognizes it as carpet powder, the kind you sprinkle on a stained rug and vacuum up. The illusion of having cleansed a problem. But after the Surfside, she'd give this one the Good Housekeeping Seal of Approval.

God, am I doing the right thing?

For one moment more, she absorbs the possibility that she might still turn back, might still wait. Then Chris, deep inside the room, makes an about-face and swings his arm wide, saying, "Look, honey, cable television."

It's not the prospect, the likelihood, of sex that halts her here in the hallway. She's not afraid of what might happen. But the ordinariness of the room is a damper on her sense that the events of this night have been fated—like taking a bite of a hot dinner she's been salivating over and discovering it to be cool in the center. How can she hold on to her sense of *meant to be* in a room so unremarkable?

It must be on her face, this indecision, because Chris sends her a look so questioning that she fears she has hurt his feelings—has introduced some element of doubt to what up until now has been mutually understood. She takes a step backward. "If this is a honeymoon, aren't you supposed to carry me over?"

There's a sudden bright flash—a jagged zip of lightning through the window. As Chris walks toward her, ready to pick her up, Ruby hears thunder roll.

The kissing is more than good. The desire to kiss—to keep on kissing—is strong. After Calvin, that's important. She feels the kiss unfold, her mouth like a night bloom opening to the dark humidity. It's one long kiss, not a series of little pecks to interrupt a jabbing tongue. Chris is a better kisser than Calvin—or is it that he's simply the right kisser for her? Maybe Calvin's kissing is right for someone else? Maybe for a boy. Maybe he won't figure out how to kiss until he kisses the kind of person he really desires.

Chris's hands are under her shirt, fingertips cold as they trail across the warm sunburned patch on her stomach, the souvenir of her few hours at the beach. When she thinks of his hands and not his mouth, she feels the panic of *moving too fast.* Her thoughts fly back to the first kiss in Alice's bedroom—he didn't ask, he just went for it. Then he lured her from the club and into his car, and now they're in a motel room. What if he's no different than Calvin, another boy with money who gets whatever he expects—

"Are you OK?" He has pulled away from her mouth, his hands have slid down her ribs to her waist. "Something just changed."

"No—"

She sits down on the edge of the bed. Thinks about the noise the springs make—will people be able to hear? *This is a family operation.* She's removing her boots, her socks, wiggling her freed feet. There's a little pop in one ankle. She cleans her toes of sand. A weird memory—Jackson used to call the dirt between his toes "little acorns."

She says, "I was thinking of when you kissed me this afternoon, back at the house."

"You tasted like beer."

"You tasted like mouthwash."

"Is my breath bad now?"

She shakes her head. "Is mine?"

"Nah. You taste great." He moves in again, but she stops him. He says, "Something *is* wrong."

"I kind of want to take a shower, before anything."

"Yeah, sure, go ahead."

She takes a few steps toward the bathroom.

He says, "I could kiss you in the doorway of the bathroom. Like old times." She turns around, taking in his shy smile. He adds, "I've always wanted to take a shower with a girl."

She's showered with Calvin but doesn't want to say so. There's such eagerness on Chris's face—that same face she's already seen high, and sad, and humiliated—that she finds she's holding her breath, as if waiting for some signal. She's going to be naked in front of him, they're going to be naked together. It's not the same as with Calvin—with him she would undress in the bathroom and get in the shower and then moments later he'd pop through the door saying. "Is the water hot yet?" and strip before she could reply.

She and Chris are going to do this side by side.

She says, "You can lose your shower virginity with me."

He moves closer. She pulls her shirt over her head, stands there in the same black bra she's worn all day. She feels the air on her skin. He stares at her.

He says, "I'm embarrassed."

"You?"

"You're so sexy, and I'm just—" He runs a finger along her neck, and down into the space between her breasts. She puts his hand on the cup of her bra, and he gently squeezes. He moves his fingers up to the strap, tugs it softly off her shoulder.

She helps him take his shirt off, too. The line from his neck to his shoulder is a strong curve, his shoulders are bony except at the cap, where the muscle is rounder.

"I'm too skinny," he says. "I can't put on bulk."

"No," she protests, though she is almost alarmed by how lean he is. His torso is a plank, stripped of any excess, skin stretched over striated muscle, bone, sinew. There's nothing to pinch. The veins stand out in his arms. He's probably always been this thin, but when she met him on their Catholic weekend she wasn't thinking about his body. Now she can't take her eyes off him—the concave chest with its two dark nipples, the scraggly dark hairs above his navel, the slanting lines of his lower abdomen, moving from his bony hips down into the waist of his jeans. She hasn't seen a lot of naked men. Calvin, of course. Her brother, careless around the apartment. Her friend Tara's boyfriend, who streaked through a slumber party, his thing sticking out stiffly.

Men's bodies are so strange, there's almost nothing soft or warm-blooded about the way they look. They are more like machines than like mammals. Their bones seem like *parts.*

She stands and then pulls him to his feet, too. She unfastens the button at his waist. She tugs downward. He is wearing navy blue boxer shorts, crumpled up inside his pants. He pushes the jeans down, and the boxers loosen around his thighs. She can see how his penis is thickening, nudging the cotton cloth away from his leg.

This is where Calvin would grab her hand, press it against him, and start the rubbing that he himself would eventually finish off. This is where she would begin to count each stroke, rhythmically, as a way to pass the time. But Chris has kept his hands at his side, letting her lead. She turns around so he can unfasten her bra. It slides off. She turns back to face him. He's still smiling. He's harder than before.

"I've always had to do all the work," he says. "With girls. Like, be the one to . . ."

She pulls his hands to her waist. He unbuttons the jeans she's wearing, his jeans, and then she's in her panties, and she takes him by the hand and leads him to the bathroom. Just to walk across a room half naked—it's not something she's done before. The only sound is the rain on the glass, coming down hard, as if someone outside is clattering an electric typewriter, writing down their story as it happens.

In the bathroom mirror she glimpses the bruise darkening on her hip, the spot where she hit the floor during the scuffle. It's a dark smudge in the bright room, with its white tiles and pastel towels, its smells of cleanser and soap.

They stand outside the tub while he adjusts the knobs and giggle as the room fills with thick vapor. It nearly obscures them from each other. And then she doesn't know who's doing what first but they're both out of their underwear and kissing, arms wrapped around each other. She's no longer worried about moving fast. He lifts her up. His grip all sinew and sharp angles. He places her in the tub. Catches her when she nearly slips. Water cascades over them, still hot but bearable, except on her stomach, where it's like fire on the sunburn. She turns away from the jets. Now he's behind her, pressing hard into the small of her back. She reaches back—for a split second she thinks that she's grabbed his wrist. He's so thick. He's bone-hard. She slides her hand and finds the head, that rubbery dome. Who was it who said—*Benjamin*, that's right, Benjamin had said to her that Chris was small.

Which is clearly untrue. Why do guys all care so much about their size? Why are they so competitive? *Phallocentrism,* that's what her women's studies professor calls it.

Chris's hands are wrapped around her, soaping her breasts, her nipples have never felt so hard, his hand moves down to her stomach, cool on the burn, and then down some more into the tangle of hair. The soap moves around. She can feel him being tentative so she puts her hand on his and lets him know to push, to clean her, she wants to be clean there, for him.

He turns her around and lets her rinse off and then, awkward, drops down to his knees and digs in with his fingers to find the lips of her vagina. She puts her hands in his hair, clamps on to him for balance. His mouth goes into the mossiness. She widens her stance, anticipating already what she hasn't ever experienced. This is not something that Calvin or anyone has done to her. A mouth on her *clint.* She's touched herself and knows what can happen, and it's like that at first, his tongue like a finger but slippery. She finds a way to brace the wall so she can lodge herself onto the force of his tongue.

"Lower," she dares to say, and then guides him with "yes, there" and "no, lower," figuring this out as best she can. Not like a finger at all, his tongue sets her trembling and arching her back. She worries she might fall. Pushes him away and nudges back to the lip of the tub. She yanks the shower curtain out of the way, the water will get everywhere, so what? Chris hasn't stopped eating her out—that's what this is, *eating out.* She feels a laugh welling up. Such a vulgar phrase, *eating out,* but now she's part of it. *He's eating me out.* It seems comical, joyous. She needs to find her balance. She grabs him by the hair, pulls him off, slides backward out of the tub—a wobbly maneuver onto the bathmat. She lays herself down. She hopes the mat is clean. She doesn't care.

Chris has crawled out of the tub after her, a diver coming up from the depths to gasp for air before plunging in again. He knows how to do this, *God, he really does, thank you, thank you.* Is that OK, to thank God for sex? Shivers and shivers, it's getting more intense, *God,* there's pine in the air mown grass blossoms sap the stickiness of leaves she's humming moaning into the wind blowing down the side of a mountain she could topple right off into the sky down and down through the air. *What is this what is happening.* Like hitting the surface of water knifing through it like velvet breathing underwater no difference between what is inside of her and what is beyond her mouth open taking in the ocean letting out a scream, *let it out*, letting him letting him letting him—

Her body, trembling.

She's being lifted, somehow he's picked her up, and he's carrying her to the bed, again, the second time tonight. She's in the air wet and naked. What were all those pictures, flying and mountains and water and velvet? Chris's wet black hair is stuck to his skin, his brown eyes are bare and open and zoomed in on her. Has anyone ever looked at her before like this? He says something, he's asking her—what, she can't hear anything but the running water of the shower or is that rain outside? She can't help it, her hand goes where his mouth was. She's wet not just with shower water but with what came from inside, her orgasm. *I had an orgasm, that's what that was.* And the laugh that welled up before now breaks like a wave, and she can't stop.

"Why are you—?"

"That felt so—"

He's pushing her legs open. She reaches out to hold on to him, there's not much of a butt to grab, skin and bones, a tiny tuft of hair at the top of his tailbone. Up front, pushing forward, is the thick shaft, the pliant head, hovering right there, where he's licked and licked. Filling her. Wait, is he going in? There's pressure, a radius of heat, sliding in. "Wait," she says, "wait, wait, wait, wait," she says. "Wait, get the rubber," she says and shoves him off her and slides away. "Don't just—"

"Sorry. Right. Of course. You're not on the pill."

"No—why would I?"

"I know. I'm just used to—" Then he's gone, fumbling through his clothes. *Used to?* What is he used to? Having sex with girls on the pill? How many girls has he had sex with? What about the kind of germs the pill can't stop? . . . He's back, he's fumbling with the foil, which says TROJENZ— she always thought it was TROJANS—wait, it's TROJAN-ENZ, what does that mean? Maybe this is some new kind. He puts it over his dick, gets it wrong, has to flip it, now it unfolds along the shaft but does not go on easily. "I'm having trouble with this," he fumbles. "It's too tight."

She sits up. "Should I help?"

"I hate these things," he says, and then with a frustrated growl, he pulls the rubber off, tosses it to the floor. He throws his legs over the side of the bed and drops his head in his hands. He pouts.

She pushes her hair back from her face, tilts her neck so the hair will stay out of the way. She sees that his cock, softening suddenly, has no foreskin, which is what she's used to, with Calvin. She lowers her mouth, puts her lips around the head of it. There's a taste from the latex—gross, medicinal—but she keeps at it, moves her wet tongue around, and the taste goes away under the wetness and the heat. She tries to figure out how to breathe.

She doesn't really know what to do here. She's done this with Calvin but not much, she never really liked it with the foreskin. She wants to make Chris feel as good as he made her feel, but really what do you do with it? It's strange, a big piece of person in your mouth, a piece of the guy machine. A big machine part. He pushes into her throat. She gags. The shock of it. "Sorry, sorry, I'm sorry," he says.

She hears the foil crinkling. He's opening another one.

"Try again?" he says, sliding hard from her mouth and fumbling again with the rubber. She lies next to him. "I want your first time to be special."

But she remembers the first time—the secret first time, Brandon, no condom, no gentle anything. The blood that time. It scared her enough to send her to her mother, a day or two later. Dorothy took her to the doctor, she meant well, she was concerned, but it was awful, the doctor touching her with hands that had hair on them. Opening her up and saying in his stern voice *you're lucky this time, your carelessness could leave you pregnant or diseased or both, don't you know what's going around out there, think about that, young lady.*

They kiss, and it feels different this time, not a sweet bloom but something raw and exposed, mouths chapped and burning as if cooked in the sun. The smells and tastes are different now. There's soap on his lips from eating her out, and there's something else there, too, which is, she guesses, her own smell. Weird to think about that. She feels in an instant daring and adult. She sees that together they could do everything, things she's only heard about and never imagined for herself. She lays back. He's got the rubber on. He gets in between her legs. She's still wet, so it goes in quickly, sliding into her inflamed vagina. She's heard of women using lubricants but never understood until now the way her body would create its own. He's moving against her. She feels pressure in every direction, forcing the breath from her lungs.

"Go slowly," she says.

"Are you OK?" He holds himself above her. She touches his skin. Nods. His skin is smooth and hot, like the door of an oven.

"Can I push a little more?" he says. "I might be about to break the—I mean, you'll probably feel—It could hurt."

Break the. Probably feel. Could hurt.

It did hurt, back then. She did feel it. The broken hymen. The doctor used that word later. She had swallowed her scream, back then.

"I'm afraid," she says, or perhaps only thinks. He doesn't seem to hear her. He pushes. She feels herself resisting, tries to relax. A deep breath, a flutter in her throat as she exhales. His hip bones press against. He is deep inside. He's shining with sweat. A switch seems to have flipped, opening something up in him. Droplets hang and release onto her. His effort is clear. That's good, she should feel to him like a virgin. "Just push," she says, and he does, deep, and she lets herself cry out. He looks worried when she does this, so she grabs him and holds him close.

They rock together. She shuts her eyes.

A whimpering. She looks at him. His lower eyelids pool with tears.

"Chris?"

"I thought I was going to die, but now I feel strong again."

She kisses him. Then it all disappears, time disappears, and thought, and worry, and only sensation is left, and it sort of feels great and sort of hurts, but mostly what she does is look at his face, which is concentrated and beautiful, the sad eyes, the scar on his lip, the tendons in his neck, the black hair flopping like a curtain in the wind, a bead of sweat along his cheekbone. He's pulling back, and then digging deeper and really going for it, he's lifted her legs with his hands and is just going for it.

And then at some point the balance goes the other way, and things aren't so good. Despite the natural lubrication, there's an irritated feeling, too. Some excess friction. "Slower," she croaks out.

"Oh, sorry, sorry, sorry." He leans in and kisses her.

"You don't have to apologize," she says.

He says, "Let me pull out," and he does. Then he says, "Oh, no."

"What?"

She sees his penis pointing up to his navel, pulsating, oozing clear gooey liquid. But there's no latex on it.

She's confused. "I thought you put it on—"

"I did. You saw it."

He's patting the bed around her. She lowers her legs, scoots backward.

He says, "Is it in you?"

"What?" She reaches down, it almost hurts to touch herself, she's so inflamed, but her fingers slip in past the hair and lips. Then she feels the curled edge. She pulls it out, a dun colored wrinkled slimy thing. She winces.

"Oh, fuck," he says. "I think that can happen if, I don't know, I heard it can happen, if it doesn't fit right." He's stammering through accelerated breath. "Do you want, I don't know, a towel or anything?"

She looks at her fingers. She never took off the ring he gave her. She says, "Let me go wipe up the blood."

"Is there?" he says, examining under the head. The clear goo dribbles down the length of the shaft. Could she get pregnant from that?

In the bathroom she runs the water, wipes herself with a warm cloth. There's no blood. She hates that she's lying. She doesn't know what else to do.

She sits on the toilet, she thinks she should pee, that if there were any sperm that got in she could pee them out. This is absurd, she knows, but she imagines it's true anyway. The urine tingles as it passes through.

When she gets back to the bed he's lying on his side. "What are we supposed to do?" she asks.

"You're upset," he says.

"Aren't you? The condom—"

"I doubt it would, I mean, I didn't actually shoot—"

"No, I'm sure it's OK." She sits down, but apart from him. He's still hard. Should she use her hand on him? No, not with Chris.

"Come here," he says, patting the bed.

She spoons into him, letting him enfold her. She's aware of the tangle of limbs, of hard parts and soft, the strangeness of trying to find the right position, the awkwardness of their breaths moving at different paces. He licks her shoulder, nibbles her ear. She feels his tongue near the scratch on her neck.

He says, "I don't want you to feel bad. This has been magical."

"Until I find out I'm pregnant."

"Shh, shhh, no. We didn't get that far."

"I'm due next week, so we'll know soon enough."

He rubs her hair, which calms her down. "Nothing bad will happen," he says. "There's something holy between us."

She takes a deep breath. He's right. It was beautiful and holy and the condom probably only came off at the end, so there's no chance—not much of a chance anyway. Nothing she can do about it now. Just be here with Chris. She thinks that she won't sleep, and then she's drifting away. Sinking.

She's awakened from a dream that disappears the moment her eyes take in the motel furniture, the drapes, their clothes scattered across the carpet. Two condom wrappers on the floor near the bed. She recognizes the whoosh of waves crashing beyond the walls before she registers a louder, closer sound: the ringing of the phone on the bedside table. It hurts her ears. She must be a little hungover. Her mouth is dry, too.

Chris lies nearer to the phone, but he remains inert, his face so calm and youthful that she can picture him at age fifteen, the boy she kissed in the woods behind the seminary, the smell of wet leaves all around them.

She reaches across him to the phone. "Hello?"

It's the guy at the front desk, telling her in a gruff voice that checkout was thirty minutes ago. She looks at the clock. 12:30. They've slept all morning! Bright light seeps through the crack between the curtains.

Unsure what to do, she asks, "Can we have this for one more night?"

"You plan on staying one more night?"

"If the room is available." She's amazed at her own composure. Could they really stay longer? What day is it, anyway?

He grumbles to himself, as if reacting to an impossible request, but then he says, "Well, I think if I move some folks around." His voice is unconvincing. He's lying to her. He just doesn't want them there. "This is the kind of thing you're supposed to request *before* checkout time," he mutters.

Chris is stirring beneath her. She covers the mouthpiece and says to him, "We slept late." He smiles at her, his eyes full of wonder, as if she's just told him something miraculous. Or maybe he's remembering last night, as she is—the tumult of their bodies together.

The manager comes back on the phone. "OK. One more night."

"Use the same card," Ruby says.

Chris raises his voice, "And tell the maid we don't need the room cleaned."

Ruby repeats, "We don't need—"

"I *heard*," the guy says and hangs up.

"I guess that's that," she says to Chris. They both grin and fall naturally back into their spooning positions. Fresh stubble on his jaw brushes her neck, which sends a shiver along her skin. She reaches behind and grabs him. For a few moments, everything is bright and cheerful. Another day together. The room paid for. This improvised honeymoon can continue. Maybe life itself will continue like this, days and nights blurring into each other indefinitely, Chris at her side, nothing but deep, contented sleep to separate one leg of time from the next.

Chris's breaths fall into a steady rhythm. Sleeping again. She's not sure she can. Her mind has become active. It was just a day ago, a little over twenty-four hours, that a different phone woke her up, a different voice on the other end: Calvin's. He was leaving his apartment, was going to get his car from the garage and then would pick her up. *Make sure you're ready, so I don't have to find parking.*

Now, just like that, the dream she awoke from comes back to her. Calvin was in it, knocking on the door, saying, "Ruby, I know you're in there." She didn't answer, but he persisted. His voice boomed through the door: "Just come out so we can talk about the baby." The baby!

Involuntarily, she twitches, and Chris mumbles. "I slept again."

"I'm awake," she says.

"So, what're we gonna do to get our thirty-five dollars' worth?"

In an earlier part of the dream Calvin was saying, "I have to drive you back up the Garden State Parkway. It's Sunday. We have to go to church." Alice was part of it, too. Ruby was pleading with her, "Alice, you're a woman, you understand. I have to find Chris. I have to get to Chris." The hotel room became her bedroom in Greenlawn. On the nightstand was the lamp shaped like a ballerina with its hollow bottom.

She gasps, remembering suddenly. "It's Sunday! It's my brother's birthday."

"Do you want to call him?"

"Not *Robin*." She pulls herself upright, struggling to reorient herself. What is she doing here? She's out of her mind. She's supposed to be driving back to Manhattan with Calvin. There was this idea about stopping at the cemetery—it was her idea in the first place. They were going to end up at Dorothy's in time for supper. It's Father's Day, too. She can't remember, did she tell Clark she'd stop by on her way home?

"I have to go back to Alice's."

"Seriously?" Chris says, "I don't understand."

"Calvin has my bag, with all my clothes and toiletries—"

"He'll bring it back to New York, and you can just meet up with him later."

"No. I mean, yes, I could, but—"

"We just paid for another night here."

She drops her head in her hands. "I think I really messed up . . ."

"Are you mad at me?" he asks, an urgency in his voice that bothers her. This isn't about him, why is he trying to take this on?

"I just have to deal with this."

She gets up and scavenges the room for her purse, finally locating it in the bathroom. Inside is a scrap of paper that has Alice's number. When she returns and picks up the phone, Chris rolls away from her.

On the other end of the line, endless ringing. No answer.

She hangs up. Have they all left the party? Did the rental end today?

She dials again and waits through more ringing. At last, someone picks up. A female voice, loud and slurred, says, "Hello?"

"Is this Alice?"

"Hi, Alice. Wanna come to a party?"

"No, this is Ruby. Is Alice there?"

The voice calls out, "Which one of you stuck-up bitches is Alice?" and then the phone drops, and the muffled sounds of the party filter through the line—voices, laughter, another bad pop song she recognizes but can't name. It seems impossible that the house is still full of people. She waits, frustrated, her fingers tight around the receiver, as Chris rises and walks naked across the room. He closes himself in the bathroom. Maybe he's right. Maybe it's a bad idea to go back there.

Eventually she hears a click, and then the automated voice saying, "If you'd like to make a call, please hang up and try again." She puts down the receiver, redials, and gets a busy signal.

Chris emerges from the bathroom, water droplets running off his face and neck onto his bare torso. His lean body glows from behind, like a saint in a religious painting. As he approaches her, his eyes seem to plead: Not yet. Let's not break from this yet. She doesn't want to, but what about all those plans? Then he squats down next to her and looks her in the eyes. "I don't care what we do. I just want to be with you."

"I was going to visit my brother's grave today," she says.

"Where?"

"Near where my Dad lives. Paramus."

"Do you want me to take you?"

She thinks about it. She nods. Yes.

Their hands reach out to each other and meet with a tick of static electricity, which seems to seal the agreement. She feels panic slip away. Chris will take her to the cemetery. She'll get herself home eventually.

So they've bought themselves some more time. They embrace, and he nudges her back toward the bed, pulls her down into the sheets. For another hour, she forgets about everything outside this room. They try different positions this time. Even through her hangover, it feels clearer in the light of day, more intense. He pants her name as he comes. This time, the condom stays on.

They cruise in Chris's car down Ocean Avenue, along the promenade. The streets are Sunday-crowded with jaywalking pedestrians, slowing progress to a crawl. Chris swerves into the first open parking spot they see, which is closer to the boardwalk than to Alice's house. "You wanna?" he asks, cocking his head toward the ocean.

"No, we should, I mean, *I* should—"

"Ten minutes," he says, taking her hand. "One last blast."

She nods, not at all sure why she's agreeing, and then just like that, they're flowing toward the music, the rides, the smoke of an Italian sausage stand, the din of the ocean. He's right, what's ten more minutes? She clings to his hand, as if to let go would set her adrift in this sea of bodies, never to find him again. She imagines that any passerby who notices them would definitely think they were made for each other, with their matching hair and matching jeans and what must be twin expressions on their faces—a little bit satisfied and a little bit selfish, understanding themselves to be apart from the rest of the world. It must be obvious to anyone who looks closely that they've just pulled themselves from bed. That they are lovers.

Chris says, "It's the first day of your post-virgin life."

She nods vaguely. "Now we never have to talk about it again."

The squeeze he gives her hand is a great relief.

Chris pulls out his wallet to pay for their boardwalk tickets—in a passing glance Ruby notices that twenties are bursting from the billfold. He said last night that he had a lot of cash, but this is really a lot.

Should she have asked for some for the motel? He should have offered to split the charge. A dark thought—this money was related to wanting to kill himself. Maybe he was going to give away all his money on the last day of his life. Or something.

She puts it out of her mind as he takes her hand and leads her onto the Funtown Pier, toward the Ferris wheel, and they dodge little kids and harried parents and groups of teenagers making noise and blocking the way. They are cut off by a rushing group of girls chanting among themselves, "Walk fast, beat ten people, walk fast, beat ten people," and then whooping as they secure a place near the front of the line. They remind Ruby of a certain kind of classmate at Barnard—athletic, nerdy, peppy to the point of annoying. Young for their age. There's one boy among this group, in white OP shorts and a T-shirt that reads IT'S FUN TO WORK AT CHICK FIL'A. His blond hair is feathered, his face lightly freckled. His voice, as he gossips breathlessly with the girls, is pitched high. He reminds her of Robin—of Robin a few years ago, in high school, when he was a little softer, a little—for lack of a better word—gayer.

Robin! She called him, last night, from a pay phone—she'd almost forgotten about that. Left some kind of half-drunken message. She should try him again, in case she said anything odd—though it's not likely he would worry about her, even if she did sound plastered. He's so wrapped up in his own life, he probably didn't give the message a second thought.

The line for the Ferris wheel moves fast. They slide into a two-person seat, behind a safety bar, which she lowers carefully, remembering Wendy's broken nail. Then they begin the lurch upward. The wheel stops and starts along the rotation as the seats fill up, until finally they're in motion, gathering enough speed to make her feel a little queasy. She put her body through so much yesterday. Chris is smiling, a brighter smile than she's ever seen take hold of his face. He's enjoying the rush of being raised up so high. He even lifts himself from the bench, as if he would take the whole ride standing, and she yanks him back with a playful slap, giggling as if she finds this funny. In fact, for a moment her imagination had turned sinister—she saw Chris jumping out, arcing through the air over the amusement park, clearing the planks of the boardwalk, plummeting toward the churning water down below. It's Jackson all over again—a fall that happened right before her eyes. So many years ago, but the fresh pain in her gut reminds her how quickly she can be taken back to those days. The worst time ever.

"OK, now we definitely have to get going," she tells Chris, as she finds her footing on the pier and feels some sense of balance returning.

"OK," he says. "If we walk fast, we'll beat ten people."

"You're a geek." As she smiles, she catches sight of a sturdy, dark-haired girl in a black skirt up ahead. As she turns her head, the flat features of her face, the catlike eyes, reveal themselves. "Hold on," she says to Chris. "It's Joanne."

She's strolling with a guy, her arm hooked through his in a strangely old-fashioned way. Ruby calls her name. Joanne turns and lets out a shriek of recognition. She pulls away from her man. The two of them, Ruby and Joanne, rush toward each other and fall into a hug like sisters at a family reunion.

"*Oh my God*, I am *so psyched* to see you," Joanne exclaims, enunciating dramatically and sounding at the same time absolutely genuine. "Hey—this is Tony," she adds, as her boyfriend catches up to them. He's about the same height she is, though factoring in her teased-up hair, he appears to be inches shorter. He's wide around the middle—side by side they're like an unbreachable human wall. Joanne nuzzles into his chest as if she's trying to shrink herself.

Ruby pulls Chris closer, and Joanne shakes his hand vigorously, saying, "How perfect is this?"

Ruby starts to explain that Joanne rescued her from Dorian last night, and Chris says with a smirk, "Yeah, I saw how that wound up."

Ruby says, "I can't believe I ran into you."

"Dis place ain't dat big," Tony says in an accent thick as the crust on a Jersey pizza.

Joanne says, "I didn't win anything last night. Remember? So I gotta win something for my birthday."

Ruby says, "Oh, that's right! It's today."

Tony says, "She'll celebrate for a frickin' week. She acts like it's frickin' *CHONNA-ker*—"

"Like what?" Chris asks.

"Like she's a Jew at Christmas and wants a stuffed animal a day for eight frickin' days."

"Oh, *Chonnaker,*" Chris says. "I always wondered how to pronounce that."

Ruby can tell that Chris is suppressing laughter. She squeezes his hand, wanting him to be kind.

Joanne says, "I believe in birthweeks. A whole week to celebrate."

Tony says, "'Cept with you it totally is *weeks*. Like, as in *plurals.*"

Now Chris's laughter begins to leak out. Tony breaks into a smile.

Joanne looks at Ruby and rolls her eyes. *Men*, she seems to huff. "Oh, Rubes, listen. Wendy? From last night."

"Wendy, yeah. What about—"

"Totally in trouble. Her cousin was there. At XS. He saw the whole thing, and he totally told his mom, who is Wend's Aunt Marie, so she told Wendy's mom, and like, *in trouble.*"

"I'm so sorry," Ruby says.

"Oh, come on! It's not your fault someone's mother punishes her."

But Ruby's apology is not only for Wendy's situation but also for Chris's behavior, as he continues to snicker uncontrollably, with no sign of stopping.

Joanne rambles on about Wendy coming home drunk and disheveled and facing her mother's wrath: "Totally grounded, totally took away the keys to the Datsun, which is like Wend's car bought and paid for with her own money, and plus on top of it had to go to mass at like 10 A.M. in the morning."

Ruby drops Chris's hand. Even Calvin, at his most vocally critical moments, was never rude to someone's face. Chris's unstoppable laughter is *at*, not *with*. Tony seems to have picked up on it, staring at Chris with a hardening look in his eyes.

Finally Joanne lowers her voice and says, "Rubes, is he *on* somethin'?"

"I think he's just punchy."

"Maybe someone oughtta punch *him*," Tony says.

"We didn't get a lot of sleep," Ruby says. Joanne squeals in obvious delight.

Joanne invites them to join her and Tony at Club XS for happy hour, but Ruby insists they need to get going. It clicks with Ruby in a way it didn't last night that Joanne is a local girl, that Club XS isn't some vacation hangout she stumbled upon but a regular part of her nightlife. It's not so different than when she herself goes below 14th Street in Manhattan looking for a good time. Joanne and Tony and Wendy are the "townies" Alice was disparaging yesterday. The term is supposed to be laced with pathos—these poor people stuck in this hick resort town, relying on wheels of fortune for birthday thrills. But of course there's nothing sad about Joanne. She's living her life just fine. She offers Ruby another sisterly embrace with a promise to stay in touch.

Tony continues to eye Chris, who at last has calmed and is straightening himself back up. "It's been real," he says, through sputtering breath. "Don't mind me, I'm just . . ." He doesn't finish.

When they're barely out of earshot, Chris says, "Dat was a *pisser*."

Ruby turns away from him. Without waiting, she moves toward the street.

"Wait up."

"We've wasted enough time already—" she snaps.

"They were *your* friends."

"So you could have tried to be friendly."

"That guy was ridiculous. I couldn't help laughing a little."

"A little?" She keeps up her pace.

Chris catches up to her. "Don't be mad at me," he says. She turns to meet his face. His wounded expression melts her anger. She doesn't want to fight—it ruins everything. But she hates snobbery. Her mother can be such a snob—so many expectations.

"Let's get to the house," she says. "Let's get this over with."

He nods and takes her hand again.

But when they turn the corner and Alice's rental comes into view, Ruby pulls from his grasp, with the excuse of pushing a flyaway strand of hair from her face, and then she creates a little physical distance between them. Chris says nothing. He probably understands that this could be awkward. She hopes he does. Calvin could be there.

They pass by the Deadheads and climb the front steps of Alice's house, passing the keg, overturned on the porch in a dirty puddle. Pop music blares through the screen door, a yearning male voice singing, *"I can dream about you, if I can't hold you tonight."* The house is emptier than Ruby had expected, and it's thoroughly trashed. Long-stemmed roses wilt in a browning heap atop chunks of glass. Empty liquor bottles lie scattered in every corner. On the same couch where she sat yesterday with Calvin, an unfamiliar guy snores heavily, drooling onto the shoulder of his blue football jersey. A sour smell permeates the air and seems to intensify the continuing pressure inside her skull. She should have asked Chris for more aspirin.

Chris is looking through the archway to the dining room, where Benjamin drops his face close to the table and emerges a few seconds later wiping his nose. So there's still coke in the house. Did he ever come down? Cicely is there, too, and Fuckin' Nick, shirtless now, rolling dice on the table, playing some kind of game. Alice blasts into the dining room, coming into view so quickly it's like she'd been shoved from the kitchen. Her hands are covered in yellow rubber gloves. She holds a squirt bottle in one hand and a sponge in the other and immediately leans over the table and begins spritzing and wiping. "Hey!" Benjamin shouts. "Back off, Mrs. Clean!"

"Alice?" Ruby calls out, to no reply. Louder, "Alice! Um, it's me."

All heads turn. Alice covers her nose and mouth, her eyes darting around in alarm, as if the room had just been swarmed by a SWAT team. And then clarity takes hold and she's immediately rushing toward Ruby. "I thought you were raped and left for dead in a Dumpster!" She clutches Ruby in a waft of ammonia that Ruby recoils from. "Where were you?"

Before Ruby can reply, Alice shoots a look at Chris, and her face darkens. "I knew it," she says.

"Nice to see you, too," Chris says.

Alice pulls Ruby toward the dining room table. "Come with me!"

Benjamin's bugged-out eyes scan back and forth from Ruby to Chris. His mouth takes on a twisted grin. His hair is an unkempt mop, a hundred little antennae sticking out every which way. He says, "What a gruesome twosome you are."

"What's happening, Ben," Chris mutters, nodding toward the powder shining on the table.

Benjamin says, "None of this for you unless you're nice to me."

"Is Calvin here?" Ruby asks.

"That's a fine question," Benjamin says.

"He's fuckin' looking for you and shit," Nick says.

"He's been looking for you all night," Alice adds. "No one knew where you were!"

Ruby feels her stomach tighten. "I called this morning. Someone picked up the phone."

"You called here?"

"I asked for you by name."

Alice says, "It was probably one of the Smurfs. We were invaded by Smurfs, an army of trashy boys dressed in blue. There was Jack Daniel's Smurf and Pizza Face Smurf—"

"And Loverboy Smurf," Cicely adds, "Last seen with Dorian." She motions with her head toward the bedrooms.

"We'll call him Date Rape Smurf," Benjamin says.

"Some girl answered the phone," Ruby offers.

"Fuckin' Smurfette," Nick says. Ruby notices that he's got a bruise the size of a postcard on his shoulder, as if he's fallen or been punched. Then she thinks of the scratch on her neck and reflexively pulls her hair forward to conceal it. She suddenly thinks of Dorian's clothes, discarded last night. In a parking lot. Where *was* that?

Alice reaches her arms wide. "The Smurfside Heights Varsity Football Date Rape Army! They totally stomped all over our lovely house. What about my security deposit? No one else is leaving until this place is spic-and-span!" Alice waves the squirt bottle like a wand, its nozzle dribbling onto the carpet. "I repeat. *No. One. Leaves.*"

Ruby says, "I just want to get my stuff from Calvin."

Cicely looks up from the table. "I'll help you, Alice."

Alice says, "Do a little blow, you'll get your energy back."

Chris says, "Ben, how much have *you* done?"

"It sounds like criticism when you talk that way. Come on, Christopher—have one for old times' sake."

"Old times being yesterday," Alice says, shooting a daggered look at Chris. "Ruby, let me make you a drinkie."

"I drank enough yesterday for the whole summer."

"But I went to the A&P and bought all the fixings for Bloody Marys. You know, there are tons of vitamins in the tomato juice, plus celery, orange slices, olives, and green peppers. It's liquid salad! Wait—do we have any vodka left?"

Alice runs to the kitchen, Ruby calls out after her, "Make mine a Virgin Mary."

"That's appropriate," Cicely says with a giggle, as Nick, at her side, chuckles along with her.

"Is it?" Benjamin asks. "Still?"

Ignore them. "If Calvin doesn't come back soon," she says, "I'm going to have to go. We don't want to drive in the dark."

"Relax," Benjamin says. "Pull up a chair." He kicks at the chair next to him and sends it tumbling backward with a thud onto the carpet.

Chris lifts it up and sits down, a simple gesture that Ruby can't help but find worrisome.

"That's better," Benjamin continues. "We can entertain each other with stories of our evenings. I'll start. Let's see, after we last saw you, I brought Dorian back here and held her hand while she puked in the toilet."

"I'm sure you completely did not," Cicely says. "I was the one who stayed with her."

"In my mind I was very helpful," Benjamin says. He turns to Ruby. "OK, now your turn."

His face, even in its amped-up state, still manages to convey such pleasure, such gloating, that she finds herself saying with a kind of spiteful pride, "It's none of your business where we spent the night."

Benjamin tsk-tsks and shakes his head in exaggerated disapproval. "I sense a new alliance here. I smell . . . consummation."

"Don't push it, Ben," Chris says. He adds, "Ruby, we can wait out front if you want." But he reaches for her, pulling her onto his lap. She sits stiffly, his thighbone a hard shelf under her rear end, wishing she had listened to him back in the hotel room, that they had skipped the house and just gotten on the road.

Alice reappears carrying a tray of pint glasses sloshing red liquid, each topped off with so many wedges of fruit and vegetables they could be tall, whimsical Easter bonnets. "This one's yours," Alice says, handing a slippery glass to Ruby. "I made it weak. What should we toast to?"

Cicely says, "To Ruby being safe and sound," and there's something so sincere in the tone of her voice that Ruby finds herself going along and clinking her glass with the rest of them. She's suddenly aware that her mouth is watering, ravenous for sustenance. The drink, it turns out, is loaded with vodka.

Benjamin raises his glass again. "To the last American virgin."

"Ben, I want to talk to you," Chris says. "Ruby, give me a minute, OK?"

She nods as Benjamin, with a theatrical flourish, rises from the table and disappears with Chris down the hall toward the bedrooms.

Alice turns to Nick. "Shoo. Time for girl talk."

"Like I fuckin' care?" he says. Ruby watches him stumble, shirtless and bruised, into the living room, where he rummages behind the couch and finds a telephone, receiver off the hook. He wanders onto the front porch with the phone in hand, stretching the cord to its limit.

She watches her chance to call her parents slip out the door with it. Another delay.

She reluctantly takes a seat. She gulps the Bloody Mary, vodka and all. Girl talk is not what she needs. What she needs is to get out of here, quickly. What she needs is to turn back the clock a few hours to place the calls to her parents that she failed to make. And then on top of that the irony of sitting here waiting for Calvin after having blown him off all night! She feels the liquor prickling her belly. Maybe it will actually help her hangover. Hair of the dog. She's heard her mother speak of that.

Alice leans close and asks, "Did you? With him?"

"I don't feel comfortable talking about it."

"You did!"

"That's between me and—"

"Poor Calvin," Cicely says.

"He's going to be crushed," Alice adds.

Ruby chomps at a celery stalk. The crunching reverberates inside her skull, drowning out the chatter, for a moment.

"It hasn't been working out," Ruby says, washing down the celery with another gulp. "I don't know what he's told you, but things between us—"

"So was it honestly your first time?" Cicely interrupts.

"What?"

"Last night, you and Christopher?"

"We relate to each other," Ruby offers. "That's all I'll say."

"Your soul must be as dark as his, then," Alice says. "I would not want my first time to be with Christopher. I dated him, I should know. Not to mention the size of it." She looks at Cicely and fans the air, as if cooling off a good sweat.

"You used to call it *the cucumber*," Cicely says, pulling a cucumber spear from her glass and giving it an obscene shake.

"You guys, stop, please," Ruby says. How could Chris have been with Alice—okay, she's pretty, in a blond, emaciated way—but how could he have allowed her access to his body? Whatever went on between them was some other thing, unlike what she shared last night. It *must* have been—Alice could not have drawn that kind of tenderness and attention from Chris. No way.

"I want to know what position," Cicely says.

"I'm not talking about it—"

"Did it hurt?"

"I guess."

"You *guess?*"

"Did you bleed a lot?"

"Well . . ."

"No?" Alice shoots Cicely a look. "Did he put it all the way in?"

"I'm not talking about this!" Ruby stands, drink in hand, and begins to move toward the hallway. She'll find Chris and they'll just get out of here, forget about Calvin and her overnight bag, enough is enough—but someone is suddenly right there, nearly crashing into her. The Bloody Mary bobbles in her hand. She looks up and comes face-to-face with Dorian.

"Watch it!" Dorian says, and then, "Oh, *you.*"

Ruby steps away from her, shaking tomato juice off her fingers. "I'm not looking for trouble."

Dorian stares, blinks, swallows. Her face looks drawn, mouth slack. Small crescents of white show under her irises as if her eyeballs are threatening to roll back into her skull. She wears a long T-shirt that barely covers her panties. Her stick-like legs are splotchy, as if they've been slapped.

She steps past Ruby and joins the others at the table. "What's she doing here?"

"Dodo, be nice," Cicely says. "Ruby lost her virginity last night."

"To Christopher," Alice snarls.

Dorian stares at Ruby and then says without much inflection, "Hooray." Ruby stands frozen in the doorway, ready for anything. Dorian adds, "Are you going to the kitchen? Can you bring me something to drink? Anything. Anything with alcohol in it."

"Um, OK," Ruby says, releasing a pent-up breath. Is this a truce? She turns once again toward the kitchen—and again nearly walks into someone, a guy in a blue football jersey, who has also emerged from the sleeping wing of the house. He must be the one who was with Dorian in the bedroom. Date Rape Smurf.

He mutters, "Sorry," and keeps moving. Through the dining room, into the living room. He leans over the couch and shakes the guy sleeping there. "Get up, Woz. We're outta here like Vladimir."

Ruby carries the open vodka bottle back to the dining room table, with a few plastic cups. Dorian pours a shot and downs it. She doesn't grimace, doesn't choke. She simply breathes deeply through her nose and sits up a little straighter.

The two remaining Smurfs leave through the front door. Dorian follows them with her eyes, and then turns to Alice and Cicely and says, "Do you think I'll get VD from him?"

"He's kinda the type," Cicely says. "You didn't use a rubber?"

"Give me a percentage. Fifty percent chance?"

Ruby sits down again, remembering the press of Chris's body on hers, the latex that came off inside. How long had he been thrusting without it? How worried should she be? "Have any of you ever—have you had it happen where the rubber comes off, while the guy is still—"

"Fucking you?" Dorian says.

With a kind of awe in her voice, Alice says, "That's a new one."

Cicely says, "If it came off and it was, like, *full,* then I'd be worried."

Dorian says, "Wanna come with me to the clinic? We can get our insides examined together. Female bonding. God, I do not want to have another abortion."

With each statement, Ruby feels a fissure moving up through her body, like a hairline on a thin sheet of glass, lengthening and fracturing into a delta, a web. A pain in her guts moves with it, expanding.

Alice says, "Ruby, if you're pregnant from Christopher, *promise me* you'll get an abortion."

"Can we change the subject?"

"It's not that bad," Cicely adds. "as long you don't think about what it really *is*."

"I know how to take care of myself," she hears herself saying, though the words are muted by the increasing feeling that her body is splitting into pieces.

"That's a horrible gene pool to pass on," Alice says. "I felt dirty after he fucked me."

Smash. Fragments splinter inside her, and then, without warning, she hears a noise escape up through her throat—a kind of moan like from an injured animal. The three girls stare at her, baffled.

"Why are you all so mean to me? Why?" Her voice shakes.

"No, no, no." Cicely scurries to her and attempts a hug. "We're looking out for you. These guys are all users. I mean, they're our friends, but they're totally users, too. Only your girlfriends will look out for you."

"You're not looking out for me—"

"Here, here, here," Alice says, pouring a shot of vodka and giving it to her. "You need to numb your feelings. It's too much to handle, I understand."

Ruby takes the cup and downs the shot and it's awful, the worst taste in the world, and it stings her insides as if invading open wounds. Alice grabs Ruby's Bloody Mary, plucks out the cucumber and the bell pepper and the orange wedge and the lime, and slides it over to her, and Ruby, sniffling, just drinks the whole thing down, coughing wetly when she's done. Her nose is runny, she's a mess all over again, leaking.

"I admit, I was a bitch," Dorian says. "But I don't believe you, that you're a virgin. That you were. I'm sorry, I just don't."

"What does it matter to you?" Ruby sniffs. "What if I wasn't?"

"I'm just an honest person," Dorian says. "I promote honesty."

"You weren't?" Alice says to Ruby.

"What?"

"That's why you didn't bleed."

Ruby stands up and pushes back from the table. "Not everyone bleeds." That's true, isn't it? She's heard that, hasn't she?

They keep talking, Alice, Dorian, and Cicely, about penetration and bleeding and virginity, about her and her night with Christopher, but she can hardly hear them beneath the noise emanating from deep inside her, a humming vibration, a kind of aftershock that is both sound and sensation moving along her nerves. Something's happening to me, she thinks, and then she looks up and sees that Chris is standing in the doorway.

He looks at her and says, "You weren't?"

"What?" She can barely register his presence. How long has he been there? What has he heard?

"Last night wasn't your first time?"

"I didn't say that."

"So you were? Or you weren't?"

"Why does it matter?"

Dorian says, "I knew it."

There's something wrong with him, she can see it in his eyes, but she can't put her finger on it, and then Benjamin walks in and he looks absolutely crazed, his mouth flapping, teeth grinding, and she realizes that they were doing coke together.

Ruby shoves Chris out of the way and runs down the dark hallway.

Where's the bathroom, where is it? She tries a door—it's a closet—then another. Someone is coming up from behind her, maybe it's Chris—no, it's Cicely, who follows her into the bathroom.

"Leave me alone," Ruby says, and then a wave rises up inside her, all the churning water beneath that cracked icy surface, it's rising up like an ocean wave. She snaps up the toilet lid, leans forward, and out comes a wash of tomato-red vomit.

She hears the door close, and then feels Cicely pulling her hair off her face, and she's grateful, so grateful for this small kindness, as another wave lets loose, and then another, her body rejecting the pressure she has subjected it to. Releasing the poison. It's as though her entire being has fallen into pieces, and everything old and ugly is forcing its way out.

Robin follows Calvin toward a cluster of three shabby houses, the rundown rentals on the block. The nearest one has a few long-haired boys hanging out in front on lawn chairs, glassy-eyed dudes in baggy shorts and tie-dye shirts, staring at the street as if waiting for something to appear. Does anyone still wear tie-dye? Then he sees that one of the shirts features a Grateful Dead logo on it, and it all makes sense. One of them raises his hand, less a wave than a signal. He pulls himself from the chair and ambles over, zeroing in on George and addressing him with, "Hey, brother. What's doing with you?"

George takes a step backward, checking the guy out. He's got a few blond dreads pulled back with a rubber band, and long stick arms and legs poking out of torn-up Army-issue shorts. The guy shifts his weight from foot to foot as he talks and swings his limbs like a rag doll shaken by the wind. "Brother, just wondering if you might know how to set us up with some ganja?"

"What are you," George asks, "a cop?"

The guy huffs out some surprised laughter. "Most definitely not."

"But you think I'm a dealer?"

"Naw, man. It's not like that. Just looking for some kind bud." He gestures toward his buddies. "We've got lots of brew, if you wanna swap."

The guy is sort of cute in a sloppy, dirtbag way, the kind of kid you see playing hacky sack outside the dorms, eating breakfast in the middle of the afternoon, sleeping in lecture hall. Robin knows a few of them from the drama department who build sets and work on the lighting board, wealthy white boys with dreads. Trustafarians. They're harmless. But the look in George's eyes is neither amused nor familiar. His gaze hardens and he pushes ahead, telling Calvin, "Come on."

The Deadhead calls after them, "No sweat, man. Have an excellent day."

Robin can see the tension in George's shoulders and back, his entire torso defensively coiling into itself. A pang of protectiveness hits him. He's dragged George into this mess, through this long day of insults, where everyone is projecting something on to him.

On the front porch of the next house, a guy, not wearing a shirt, sits astride a beer keg, talking on the phone. His shoulder is bruised, a yellowy purple blotch on alabaster skin. There's something sexy about this. The boy gives Calvin a nod of recognition, and mutters into the phone, "Calvin just brought over more fuckin' people and shit."

They have to step over the cord to get into the house. Following Calvin through the screen door, Robin feels a rush of something uncomfortable crash over him, a blindsiding wave. It could be fear, it could be sorrow, it could simply be a sense of being overcome by the unknown, but it has everything to do with trying, and failing, to connect his sister to this derelict place, which smells like spilled beer and spoiled food and looks like it's been vandalized by thieves. When he calls the cops, they're going to take one look around and want to arrest someone.

A tall, twitchy blond girl approaches them, her hands wrapped in yellow rubber gloves. "We found her, we found her."

"You found Ruby?" Calvin asks, and the girl, who must be his sister, nods.

"Is she OK?" Robin asks.

"She's in the bathroom."

"Where? Let me see her."

"Alice, this is Ruby's brother," Calvin says.

Alice covers her mouth with one yellow paw. She looks away from Robin and shakes her head as if she doesn't want to say anything more.

Another guy, with coked-out eyes and finger-in-the-socket hair, steps up alongside her. "So you're the notorious gay brother."

"Excuse me?" he says.

The guy turns to George, who stands behind Robin, his arms crossed, legs firmly planted, and asks, "And who are you?"

Calvin answers quickly, "This is George. He's the brains of the operation."

"Actually," George says, "I'm the muscle."

"So Calvin brought the A-Team?"

"What'd you just say?" Robin asks, feeling his patience stretched—for George's sake, as much as his own—feeling himself ready to snap if someone doesn't direct him to his sister.

"Hey, Frizzy," George says, taking an intimidating step forward. "Pipe down."

"A joke. Can't anyone take a joke?"

Robin says, "They always call it a joke after they insult you."

This guy rolls his eyes, muttering what sounds like "Eat my shorts," to which Calvin says, "Come on, Benjamin. Don't start anything."

Robin lets out a slow breath. He'd been wondering, for a single sickening moment, if this guy was the mysterious Chris.

Alice remains in front of them, shaking. She points toward the back of the house, saying, "Bathroom," and adding, "I am so, so sorry."

"Why? What happened?" Robin asks.

Alice sticks a finger in her mouth.

Robin marches past a dining table, where a skinny girl is pulling an oversized T-shirt over her knees as if made modest under Robin's glare, and frizzy-haired Benjamin nibbles on a fingernail as if he might chew it clean off. Like the bruised boy they passed on the front porch, these two might be good-looking if they weren't so sleep-deprived and haggard. Everyone here looks older than they are, as if they're already ruined by life.

Down the dimly lit hallway, Robin spies a scrawny boy in black knocking steadily against a closed door, repeating Ruby's name in a soft, plaintive voice. So this is Chris. It takes all the will Robin can muster not to shove him to the ground, like he did Douglas.

"I'm her brother," he announces.

"Oh, hey." Chris squints at him. "I can see the resemblance."

"You definitely want to move out of my way now." Chris does so, and Robin takes his place at the door. "Ruby? It's me. It's Robin. Will you let me in?"

There's some shuffling and mumbling from inside. The toilet flushes. Then the door pushes open just a crack, and a girl peeks out.

"Hi, I'm Cicely."

"Great to meet you, Cicely."

She seems to register the edge in his voice, seems to take this as a cue to let herself out. In a tone that reminds him of hospital nurses speaking in bone-chilling euphemism, Cicely says, "It's been a little bumpy in there."

He steps forcefully into the bathroom, closing the door behind him, banishing Chris to the hall with the click of the lock.

She's on the floor, at the base of the toilet, her arms wrapped around her stomach.

She's not moving, and for a moment he isn't sure she's breathing. Then, from beneath her limp black bangs, her glassy eyes seem to fix upon him. She wipes her lips with a finger.

Robin catches his breath. Good. OK. She's OK.

Her clothes are splashed with what he hopes is water and not puke. He doesn't even want to think about the soiled floor she's sprawled upon. There's nothing resembling a clean towel anywhere. He's disgusted to find her like this. How did this happen? How could she let herself? But then she says, "It's *you*," and there's a lilt of wonderment in her voice that completely dissolves his fury.

"Yeah, me." His throat constricts, emotion caught there, hard to swallow. He helps her sit up.

Miraculously, there's a fresh roll of toilet paper on the back of the tank. He wraps a soft, thick wad around his hand, dampens it in the sink, and pats down Ruby's face. She feels warm and dry, almost feverish. "You need some water."

"I haven't had any."

"Maybe that's why you're so sick." The plastic cup in the toothbrush holder has about a inch of brown liquid in it. He dumps it into the sink. The frayed end of a cigarette butt spills out, joining the other cigarette butts already dissolving against the porcelain like dark, tiny worms. He rinses the cup, doing his best to scrub it out, even without soap, then fills it. "Don't sip," he tells her. "Gulp." He looks at her throat as the water passes into her. Sees her start to revive. He feels in this moment more clearheaded than he has all day, all weekend, maybe for even longer than that: The ability to help someone clearly in need seems to organize all the confusion of the world into simple, identifiable tasks.

From somewhere in the house comes the sudden noise of a scuffle. Voices are raised, chairs scrape the floor, something crashes into something else. Calvin is shouting. Chris is shouting back. Then George's voice breaks in, commanding, "Hey! Hey!" and there's an abrupt, loud, hollow thud that could be the impact of a body against a wall, followed by a piercing scream from one of the girls.

"What's that?" Ruby asks.

"Don't worry," Robin says, though he hopes it's Calvin beating the hell out of Chris.

"I can't stay here with these people," she says.

"I'm with George. We have his car."

"We have to . . ." She mumbles words that he can't make out, but when he doesn't respond, she clears her throat and repeats, "*We have to go to the grave.*"

"OK," he says. "One thing at a time."

"Did I tell you 'bout the last time I went to Jackson's grave?"

"I don't know, Ruby. Can we talk about this later?"

She bobs her head in apparent agreement, though he sees some complicated pain in her eyes, some unexpressed emotion passing across her face. Then she says, "Chris."

"What about him?"

"He needs me."

"I'm not so sure about that."

"He *does*. You don't understand." One hand on the lip of the sink, she pulls herself up, shaking off Robin's hand when he tries to help.

Their eyes meet in the mirror, and he sees so clearly what Chris had just noticed, how much they resemble each other. There are traces of each of their parents in both of their faces, arranged in different proportions. They'll always have this similarity, this undeniable bond that marks them as brother and sister. And then he sees that there's a tiny bite mark above her collarbone, and another scratch on her neck, a little pink welt, and he feels himself pull away from her, resisting that bond. Maybe she notices, because her expression changes, too. She comes to alertness, steeling herself against him. So she's serious about this boy. It doesn't make any sense to Robin, because if it weren't for Chris, would she even be in this state right now? She's acting against her own interests, he's sure of it, which means that right now he simply knows better than her. It's a feeling that's more parental than brotherly.

"You wash up," he says, heading back into the hallway. "I'll deal with Chris."

* * *

As he makes his way toward the kitchen he hears sobbing.

Alice stands near the refrigerator, weeping into Cicely's chest, as the larger girl runs a comforting hand through her hair. The other boy is there, the coked-out nail-biter. When he sees Robin, he announces, "All hell just broke loose," with just enough of a wicked smile on his face to send a shiver down Robin's spine. His eyes dart to the dining room, where the shirtless boy is picking up chairs that have been knocked over. There's a *National Enquirer* spread open to a headline reading "Rock Hudson's Secret Life." A rolled ten-dollar bill rests on top of it. A spattering of Bloody Mary gives the place the look of a massacre.

"Where's Chris?" Robin asks.

Alice breaks from her wailing. "He's never allowed back here again!"

Cicely adds, "Calvin kicked him out."

"What the fuck kind of party is this?" Robin asks. "Someone should call the fucking cops on you."

Alice's eyes go wide. "They've already been here once."

"When?"

"In the middle of the night."

"Did anyone happen to tell them that my sister was missing?"

Alice leans back into Cicely and resumes her sobbing. Cicely shakes her head reproachfully, glaring at Robin.

The nail-biter says, "Your sister sure knows how to stir up trouble."

"Don't say one fucking word about her," Robin answers. "Not a word."

In the living room, he finds George sitting on the couch alongside Calvin, who is applying pressure to his nose with a bloodstained dishrag. "I don't think you broke it," George is saying. "Keep the pressure on."

"It hurts," Calvin says.

"I want to take my sister home," Robin says, stepping closer to George.

"To Manhattan?"

"No, I think to Greenlawn. For starters, anyway."

"Aren't you supposed to be back at work tomorrow?"

"I can't think about that right now," Robin says, though what he's thinking, and what George likely realizes, too, is that if Robin doesn't show up, he'll be fired. Probation violated, end of story. A chain reaction of consequences tumbles forth from there: no rent money, no way to stay in Philly without a job, no more living with George.

He says, "I can't let any of these boys drive Ruby home. No way."

"It's cool, I get it," George says.

"So you'll take us?"

George nods. "I'm with you." There's sweat on his brow, the sheen of whatever effort he just expended.

Robin puts his hand on George's shoulder. "I'm sorry about all of this. I'm sorry I keep having to find reasons to say I'm sorry." He feels himself just barely holding back everything tender he wants to express. This is no time for emotion, here in this room, amid this chaos.

From behind them, Calvin's voice: "I think it stopped."

Robin pivots to see him standing, his nose crusted in blood, a smear of crimson on his cheek. And then he sees that Calvin is staring across the room. At Ruby.

She stands in the hallway, pale and quiet, a ghostly version of herself. Her eyes dart about nervously.

Calvin stares at her. "We gotta talk, Ruby."

"My bag is still in your car," she says.

"Come with me. I'll drive you back to the city."

"I can't go with you."

"Why not?"

Robin steps between them. "Ruby, I don't want you leaving my sight. George is driving us back to Greenlawn."

Calvin throws his arms wide, raises his voice melodramatically. "So that's it? 'Get my bag, Calvin.' And then I just sit here bleeding? Ruby, where the fuck have you been? With that guy? That maniac? What the fuck?"

Robin says, "Calvin, don't push it." But he sees that Ruby hasn't flinched, even in the face of this outburst.

"I apologize," she says.

"Great. That's fucking great. I'm sorry, too, Ruby, I'm sorry I ever got involved with a bitch like you." He spins around, almost a full rotation, as Robin had seen him do back at the bar, his frustration like an involuntary spasm. "You, too. Fuck off, Robin."

Robin calls after him, but Calvin is already out the door and down the steps, his long legs taking him quickly away. Ruby follows Calvin with her eyes, and Robin sees how unnervingly calm she is, how seemingly without remorse at the end of this relationship. She lets her gaze travel once again across the wreckage of the party, like she's committing the place to memory. The finality of this is almost chilling.

He tells her to stay put, tells George to remain here with her, and then he heads out the door after Calvin, promising to return with Ruby's bag.

On the sidewalk he has to jog to catch up, and by the time he gets to Calvin, he's winded.

"Slow down."

"Why should I?"

"Come on." Robin pulls out his cigarettes, waves them at Calvin. This does the trick; at last he stops. "Look, you did a good thing," Robin says, lighting one for each of them, remembering his lessons: *become like the person you need to impress*. "I know this is messed up, I know you're pissed—"

"She's rejecting me. That's what's going on. For that slime bag. You have no idea what that feels like."

Robin exhales and says, "Actually, I just got dumped yesterday."

"Really?" Calvin looks him in the eye. "That guy, the one I met at your play?"

"Yeah, that one. And for all I know he's off with someone else already."

"That's so unfair," Calvin moans.

It *is* unfair, Robin thinks. But there sometimes seems to be a finite amount of fairness in the world, as if no one can gain unless someone else loses, all of them kept in cruel balance with each other.

"For all I know, Peter did me a favor. Maybe Ruby's doing you a favor."

Calvin waves dismissively and resumes walking down the street, at last locating his car, a newish Saab parked too close to the corner. A parking ticket is stuck under the wipers. "Fucking great," Calvin mumbles, throwing the ticket into the front seat, where it lands on another one. "I'll just send that to your sister."

He pops the trunk and pulls out a bag. Robin recognizes it as one he gave to Ruby for her birthday, black leather bands around gray canvas, still in good shape. He remembers writing in the card: "For your next adventure." He'd imagined her traveling overseas, or maybe out west, to California, anywhere beyond New York and New Jersey, where she's spent her entire life.

Calvin is staring at the bag as if he wants to plant a bomb in it and send it back to Ruby with a ticking timer inside.

"Calvin, I'm sure there's someone else for you, a better fit. I'm sure."

"Right. Like anyone would go out with me." He slumps against the car, puffing at the cigarette.

"What's that supposed to mean?"

"People hate me."

"Come on."

"It's not a big fucking secret. I can handle it, you know? I'm an outsider."

"I don't hate you. You can be a big baby, like you're being now—" Calvin frowns, and Robin adds quickly, "—but you're a good person. You did a good thing, calling me, searching for Ruby. Just because she's not grateful doesn't mean it wasn't the right thing to do."

"What kills me is she spent the night with that guy. She probably gave it up for him."

Robin exhales. "Calvin, you'll have some good sex in your life, don't worry." He rests his hand on Calvin's arm, wanting to calm him down, and wanting to get back to the house.

Calvin stares at Robin's hand, long enough that Robin has to wonder what exactly he's thinking. Then Calvin says quickly, "You know I'm bisexual?"

Robin coughs. He almost loosens his grip, then decides to hold steady. "You are? I mean, sure, I kind of figured—"

"I was going to tell Ruby. But I was afraid she'd break up with me. Ha!"

"Have you . . . done anything?"

"I messed around with one guy. He was there, just now."

"It wasn't Chris, was it?" He drops his arm.

"No. Benjamin."

The nail-biter. Of course.

"It didn't mean anything. But, yeah, we messed around a little last summer. I made the move. Before I met Ruby."

"Maybe you'll get to explore this side—"

"It's not a big deal," Calvin says, suddenly brusque. "Everyone's bisexual. I've been reading a lot of theory. Marcuse calls it polymorphous perversity. Everyone in an ideal world would be able to express it. Bisexuality is inherently a critique, because it refuses the dualistic labeling of sexuality."

"Right. Kinsey said we're all on a scale somewhere."

"I'm not saying I'm smack in the middle. I mean, I still like a nice set of tits."

"Of course."

Robin looks up the block. He's ready to go now, worried that he's been away from Ruby again for too long. George is with her, though. George will take care of things.

Calvin says, "You figured it out? That's what you said, just now."

"The script," Robin says. "Look, I really need to get back to—"

Calvin snaps his fingers. "The best thing that could come out of this is that my script gets a jolt of new energy. I'm thinking I should have Agnetha take off with some other guy, while Carter goes looking for her. Do you think that would work? I mean, based on what you read?"

"It could . . ."

"Because you get the undertone that runs through it, that Carter's really lusting after his friend, right?"

"Oh, yes, that was apparent." Seems even more apparent now, knowing that Bennett in the script comes from Benjamin in life. But, really, Benjamin, that wiseass? The one who was so quick to label Robin gay as soon as he met him, who insulted George with that Mr. T. crack? Calvin seems to lack the capacity for good judgment. "Why don't you let Carter become more aware at the end?"

"You mean in the bathroom? It's supposed to be ambiguous."

"But it's kind of a cliché. The whole thing with the razor."

"It is? Because I'm, like, morally opposed to cliché."

"So don't make the sexually confused guy come off as *weak*. It's not the 1950s, you know." And then he says something he hadn't planned to say, though as soon as he does it seems true. "I'd like to play a character who's more ready to deal with being gay. Or bi. Whatever you want to call it."

"See, this is why I knew you needed to take that role, because you're in tune with the themes and motifs I'm interweaving into this, and the social context of imagery and so forth." Calvin opens the Saab's back door and pulls a notebook off the floor. "I'm going to stay here and write some of these new ideas down."

"Good. I'll take the bag and get Ruby. Do you want me to give her a message?"

"No, fuck her. Sorry. I mean—tell her if she wants to maintain any sort of friendship she's going to have to make it up to me. I'm serious.

I'm not gonna go sniffing after her like some kind of pussywhipped guy."

"Will do."

Robin gives Calvin another squeeze on the arm. Calvin looks up at him and beams. It's surprising, this genuine affection. But it passes soon enough, and he returns his attention to his notebook, his hand looping across the lined pages in a fit of inspiration.

Robin turns and moves back down the street, his sister's case in his grip. The bag is remarkably heavy, as if she had packed for a longer journey.

From the front porch, she calls out to the Deadheads in the lawn chairs, "Did you see a guy come out here—black hair, red T-shirt?" They send her vacant stares and shrugs. She looks up and down the street. Only a few trees. Little shade or shelter. Nowhere to hide, but no sign of Chris.

She can't be sure he hasn't left for good. He knows she lied to him. Then Cicely wouldn't let him in the bathroom. Then Calvin picked a fight and might have hurt him. He could have decided enough was enough. And if she's right—that he got high with Benjamin—he could have followed that buzzing energy anywhere. She takes a few steps into the front yard, a plot of arid ground between the stoop and the sidewalk, more gravel than grass. There's a wobble to her step, some leftover dizziness. She wonders if that was alcohol poisoning. A hot merciless wind sends a wad of Kleenex sputtering along the sidewalk. The toe of her boot snags on something in the dirt. She reaches down and with one finger pries up what seems to be the lower half of a bikini, a riot of color, coated in filth. At that moment she senses eyes upon her. A woman her mother's age is sweeping the sidewalk a few houses down, scrutinizing her.

"Day and night, nothing but a racket," the woman snarls. "You should be ashamed."

"No, I'm not part of this—" Ruby begins and then stops, because the woman's accusatory expression doesn't change, and really, why would it? To her, Ruby is just one more troublemaker here for the weekend, blazing a path of destruction in the name of partying. And anyway, Ruby *is* part of this. She's smack in the middle of it.

The soiled bikini bottom dangles from her finger. In a flash she remembers a preposterous thought that soared across her mind as she leaned over the porcelain bowl and emptied herself out—the idea that throwing up would somehow protect her from pregnancy. That the violence of the act would—what? Loosen any fertilized egg that wanted to attach itself inside of her? She feels a repulsive shudder travel down her back. She flicks the bikini to the ground again. The woman with the broom, still watching, lets out a disapproving grunt. Ruby drags the cloth with her boot toward the porch steps, as if this might make a difference. What if she is pregnant and she never sees him again? What if he kills himself—would she have to keep the baby, to keep him alive?

"Hey, Ruby—over here."

She recognizes his voice before she sees him—already she knows what her name sounds like coming from his mouth—and then there he is, just a little ways down, sitting on the hood of a car, exactly as he'd done outside the club. Sitting and waiting. *Thank you, God.* She has the strong impulse to run to him, grab his hand, and drag him away. To disappear together once more and not tell anyone. Wasn't everything fine until they came back here? The room at the Island Beach Motor Lodge is paid for. She can go home tomorrow, after another night with Chris. She can visit Jackson's grave tomorrow, too. A day late, yes, but she can memorialize his *birthweek.* She walks slowly to him, her steps controlled.

Chris's face is puffy on one side. There's a bright red patch where his jaw meets his neck—is that from Calvin? It nearly mirrors the scratch Dorian gave her last night. It repulses her, all this fighting. They're supposed to be adults, but they're as primitive as wild animals.

"You and me," he says. "That's all I care about." He slides off the hood and reaches for her hand. He wants to take her away. Already she can read his intention in a single gesture. The desire apparent in his body language. There's something so powerful in that knowledge. But she stops short. Because it's not last night anymore, and now there are too many questions.

"Did you?" she asks.

"What?"

"Did you do coke with Benjamin? Just before, in the house?"

"Benjamin's always got coke. Fucking Scarface."

She press her lips together, waiting.

He hunches his shoulders guiltily. "I did one little half-line. I was just trying to slow him down."

"Slow him down?"

He drops his head, looks at his hands. "I was confused. He was talking all kinds of shit. About you. That you weren't really—"

"What? A virgin?"

He shakes his head. "Never mind."

"That's what he said, right?"

"Is it true?"

Now she finds herself looking away, trying to come up with the words. "It has nothing to do with you."

A grunt, the sound of pain being absorbed, releases from his throat. "Just tell me it wasn't Calvin."

"It wasn't."

"Because for all you know he has AIDS."

"Why would you say that?"

"Because he's got homo tendencies! Everyone knows that."

He's clearly still wired, his mind unsettled, his thoughts spinning like a boardwalk wheel of fortune, round and round he goes and where he'll land nobody knows. In the periphery of her vision Ruby sees the woman with the broom standing still, taking all of this in. Ruby steps closer to him and deliberately lowers her voice. "You were the one who didn't want to keep the condom on. So don't talk to me about AIDS."

"At least I'm not a liar. You let me think you were—that you hadn't—"

"Why does it matter to you?"

"You said I was the first." He really does sound upset—she understands why. She let him believe it.

But her anger is strong, too. "You're just mad that you didn't get to screw a virgin. You'd say anything to get in my pants, wouldn't you? You probably didn't even plan to kill yourself."

"How can you say these things to me?"

"Because I don't know you!"

There's a clang from across the street, the metal lid of a garbage can banging into place. The woman there yells, "I'll call the cops on you!"

"Fuck you," Ruby screams. "You're not my mother!"

The woman drags the back of her hand up her throat, flicking out a fuck-you, and then she scurries off into her house. Maybe she will call the cops. Maybe they'll be here any minute.

Chris is staring at her through his droopy bangs, and what she can see in his eyes is pure pain. She thinks she should take back the words she just shouted at him, but she can't. It doesn't work that way.

At last, he says, "OK, maybe I did a little tiny line, like that long and that wide." He holds two fingers together, a sliver of air between them. "But I'm not like Benjamin, I'm not a fucking cokehead. I'll stop. I'll never do it again if you don't want me to. I didn't know it would bother you." He drops his head in his hands, whimpering, "I'll totally stop, if you'll be my girlfriend. If you wanted me to never do coke, or any other drug, ever again, and that meant we could spend all our time together—that I could be your *boyfriend,* for real—I would stop."

"I don't need a boyfriend, I need a lover." For a split second she isn't sure if she's said these words aloud or simply thought them. But then he shakes his head and without warning begins to walk away. She doesn't want to chase after him but she can't let him leave like this. "Chris—wait! I just meant—"

Over his shoulder, he says, "No, I get it now. You're not a sign. You're a temptation I was supposed to resist."

She rushes to him, grabs him by the arm, halts his retreat.

"You can pretend this never happened," he says, voice drained of emotion. "Pretend you're a virgin and find another stupid guy to fall in love with you."

His face is a mask, is stone, but even in his impassivity she sees the face she fell in love with last night—she did fall in love, didn't she? What else could she call it? Would they be tearing each other apart if it was anything else?

"Listen, Robin wants me to go with him."

"I thought I was taking you—"

"I can't get in the car with you. Not if you're high."

He drops to the sidewalk. Just crumples so that he's sitting on the curb, his head in his hands. From above, she watches as he begins shaking. "Who's going to take care of me? I don't have anyone."

"Ruby!"

She raises her eyes and sees her brother, standing at the curb, with George nearby. She'd been so intent on Chris she'd forgotten that all of this was in view of Alice's house. And she hadn't realized that the rest of them were there, too, the whole sordid gang—Alice, Benjamin, Dorian, Cicely, Nick—gathered on the porch like they're posing for a yearbook photo. The Wasted Club. Mean Kids of America. The Young and the Useless. All of them, taking in the show. Captivated. At least Calvin is not among them—a small blessing. *Thank you, God.*

Robin marches toward her, carrying her overnight bag. "It's time," he says. "I just put in a call to Clark."

"You did?"

"He said thanks for making his Father's Day so special."

She scowls, certain that this isn't true. Clark isn't sarcastic like that. She wants Robin to understand what she's been through. "OK, OK, we'll go. But you haven't met Chris yet, have you?"

Robin looks down at Chris, slumped beneath them. "We met," he says, icily.

Chris's smooth, pale face is now damp with tears. "I was hoping Ruby could stay," he mutters. He lifts his arm to Ruby, as if to keep from sinking.

George is there, next to Robin. Always at his side. Why is *George* here, anyway? Why did Robin have to bring him? George, however, does something remarkable. He crouches down next to Chris and very gently but clearly says, "Hey, brother, listen. It's just not the right time, OK?"

Chris flicks his head toward George. He casts his sad eyes upon them all. "Guys, you don't know me, so maybe you won't believe me, but—I'm in love with Ruby."

So it is true. He's feeling what she's feeling. He's going to forgive her.

"That's great," Robin says, not very convincingly. "But how about some perspective, OK? If you love somebody, set them free, right?"

"Right," George adds. "Love is patient. Love conquers all."

Ruby tightens her hand around Chris's. "Why are you guys being such jerks?"

Robin begins to back away, but he keeps his eyes on her. "I'm giving you one more minute. *One*."

She can see that she really has to go.

"What are you going to do?" she asks Chris.

"Go back to the motel, I guess. The sheets still have you in them."

She leans in for one more kiss, taking his face in her hands. His mouth responds desperately. They sink into each other. At the same time she feels herself carried up and away from the lies and the angry words, from the pain. She is free again, free from doubt, as she'd been last night, when she put her trust in him. This has all been a test—this kiss is the proof that they have passed. Are the others still watching?

Let them. Let them see there's something strong here, stronger than what any of them have ever known. Let them witness this. True love should have a witness.

"Damn, that scene was *white*," George says as the three of them move down the sidewalk, "White people, white music, white drugs."

"Now you know why I didn't stick around last night," Ruby says.

"Because you're *not* white?"

She flinches at George's sarcasm, which is so unlike him. "Because it was gross," she says.

They reach a big gray Cadillac, which Ruby recognizes as George's, going all the way back to Greenlawn. His parents always had Cadillacs. They passed the old ones on to their kids and bought a new one every few years. It seemed so showy at the time, all those big boats. But now the body is dinged and scratched, the back bumper dented. Age—or West Philly—has taken its toll.

"Can I have shotgun?" she asks. "So I don't get sick again?"

"No. You can't," Robin says, and gets in the passenger side.

She looks at George as if he might help, but he simply slips in behind the wheel.

For the first time it occurs to her to wonder how the two of them wound up here. There was no plan for this. Someone called Robin. Someone called because she was missing. Which means this whole thing got bigger than she ever stopped to consider.

As soon as George steers the car toward the long, broad bridge that spans the bay, Robin spins around in his seat. "Do you mind telling me what the fuck you've been thinking?"

So condescending. So aggressive. So *Robin*. He could have just eased into a conversation instead of going for the jugular. Now she has to defend herself, after he's seen her leaning over the toilet, seen the coke on the table, the empty keg on the porch, the bottles everywhere all over the house. Seen the results of punches thrown, and Chris in tears. She says. "I didn't ask you to come here."

"No, your *boyfriend* did."

"Things are over between me and Calvin."

"You should thank him," Robin says. "He was worried about you."

"You're just taking his side—"

"There are no *sides* here, Ruby."

"—because you want to be in his dumb movie."

"That's ridiculous."

"He's never going to make a movie, Robin. He's all talk. He never *works* for anything."

"He worked pretty hard to find you." She hears a quivering in Robin's voice that tells her she has rattled him. He *does* care about Calvin's movie. It's not surprising—he's so focused on what he wants, he hasn't considered that getting involved with Calvin would impact her. Robin adds, "For all his faults, Calvin means well."

"Too bad he's such a lousy kisser."

From the driver's seat, George lets out a low whistle. "Harsh."

She hates that George is here, that Robin has an ally while she's on her own. It's like when she first started dressing the way she wanted to, and Dorothy called in Nana so they could gang up on her. Not good cop/bad cop, but bad cop times two. Maybe it's better if she says nothing at all. She doesn't owe them anything.

But Robin persists. Did she have this all planned out ahead of time? Was she with him all night? Nobody knew where she was! She was facedown in the bathroom! On and on like that, until she snaps, "I'm not some damsel in distress, so stop trying to play the hero."

George catches her eye in the rearview mirror. "You got in a *bar brawl.*"

Robin adds, "George left his shift early, so we could find you."

"I didn't ask George to get involved."

"But he *did.* Doesn't that mean anything to you?"

George says, "I seem to remember a message on our machine—"

"That message was for Robin. This is between me and my brother."

George says, "I just thought you might appreciate another point of view."

"Since when is your view any different from his? You follow him around like a puppy."

"*Excuse* me?" He pivots and glares at her—it's nerve-racking, the way he takes his eyes off the road. She's aware now of the traffic thickening around them as they approach the bridge.

"I'm just saying, George, speak for yourself."

"Speaking for myself, how about I kick you out of my car?"

"Fine with me. I'll call Chris."

Robin says, "Ruby, stop being so obstinate."

Obstinate? she wants to shout. *I'm trying to stand up for myself.* But saying this out loud would sound childish, like "You're not the boss of me," and they won't be convinced, anyway. They pushed her into an argument that she can't win, and now whatever she says will only prove to them that she's at fault. At fault for what? Causing worry? Is that such a crime?

She takes a deep breath. Scrambles for another tactic. Says, "You've been doing what you want your whole life, Robin. Without telling anyone where you were going or who you were with. So don't *moralize*."

He is silent for a moment. Then he says, "That's different." But there's not much strength in the statement.

A point for me. Finally. "Look, my head is pounding, and I just puked my guts out. You don't even know what I've been through."

She expects him to just leave her be, but of course, her brother never lets anyone else have the last word. He always has to win. So she's not surprised when he says, "We've been through some shit, too." And she's also not surprised when he punctuates this by turning on the radio and with an angry flick of his wrist, cranking the volume. It must have been tuned to some other station, now out of reach, because a blast of static erupts. She watches him spin the knob until he picks up something familiar, the "*Hey, hey, hey, hey*" of that song from *The Breakfast Club*. She can picture the singer in the video, in his sharp suit and floppy hair, encircled by monitors, faces whizzing by as if everything in his life is closing in.

Why did she get in the car with them? Why didn't she stay with Chris? This is torture. She *chose* this, instead of doing what Chris had asked—she could have gone back to their room, spent another night being treated like someone special instead of someone being blamed for everything. Instead, she left things with him on shaky ground. All those accusations. He was trying to forgive her, and she was such a bitch. But that last kiss. Maybe that was enough to let him understand.

She glances through the back window at the receding town—water tower, squat little houses, billboards advertising real estate. There's the Ferris wheel in the distance, looping people round and round, dropping them off where they started. She has the sensation of being pulled in two directions at once—toward her family and toward her lover. She looks at the ring on her finger, the fake red stone, wishing it was a crystal ball that would reveal to her his face, his state of mind. Is he at the motel already? Is he lying in their bed and thinking of her? Is he mad, upset, afraid? What if he's miserable, feeling hopeless, what if he's given up on her? She forms an image of him walking out of their hotel room, across the beach, toward the ocean. He passes oblivious families and girls in bikinis rubbing Coppertone on each other's shoulders, the lifeguards unaware that the boy in the black jeans has rocks in his pockets. Would anyone stop him? Or will the riptide pull him in and under, his last steps invisible to every living soul? *Please, God,* she starts, a plea for his safety. But she cuts off her own thought. There is no assurance from above, from the great beyond. When has there ever been? God won't save Chris. Only she can.

What is she thinking there, in the backseat, her head turned toward the ocean, her gaze upon the town they've left behind? Is she retracing her steps, wishing she had made better decisions, wishing that she hadn't vanished for a night and a day? Is there any sense of remorse in her, or is she simply mooning over that messed-up boy? Robin wants to yell at her again, and keep at it, until there's some sign that she gets just how much disruption she caused and how dangerous it was to go off with a stranger like that. On this day, of all days! And yet, the fact that she's here with him, that they're in the car together, driving away, is such an enormous relief that he wants simply to embrace her. Really, the way she looked on that bathroom floor, he feared for a moment she might be dead.

It was petty of him, not letting her have the front seat. He remembers all too well her motion sickness from when they were little kids. Long trips were always a problem. She'd hit a point where her face would drain to a sudden pale green, as if her blood had been replaced by poison, and they'd have to pull over quickly. Sometimes she threw up. Sometimes she just needed to stand still and breathe fresh air for a while. Then she'd take the passenger seat, and Dorothy would switch to the back. Robin would take the hump in the middle, because even though Jackson was smaller he could never sit still and he would drive Dorothy crazy as he bounced up and down, chattering nonstop.

Not long before Dorothy and Clark announced their separation there was a road trip to Massachusetts to see Nana in Northampton. There was no Jackson then. There was the abyss where he had been, a vacuum, a force without shape. An hour into the journey, Dorothy, sitting up front, lit a cigarette. Her smoking, which for years had been covert and intermittent, had emerged after the funeral as a regular habit. A minute later, Ruby was complaining, "It's giving me a headache," to which Dorothy said, "It's psychosomatic," a word Robin had never heard before, though he instantly grasped Dorothy's meaning: Ruby wasn't really feeling sick from the smoke, she simply didn't like it, and she was making it worse for herself. But as Ruby began to moan, Robin saw that it was his mother who was making it worse. "Dad," Robin said, speaking up for his sister, "you might have to pull the car over." Since they were on the highway, a quick stop was impossible, so Clark yelled at Dorothy to put it out. "I'm exhaling out the window," she said, "it's not even reaching the backseat." She took a few final fitful puffs, before flicking her fingers and sending the butt flying to the road. For the rest of the day, Ruby sulked, and Dorothy found reasons to snap at her.

That day for Robin came to be a marker: the start of a long period of open hostility between his mother and his sister. It got so bad that when Dorothy first told him she had found an apartment in Manhattan, he was afraid she wouldn't take Ruby along with them, would leave her in Greenlawn with Clark. There was never any real chance of this happening, but the notion had power. A foundation of doubt had solidified, and until all three of them actually relocated, he found himself asking his mother again and again about her plans for Ruby: what school would she go to, how would she get to school, what would her new bedroom be like, was the kitchen large enough for a table they all could sit at together? Each answer was a bulwark against an even greater splitting of their family. He knew he couldn't keep his parents together, but his sister was his responsibility.

So what do you say to your little sister when she has clearly fucked up, but you've spent most of your life trying to shield her from harm? Shouldn't he just forget everything that happened over the past day? She wasn't kidnapped or raped; she'd emerged with only a scratch and some nausea. She would recover from drinking too much. He will get her back to safety, and they'll be together on Jackson's birthday, as she wanted all along.

Don't you forget about me, I'll be alone, dancing you know it baby. He likes this song, likes the catchy way it ends in a string of *la-la-la-la.* He sings along, tries to take his mind off all this drama.

But it's that boy. Chris. It's the fact that *he* didn't keep her from harm. It's the sight of the two of them arguing in the middle of the street one minute and then making out the next. Who does that? One of those creepy straight boys expecting a girl to take care of him, even when she's someone else's girlfriend. The type who claims to be in love to justify the fact that he pressured her into sex. Ugh, did Ruby have sex with him? She never did with Calvin; there was only that one brute in high school, the one who pressured her into sex without a condom. Did she use a condom with Chris? In the message she left on the answering machine, Ruby said something about knowing this guy from her God Squad days. If he's a Catholic, maybe he doesn't believe in birth control. The Roman Catholics have been railing against condom use, even with the news that it can stop AIDS. Robin has memories of her on the phone with a boy back then, lengthy conversations behind closed doors. So this strung-out character is the same one she met at a Catholic retreat all those years ago? Unbelievable.

George is watching him, reading the worry on Robin's face, reaching across to stroke the back of his hair. Their eyes hold.

Hours ago, during the ride into Seaside, anger had flared between them; now, heading out into the slow-moving exodus, they are once again on the same team. Ruby's troubles have given them a way to stand together. He closes his eyes and accepts what George is offering: a sensation of being held in the palm of his hand.

George looks into the rearview mirror. "I think Her Highness fell asleep."

Indeed, her eyes are closed; her breath makes a soft whistling sound. Her face still carries some tension, as if she's fallen off in the midst of bad emotion.

"You know how all of this could have been avoided?" George asks.

"How's that?"

"If we all had car phones. She could have reached us here, and we could have turned around hours ago."

"Ha! But that still would've depended on Ruby actually calling someone."

"My Pop was talking about getting one. His guy at the Cadillac dealer says you can get one for the car that runs off the lighter. It's the wave of the future."

"I hope I live to see it," Robin says.

"What's that mean?"

"Nothing."

As they merge onto the Garden State Parkway, the evening is still bright as the early afternoon, maybe even brighter, now that the final traces of last night's storm clouds have been blown from the sky, leaving pale blue in every direction. If the traffic isn't too bad, they'll get to Greenlawn before darkness falls.

June 16th. It's one of the longest days of the year, and it feels like it, like the daylight will never fade, like the night will never come and put all of this to rest.

Robin looks into the backseat again. "I think she really is sleeping."

George says, "You missed the craziest part of the whole thing. When Calvin threw a chair at the other guy."

"Actually threw it?"

"Picked it up and just—" He makes a thrusting gesture, as if he was ramming the steering wheel into the dashboard. "And what's his name, Chris? He was only a few feet away so it really knocked him into the wall. Calvin just stood there, like he couldn't believe his own strength. But then, *wham*, Chris just charged at him. Most people, if someone threatens them, they back away, just by instinct, right? This guy was the total opposite. He just went for it. Came back swinging, and one of them connected with Calvin's face."

"He's totally bad news. I mean, anyone who makes *Calvin* look responsible . . ." Robin checks once again to be sure Ruby is out, then says to George, "You know what he told me? Calvin?"

"That he's secretly in love with you."

"Close."

George's eyes go wide. "I was joking."

"No joke. He said he's bisexual."

"Really? Did he use that word?"

Robin nods.

"Did you tell him, '*Bisexual is just another word for closeted*'?" George says this in a voice that Robin realizes is mimicking his own, slightly high pitched and superior. It's embarrassing. But George cracks a tiny smile, which is a good sign, because Robin does indeed remember saying something like that when George first came out to him, after which they didn't talk for weeks. It turned out to be true, for George, anyway. Bisexuality was a way station. Maybe not for Calvin. It's hard to imagine Calvin as completely gay, or completely straight.

George's laugh turns into a yawn. He shakes his head, back to alertness.

"Are you OK to drive?"

"Why, you think I'd turn my car over to your unlicensed ass?"

"Better than falling asleep at the wheel."

"Better would be to get a license."

"OK, whatever you say, Peter."

"Ouch!" George's eyes shine. "I got it! Let's make Ruby drive."

"Yeah. We can sprawl out in the backseat and suck down cocktails."

"Or something."

A few days ago, a casually flirtatious remark like that would have made Robin laugh; now he's tongue-tied and blushing. It's the same for George. So now what? Robin's thoughts leap ahead, to where the two of them are going to end up tonight. Taking a look at the slow-moving traffic on the southbound side of the Parkway, he says, "There's no way we're driving all the way back to Philly."

"I can drop you off at your father's, and then go to my parents'. I hadn't planned on telling them I was coming to town, but . . ." George sighs, a labored sound that only hints at much deeper frustration. Robin remembers the earlier phone call from Mrs. Lincoln. He remembers, after George got off the phone with her, hearing him sigh in much the same way.

"I never mentioned this to you, because I didn't want the pressure," George says, "but I promised myself I would tell them *everything,* once I turned twenty-one."

"Which was May 18th."

"Yeah, I'm about to hit the thirty-day statute of limitations." George shakes his head. "You're lucky, Robin, to have parents who accept you. That's pretty rare."

"Dorothy's had a lot of time to get used to it. She claims she's known I was gay since I was two years old."

"Really?"

"I told her it's her fault. The first movie she took me to was *Funny Girl.* I remember thinking it seemed so *real,* because I'd been on the Staten Island Ferry, just like Barbra Streisand. I thought I could just walk into the screen."

"My first movie was *Willy Wonka.* I remember thinking it all seemed really fake."

"That's called fantasy."

"I guess I'm built for reality."

"And Clark's fine as long as I don't talk about it."

"I can't imagine my parents being fine with it under any circumstances," George says. "Churchgoing folks hear another message, you know."

"When's the last time your father went to church?"

"It's a cultural thing," George says. "It's deep."

For a moment, the comment stings, as if it's meant to be yet another reminder of this essential difference between them, a gap Robin wonders if he is even allowed to cross. But the sensation of George's hand on his head, that comfort offered just moments again, is still with him, and he thinks, *Wait*. Clarity takes hold: He's not trying to push you away. He's trying draw you in. To get you to see what you haven't seen before, but still might.

"It's hard to see ourselves from other people's eyes," Robin says, not sure this is exactly what he wants to say, trying to make the words work for him. "I mean, we want to see everything the way we already see it."

"Yeah," George agrees. "Yeah, that's part of the problem. But that's why we keep our friends around, right? To call us on our shit?"

"Or something," Robin says.

"Or something."

Driving all the way back to Philly tonight would take at least until midnight. The very thought is exhausting: hours and hours of dealing with Sunday traffic, reversing the path they've been on all day. So tonight, he and George will likely stay at their separate homes in Greenlawn, with their very different families, like they were still freshmen in high school, 1978 all over again. He thinks with some embarrassment of the condoms and lube he packed; in the midst of the rush to get out the door and rescue his sister, he found time to prepare for more sex with George. As if there was anywhere for them to be together. Was he imagining that they'd check into a hotel room?

Ruby went to a hotel with Chris. She must have, though she didn't actually say so. But what else would you do if you wanted to be together? Where else could you find enough privacy?

He looks again at her sleeping face, and has a moment, as he did earlier with George, where he sees someone between two incarnations, an old and a new self. And then his mind makes another leap and he and Ruby are young again, two little blond kids playing a game of hide-and-seek in the backyard. He preferred this game to other neighborhood games, the ones requiring balls that he would inevitably bobble and drop or swing at and miss. Running and hiding he could do. There was something so exciting about waiting quietly while the person who was "it" went searching; you wanted to peek and see if he was near, but it was better not to risk exposure, to be patient and wait it out. On this one day, a boy from down the street named Jimmy was "it"; the other kids all scattered, but Ruby hovered at Robin's side. "Go away," he told her. "Find your own place." But she followed him behind the garage, and he was so aware of her on his tail that he didn't see Jimmy sneak around from the other side, and then she was in his way when he tried to escape. Jimmy tagged him. Robin was so mad at Ruby that when he finished counting to ten, he went straight for her. He chased her down at full speed, and when he reached her, he crowed, "Now *you're* it," and smacked her shoulder so hard she stumbled to the grass. On the spot, she quit the game and walked away. "Don't be a baby," he shouted after her. "I'm not a baby," she said, with a coolness that stunned him. "You're a jerk."

It made an impression, the word "jerk" like a sudden jolt, an impact. The jerk is the one who upsets things, the one heedless of other people's feelings. He carried her admonishment around as warning, the danger of being selfish, of being petty, even vengeful. When his mother had smoked cigarettes in the car despite the fact that it was making Ruby sick, he understood that *she* was being a jerk. Last night, Peter had been a jerk, but Robin had only made it worse by exploding. Earlier in the car, his own defensiveness with George caused him to act like a jerk again. Had he done it again with Ruby, by yanking her away from a boy she seemed to feel something for? Or have the roles reversed, and is Ruby, for a change, the one who has selfishly knocked everything out of place?

Traffic clogs and opens up, clogs and opens up, all along the drive northward, as the shore roads empty onto the Garden State Parkway. As highways go, it's not a bad one to be stuck on. Rolling green slopes line either side, and a wide grassy median separates north and southbound lanes. There are wooden guardrails instead of metal and no billboards. Still, New Jersey drivers are infamous for a reason, and Robin tenses up as cars shift across multiple lanes without warning. George's driving is as bad as anyone's. The long day seems to be wearing on him, and he's become impatient, heavy on both the brake and the gas, taken to muttering, and sometimes shouting, "asshole" and "idiot."

There's a truly scary moment when a car on the shoulder makes a move back onto the road, jutting quickly in front of them. George speeds up, even though the other guy is clearly about to merge, and lands his fist on the horn as he swerves. Robin gets thrown from side to side, grasping for equilibrium. George says, "Sorry," but it sounds more like a challenge than an apology.

From behind him, Ruby stirs.

"I don't feel good," she says. "Can we pull over?"

"Are you going to be sick?"

"I need some air."

"There's a place coming up," George says, reading the sign for the Cheesequake Service Area.

Robin sings, "Cheesequake, hit the brakes, let's go eat a piece of cake." The lyrics burst forth unbidden, a little tune invented during a family vacation, way back when. He seems to remember that his father, who is more prone to corniness than his mother, was the one who made it up, but he's not entirely sure. The song is a mystery, like the word Cheesequake itself (which could be derived from some Indian language, butchered by white people, or could also be nonsense). He looks back at Ruby to see if she's remembered this song, too, but she doesn't seem to be paying attention. She's looking more than a little green.

As soon as George moves them into a parking spot, Ruby bounds out of the car toward the restrooms.

Inside, a crowd lines up for fast food; another group mills around at a little gift counter, perusing bumper stickers and T-shirts with the slogan NEW JERSEY AND YOU, PERFECT TOGETHER.

Robin looks through the racks, hoping to find a Father's Day card. No luck. So he buys an oversized postcard with a picture of the Cheesequake Service Area. On the back, he writes, "Dad, Here's a trip down memory lane for Father's Day. Love, your prodigal children."

Next stop is the men's room. Along a wall of urinals, a couple old men are spaced intermittently; a father in a baseball cap keeps an eye on his young son at the kid-sized pisser. Robin heads for the farthest one. George takes the spot next to him.

He can hear their streams hit the porcelain at the exact same time, which secretly pleases him. Sometimes, pissing in public, he becomes inexplicably pee-shy, and no matter how bad he has to go, it takes forever to start up. But since moving in with George, this hasn't been a problem. They're sometimes in the bathroom at the same time, one of them peeing while the other brushes his teeth, and though it's not something they've bothered to talk about, Robin figures George probably takes the same kind of comfort in this brotherly intimacy as he does. Brotherly, because it reminds him of Jackson. Some of his earliest memories are of the two of them "crossing streams" into the bowl in the upstairs bathroom, the one with the fuzzy gold bathmat always bunched up against the tub, and talking with playful fascination about arcs and splashes, the varying smells and colors. It was their game, regular and unremarkable, and no one knew about it. How long would it have continued, if Jackson had lived? Or would having a gay brother have driven Jackson away from anything resembling physical closeness?

George is the nearest thing to a brother in his life now. And maybe that's what's so confusing about the line they stepped over last night. You put people into compartments, but they break out of them, and then what? Can you seal yourself back in, or are you forever changed?

At this very moment he can glimpse George's cock as George shakes off, which should be no big deal but after last night seems tinged with taboo. George senses it, too, if the quick eye contact he makes with Robin is any indication.

Down the wall, father and son have departed, and one by one the old men leave; and then it's only the two of them inside the cavernous, tiled room. Now the eye contact is not so subtle. Their glances drift across each other, mischievous, expectant.

George turns sideways. He thrusts his pelvis out. He slaps his cock onto Robin's, saying, "Swordfight."

Robin's mouth drops open, giddy with the audacity of it.

George does it again. Slap, slap, slap. And then he steps closer, lingering, more gentle. Rub, slide, rub.

But that's all. There's the squeal of a door hinge, the sound of entering footsteps. Robin moves back to his urinal and shields his crotch. His heartbeat quickens in the rush of nearly being caught.

George flushes. "Meet you outside."

Robin spots him near the curb, standing in profile studying an oversized map under glass. The sun hits him softly from behind, hugs the solidity of his neck, highlights the texture of the twists in his hair. There's the undeniably beautiful way the arch of his lower back becomes the curve of his muscular ass.

George finally sees him and waves him over. "I had you speechless in there," he says through a smile.

"Definitely."

"Is something wrong?" George asks. "You've got some look in your eyes."

"I guess I'm just thinking about last night."

"Is that a good thing?"

Robin nods. Speechless again.

George glances around. There's no one in close range, but people and cars are coming and going every which way. "Fuck. This is crazy! We've created a problem." He looks down at his pants, where Robin can see that the *problem* isn't easily concealed. "You need to walk away and let me think about something else."

"Gotcha." Robin steps back, scans the parking lot, remembers where they are, what they're in the midst of. "I'll go find my sister. Have you seen her?"

George shakes his head. "Actually, for a minute I forgot all about her."

She hasn't eaten meat in years, but impulsively, guiltily she orders a bacon cheeseburger and devours its fatty, salty bulk in record time.

While she sucks a Cherry Coke through a straw, all the way down to the ice, she hurries to the pay phone and dials the Island Beach Motor Lodge. The old guy at the desk puts her through to the room.

The phone rings and rings. Eventually he comes back on the line and states the obvious, "No answer."

"Did you see him come in? The guy I was with last night?"

"What's a'matter, honey, lost your *husband* already?"

"I'm not your *honey,*" she snaps. "That's totally sexist."

"Oh, I got a real women's libber here," he says.

"How about I call the Better Business Bureau on you?"

He begins an answer, but she hangs up without hearing the rest of it. And immediately she's wishing she'd ignored his condescension. Her anger today is an undertow. She's barely aware of it until it's pulling her in deep.

Collecting herself, she calls back. She swallows her pride and apologizes, and in the sweetest voice she can muster she asks him if he'll leave a message for Chris. She can only hope that he actually writes down the phone number, Clark's phone number in Greenlawn, which she recites carefully.

At the next phone, a young mother—flowered bikini top, dingy white shorts, sandals too tight for her doughy feet—rocks a baby over her shoulder while carrying on a loud conversation, the receiver balanced against her neck. The baby stares with unblinking eyes at Ruby as a string of spittle falls from its tiny mouth to a discolored towel on its mother's bare shoulder. Ruby smiles at the smooth, blank face, trying to draw out a happy reaction, but all she gets is a wince that quickly turns into tears. The mother shifts her child around, shushing the sudden wailing without halting her own irate conversation. Ruby hears "child support" and "delinquent" and "You don't know a fucking thing," and in glimpses she comes to see just how young this "woman" is, maybe even younger than she is. A teenager. Suddenly it all seems shocking—the foul language, the crying baby, the tacky clothes. Then the girl catches Ruby's stare and squints suspiciously, and Ruby turns away, ashamed.

There are kids everywhere she looks. Little kids being dragged along by their mothers. Sleepy kids being lifted by their fathers. Boys shouting as they dash into the parking lot without looking—that's the kind of kid Jackson was, untamable. She roots around her purse for more change. She might have enough to call home, though she dreads the idea, and anyway Robin said he talked to Clark, so there's no need to call now. She'll see her father soon enough.

Still there's this urge to talk to *someone*. Among the clutter at the bottom of her purse she finds Wendy's phone number. She dials, wondering why she's even bothering.

"Hi, this is Ruby, from last night?"

"Holy shit! What's happening?"

"Well, I never checked in with you again, so—"

"Are you still with that guy?"

"I was with him all day. We ran into Joanne on the boardwalk."

"Really? I'll get the scoop from her, you can be sure."

"She told me you got in trouble."

"Yeah, you owe me a total apology."

"Oh, I'm really sorry—"

"*Psych!*" Wendy exclaims. "J.K.—just kidding. Don't worry about it, my mother always grounds me. It lasts for like two days. It's her way to get me to do a bunch of housework for her. I call her the Sheriff, 'cause she totally runs a jail around here."

She listens to Wendy launch into the same story that Joanne told her today. (Recalls, too, how rude Chris had been in that moment. What was that about? As soon as they left the hotel room, their problems began.) Finally, she gets a chance to interrupt. "Listen, I didn't get to thank you. You guys saved me."

"Aw, you're so sweet. That was so fun last night. I'm psyched we ran into you."

"You are?"

"You're the coolest person I've met here all summer. Most people who come down here, I can't *stand* 'em."

Ruby laughs. Such a relief to know there's one person in the world who wasn't put out by her behavior.

She looks up and sees Robin coming her way. He calls out, "Train's leaving the station."

"Wendy, I gotta go. *My* sheriff just blew his whistle." They say goodbye with promises to keep in touch. Maybe we will, Ruby thinks. I could use some new friends.

She catches up to Robin and walks alongside him, out of the building onto the hot pavement. The uncomfortable silence between them is hard to bear. When he showed up at Alice's, she was so happy, felt like finally she'd be able to emerge from the purgatory of the party, wouldn't simply be sliced to ribbons by the cats clawing at her from every direction. Why did it go downhill from there? Because Robin was convinced she'd done the wrong thing. Because he wouldn't give Chris a chance. Because he still treats her like his baby sister, still bosses her around and expects her to yield.

"Sign this," he says to her. He's holding out a postcard. A picture of the rest area and the Parkway. The kind of postcard you see and think, who would buy that? She turns it over, reads the message and smiles. *Prodigal children.*

"I know, it's pathetic," he says, looking so crestfallen that even though she's mad at him, she feels the need to reassure.

"That's OK, we're both pathetic, today. It's the thought that counts."

He throws an arm around her shoulder, pulls her towards him, squeezes. Just for a moment, it makes things better.

It wasn't fair of her, she knows, to make that crack about Calvin's movie. Robin doesn't need Calvin—he just got into that London program. He'll probably wind up in some costumed Shakespearean tragedy, a doomed prince soaking up applause. Or he'll catch the eye of some art-film director looking to fill the role of a sensitive American boy. Robin'll do well. He always does, eventually. His successes have seemed like hers, too, by association. His exploits, for better or worse, have been hers, vicariously. But that's the problem, right? This—all of this—isn't *his*. It's hers, hers alone.

She can read him so well, knows his moods, the subtleties of his expression. She's pretty sure that there's more on his mind besides her. It's something about the way his overly responsible attitude reads like a role, like he's playing the part of big brother—"Big *Bother*" was a name she'd once called him after he'd grilled her about one of her early dates with Calvin.

In the car, in the backseat again, moving onto the Parkway, that queasy feeling bubbles up, like the red light pulsing on the answering machine, a message you've been avoiding but will be forced to listen to sooner or later. The radio is filling the dead air of the car with another inescapable pop song: *I can tell you, my love for you will still be strong, after the boys of summer have gone.* What is it about the summer that makes people nostalgic for it even before it's over? All those romantic feelings, ignited by long days and warm nights—must they all end once temperatures drop and days shorten? And yet she can't deny that things *do* disappear. Things you can't imagine ever not being there can wither, dry out, crumble. Is she going to lose Chris? A year ago, it would have been hard to imagine hating Calvin the way she does now. Not hating, but—what is it? Just having nothing left for him, no patience, no tolerance, no interest, really. It was so easy to watch him walk out the door of that house.

The music is loud enough that she can't hear what's being said up front. But she sees, in the space between the seats, Robin's hand resting on George's thigh, lingering there. And then George's hand falls on his and stays. Both boys stare straight ahead, which only confirms for Ruby that this is more than just a friendly pat. Has she ever seen this kind of touch between them? She's never even imagined it, in part because George has never really seemed gay to her—not the way Robin does. Robin's not a flamer, but there's a pitch to his voice and a fluidity to his gestures, plus his enthusiasm for dance music and fashion and—well, if you can pick up on that kind of thing—if you have what he calls *gaydar*—you can't miss it. But George has always seemed so serious, bookish, almost asexual. The gayest thing about him has been his friendship with Robin. Of course, now that she thinks about it, George seems different—he has attitude. He has big arm muscles and fuzz on his chest. The dreads in his hair are so carefully twisted and evenly spaced out that they don't so much look like a Rasta statement as a fashion choice.

George is looking at her in the rearview mirror. Caught her staring. "Are you OK?" he asks.

"I don't know," she says. Something isn't right with her stomach. The bacon cheeseburger and Coke were a mistake. Her gut is expanding with what she imagines to be fist-sized bubbles of sugar and fat, pressing against the lining of her intestines. The sensation of trying to suppress it is leaving her light-headed. She closes her eyes, but all she can form is the image of those floppy strips of bacon and that overdone beef patty transforming themselves into noxious gas. And then suddenly it's upon her, the very sensation she felt back at Alice's house, and she has cover her mouth for fear that she'll lose it all.

"Pull over," she croaks through her fingers. "I need to pull over."

"What?" George says. "Now?"

"Please."

Robin is looking back at her in alarm. "Hold on, OK? He can't just—"

Oh God oh God oh God—

The lurching of the car toward the side of the road, the crunching of the pebbly surface beneath the wheels, the rush of air as she pushes open the door while they're still moving—

She hears Robin command, "Wait! Until we stop!" but it sounds like it's coming from very far away, on the other side of a membrane that's formed between them, and before they've completely halted she's tumbling from the car. She gets knocked to her knees, crawls to get away from the road and then, with a pain like a spear rising up from her stomach, the enlarged bubble forces itself through her throat into her mouth. She tastes it in a hot wet stream rushing across her tongue and teeth. It shoots through the air—*splurshhh*—a bulging wet beast forcing itself out. Chunks splatter across dried grass and bleached-out garbage and the splintered wooden guardrail.

Just one big blast. She braces herself for more. Her throat is on fire, her lips sting.

Behind her, cars zoom by with the speed of missiles.

Robin is beside her. He's holding out a bottle of Diet Coke. One perfumey whiff and her throat convulses all over again—why do they drink so much of this stuff?—but this time nothing comes up—a dry heave, like a screw tightening in her skull. Robin comes back a moment later with a different bottle. She gulps warm water from the bottom, then fills her mouth again and swishes out the sourness.

She can breathe again, deeply. It's like her head has been released from too long underwater. "I think that's all."

"Take your time," Robin says. She can hear the concern in his voice.

She stands up. "We should go."

"I should have given you the front," he says.

"Yeah."

"I'm sorry."

"Well . . ." She's not feeling particularly forgiving. She knows she could push it if she wanted to, if she had any strength left to argue. So let him feel bad. He could definitely stand to remember that he's far from perfect.

The idea comes upon Robin suddenly. "Take this exit," he tells George.

"This isn't ours."

"Just—please? I want to make a stop." He hadn't been planning on it, but now it seems like a must. Especially after seeing Ruby like that. He feels like he owes her this.

George decelerates through the toll plaza, aims a quarter into the basket, and then they're swerving around the off-ramp and onto Route 4 in Paramus. One billboard after another clamors for attention: Visit the Burlington Coat Factory. Jennifer Convertibles: Do You Have One? Wendy's, still pushing "Where's the Beef?" This road is as dense as the Parkway was open: department stores ringed in parking lots; multicolored pennants flapping in the wind over car dealerships; the movie theater that used to be ten screens and now boasts fourteen: *A View to a Kill, Cocoon, The Goonies*. "Do you have any desire to see *St. Elmo's Fire*?" George asks him.

From the front seat Ruby releases an inexplicable grunt.

"What?" Robin prompts.

"Nothing."

"Where are we going?" George asks.

"Take the exit by the Fashion Center," Robin says.

Ruby spins around, surprised. "Are we? Now?"

"I figured, while we're over here . . . You still want to?"

She nods and faces front again. She seems to dip down in the seat, making herself small. He can't quite read her body language. Has she for some reason changed her mind about this? For years, Ruby was the one member of the family who wanted to visit Jackson's grave. It must have been something that Nana, the cross-bearing Catholic of the family, put in her mind.

After they left New Jersey, visiting the grave seemed to become more important to their mother. It became a task for holidays: on a day near Christmas, and again near Easter, and on Jackson's birthday, too, Dorothy would drive them to the wooded cemetery off Route 4. He can't remember any conversations they ever had about these cemetery visits, can't remember voicing the feelings that got dredged up. He remembers that he would sometimes stare at his mother and feel something close to hatred, for dragging them to the gravesite. They were just going through the motions, but toward what end? It occurs to him that they still haven't called Dorothy; he doesn't know why he's avoiding her, now that things have been resolved.

George steers into the cemetery, and they make their way along a curving drive to the newest section, where Jackson is buried. The three of them walk silently through rows of granite stones, new enough to reflect glints of sunlight dappling through the overhanging trees. In the background are the mausoleums and ostentatious monuments of the past: weeping angels, lions in repose, a larger-than-life crucifix featuring a Jesus whose agonized face is coated in years of soot. And then they come upon the simple rectangle that marks Jackson's burial.

JACKSON LEOPOLD MACKENZIE
JUNE 16, 1967—DECEMBER 15, 1978
SON, BROTHER, SLUGGER

"Leopold" for Dorothy's father; "Jackson" for some whim of Dorothy's, enforced from birth by the edict that he never be nicknamed "Jack," as "Robin" was never to be called "Rob" or, heaven forbid, "Bobby." "Slugger" was Clark's touch. Robin remembers Dorothy in tears begging Clark not to include it, insisting it was undignified and sentimental, to which Clark, his eyes hardened, his jaw set, hissed out the words, "Deal with it, Dottie." Arguing for an hour over their dead son's tombstone. Dorothy: "Couldn't we go with *athlete*?" Clark: "He was the Little League home run champ!"

George, at Robin's side, says, "I forgot all about that: December 15th."

"Yeah, well."

December 15, Robin's own birthday, the cosmic unfairness of it never lost on him. Even now he feels a clench in his gut, the way he's been marked doubly, not just by loss but also by blame. And mixed in with it all, the residual resentment, as if the timing had been by design, as if Jackson *chose* to pass over from coma to death on that particular day so that Robin's progress through life would be inextricably linked to Jackson's erasure from it.

Ruby has kneeled down at the base of the grave, her hands raking stray leaves. She must be praying.

Robin lowers his head and tries to come up with something appropriate. *Dear God, please look over Jackson, wherever he is.* The thought can hardly take hold: Look over him, where? He doesn't exist anywhere but right here at their feet. His body, damaged, withered and shrunken after all those weeks in the coma, and then buried in this spot, has rotted away to nothing. Food for worms. Nutrients for the cemetery lawn. Flesh into dust.

A residual terror starts his legs trembling. It's not just the vision of Jackson there, buried in the earth, decomposing; it's the understanding that this is what's waiting for *him.* Death is hissing all the time from the shadows, and in those moments when he lets himself confront this darkness what he sees is a scene from a science fiction movie, a parade of once-handsome lovers gone blotchy and skeletal, like the survivors of an atomic bomb exploded in the air over Manhattan. Not dead but dying; ill; *infected*—that horrible, spiky word. It is the horror of this suffering that has struck him with such great force over the last few years, a suffering that it seems he might not be able to avoid, because he's done the same things that all those men did, not knowing the consequences. But until now he has never let himself follow these cluttered, terrifying thoughts all the way to this final truth: the image of a grave with his own name on it, perhaps right here, next to his brother's. Involuntarily, he gasps for air, so audibly that Ruby turns around to look at him. And then he wonders if perhaps she hadn't been praying, because her attention seems elsewhere, her eyes are darting around, as if she's on the lookout for something.

She says, "Did I ever tell you about the last time I was here?"

"You mentioned it, in Seaside."

"Clark and I came here together, and there was a woman visiting another grave, just over there. She told us she saw a groundhog—I mean, she said it was a groundhog, but I don't know. Could have been a mole, or some other rodent. So she went and told the workers, the groundskeeper guys. They went looking around for it, and they found it, not very far from here. And then one of them whacked it on the head with a shovel." Then she says, "Whack-A-Mole," and lets out a strange, bitter laugh. Her expression falls, and she begins twisting the toy ring on her finger.

"That happened right in front of you?" he asks.

"Yes. I'm not sure they realized that we were here, but I screamed, and they stopped. And then we could see the poor thing stumbling around half-dead. I didn't see blood, but the guy had hit it really hard. Clark just started yelling at them. 'Don't let it suffer!' And the guy went back over with the shovel. We watched them bash it to death."

"What a nightmare."

George asks, "What happened to that other woman?"

"She had already left. So we were the only witnesses." Ruby glances at the tombstone. "I haven't been back here since then. Nearly two years."

Robin pictures his sister two years ago. It's easy enough to strip away the black hair dye and the gothic wardrobe; it's not so easy to remember her without the new attitude she wears, the toughness, her quick suspicion of things others take for granted. Two years ago she was so much less burdened. "Was that when you stopped going to church?" he asks.

She nods. "For a while I thought that God had shown us that mole getting killed as a sign—a sign that if Jackson hadn't died, he would have gone on suffering, which would have been worse."

"I think about that a lot, too," he tells her.

"But then I thought, no, it's not a sign. God doesn't care about sending me *signs.* It was just an example of cruelty." She is silent for a while. "That was also right around the time I was with that guy, Brandon, the one I had sex with? He was such an asshole. And I think I just started to feel bad about everything."

"I never put all that together."

"You were leaving for college."

George takes his hand and squeezes tightly; it's only then that Robin realizes that he has just shivered. Their fingers braid together. The sensation of it briefly sends Robin back to the night before (was it only last night?): the two of them holding hands in the bushes, amid the broken moonlight, waiting out the police, scared shitless. He had suggested "surrendering," just another word for giving up. Such a cowardly thing to say.

He meets Ruby's eyes, pale and blue and watery with grief, and something inside him splinters, and his eyes well up and overflow, too. Because he sees not the young woman who has frustrated him all day long but the little girl who stood in this very spot with him on a cold December day eight years ago, both of them trying to face the incomprehensible truth that their brother was gone forever, and that they were in some way a part of that, witnesses to the accident if not actually responsible for it. Both of them trying to face the truth of capital-D-death, of once-and-for-all finality, which even now, even still, is the greatest mystery. So here it is again, that eternal resemblance, the way her life will always reflect his, not only on her face, but beneath that, too, in the knowledge that they share.

And then Ruby steals a glimpse at where his hand is intertwined with George's; she doesn't appear to be surprised, and if anything, some sadness seems to clear from her face for a moment. This feels to Robin, in some small way, like a blessing.

At last he knows what he wants to convey here, in his thoughts.

Not a prayer for his brother, dead and gone, but a wish for himself and his sister, to find a way out of the past, once and for all.

To find forgiveness.

Greenlawn. The leafy elms and oaks that line Valley Road. The split-level homes and two-story colonials flying American flags from their porches. Pairs of joggers running in the road, skin varnished in light sweat.

Through the open backseat window, Robin takes in the humid breeze, carrying honeysuckle and cut grass and barbecue smoke. He knows every structure along this route, the configuration of every corner, so that when something new appears, he can't help but comment out loud.

"The Continental House is now called the Tuscan Caffé?" he asks, as they pass the place once known for hiring all the local fifteen-year-olds for their first jobs bussing tables. "With two f's?"

"My dad says that there are a lot of investment bankers and junk-bond types moving here from the city," George replies.

"Greenlawn is getting fancy."

From the passenger seat, Ruby mutters, "That'll be the day." Her first words since the cemetery. She clears her throat as if ready to say something more, then seems to think better of it.

He wonders if she's saving her strength for whatever awaits at the house. He wonders, too, if he should be rehearsing his own speech for his father. How much scrutiny will he face for his actions? Will they say he waited too long to contact them? That he was irresponsible not to call the cops?

As George makes one turn and then another, bringing them closer to the house, the balmy summer sweetness splits apart like skin on ripe fruit, and beneath it Robin feels once again the pit of dread that is always part of coming back to Greenlawn. He moved away at fifteen; when he returns, he is fifteen again. Coma Boy's Brother.

On Bergen Avenue, George slows down, clicks on the blinker as if to turn in to the driveway. But there's a car already there: Dorothy's Maxima.

"Mom's here?" Ruby asks.

"I guess she's in the house."

Ruby groans. "I must be in major trouble, if she's waiting *inside.*"

Robin looks at George. "Not sure you're going to want to stay for this."

"Your mom'll be pissed if I don't say hello."

They wander up the driveway, which is a fresh, deep black; Clark had it repaved after the winter snow melted. Robin lags behind Ruby. It's her day. Her mess. She can lead the parade. She lugs her bag as if it weighs a hundred pounds.

When they turn into the backyard, they meet the sight of their mother, atop the stoop, her arm holding the screen ajar. Such a familiar sight: all those times he came up the driveway to find her in this doorway, stopping him before he could enter so that she could say whatever absolutely had to be said, right away. But today, this strategic motherly ambush is not directed his way.

"Ruby Regina MacKenzie," Dorothy says. "You scared me to death."

Ruby for her part says only, "Where's Dad?" The audacity of this strikes Robin as almost cruel. It's Clark's house now, she seems to imply. I answer to him.

"He's in his office."

"I need to clean up." Ruby steps into the doorway, forcing Dorothy to make room for her and her bag, and passes into the kitchen.

"She got carsick," Robin offers.

"Is she all right?"

"I think so," Robin says gently, kissing his mother on the cheek and following his sister inside.

Dorothy says, "George, maybe you can enlighten me?"

"I'm just the driver," he says.

"I promise, I won't kill the messenger."

"Everyone chill out," Ruby calls from the kitchen, which strikes Robin as unnecessary, since Dorothy is maintaining a surprising level of composure. Ruby vanishes into the living room. A moment later he hears her footsteps heading upstairs, and then the sound of water moving through the pipes. The house, an eighty-year-old wooden structure, has always been a collection of creaks and groans, and the older it gets, the less it conceals.

Robin says, "Mom, you should try to get her to talk."

"She just flew right past me!"

"She's kinda stressed out."

Dorothy narrows her eyes at him. "Of course you're sticking up for her."

He *is*, he realizes; he hadn't actually made a decision to do so, but something about being back in the house, in this kitchen, the site of so many arguments in the past, brings out an urge to pacify. "I've already given her a hard time."

"She'll listen to your father." She calls out, "Clark! They're here!"

Now he can hear his father's voice carrying through the wall from his office. Robin is seized by the idea Clark is in there with Annie, his girlfriend, that she's lounging on the daybed in a bathrobe, cooing, "Clark, take care of your family and then come back to me, baby . . ." The anxious fantasy dissolves as Robin realizes Clark is talking on the phone. But now that he's imagined it, he can't quite shake the idea that this mystery woman is somewhere in the house. Does his mother even know that his father is dating? Would it bother her? It's been five years since the divorce, enough time to get over it. But is she? For a while, it was very ugly; Dorothy would sit at the edge of Robin's bed and tell him through tears how miserly Clark was, how little he wanted to spend on child support, on tuition; and Clark would counter, on the weekends, with brutal one-liners: "Your mother has always had her own version of the truth."

The reality of all four of them here under the same roof again makes him want to flee. He looks to George, whose expression says that he, too, is braced for confrontation

Dorothy says, "Well, how are you? How's Peter? How's his dissertation?"

"Peter is on my S-H-I-T list."

"Whatever for?"

"We broke up. He might have been cheating on me."

"Are you sure?" she asks. The way her mouth drops open makes Robin swell with love for her, for being on his side, for embracing his romantic well-being. She turns to George as if for confirmation, and he nods. Robin remembers what George said, that he's lucky to have his parents: This bright truth smacks up against the old ghosts still lingering, hissing the conflicts of the past.

"I saw him making out with someone," Robin says. "But then there was a message from him on the machine, saying I got it wrong."

George says, "What message?"

"When I checked the machine . . ." He wishes now that he hadn't kept this from George all day. "He wants an apology. He almost made it sound like, if I did, maybe we might get back together in the fall."

Dorothy says, "Don't throw it away. Peter's a catch. I always thought a scholar was a good match for you."

George shakes his head in disapproval. There's a challenge in his eyes that says, *There will be no apologies to Peter, no getting back together, not if I have anything to say about it.*

And Robin has to ask himself: So why didn't you tell George about the message when you first heard it? Are you still hoping you have a chance with Peter?

To his relief, Clark appears. Robin hasn't seen him since Christmas. Unlike Dorothy, who has filled out, his father seems as lean as ever, perhaps even fitter; he's been jogging again and is talking of running a marathon next year, a feat that Robin finds more impressive every time he himself wakes up in the morning coughing up last night's cigarettes. Clark's hair went silver back when he and Dorothy only communicated through their lawyers—Clark ruefully dubbed it "litigation white"—but his face hasn't changed. He greets Robin with a hug and extends his hand to George. There's a round of pleasantries about Philadelphia, and college, and it's-not-the-heat-it's-the-humidity, before he finally looks around and says, "Where's the fugitive?"

"Clark, talk to her," Dorothy says, slumping into a seat at the table. "She's upstairs."

George clears his throat. "I guess I should go?" He pauses, uncertain. "Can I use your phone?"

Dorothy says, "Of course," and then catches herself. "I'm sure it's—Clark won't mind. Clark, where is that thing?"

Clark hands George the handset of a cordless phone. Robin glances to the wall where their old rotary phone, with its long, coiled wire, used to hang. The phone base is mounted there, a hunk of bright, white plastic

Robin's attention splits between George on the phone with Mrs. Lincoln, and Dorothy pushing Clark to go upstairs to Ruby. Both conversations make Robin uneasy. So he steps out into the backyard and lights a cigarette and stares across the lawn, which is thick and green and trim, healthier than it's looked since Robin himself used to mow it (a chore left behind with the suburbs), and he stares at the house beyond the hedge.

The Spicers used to live there, though they haven't for several years: Victoria Spicer was once his best friend, but became a stranger to him even before he moved to New York; their friendship fell apart during Jackson's hospitalization, though he couldn't say why. He remembers no defining break, no argument, just a general air of estrangement, of disappointment. It had something to do with Todd, her older brother, with his lean body and his long hair and his stoned eyes that could turn hard and cruel without warning. Todd who could be a bully towering above him, tormenting him, or who might be on his knees sucking Robin's dick in his bedroom. Victoria never knew what was going on between Robin and Todd, but maybe she suspected. Maybe she even knew that Todd was half-queer then. And now he might have turned completely queer. That was the rumor anyway, as Robin had heard it from Ruby who heard it from one of her old Greenlawn High classmates who showed up at some event at Barnard with a gay boy from San Francisco. This boy said he'd "almost slept with" someone named Todd, from Greenlawn, New Jersey (it was the name, Greenlawn, that had triggered the story), who worked on Castro Street, busing tables at a café with an entirely gay clientele. He had pierced ears and a lion tattoo on his shoulder, and he drove some old muscle car, and he was apprenticing with a metalsmith who made jewelry out of silver. Robin has imagined San Francisco for years, a kind of frivolous, fantasy city always hosting a parade or a protest march, but he can't imagine Todd Spicer in the midst of it. He doesn't fully believe that this tattooed guy working at this café was *his* Todd; but he doesn't disbelieve it, either, because the story is much like Todd himself always was: available only in pieces, an accumulation of surface details open to interpretation. If he met him face-to-face, he'd know what to think: the gaydar would be set off, or not. And if it wasn't even a matter of gaydar, if Todd had actually come out, what then? Would Robin rejoice at this miraculous turn of events? Demand an apology for past mistreatments? Sit down and have a heart-to-heart with him? The boy who'd been the source of the story couldn't offer any more details; he wasn't going back to San Francisco, he said. He called it "the elephant graveyard."

George enters the yard and says, "I'm heading over to my mom's." He makes his hand into a gun and shoots himself in the temple.

"Save a bullet for me," Robin says.

"So, are you staying overnight?"

"Let's see how it goes. Are you?"

"Let's see how it goes."

Robin walks him to the street. After all this, it seems impossible that they're parting company. It feels like the end of a date, where you've entertained the idea of continuing into the night but instead, through circumstance or sensibility, have decided to hold off. He flips backward through the day: the look in George's eyes at the Parkway rest stop when he called "swordfight"; the sweat on his brow after he broke up the scuffle at Alice's house; the hurt and anger on his face when they were tailed by a cop and Robin told him he was being too sensitive. At last he lands on the one moment that is tugging at his insides, the one that makes what should be a nonevent, this good-bye-for-the-night between best friends, something more tumultuous. It was a moment in the Cadillac, just after listening to Al Green, when George said, "I predict you're going to be over Peter really soon," a prediction which now seems to have come true, because he is, isn't he? Over Peter: over the hope of reunion, maybe even over the desire for it, no matter what thoughts just flashed through his mind in the kitchen. George knew it right away; he might have known also who would replace Peter in his imagination: George himself. That was the unspoken part. Peter's exit cleared the way, at last, for something to emerge between them that had never before had the room to grow.

But he can't say anything like this to George. You can't fall for your best friend. Everyone knows that. So they hug, and Robin thanks him, "for everything," and says, in a grand flourish of understatement, "Well, we got through the day."

George says, "It's not over yet."

Back in the kitchen, Robin realizes how hungry he is. He asks his mother, "Did you bring that paella and gazpacho you were talking about?"

"It's at home. I'm saving it for someone who'll appreciate it."

"So you're punishing Ruby for not showing up?"

She smiles. "I'm not *that* petty. No, I decided I'd offer it to the young man who lives upstairs. Do you remember him? Donovan?"

He nods. "The gay guy."

"Well, I wouldn't want to make assumptions."

"Pretty safe bet, Dorothy."

There's an awkward silence, and then they both try to say something at once. He prompts her to go first.

"Are you being careful, Robin?"

And of course he knows what she means, and why she brought this up right now, in the context of their neighbor who is not well. But the last thing he wants to do is talk with his mother about the dangers of his sex life.

"Nothing to worry about," he says.

"Of course there's something to worry about. You're aware of what's going on among homosexuals."

"Don't say *homosexuals*."

"This is not a semantic issue, dear." She lays her hand on his. "You can talk to me."

"I know." He pulls away from her. How could he possibly talk to his mother about everything he fears, every dark thought that crosses his mind? And yet, were the worst to happen, how would he possibly go forward without her?

He stands up and heads to the fridge. "You think Clark keeps any provisions around here?"

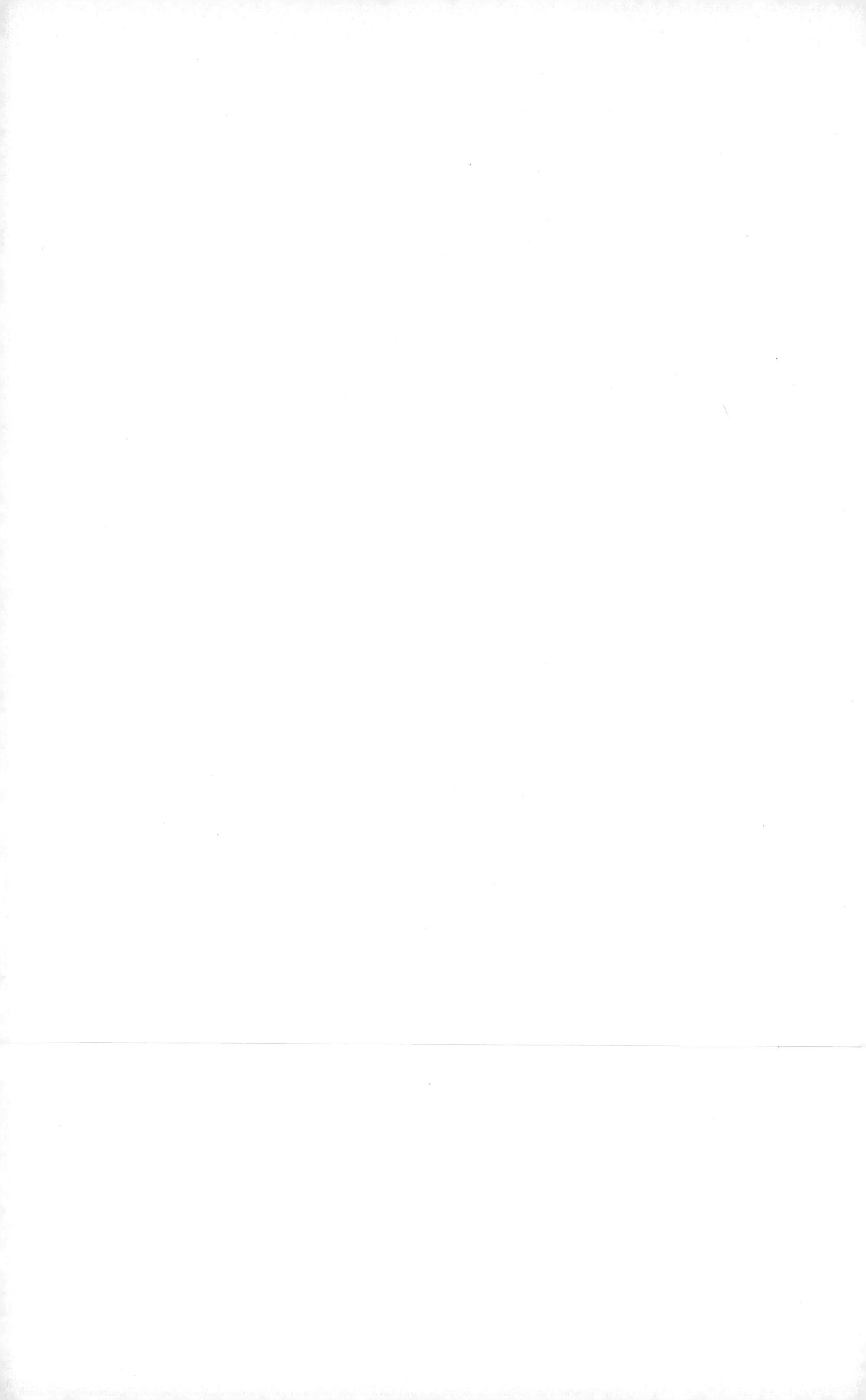

Another bathroom, another shower. Everywhere she goes, she's washing off the mess of where she has been. She'd prefer to be cleaning up in Manhattan, where Dorothy recently badgered the landlord to upgrade the fixtures, and where they now have a shower with a built-in massager. This bathroom, off the upstairs hallway, next to her childhood bedroom, has been the same for as long as she can remember. Gold-flecked wallpaper, a toilet that runs too long after you flush it, a mirror with a chip in it at exactly the level of her eyes, so that she has to shift around as she applies her makeup. Her father has made changes all over the house but not here, which strikes her as just like a man. A woman would make sure to renovate *the facilities,* as her mother likes to call them, before repaving the driveway. Not a very feminist thing to say, but there you go. Not even a women's studies curriculum is going to erase her desire to look presentable.

She showers and wraps herself in a towel and is moving through the hall back to her bedroom when she sees, at the top of the stairs, leaning on the banister, her father. He's clearly been waiting for her. "They sent me up here for you," he says, averting his eyes.

"I'm getting dressed." She scurries into her bedroom and closes the door.

Nothing has changed in here. Ever. Robin had his room redone, and she always expected she would, too. The excuse was that his room had been Jackson's—they had to clear the air of the memories, or something. But she, too, has memories, stuck to the walls like the flowery pink wallpaper. She'd like to clear them out. But first she'd like to climb into bed and sleep for two days.

"Notice anything different?"

"I'll be down in a minute!" she snaps, in disbelief that he's still standing out there, waiting for her.

"I added a light fixture by the bed."

"Oh. I see it." She used to complain that she wanted to be able to turn off the overhead light from her bed. So he did that for her. There's a new switch within arm's reach.

"Figured you'd want more control."

"Yeah, it's great." She still has some clothes here, even though the formal joint custody visits ended more than a year ago, on her eighteenth birthday. She finds a pair of loose sweatpants and a T-shirt, white, with three-quarter-length black sleeves and the logo of Doris & Georgie's Sweet Shoppe, an ice cream parlor in Greenlawn where she worked one summer while she lived with Clark. It's a little tight, and has a few stains, but it's better than the other option, a big baggy thing with a Ziggy cartoon on it that says, IT'S EASY BEING ME . . . BECAUSE I'M ALL I GOT!

"Clark, don't stand there waiting for me, you're making me nervous."

Finally, she hears him step away.

But when she comes back downstairs, many minutes later, he's hovering near the bottom of the banister. "So are you ready to talk?"

"What do you want me to say?"

He throws his arms wide. He's not the most articulate person, her dad. He's not hyperverbal like her mother or her brother. She decides that her first priority is settling her still-knotted stomach. She swallowed two Anacin in the bathroom for her headache, but they're already churning in her gut like sand in salt water. She entertains the passing thought that there's something physically wrong with her, beyond even being sick to her stomach. Maybe it's also a touch of sun poisoning—the burned skin on her stomach has begun to tingle and itch.

Dorothy is at the kitchen table—sitting in the same chair that used to be "hers," with a cup and saucer in front of her, a few crumbs on a plate. "Come sit with me," she says, patting the chair next to her.

The way the light slants in from the window over the sink is no different than light falling on her five, six, ten years ago—Ruby can peel away the extra weight on her mother's body, dress her in a chic, tailored blouse like she used to wear instead of the loose tunics she favors now, imagine her hair bigger and brighter, as it once was—and the effect is of a figure from a dream emerging in the flesh. Or from a nightmare, in which Ruby is still a boxed-in little girl, doing what she was told and praying faithfully for intervention because she had no will of her own.

Dorothy looks comfortable, her posture relaxed, as if sitting down to tea with Clark is a usual occurrence. There was a time when the only words that passed between her parents were angry ones. It embarrassed Ruby to see her father in those days, looking beaten down. Later, during the divorce, her mother questioned each legal detail, made everything more difficult than it had to be, until she brought out the fight in Clark. Enough time has now gone by, it seems. They can be in the same room without lawyers present, without seething at each other. What have they been talking about? About her, probably.

Ruby pulls a box of Lipton tea from the cupboard, then goes to the stove to turn on the kettle. Robin stands near the back door, leaning against the wall with his arms crossed. Clark is in the other doorway, to the dining room. She's surrounded.

With her back to them all, she asks, "Why can't anyone be happy for me?"

Dorothy answers, "How can I be happy for you if I don't even know what happened?"

"The circumstances seem pretty clear—" Clark begins.

"You don't know the circumstances. You weren't there."

"Don't give me attitude, young lady!"

"I'm not a *lady,* this isn't the nineteenth century. I'm a woman."

"You're not even twenty, and you're acting like you're ten." Clark says, "And tell me, what kinda example do you set when you run off like that?"

"What's that supposed to mean?"

"No one knew where you were!" Clark says. "You were supposed to be staying at the beach house."

Ruby looks to Robin, and he must see the plea in her eyes, because he speaks up. "Dad, that place should be condemned. The party was going on nonstop." He adds, "She called me last night, so she did *try* to get in touch."

"I stayed in a hotel room."

"Let me guess," Clark says. "It's on the credit card I pay for."

"For emergencies, which this *was.*" She crosses her arms and leans back against the counter. This is not how it's supposed to be, her *fa-*

ther on a rampage. She'd expected Dorothy's anger, but Clark has always been her ally during mother-daughter duels. Setting an example for whom? No one has ever looked to her for anything, and now that she has done something she wanted to, without checking in and seeking permission, now she's guilty of falling short of standards?

Dorothy appears to be perplexed by something. "Were you with Calvin at this hotel?"

"No." Then, quickly, Ruby says, "There was a guy at the party—"

"What guy?"

"—I knew him from Crossroads."

"The Catholic program?"

"Yes. His name's Chris. We lost touch, but we still have—I don't know how to explain it. He was there, and I stayed with him."

"Just the two of you?" Dorothy asks.

Ruby nods.

"Since when are you sexually active?"

"Since last night! OK? The entire world now knows. My parents, my ex-boyfriend, my brother, George, a whole party full of people I don't even like. Everyone knows I had sex last night."

Silence. No one seems to know what to say or where to look. After a moment, Robin speaks up, a forced levity in his voice. "When I first had sex, I kept it as quiet as possible."

This actually makes her want to laugh—nervous relief—but Clark wrinkles his nose and says, "Aw, Robin. Come *on*," and she can see Robin's posture shift, so that he's now looking almost as defensive as she is.

Dorothy says to Ruby, "You did use protection, didn't you?"

"Yes." She feels her face warming up. This is really too much.

"I mean, with everything going around these days—"

"I said yes, Dorothy."

The phone rings—a light, electronic trill, so unlike the old mechanical ring from their rotary phone. Clark answers and they all hear him say, "Yes, she's right here. But we're having a family discussion right now."

Ruby feels a jump in her chest. *It's him.* "Give that to me."

"Look, Ruby, we're not done here." Clark speaks into the phone again, saying, "Hold on, Calvin."

Calvin?

She holds out her hands, mouthing, *no*. She looks to Robin again for intervention. He peels himself from the wall and takes the handset from Clark. "Hey, it's me. . . . Yeah, but we're in the middle of some family, um, negotiations. . . . Mm-hmm, it's like Reagan and Gorbachev here. . . . What? . . . No, of course I didn't."

It's annoying to have to witness them bonding like this, but he's doing her a favor, he's saving her from a really awkward conversation. There's a hollow grinding away inside her. Anxiety about Chris, about where he is, what he's doing, what he might have already done.

When Robin hangs up, he announces, "Calvin says he'll be home later, and he wants to speak to you."

All of a sudden both of her parents are talking at once, weighing in on Calvin's call—their words mercifully drowned out by the wail of the kettle. She turns off the flame, pours water over a tea bag in the mug, lets it saturate and drop to the bottom. "I'm not taking relationship advice from my divorced parents," she says.

"Harsh," Robin says, as they all fall silent.

She picks up her tea, grabs the cordless phone, and leaves the room. Enough is enough.

Ruby's exit has both of his parents looking to Robin, as if they're the confused children and he's the adult with the answers. He knows what Ruby just went through; he's been grilled like this before, long ago in this kitchen, for his own transgressions. He was ready to mediate, if need be, but she didn't exactly make it easy. Now he expects to be reprimanded, to take the heat because she won't. They'll surely find something wrong with what *he* did today, and they'll jump on him for it. But, no, they just look at him, helplessness on their faces. Is it actually possible that he will get through all of this blamelessly, that Ruby, who never gets blamed for anything, is going to absorb all the bad feeling in the family?

Clark shakes his head. "Could you imagine if your brother was alive to see this?"

"He'd probably have been down the shore this weekend, too," Robin says, "raising hell like the rest of them."

Clark throws up his hands, and Dorothy admonishes, "*Robin.*"

At first he thinks it's "hell" that has upset them, because who wants to be reminded about eternal damnation when you're remembering your dead son? (And for all he knows, his parents, who have always struck him, more or less, as being atheists, might still entertain the notion of the afterlife.)

But then Clark says, "He was a good kid, he had a real love for life," and Dorothy says, "He truly enjoyed himself, didn't he?" and Clark adds, "If he'd only had the chance to grow up," and Robin sees that it was a mistake to even insinuate that a grown-up Jackson would have been just another problem child.

The more time that passes, the more Jackson, in his father's eyes, and maybe in his mother's, too, has been turned into an angel, beatified as the *slugger* who was destined to be a source of pride, had he not been cut down at the dawn of his potential. If he'd had the chance, he would have grown into the kind of young adult who wouldn't let them down, as Robin has always done, as Ruby has shown she's more than capable of as well. This is so far from what Robin imagines, when he imagines Jackson grown up: definitely a jock, certainly socially aggressive, probably embarrassed to be saddled with a gay brother and a weird sister. Someone who loved his own life but couldn't be counted on to love Robin's, or Ruby's. There's a divergence in these visions that can't be bridged, because it's all speculation anyway, speculation hardening into something like a fact. The might-have-been.

If he'd had the chance . . . And whose fault was it, that he hadn't? The fact that they were both there, Robin and Ruby, at the moment Jackson fell, is never, ever discussed, but none of them have forgotten.

He finds that he wants another cigarette. Wants to call George. Wants to disappear. Little desires flying by in a fraction of a second.

Dorothy stands and dusts off her lap. "It's been a long time since my daughter listened to me," she says, "but I'm going to give it one more try."

Robin says, "Why don't you listen to *her*?"

She cocks her head to the side, as if to more fully receive the idea. "Maybe I will," she says.

Clark gives her a thumbs-up, and Dorothy rather self-consciously returns it, an exchange so unlikely it leaves Robin staring at them both. And then off Dorothy goes into the living room, the path of her footsteps following Ruby's.

And so Robin finds himself alone with his father for the first time in ages. They look at each other, both aware of this.

"Oh!" Robin says, remembering. "I have something." He picks up his bag and pulls out the postcard. "Happy Father's Day."

Clark looks it over, front and back. It's hard to read his expression. "Cheesequake! That brings back memories. Your mother used to sing that song."

"I thought it was your song."

"Your mother was the one with the voice." Clark places the card under a magnet on the fridge. He puts the photo facedown, the inscription facing out. The "prodigal" joke seems to Robin lukewarm, an *almost*.

"So," Clark says, "Wanna see my fax machine?"

The machine, a big beige contraption with a phone and a keypad built into it, sits on a file cabinet in the office, next to a surprisingly modern-looking black desk. "I dial the number of the other machine," Clark demonstrates, fingers tapping, "and then I feed in my document here." On a piece of paper, Clark has written in big letters, "Someone is thinking of you!" With a sheepish grin, he explains, "Annie's got a machine at home, too." Robin listens to the oddly melodic pattern of the numbers with their individual tones, the hiss and beep as the connection is made, the efficient clip and slide of the paper getting sucked inside the machine. The sound of his father sending a love note. "It takes a few minutes, but pretty soon a confirmation comes out the other side, in the tray."

"Cool. Bet that wasn't cheap."

"Company paid for it." He says this with pride, evidence of something earned. "Plus, I bought stock in Xerox," he says, pointing to the logo on the console.

Robin takes in the scope of the office, the comfy order his father has created here, in this room that was once meant for their brother's recovery, and then became a place to escape. Last time Robin was here, his father was excited to show him a new computer, something made by IBM. Clark's interest in technology has seemed to Robin a curiosity, but today he's encouraged by it. After all those years of inertia, he's making room for the future, for possibility.

He glances back toward the dining room, as if Dorothy might still be there, and even though she isn't, he lowers his voice. "So, Annie was here earlier when I called . . ."

"She decided to leave. She could feel the temperature rising, with all of you closing in." He chuckles.

"You didn't want her to meet Dorothy?"

"They've already met."

"When?"

"At your Uncle Stan's wedding."

"That already happened?"

"Last Sunday. Apparently, ahem, you didn't get around to RSVP."

Robin makes an excuse about his mail getting lost in the shuffle between Pittsburgh and Philly, but he knows where the invitation to his uncle's wedding is: exiled to a pile of unopened letters at the bottom of his steamer trunk. He had no intention of celebrating with Stan,

Dorothy's brother, the blowhard of the family, the kind of guy who never once visited them in Manhattan because "the city is full of ingrates." The kind of guy who says "ingrate" because he knows you won't let him get away with saying "nigger" or "queer." Why his father has stayed close to Stan even after the divorce has always been a puzzle, a notch against him. But the real shock of this news isn't that the wedding has already come and gone with both of them there, but that Dorothy hadn't mentioned it. He realizes that they missed their weekly phone call last Sunday, and that today's call got swallowed up by Jackson's birthday.

Clark pushes the door shut, blocking the living room and dining room from view. Robin feels himself on alert now. Clark says, "The wedding was pretty nice. Your mother and I got along just fine, even with both of us having dates."

"Who did *she* bring?"

"A fellow named Stewart. Nice guy. Insurance. Not sure how they met."

"She mentioned him to me, I think." What she'd mentioned, he recalls now, is that she'd placed a personal ad some time ago; but he didn't know about any insurance man. "I guess I haven't been keeping up," Robin adds.

"You kids live your lives," Clark says, as he runs a finger over the fax machine, wiping off dust that doesn't actually seem to be there, "and we live ours."

There might have been a time when the possibility of his parents, dating other people, meeting face-to-face, would have filled him with agony. Now it's come and gone, out of sight, out of mind. A nonevent. And maybe that's not so surprising, because as much bad feeling was stirred up by the divorce, at its heart it was never about unfaithfulness. Neither one of them had an affair. There was no injured party. There were only "irreconcilable differences." *I just couldn't seem to do anything right in your mother's eyes* was Clark's way of talking about it. *Your father pulled away from me,* was Dorothy's. *She became such a critical person,* he said. *He's so shut down,* she said. *He wasn't/She wasn't the person I married.* For a time, they had confessed to him, over and over. But that was years ago.

And then he remembers what had angered him about Stan's wedding invitation, why he looked at the envelope but decided he wouldn't open it. "I wasn't invited with a date," Robin says. "Ruby got a plus-one, but I didn't."

"Ruby didn't come, either. Two no-shows."

"But you know I've been dating someone, right?"

Clark doesn't say anything, doesn't exactly meet Robin's eyes, either, which only pushes Robin to forge ahead, to make a point. In a rush of words he talks about Peter, how they met, their life together in Pittsburgh, how it got "serious," none of which he's mentioned to Clark before. He takes him all the way through to the breakup. "Just yesterday," Robin says.

Clark mumbles something, impossible to make out but with enough of an encouraging tone that Robin keeps going.

"You know that George is gay, too, don't you?"

"It was great to see George again. I've always liked him." With an uneasy laugh, Clark adds, "Not sure what he's doing with his hair, though."

"He's growing dreadlocks," Robin says.

No response.

"I assumed you knew about George, but maybe you haven't thought about it." He pauses, every second like a full minute ticking by, demanding to be filled with words. "But, see, the thing is, we've been best friends for so long, but now, I'm wondering if maybe we might be more than friends . . ."

Clark blows a bunch of air through his lips. His head hangs a bit, and his eyes stay on the fax machine.

Robin feels his own face heating up in embarrassment. This conversation started out okay, but now . . . Why'd you have to go and ruin a perfectly good moment? He's angry with his father, with himself, too, and it comes out in his tone of voice: "Are you going to say anything, Clark?"

Clark turns to him with a pained look, though he seems to be working to contain it, to put a braver face forward. "One thing I've learned over the years, sometimes less is more. If you shoot off your mouth, it's hard to unshoot it."

"If you need to say something to me, let's just have it out."

Clark waves his hand, as if wiping steam off a bathroom mirror. "Annie told me something recently. She said life is about expansion. Pretty good, huh?"

"I guess."

"Because as you go along, you have to hold more and more in your head. You meet new people, come across some new ideas, adjust to new circumstances. You can't say, 'Nope, that's all there is, I already know everything I need to know, nothing new for me, end of story.' Because where does that leave you? So, yeah. Life's about expansion."

"All right," Robin says, because he feels like he has to say something agreeable. What he wants to say is *What does that have to do with George and me?* But he knows: A gay son is still a new idea for Clark. A black boyfriend on top of that is newer still. This is what George was predicting, in the car today: *If I was your boyfriend we'd see how racist they were . . .*

I'm not there yet, his father is saying, but I'm trying. So be patient. Don't expect too much from me, not yet.

Is this the burden of coming out? Wait for them to catch up, while they *try* to understand who you are and how your heart works. It's not exactly the father-son moment he thought they were about to have, a few minutes ago when Clark closed the door as if to signal a new alliance. It's not the advice he maybe thought he might get when he brought up Peter, and George. Because that's what he could use, he realizes. Advice. A way out of the thicket. Not "I'm trying to expand so I can fit you in," but "I have enough room for you now."

In acting class, his professor told them to identify the moment when they freeze up, when they can't go any deeper. At those moments, ask yourself: What am I afraid of? This is one of those moments: He can't find a way to play his part, the good son following the father's lead. *What are you afraid of?* His mind flies back to Jackson's grave.

"I'm afraid if I get sick you'll abandon me," he says. He says this out loud, though it could have remained an unspoken thought, an exercise.

Clark looks bewildered, and then the words sink in, and his look turns stricken.

"I'm not sick," Robin says. "I mean, I don't think I am. But it scares me."

"I don't know much about it," Clark says, in a clear voice.

Robin waits for something more, but there's only silence that can't yet be filled in.

"Never mind," Robin says and makes a move for the door. "This is the wrong time—"

He's shot off his mouth, and now he can't unshoot it.

Clark extends his arm, as if to stop Robin from leaving, but his reach falls short, and so Robin keeps going.

Behind Ruby's bedroom door, Robin hears them going at it, his mother and his sister, loud enough that he considers listening in for the blow-by-blow, loud enough that he decides to keep on moving.

In his bedroom, he flips the light switch and is assaulted by the flashy, silver Art Deco wallpaper he chose years ago. It seemed like a good idea at the time. Jackson's bed had been taken out, and the room was Robin's alone. (He never asked where all of Jackson's things went. Were they thrown out? Or is there a box in the basement packed with the baseball trophies that used to line a shelf over Jackson's bed, brass-plated figurines of boys with raised bats that glinted in the morning sunlight while Jackson lay sleeping beneath, a bubble of spit at his lips? Robin remembers how he used to wake up early and read quietly in bed, getting a half hour to himself before Jackson bolted up and began talking right away: "Wanna play *Star Wars*? Wanna play Army? Wanna play *Planet of the Apes*?")

The wallpaper makes him cringe now: a busy pattern of strong vertical lines blooming into shells, flowers, butterfly wings that makes the walls look they are leaning inward, threatening to collapse. He'd picked it out during a brief, intense phase when he became obsessed by everything Art Deco. Living in Manhattan had attuned his eye not only to the majestic Chrysler Building but also to other buildings done in that style, sturdy banks and elegant apartment houses, and the decorative details that popped up everywhere, like on the sidewalks around Rockefeller Center, where the trees grew out of pewter grilles shaped like crescent moons. He saw himself in those earliest New York days as a refugee from the suburbs, from the rituals and routines of boys he didn't like and didn't understand. This was his dandified, Oscar Wilde period, when he addressed his friends as "darling" and wore velvet pants he'd begged his mother to buy him from Macy's. Transporting this aesthetic back to his weekend bedroom in Greenlawn was a way to extend the vision he'd created for himself as a young urbanite, a student of theater, finally living in a suitable place, awash in grand style and sharp decor.

New York proved to be grimier and harder-edged than he'd first let himself see. The city was still recovering from financial bankruptcy, was famous for potholes and gridlock, was under the weight of constant crime no longer confined to "bad neighborhoods" but potentially waiting around any corner. His feminine getups, which gave him a certain luster among the other drama students at Washington Irving, also attracted the very same insults he thought he was leaving behind in New Jersey, and he soon enough switched gears and began wearing olive drab bought in Army & Navy stores and Converse high-tops with argyle socks. Now the wallpaper seems not to point to New York's lost grandeur, but to his own tarnished vision of the fabulous life he'd expected. And it's also wildly out of place in this old house, like a silver buckle on a broken-in work boot.

He can see now that there was something remarkable about his father letting him choose this paper. When they had stood side by side, slopping the paste on the back, then hanging and smoothing it together, Robin was aware of it only as work, not as a gift, which it surely was. Clark was letting him have his little bit of glamour, even if it was a folly. It must have been difficult for his father to hold his tongue. He wonders if he ever thanked him.

Next to his bed is a nightstand that was also part of the redecoration, with a bit of Deco flair: curved corners and sculpted feet. It has a little locked cabinet in it. Robin reaches his hand around the back of the nightstand, where the key hangs on a hook. He knows what he'll find inside the cabinet: a pile of diaries that he kept during high school. He used to fill them up, and then bring them to New Jersey and keep them hidden here, away from the prying eyes of his mother, who would read them, he was sure, if she had the chance.

He scans across pages of his cursive handwriting, fatter and loopier than the way he writes today. The words are large and spread out on the page, as if his every thought deserved headline treatment. There are details about his classes, arguments with his mother about his curfew and his chores, breathless accounts of shows he'd seen: *Children of a Lesser God, 42nd Street, Baryshnikov on Broadway.* But this isn't what he wants to read.

He wants to read about falling in love. He wants to read about Alton.

There's this girl named Michelle who wants to go out with me, but I told her I didn't want to. Alton said his new special nickname for me is "Heartbreaker." . . . I went with Alton to get his ear pierced at a store in the West Village. His father's going to disown him when he sees it. . . . Alton told me I was good looking enough to act in movies. He said his cousin knew an agent and I should talk to him. . . . Alton and his fake girlfriend Carolyn and me went and saw The Shining, *which was creepy. She hid her eyes the whole time on his shoulder. She was totally faking being way more scared than she really was. She's jealous of his friendship with me. . . . I told Alton his curls were cute, and he let me put my fingers in his hair.*

Eleventh grade, Washington Irving High School. He thought at the time that he'd found a "soul mate" in Alton. *I finally told him about the stuff I've done with other guys. I told him about my piano "lessons." I figured I'd shock him, but he didn't say much.* His silence at the time seemed like acceptance; now Robin can see how quietly freaked out Alton had been, in part because he was so intrigued. *He said we should be totally open with each other. And he said "I would only do that with someone if it was love."* He flips ahead, looking for the entry about the weekend spent at Alton's family vacation home in the Hamptons. The night Alton climbed into bed with him, and after months of flirtation, and teasing, and circular conversations about beauty and bisexuality, they finally had sex.

I'm afraid to even write this because I might jinx it or someone might find it, but I'm not going to hold back. Alton rubbed Vaseline on his dick and put it inside me. I told him I'd never done it before and he said "You love me, so why not?" It hurt especially when he got faster but love hurts they say. I think that this was the most special thing that's ever happened to me. I can't believe we DID IT. I wish we kissed more. He was weird the next day in front of his parents at breakfast.

And then weeks of worry and pining: *He's been so busy we haven't had any time together. . . . We're not in the same workshop this quarter so we don't have much to talk about. . . . He said he's "resetting his priorities" whatever that's supposed to mean. . . . I asked what I did wrong and he didn't answer. . . . He said he has a lot of pressure on him.* No more trips to the West Village, no more weekends in the Hamptons, no more tagging along on dates with Carolyn, no more special nicknames. He remembers all of it clearly, remembers how he'd keep himself awake at night, crying under his pillow. The surprise is this: between the first diary entry and the last, only six months went by. The great obsession of his high school years flourished and died in half a year. That's less time than he spent with Peter, though it somehow has the weight of something longer.

And then there's this, the final entry in this diary, dated June 25, 1981, almost four years ago to the week:

> *George says I let my feelings take over with Alton. He said sex is an animal act. Humans are animals and have basic needs that are biological or chemical. Alton's tendencies were probably "experimenting" even though he said he loved me. George said for me it was more of an "orientation" being gay, based on the way my brain is wired, and I agreed, which was more than I ever admitted to George before. He is such a good friend. He never says anything mean to me and actually never fills my head with compliments, which maybe is the sign of a true friend, unlike a user who is always buttering you up. I didn't really get until now what a user Alton truly was. George is honest. I asked George if he would ever "experiment" and he said "I would never rule it out" which is* so *George. I almost said do you want to mess around, because I'm horny (like an animal, ha ha). Though I don't need to fall for another straight boy.*

At first, he doesn't remember writing this, though with every sentence the moment comes into focus. George had come into the city that day, and the two of them rode the subway downtown. They paid the quarter for the Staten Island Ferry, traveled there and back in the salty harbor air, and then went up to the observation deck at the World Trade Center, which was the closest he'd ever been to the top of the world. They stayed there through sunset, watching the lights come on all over the city, and were the last to get kicked out by the guards. While Robin confessed about Alton, George looked him in the eyes and listened, and that made it easier to speak.

Dorothy says that George is going to be really handsome when he gets older. Some people are late bloomers. Too bad George isn't my boyfriend. He knows me so well. Better than anyone in the world.

When they parted earlier, he wanted to say more to George, wanted to blurt out, "Let's be lovers." But somehow he couldn't. When Peter dumped him in the restaurant, he didn't speak in his own defense. When his father, just a little while ago, wouldn't assure him, I won't abandon you if you get sick, Robin kept quiet again. He often thinks of himself as a open book, all his feelings on the surface, but now he sees that over and over, where his heart is concerned, he has failed to speak his truth. It's there on these pages about Alton. It was there even when he lived in this house, when his friendship with Scott Schatz became sexual at the same time his crush on Todd Spicer became sexual, too, and each of them, in their own way, stifled his affection, chastising, "Why do you always have to *talk* about everything? You're acting like a girl." The message is clear: Don't tell another guy what you feel, if you don't want your feelings hurt. Don't ask for more than he's willing to give you, because then he'll give you nothing at all. If your heart is aching, keep it to yourself. It's your problem, not his. Alton's vision of Robin as a *heartbreaker* is exactly backward: It's his own heart that's been injured, again and again, sometimes cleaved by rejection, sometimes smothered by silence.

He looks up from the old diary, to the opposite side of the room, and he is overtaken by a jolt from the past: suddenly the Deco paper is not yet up, Jackson's trophies have not yet been cleared, and Jackson's death is new and fresh and staggering. Robin is fourteen, and feverish, lying right here, reading the copy of *Franny and Zooey* he got for Christmas. He looks up from the book to the other bed, and he understands that it will never be host to his brother again, but at the same time the bed doesn't seem exactly empty, either; and then he looks out the window, across the back yard to the Spicers' house, where a light is on in Todd's bedroom, a shadow moving across the window. The last time he'd seen Todd, he'd been humiliated in front of all his friends, Todd had actually spit beer on him and threatened to beat him up. And in that moment he couldn't tell: was his brother gone and Todd still around, but out of reach, or was Todd gone and Jackson lingering here like a ghost? What has been lost, and why, and what part of it is his fault? It is a moment of infinite disorientation: There is pain that he thinks he has caused, and pain that he thinks was thrust upon him, but he can't tell one from the other.

And now, here, today, coming back from this slide into the past, he sees that there is a difference between these various losses, these multiple pains. That for all his confusion as a fourteen-year-old, there always was. He can't bring his brother back. He can't ever undo that day on the slide in the playground. He can't change the ways he has been misunderstood, even used, by boys he has been drawn to.

But it must still be possible to love and be loved back in equal measure. It has to be. Because why else is that love put in your heart, if not to find expression? And why else do we carry on, if not to try again?

He thinks of the moment at the graveside when George took his hand.

And he wants to bow his head again, because what he wishes for, hopes for, even prays for, if that's what this is, is not forgiveness, not for the past, but courage, for what comes next.

OK, here it goes. Mother-daughter hour in her childhood bedroom. Another scolding from a member of the MacKenzie family. Ruby has already tried to beg for some time to take a nap, but Dorothy insisted on talking right now, said she'd been in Greenlawn long enough and wanted to get back to Manhattan. They could talk there or here, but they were going to talk. "OK, talk," Ruby told her. "But I'm expecting a call."

She has already tried the motel—glad to get a woman at the front desk instead of that patronizing man. Very kindly this woman told her that Chris had checked out. Yes, she was quite sure he'd gone. The maid had already turned the room. Ruby hung up the phone and stared out her window into the night sky, pitch black, except for a single star, or was it a planet, she can never be sure what she's seeing up there. The moon wasn't yet visible—that's not a sign, she tells herself, though it's hard to avoid thinking that way.

The mood is fraught—it seems like one of them will speak, and then the other, but all that comes out is a series of sighs. Ruby huddles near the headboard. Dorothy sits on the other end of the bed. Under a bright overhead light, the wear and tear of the years strain her face. People sometimes tell Ruby that she resembles Dorothy, but she hates that. She'll never be a woman like her mother, whose every worry, attitude, and opinion is so transparent. A woman marked by a failed marriage, the mess of divorce, children gone or out of reach. No way.

It occurs to her to deal with this the way Wendy did with her mother—to just take whatever is coming, and leave it at that. Not to put up a fight, because everything eventually blows over. Laugh it off.

And yet, when it comes to Dorothy, she doesn't feel very forgiving, doesn't feel it in her to cut that much slack.

Dorothy says, "Tell me about this boy," and Ruby immediately wants to explode.

"It's none of your business." She can hardly keep her voice down.

"I would like to know."

"I'm entitled to privacy."

"I wish you'd confide in me."

"Been there, done that. It didn't do me any good."

"What on earth are you referring to?"

"You know."

"I'm not clairvoyant, dear."

"When you told me to pretend I was still a virgin. *After* I had sex!"

Dorothy adjusts herself uncomfortably. "You were traumatized, Ruby. I was trying to help."

"You told me to *forget* about it."

"I wanted you to move on."

"You wanted me to lie."

In the hall she hears footsteps—Robin must be out there. He seems to pause, but then his door is opening and closing. He's blocking himself off from this. She can't blame him.

Dorothy says, "*You* didn't want anyone to know, Ruby. You were upset that Robin found out."

"Found out? You told him!"

"He knew something had happened."

"You could have *helped* me."

"I did help you, Ruby." She lowers her voice. "I went to that boy's, to Brandon's, high school and filed a complaint. I remember it very well. I was told by the counselors that his parents were called in, and that they would discipline him. I followed up, and they told me they'd keep him away from you."

Ruby hugs her pillow. This is new information—is it even true? If it was, wouldn't she have known about it by now? It's true that she never saw Brandon again at any of the school mixers. She'd thought that was a matter of luck. She was sixteen when all that happened, though it seems forever ago. If it hadn't been for Chris this weekend, Brandon would have remained buried.

Dorothy is staring at her. "Dear, I'm concerned about what you said downstairs. About last night."

"I couldn't stay a virgin forever."

Dorothy rubs her face wearily, and Ruby almost feels bad about the sarcasm.

"I don't want to be lectured, Mom."

"Yes, you've made it clear. You're not taking advice from divorcées—" She offers a tight smile. "But if you'd tell me even a little something about Chris—"

"Why should I?"

"—I'll listen."

"You never do—"

"Give me a chance! For God's sake, give me a goddamn chance." Dorothy shouts these words, and the surprise of this—because she never raises her voice, she relies on measured condescension to do the job—has its effect. Ruby takes a deep breath. Feels herself retreat from the argument. She's aware all over again of her ongoing physical discomfort—her stomach, her sunburn, a new, bloated feeling that she imagines for a wild moment to be some early warning of pregnancy—and then she does what she can to banish all this irritation, to concentrate.

"I don't know," she mumbles.

"Please," Dorothy says. "I don't want your life to be a mystery to me."

"I met him a long time ago," Ruby begins. "Do you remember Crossroads?" She talks, haltingly at first, about the retreat weekend, about the phone calls that followed and then ended without warning. "I kind of made myself forget him," she says. "But I never really did, you know?" She says it was a surprise that he was there at the party, that he recognized her first. She tells her that she thinks he's good looking, that she likes his style, that she already feels things for him she never felt for Calvin. Dorothy seems to be holding up her part of this—staying quiet, receptive—so Ruby says something she's never said aloud before—that Chris is the first person to understand all the confusion in her head about God. She doesn't mention cocaine or suicide or condoms slipping off—this is obviously not what you tell your mother, no matter how much she wants to be close to you—and anyway, these things don't seem important compared to the overwhelming sense of fate and certainty that her feelings for Chris are wrapped in.

"Was he respectful?" Dorothy asks. "Of your sexuality?"

"Yeah."

"And you did actually have sexual intercourse with him?"

"Yeah."

"And?"

"It was major."

"Major?"

Even though Dorothy keeps pressing on, Ruby senses that she's nearing the limit of what she can tell her mother, what her mother can hear. She says, "I think it's what people mean when they say 'making love,' instead of 'having sex.' "

Dorothy brushes her hand lightly along Ruby's hair. "Well, dear, that sounds like passion. That's the word for what you're describing."

Ruby wrinkles her nose. "That's something out of a romance novel. I mean—he gave me an orgasm."

"I see."

So that was the point where she went over the edge—she can see it in Dorothy's face, in her body language, the way she's rubbing her hands together now, as if smoothing in lotion. "Sorry, Mom."

"No. Don't be. Passion is physical. Romance is all the trappings, which you can whip up without real passion. You know, Clark was very romantic when we were first together, a million years ago. But when I look back on it, I don't think that we ever felt passionate about each other."

"But you married him."

"I didn't have much of a choice, dear. You know that."

"You could have gotten an abortion."

Dorothy blinks, an almost bewildered look on her face. "You can't imagine how frightening an idea that was."

"Right," Ruby says. "The coat-hanger days. But if you really wanted to—we learned all about these women's collectives in the sixties that were doing almost like an Underground Railroad for pregnant women."

"Just because you learned it in school," Dorothy says, and then swallows hard. Something passes over her face. Dorothy rubs her hands on her thighs and then stands. Ruby senses that the limit has been reached. Of course. There's always a limit.

Dorothy says, "I'd like to get on the road before it's too late. Perhaps we can continue this conversation in the car?'

"I'm not coming with you."

"Why not?" Dorothy blurts.

"I told you, I gave him this number. I need to wait for this phone call now."

"If that's what you want," she says, her voice cool—the same old Dorothy again.

"I can get back to the city by bus."

As they hug good-bye—wrapping stiff arms around each other, their cheeks brushing—the familiar smell of her mother's powdery-spicy perfume is suddenly everywhere, and Ruby almost changes her mind. It would be easy to get in the car and go back to Manhattan and sleep in her real bedroom tonight. It would be nice to imagine that the drive home would allow them to keep talking things through, and that this would be a watershed moment. They'd end the night huddled over the *New York Times* crossword puzzle, something that had once been part of their Sunday ritual. They'd eat the food Dorothy had cooked, and even sip a little wine, something Dorothy only does in moderation now. It would feel like a special occasion, and tomorrow she'd wake up refreshed, ready to start her life over again, free of Calvin, and move ahead with Chris.

But Dorothy's embrace is brief, and the awkwardness magnifies as they pull apart with nothing more to say.

The door shuts behind Dorothy and Ruby is left staring at its blank back side—wood painted white, gone dingy, full of tiny pushpin holes and scraps of Scotch tape, remnants from the teen-magazine posters that used to hang there. She's newly aware of the bloated feeling in her gut, the way her abdominal muscles ache, and above all her desire to sleep.

Lying in bed, she runs through everything she just told her mother and sees the conversation for what it is—a surprising level of honesty wrapped in a lot of avoidance. Selective details. A lack of trust in her mother's ability to respond. Dorothy isn't going to warm up to Chris, assuming she ever meets him, which is something Ruby would actually like to put off for as long as possible. And Chris might be in danger, and she couldn't tell her mother about it. So what does that say about fantasies of being *close*?

She hears Dorothy across the hall, saying good-bye to Robin, their voices muffled and conspiratorial, intimate in tone. There's a bit of light laughter between them. That's just the way it is. It's always seemed unfair that Robin has always been, will always be, the favorite. Now it strikes Ruby as a relief. A kind of freedom. She can do what she wants, and if her mother doesn't like it, well, too bad, because her influence can only go so far. If there's anything that's been made perfectly clear this weekend, it is this: no one is ready for her to grow up, to be a woman, and make her own choices. No one except Ruby herself. She is done waiting for their permission.

After a while she knocks on Robin's door. He calls her in, and there, amid all that loud wallpaper, he lies on his bed. He's flipping through a notebook—one of those speckled composition books, black-and-white, like something from middle school—but as she comes into the room, he closes it quickly and turns it facedown. She says, "I'm not going back to the city with Dorothy."

"So I heard."

"Was she pissed?"

"You know Mom. She takes everything personally."

She points to his notebook. "What's that?"

"An old diary. From high school. I used to get myself quite worked up."

"Used to?"

He smiles. He really does have a great smile—she thinks for the millionth time how Robin's life has gone the way it has because people have wanted to get closer to that face of his. If she didn't love him, she would probably hate him.

He says, "There are things in here I sort of forgot about."

"I never keep a diary. What if someone else reads it?"

"Apparently, I'm an exhibitionist." He thrusts out an arm theatrically. "When I die a famous actor, you can sell these to the tabloids. I promise to leave a beautiful corpse."

He means it as a joke, but hearing his words is like being forced to swallow more alcohol. Her stomach flips. There's just too much talk about death this weekend. It's gotten under her skin. Maybe there's no avoiding it, given what day it is. But with Chris still missing she feels the sourness of the very thought—she feels a sudden resolve.

"OK," she begins. "I guess I'm on some kind of honesty kick tonight, so—it was nice of you to come and find me, because you thought something bad had happened. I do *get* that."

"But?"

"But I'm worried that you ruined my chance to be with Chris. You came too soon."

"I'm suspicious of him, Ruby. When I met him, he was kind of in a state."

"He's just emotional."

Robin nods reluctantly. *Emotional* he seems to understand.

"I *like* him. A lot. I *care* about him. With Calvin—I always thought Calvin was cool and unique, but I never felt, you know, *passion*." She can't stop the word from coming out. Score one for Dorothy. "You understand."

"I guess."

"I want a real *lover*."

"Only one? Having just one is so passé—"

"Be serious, you queen."

This makes him smile again, and then he sits up, adjusting his posture, and announces, still smiling, though it now seems a little forced, that Peter broke off their relationship. And there's more to it than that, he starts to explain—which is when Ruby flashes to the car ride up the Parkway, and then to the cemetery, and she knows what he's going to tell her. "Does this have to do with George?"

"Yes." He grabs the notebook and reads, "*Too bad George isn't my boyfriend.* That's from high school, before I even knew he was gay." He begins to tell her about his weekend. She listens with a kind of amazement about a near fistfight in an alley, about hiding from the cops, about the two of them going back to their apartment and having sex for the first time. It's not the details that surprise her—nothing that happens to her brother really comes as a surprise, given all that she knows about who he is and what he's capable of—but rather it's the fact that their lives seem, for the first time ever, to be made up of the same material. Maybe separate from each other, but at least parallel, which is something. He tells her that it's not just the sexual connection that has been the revelation with George, but the fact that he actually possesses all the qualities Robin wanted Peter to have: stability, trustworthiness, sexual safety. He asks, "Do you think that's weird?"

"No, because you can fall in love with someone slowly, or it can hit you hard, right away. With Chris, it just was like—" She snaps her fingers.

"I've fallen in love at first sight many times. I was so into Peter when he first walked into our seminar. But that kind of thing never seems to last. Do you remember Alton?"

"How could I forget? You used to go on and on about him."

"That wasn't love. It was just, I don't know. Hormones." Robin points to the notebook and flips through a few pages. He seems to scan them as he frowns and says, "I have no idea if George is feeling it. Did it seem like that to you? Did you notice anything?"

"I noticed that George seemed, like, less sheltered?"

"He's turning into like, I don't know, an activist. But he still doesn't have a lot of experience. With guys."

She tells him, "When I saw you two you at the cemetery, I thought, I don't think I've ever seen you holding hands with a guy before."

He looks back at the notebook and says, "I guess that's probably true." He seems to drift into thought, memory—she can only guess where he's just gone.

She had been amazed by the sight of them with their hands intertwined, by its out-in-the-openness, and by how it seemed perfectly normal to her—or rather, a perfect fit for Robin. A natural expression. And even though she was sad that Chris wasn't there with her—that she had left him behind instead of figuring out a better plan than *I'll call you*—she still felt like there was some possibility for them. For her and Chris. If Robin could have this connection with George, more romantic than their usual friendship allowed, then she could find some way to fit Chris into her life, even though there were all these strikes against them.

She moves to sit down on the bed. And then she's hit by a rush. She thinks it must be the turbulence in her stomach threatening to come forth. Then she thinks, no, not my stomach, something else, lower down—it feels like her period, but it's too early for that. Then she feels the warmth, and excuses herself to go to the bathroom.

She touches herself, looks at her fingertips. Yes. There it is. She's started to bleed. She must have calculated her cycle wrong. Or maybe it's just come early—perfectly, joyously early.

She thinks, I should always have faith.

Back in her room, she lies down again, and she feels fifty pounds lighter. Cleansed. (The fact that that Clark has a girlfriend has worked in her favor. Tucked under the sink, she found what she needed. Never before has a box of Tampax seemed like such a gift.)

At last she is able to rest, to sleep. She even dreams, wild images of the ocean that are both scary and beautiful, as she floats on the surface in the sun and then dives into blue depths. There's a far-off landscape, a lush green shore, Chris is in the water with her, swimming ahead, and he's telling her, "We've got to get to the place." He keeps saying it, "That's our place," but she can't quite keep him in her sights and then he's gone and there are birds circling overhead, their calls becoming louder and menacing, mechanical. The sound of machines grinding away.

She awakes, but the dream carries noisily into the room with her. Quickly she understands that the phone is ringing. She finds it, tangled up in the blanket with her.

"Hello?"

"It's me."

It's him.

"Are you OK?" she asks.

"I'm OK," Chris says.

"I called the motel, you weren't there."

"Sorry."

"Did they give you my message?"

"I got it when I was checking out, so I had to wait to get to a phone and didn't have any change, and I couldn't find my phone card. I couldn't find my wallet."

"You lost your wallet."

"Yeah. My driver's license and my money and, well, everything."

"That sucks."

"I didn't want to call collect."

"I thought—" She's not sure she should say it. "I was starting to freak out."

"Sorry. You probably had a lot of dark thoughts. Why wouldn't you?"

"So you're not still wanting to—do anything?"

"I'm not gonna off myself." He says this a labored way, almost as if he's embarrassed, but it's hard to feel reassured, because just hearing him voice it makes the possibility of suicide reassert itself. He says, "I'm back at my mom's place now. How are you?"

"My family's been pretty difficult. But I'm trying to tell them everything's OK." She rubs her face, feeling the weight of the dream still moving in her skull. "I mean, everything between us. Isn't it?"

"Sure," Chris says.

"Really?"

"I meant what I said, Ruby. I fell in love with you all over again."

"I love you, too." She rushes to say more, because even those three important words aren't enough. "I'm sorry I said mean things."

"I have so much respect for you. No one ever fights for me."

"You're the one who fought for me. I heard that you punched Calvin."

"He threw a chair at me."

"God, I'm so done with him. I never want to see him again."

"You don't have to."

"Except now my brother's supposedly going to work with him on some dumb movie."

"Let's not talk about him. He's a chump." She laughs, but she notices he doesn't. He says, "So you really didn't have sex with him?"

"No. But—look. I don't want to talk about virginity. It's just this patriarchal construct, and it's so fucked up that people put all this value on it—"

"I wish I'd been a virgin for you," he says. "I wish I hadn't boinked a bunch of airheads I didn't care about."

"It doesn't change anything," she says. She thinks, *a bunch*? She wonders, *Do I want to know*?

He says, "I have to tell you something. I'd rather tell you in person, but I don't think I can wait."

"When can we see each other?" she asks. She starts proposing plans—should she take a bus down to Princeton? Does he want to drive up here, or could they meet in Manhattan? Should they try to find another hotel room?

He's quiet as she throws out all these ideas. Why isn't he saying yes? She feels a stab of panic—it's that dream all over again, but now she's way, way out in the ocean, and the ocean is finite, and like some kind of Old World vision it ends in a waterfall plunging into the void, and she has to swim with all her strength to avoid the fall.

Then he says, "I've been talking with my mom. She's had this plan in the works for a while. She wants me to go to this camp."

"Summer camp?"

"It's for young people with substance abuse problems."

"Really? Like, you'd be a camp counselor?"

"No . . ."

"I don't get it." She's not sure why she can't follow this.

"I'd be there to get off cocaine. Once and for all."

"Oh." And now she's out of the dream entirely. The water has gone still. Chris is there saying, *the place we have to get to,* and she's waking up all over again. There was no edge-of-the-world plunge. There is just his voice on the phone, in the darkness of her childhood bedroom, where she lies wrapped in a blanket, with the sensation of blood fresh upon her.

"My mom's been trying to get me to go to this place for a while," Chris says. "And I've been saying no, because I don't trust anyone to really help me, you know?"

"Yeah, I know that feeling."

"And actually it was one of the reasons I was thinking about killing myself. I mean, she wanted me to go to this camp, and I wanted to do anything in the world except go there. I brought all this money down the shore thinking I could do so much coke that I'd . . . I don't know. Just surpass what I'd done before. But then, when I got to the point that I was actually writing a suicide note . . ."

She feels herself recoiling for a moment. Thinks of Robin's suspicions, thinks that he was right after all, that Chris is too much trouble. And then is fighting back against that vision, which she does not want to believe.

Chris tells her that after she drove away, he spent part of the afternoon at Our Lady of Perpetual Help, on his knees, head bowed, struggling to figure out what to say. "I didn't want to pray to that mean old man on his fucking throne in the clouds. So I figured, I'll just sort of make a list of what I want, like, what's important. Like, I don't want to be high all the time. I really don't. And I can't lose you again. I almost lost you because I was high." It sounds to her like he might be crying now. There's a hoarseness to his voice, a sniffle between the words. "So now I have to do something about it, right? Because you can't just speak the truth and then ignore it."

"No."

"So, maybe I have to give this rehab camp a try."

"For how long?"

"Six weeks."

"The rest of the summer," she says quietly. It might as well be forever. How can she let him go for six whole weeks when they've only had a day together?

"Will you wait for me?" he asks.

"Why wouldn't I?"

"Because I'm a drug addict."

She pauses. "That's an intense word."

"It's a pretty big deal, Ruby. More than I probably let on." He says, "College has been one big coke party."

She listens as he tells her about this problem, its escalation, its greedy hold over him. He talks about sniffing flyaway bits of powder out of the upholstery of a sofa, of spending money meant for textbooks on buying more coke, of carrying around too much cash all the time and buying from scary men in the dark alleys behind nightclubs. He says he will probably drop out of school again, probably find some kind of job when he's done with this camp. Work for a living, keep himself busy, stay away from people like Benjamin and Alice. Stay away from temptation. She thinks this must all be a good thing, that his confession is what she needs to erase the worries she'd had about him. If she can just be with him again, look into his remarkable eyes, kiss that lip with its tender, innocent scar, she'll know that all will be well.

But this is when he tells her that camp starts tomorrow. In a Midwestern state.

He has a flight out of Newark Airport first thing in the morning.

His mother is already packing a bag for him.

And in this moment her entire life realigns. What matters and what doesn't. What is passion and what is just passing time. What everyone else has wanted for her, and what she wants for herself. I'll wait for him, she thinks. What else would I do?

They talk. They talk about everything that's happened in the hours since she left him down the shore, and then about everything that transpired in the years since their phone calls ended. "Those were our lost years," Chris says.

"I still can't believe I found you again," Ruby says.

They talk without thinking of time.

When at last Chris's mother calls him away, and they hang up—*I love you, I love you*—Ruby feels almost embarrassed—even though she's alone—to discover the snot dripping from her nose. Down below, there's been more blood. She didn't want to break away from him and now she's sticky and she wants another shower.

When she comes back from the bathroom, she sees that there's moonlight in the room. Outside the window, fat and orange and filling the sky almost magically, the moon is finally there, on the ascent. It's a different moon than last night's—already shrinking on one side, like a piece of fruit left on the counter to age.

She's aware of what a deadly quiet night it is. There's barely a car on the road. No laughter from neighbors barbecuing in their yards. All she hears is the sound of crickets, a faint musical croaking that has always been the sound of summer nights in New Jersey.

Then she picks up the gurgle of the television from downstairs. Clark must be settling in for the night. A lot of those lost years passed by right there, on the couch, near her father, with the TV on and not much being said. She has at times resented all those vanished hours, resented the split in her family that forced her to spend time here, when she might have been somewhere else, of her own choosing. But right now, in the middle of this silent summer night, drained of the energy she just gave to Chris, as she sent him off to repair himself, the comfort of the living room seems like all she can manage. She pulls herself up and heads toward the stairs, toward the sound of something familiar.

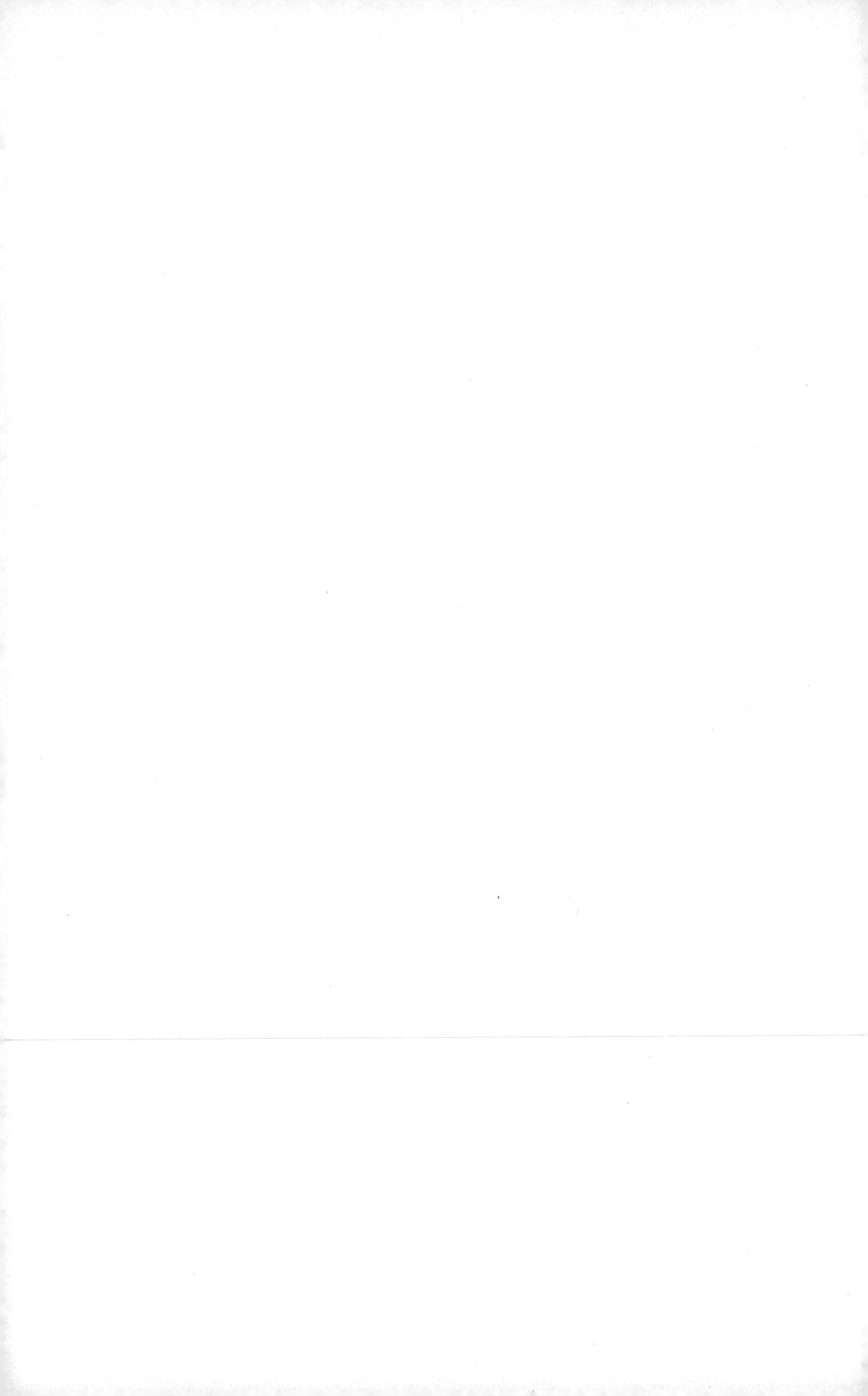

A car in the driveway brings Robin to the window. It's not just any door, but the distinctive heavy slam of the Cadillac. The yard is bright with moonlight, and George is making his way across it.

He's been poring through his diaries for a while now, feeling the distance between who he was then and is today, and also, more obviously, how time has failed to change him. All the ways he hasn't yet mastered his fears, focused his actions. He reads a line he wrote at fifteen or sixteen, like, *I'm going to try harder to reach out to Ruby,* or *I'm going to rehearse more outside of class,* or *I'm going to learn to be a better listener,* and it could just as easily have been written today at age twenty.

It's been strange to be holed up in Greenlawn, this close to Manhattan, and not go into the city. Not even feel the pull of it. When his mother left, she invited him back with her, and as he told her, no, I'm going to stay here so George and I can make an early start for Philadelphia, he could see that she wasn't quite sure how to take it; in the old days, if Dorothy was driving from Greenlawn to New York, her children were always in tow. But they're not children now, not in the same way. So some things in your life do change. External things. Inside, it seems, if these diaries contain any insight at all, you continue to be the same person. Unless you can be brave.

Home is a powerfully mysterious concept right now. Philadelphia is new and temporary. Manhattan is his official address, and yet he spends less time there than at any point in the past five years. With all of them in Greenlawn today, this place has the whiff of family life as it might have been lived had the earth not shaken under their feet all those years ago; but he could hardly call this home. Clark lives here, amid the memories, but Robin feels caught in a role between a visitor and a guest, like a squatter with an old claim who pops up from time to time for a meal and a nap. He knows he'll never again do more than pass through this house, never stay for long. He'll return to Pittsburgh in the fall, but he wonders if it will seem like Peter's turf, if he'll have to start all over, sift through friends, find new hangouts, try to resolve what is still his, as opposed to what used to be theirs. And then in the spring comes London, the big unknown, the test. He'll go. He knows that now. He has to; it's the brave choice. But London won't be home. None of these places seems solid, or permanent. He could be in any one of them and still feel like he belonged somewhere else. Or nowhere at all.

Robin takes the steps downstairs two at a time, wondering what could have brought George back so soon. In the living room, Clark and Ruby are sitting on the couch together, watching what appears to be a science fiction movie, though a rather ridiculous one, with fake-looking spaceships and a lot of overacting. They're both laughing, Clark rather heartily and Ruby almost against her better judgment. As Robin passes by, Clark says, "You gotta come back for this. It's *Buckaroo Banzai*."

George is at the back door, looking worn-out in the same T-shirt and scrubs he's worn all day. His face portrays absolute dejection. His eyes look like he's been rubbing them, as if he's been crying, which is not like him at all.

"I told them," he says.

Robin doesn't need to ask what. "Come in. I want to hear."

George drops his bag on the floor and slumps into a kitchen chair. "Is there any beer?"

Robin opens the fridge and digs among the lower shelves. In the back he finds a couple cans of Miller. "That'll do," George says. Then Robin gets another idea. In the upper cabinets he finds a bottle of Scotch, a fancy bottle in a blue velvet bag. George nods eagerly.

Robin calls out, "Clark, we're borrowing your Scotch."

"What?" Clark calls back, his voice barely carrying above the explosions from the TV.

Robin fills two glasses with ice and pours an inch of amber liquid over both of them. He finds a half liter of Diet Coke in the fridge and pours it into one of them. "Straight up for me," George says, and then adds with a rueful twist to his mouth, "So to speak."

Robin raises his glass. "Here's to one of the biggest moments of your life."

George gulps and winces as the Scotch goes down. "I hope it wasn't one of the biggest mistakes."

"Come on, you know it wasn't."

"Telling them was the only thing on my mind. I was thinking, if they had a meltdown on me, I could leave and go to a bar. There's that gay bar in River Edge, Feathers."

"The worst name for a bar ever," Robin says. "Plus, I've never gotten past the guy checking ID."

"I kept thinking of how your mom asked you about Peter. Seemed so normal. I thought, OK, it's possible for people to open up their minds."

"Hey, not to interrupt, but I'm sorry about that thing before, when I didn't tell you that Peter had left me that message. I don't want you to think—"

George sucks down some more Scotch and makes a dismissive gesture. "My mom had made a whole bunch of food, all my father's favorites, like this battered steak and mashed potatoes, so she heated some up for me. My father was saying what a great surprise it was that I showed up for Father's Day. I didn't give him the whole story, about Ruby. I just said that you and I decided we'd surprise our fathers. And he was really in a good mood. I figured, I'll build up some goodwill. Cash in on it later. And they wanted to know about school and about the restaurant and all sorts of things—"

"Did they ask about me?"

"Well, I mentioned you first, and then my mother said something."

Robin thinks that he may not want to know what that "something" was. There was a time when Mrs. Lincoln was really fond of him, but the first time she saw him visiting from New York, wrapped in some not-very-masculine outfit, she notably cooled. Now, when he talks to her on the phone, she's polite, but it's never more than small talk. "She used to like me," Robin says. "But she can smell it on me now."

"Hold on, this isn't about you."

"Sorry, sorry, sorry." His diary mocks him: *Be a better listener.*

"So then out comes the chocolate cake, and I finally just told them, 'It's time to discuss the fact that I am gay.' And my father just got this angry look on his face and said, 'When did you make this decision,' and my mother said that I've seemed confused for a while now. And I tried to give them, I don't know, a little personal history. And I told them everything I knew about science, about how it's inborn, probably genetic, so it wasn't a decision to be gay, and my father said, 'There are no homosexuals in our family,' and he said I'd lost my way. I was like, 'There's Rosellen, she's a lesbian,' and they just acted shocked. I mean, come on! Then my mother admitted that she'd been worried about me, and she went to our pastor once to ask him about homosexuality, and he said something about love-the-sinner-hate-the-sin. And my father said the sin was leading to disease."

"You got it from every angle," Robin says.

"I was ready to fight. I mean, I was *prepared,* I had my facts and figures, you know? I said that the government had to do something to educate people about this medical crisis, and that there were people doing research, and the government wasn't funding it. 'How do you know the government didn't *cause* it?' my father said. 'I don't,' I said. And because my folks are such die-hard Democrats and despise Ronald Reagan, I got some glimmer that maybe they might understand the situation that way. So that was the best I could do. But they could not understand that I was telling them, this is who I am. I mean, they basically told me I *couldn't* be gay. That takes a lot of nerve."

George empties the glass. The ice cubes settle into the bottom.

The sound brings Robin back to the Greek restaurant, to Peter. The sound of dissolution. He reaches across the table and pries George's hand from his glass, holds on to his fingers, which are chilled. "Parents are always telling their kids who they are," he says.

"Not your parents."

"Well, not as much as they used to," Robin says.

In his last conversation with Dorothy before she left, when she came into his bedroom still trembling from the words that had gone back and forth between her and Ruby, Robin told her that he had had a talk with Clark. And he told her then that he had expressed this fear to Clark, that if he got sick Clark would reject him, and Dorothy had said, with steel in her voice, "I won't let him." And Robin found that he believed her, because she and Clark were communicating again, had approached something like a truce, would perhaps rebuild a civil relationship and maybe even turn to each other when needed, if required. But a mother who is willing to stand with her adult child, no matter who he has turned out to be, is a mother who has gotten used to her child as an adult. There has been a reckoning, and an acclimation. He tries to tell George this, that his parents will come around, some day, but there's no way for George to take comfort. The rejection still burns hot.

"That's not my home anymore," George says. "So I'm here to drive you back to Philly tonight."

"I thought you were here to get drunk." Robin pours more Scotch into George's glass. "Stay over," he says.

"Will your dad mind?"

"He doesn't even know what's in his liquor cabinet."

"No, will he mind me *staying*?"

Robin shakes his head, thinking that he won't give Clark the chance to say no, if it comes to that. "Come on," he says. "They're in the living room."

Clark and Ruby wave hello to George but remain fixed on the television screen, which shows a close up of a remarkably handsome actor with sharply chiseled features, gelled hair, a sexy space-age suit. He seems to be a scientist but is also singing in a rock band. "Who's *that*?" Robin asks, not recognizing the actor.

Clark says, "That's Buckaroo Banzai."

Ruby offers a sly smile, understanding from the tone of Robin's voice what he was actually asking.

There's another character, a black guy with a Jamaican accent and foot-long dreadlocks hanging down his back, who is saying, "The situation is explosive."

"You planning on wearing your hair like that?" Clark says to George, with a slight chuckle as if the idea is more comical than anything else.

"Anything could happen," George says.

"How much time do you think that takes, for that length?"

"Depends how quickly it grows."

"Well, we like you just the way you are."

"Dad," Robin says, "how about making room for some expansion."

"Fair enough," Clark says. "Fair enough."

Robin tugs George on the arm. "George is staying over," he announces, and they move toward the stairs.

On the TV, Buckaroo Banzai is saying, "Wherever you go, there you are."

Ruby makes a sarcastic click with her mouth. "Profound," she says.

Robin looks to her, and she glances toward George, making his ascent. Without a sound, she mouths the words, "Sweet dreams."

* * *

They stand together inside the garish bedroom, the silver vertical lines making a kind of cage around them. George is staring at the single bed. "So, we flip a coin to see who gets the floor? Or should I just sleep on the couch downstairs?"

Robin takes him by the shoulders and pushes him backward. They fall one then the other onto the blanket. Robin drapes himself across George, feeling how solid he is, and how warm, and how the smell of his body is strong and familiar. Robin lowers his face, close enough to kiss. But George unexpectedly turns his head.

"What?" Robin asks.

"There's something else I didn't tell you," George says. "Yesterday at work, before I left early, that guy Matthias called the restaurant. He wanted me to come over again."

"Did you tell him you found someone better to have sex with?" He makes sure George can see that he's smiling, though in fact he feels something like jealousy.

"I told him I was *busy*. Then I felt bad for not speaking up for myself. Because I wanted to say, 'I'm not interested in being sexually colonized.'"

"They sure teach you a lot of big words at that Ivy League school."

George frowns, "You don't think I'm serious?"

"Of course you're serious. You're always *serious.*" Robin rolls off George, finding room alongside him on the bed. "Look, if a guy says something idiotic to you, sometimes you gotta just laugh it off. A guy like Matthias—just tell him he's an idiot. And that he's not much of a lover."

George seems to take this in. "I think it's more complicated than that."

Robin waits another moment and says, "At the risk of saying the wrong thing for like the ten-thousandth time this weekend—"

"Why hold back now?"

"You need to know, George, that you're turning into a babe. All those push-ups you're doing are working."

"Shut up. I'm a short black guy with glasses and no fashion sense."

"No, *you* shut up. I'm telling you, you're gonna get a lot more attention. And some of the guys are going to be jerks. Racial stuff is part of it. But sex is just like that. The way people treat each other, it's not always about respect. You should trust me on this one."

"Well . . ."

"Well, what?'

George is quiet for a while, so Robin prods him to speak. "OK," George starts, pushing up his glasses. "Last night, you went back to your bed."

"What are you talking about?"

"We fell asleep together, but you snuck out and then you sort of tried to avoid the subject."

So that's it. "Your bed was too small," he tries. But George is waiting for more. "I didn't know that would bother you."

"It didn't seem very respectful."

Looking into the soft brown of George's eyes, Robin admits, "Last night stirred up a lot of feelings for me."

"So sex has an emotional component for you," George says.

"Doesn't it for you? Doesn't it for everyone?"

"Even casual sex?"

"That wasn't *casual!*"

"Oh."

"If it was, you wouldn't be mad that I left your bed."

"I guess you're right," George says. "That's what makes it so baffling."

Robin realizes that he's starting to get worked up, that this is moving in a direction that scares him. He just wants everything to be all right. More than all right. He wants this to move forward, not to stop. He feels his heart thumping against his skin where he's pressed up against the bed. He feels like he might implode for all the churning in his blood.

Perhaps George picks up on this, because at last he moves closer, and rests his body against Robin's. Robin feels himself begin to calm immediately.

"If we keep having sex," George says, "we can't let it ruin our friendship."

"Definitely not."

"Because what I want, is for sex to make our friendship better."

"Me too," Robin says. He thinks: Better, yes. But it won't be the same. And we won't know what that means until we get there.

Later that night, the room dark except for last slanting ray of moonlight, Robin lies on his side, his arms wrapped around a sleeping George, replaying their words, realizing he's just had sex, for the first time ever, in this bed, in this house. With George Lincoln. His friend, roommate, coworker, lover. Tomorrow they rise early and head back to Philadelphia, so Robin can get to work, can save his job. Can stay with George, for a while. The summer only lasts two more months, which seems like nothing and like forever, because they're on the verge of everything new. It's impossible to predict what might change during this next short window of time, impossible *not* to imagine that everything could turn over, all over again. Right now there is just this: George sleeping trustfully against him. There is the security of that.

For the first time in a long time, Robin falls asleep thinking, You're going to be OK.

The last thing he hears is the sound of the television clicking off downstairs. He hears his sister's heavy footsteps climbing the stairs. He listens as she pauses at the entrance to her bedroom, and right before the door clicks shut behind her, he hears that she is crying.

Acknowledgments

A writer needs time and space to create. For the gift of peace and quiet, and a table where I could set down my laptop and get to work, I thank these gracious hosts: Christine Murray and John Rossell; Vince Constabileo and Peter Howells; Lawrence Mendenhall and Rich Horan; Paul Festa and James Harker; and Maria Maggenti. And for allowing me to spend hours nursing coffee while I wrote, I send my appreciation to a long list of baristas in San Francisco, in particular Sal Flores at Jumpin' Java and Kevin Cheeseman at Maxfield's.

Various parts of this novel required research to come alive. For help with this, I thank Pat Kuchon, who gave me an insider's tour of Seaside Heights; Ricky Paul, for sharing stories of Philadelphia; as well as Joe Elwin, Monique Jenkinson, and Blake Woodhull, whose memories illuminated my characters and settings.

David Booth, Catherine Brady, Elizabeth Costello, and John Vlahides encouraged me through a difficult period of doubt, for which I can't say "thank you" forcefully enough; their attentiveness to my earliest drafts made all the difference. My gratitude also to these friends and colleagues who read this book in manuscript form and responded quickly, with generosity and intelligence: Kevin Clarke, Rose Haynes, Dave Hickey, PJ Jones, Christine Murray, Will Rountree, and Sonia Stamm. A special thanks to Liam Passmore, for knowing just when and how to *ping*. I'm happy also to acknowledge my father, Karl, and my sisters, Karen and Kim, for a lifetime of enthusiasm.

My collaborative relationships with Jandy Nelson at Manus & Associates Literary Agency and John Scognamiglio at Kensington Books have been the foundation of my writing life for a decade. I offer my enduring gratitude, respect, and admiration.

Finally, to Kevin: I don't know what I did to deserve you. You lived this along with me. All acknowledgment leads back to you.